To Lois:

Bad Day

for a

Bombshell

All the Best!

Cindy Vincent

Also by Cindy Vincent

The Case of the Cat Show Princess:
A Buckley and Bogey Cat Detective Caper

The Case of the Crafty Christmas Crooks:
A Buckley and Bogey Cat Detective Caper

The Case of the Jewel Covered Cat Statues:
A Buckley and Bogey Cat Detective Caper

The Case of the Clever Secret Code:
A Buckley and Bogey Cat Detective Caper

The Mystery of the Missing Ming:
A Daisy Diamond Detective Novel

The Case of the Rising Star Ruby:
A Daisy Diamond Detective Novel

Makeover For Murder:
A Kate Bundeen Mystery

Cats Are Part of His Kingdom, Too:
33 Daily Devotions to Show God's Love

Bad Day for a Bombshell

A Tracy Truworth,
Apprentice P.I.
1940s Homefront Mystery

Cindy Vincent

Whodunit Press
Houston

Bad Day for a Bombshell

A Tracy Truworth, Apprentice P.I.

1940s Homefront Mystery

Published by Whodunit Press

A Division of Mysteries by Vincent, LLC

For information, please contact:

Whodunit Press

c/o Mysteries by Vincent

Mysteriesbyvincent.com

**This is a work of fiction. All events, locations, institutions, themes,
persons, characters and plot are completely fictional. Any
resemblance to places or persons, living or deceased, are of the
invention of the author.**

ISBN: 978-1-932169-42-3

Printed in the United States of America

Dedication

*To my own partner in crime, my husband, Rob.
Thanks for making memories with me!*

*And to those who work hard to keep the memory of
the "Greatest Generation" alive in our hearts and
minds. Thank you for your dedication.*

December 5th, 1941

CHAPTER 1

Shifty Eyes and Shady Characters

Two days before waves of Imperial Japanese Navy planes blasted our warships into fireballs at Pearl Harbor, my mother and I were balancing hatboxes and shopping bags in the back of a taxicab while it raced through downtown Dallas, the fashion center of the Southwest. As usual, my mother had squeezed in every last second of shopping possible, and we'd left way past the time when we should have said our so-longs. We'd just spent the last few days traversing the hallowed halls of Neiman-Marcus, relieving them of their inventory as we stocked up on everything from evening gowns to silk stockings, and from shoes to gloves. Now we had mere minutes to race to Union Station and catch the five o'clock train home to Houston.

The cab driver's eyes had said it all when he'd pulled up to the store's entrance on Ervay Street and surveyed the mountain of boxes and bags stacked beside us. "Are all these things going with you?"

I gave him a small smile. "I'm afraid so."

His mouth dropped open and the cigarette fell from his lips. "And you're on the five o'clock train?"

My mother glared at him. "Of course. Now, do you intend to stand there all day just gawking? Or do you intend to do your job?"

Since we were on such an impossibly tight schedule, I decided to pitch in and help him load the haul. But it soon became apparent that I was only in the way. So instead, I stepped back and watched the cabbie stash everything into his DeSoto with the speed of Superman. For a moment there, I almost expected him to whip off his glasses and rip open his shirt, thus revealing a large "S" on a costume underneath. But I figured the man probably didn't have any *actual* superhuman powers. Instead he was most likely spurred on by the lightning that suddenly flashed through the sky, followed by a thunder boom that echoed off the sides of the buildings. It was enough to make me jump and send our driver into a panic. In under sixty seconds, he had the trunk loaded with luggage and parcels and shopping bags.

He slammed the trunk shut and then helped Mother and me into the backseat with as many boxes and bags as we could fit, before he stashed the overflow into the front seat. It was a miracle the man could even drive with all that stuff pushed up beside him.

Such a miracle seemed to be lost on my mother as we rode to the station. With breath that still reeked from the five glasses of champagne she'd managed to procure at lunch, she pulled off her gloves, snatched a nail file from her purse, and started to smooth her nails with rapid strokes. Her nose tilted upward while her mouth tilted downward. She was clearly not pleased.

For the life of me, I could *not* understand why. We'd been treated like royalty for days in Dallas, with the salesgirls at the store waiting on us hand and foot . . . and head, for that matter, in the Hat Department. We'd just bought the latest of the latest in fashions, and we were coming home with dresses and accessories that most women in America would swoon over.

I instantly thought of some of my friends and former college classmates, those who weren't of "our set," as my mother would say. They were resilient young women who scraped, sacrificed, and saved every penny just to get by. To them, a trip like ours would be the thrill of a lifetime. So I was well aware that most 23-year-olds didn't get to pick out an entire new wardrobe in one fell swoop like I had.

My mother dropped her file into her purse. Then she patted her braided, brunette updo and repositioned her hat. "I still can't fathom why we've been reduced to shopping domestically." Her words came out slurred, making me wonder if she had a flask of "something" in her purse. "After all, the United States isn't part of this war, such as it is. And I certainly hope President Roosevelt doesn't do something ridiculous, like trying to force us to participate. And as long as we stay out of things, I don't understand why we aren't allowed into Paris to shop."

I glanced at the traffic outside. "The House of Chanel is closed, Mother. Most of France is under Nazi rule. I don't think it would be a nice place to visit right now. Especially since the U.S. has clearly taken sides and we've been supporting England. We're not as neutral as we claim to be."

More lightning flashed through the sky and the wind suddenly picked up.

"Well, it's absurd," she insisted. "And it needs to stop. It's time the world got back to normal. Especially when we run the risk of wearing styles that someone else might have seen already. These are such harrowing times."

I rolled my eyes. It didn't bother me that my mother was a staunch Isolationist. Lots of Americans were. They didn't want us to enter the war, not with memories of the Great War still raw in their minds. But the tide had been turning just recently, and more and more Americans had been changing their minds, with Isolationists becoming Interventionists. In fact, I knew plenty of fellas who were absolutely itching to fight by now. Especially with all the horrific pictures in the papers and the terrifying scenes shown in newsreels at the movies. Besides that, it was becoming more and more obvious that we weren't quite as isolated from the conflicts in Europe and the Pacific as we'd once thought. The oceans surrounding our country weren't as big as they used to be, and they really weren't enough to stop an enemy from invading.

If they really wanted to.

But in my mother's case, it was the *reason* she was an Isolationist that disturbed me. My mother was opposed to war because, when Hitler had goose-stepped his soldiers right on into France, her annual shopping trip to Paris to stock up on her Haute Couture had come to a halt. Now, thanks to those pesky Germans mucking things up, my mother had been forced to shop right here in the good old U.S. of A. So instead of traveling by plane and then the glitz of a luxury ocean liner, we were about to board a train. Something common folk did. Never mind all that torture and starvation and fear the poor French citizens experienced everyday. My mother's shopping had been reduced to that of *any* wealthy woman, instead of something befitting the American royalty she believed herself to be. In her mind, thanks to all these military hijinks, she had been forced to suffer. And believe me, she had no intention of doing one bit of that suffering in silence.

She squinted at the driver's reflection in the rearview mirror. "Is there some particular reason you're driving this antiquated heap with the speed of a sea slug?"

I was always amazed at how she could drawl out her words so delicately and yet sound so horrifying at the same time.

Something in her tone must have hit its intended mark. I hadn't thought the driver could go much faster, judging by the way he'd been maneuvering in and out of traffic. Apparently I had been wrong. Because he shifted gears and hit the gas pedal with renewed fervor. Naturally, he was greeted with similar fervor from other drivers around us as they hit their brakes and pounded on their horns. At the same time, huge raindrops began to pelt the vehicle, and the driver pushed the lever to set his meager windshield wipers swishing away. Soon the rain was hitting the roof so hard that it sounded like we were being bombarded with rocks.

Another brilliant flash of lightning made my heart skip a beat. Especially when the driver pushed the gas pedal to the floor, and switched in and out of lanes again. For a second or two, I was pretty sure the car had tilted so far to the right that we were driving on only two wheels. That was, until he made a sharp correction with the steering wheel and put us back on all four tires again.

I grabbed onto the back of the front seat with one hand and held my hat in place with the other. "Mother, there's no use getting us killed before we even get to the station," I hollered above the nearly deafening raindrops. "If we'd left twenty minutes ago, we wouldn't be in such a mad dash."

She shot a venomous glare my way and shouted back. "In my day, privileged young ladies didn't sass their mothers. So I expect you to bite your tongue and show some manners. Was it my fault that incompetent saleslady was so slow? When I asked her to wrap up that last beaded bag I bought?"

Naturally, I found it a challenge to bite my tongue and answer her question at the same time. History had taught me that silence would have been my best option right at that moment. And at my age, I should have known better than to poke the bear, as they say.

But clearly I still had a lot to learn.

"That poor salesgirl was rushing just as fast as she could. You gave her all of a minute to take care of things," I argued, and immediately wished I hadn't.

"Teresina Anne Truworth! How dare you!"

Oh, swell. There it was. She'd spat out my full name. The number one indicator that her temper had just gone from mad to mean. People usually called me "Tracy," and I preferred that, especially since I'd never even met another Teresina in my entire life. It had been a name my mother had heard on a trip through the Greek Isles a few years before the stork had mistakenly dropped me off at the family mansion in the Heights, several years before my paternal grandfather had built a new mansion in Houston's experiment of a community, River Oaks.

My grandfather, or Gramps, as I called him, had happily grown up on a Texas cattle ranch with nothing but the basic necessities. Then, later in life, he invented some oilfield tool that made him rich, rich, rich. Yet he and my grandmother — also of humble beginnings — never forgot how they met and danced for the first time at the county fair, and they never forgot where they came from. While they certainly didn't starve during the Great Depression, they didn't stand idly by when others did. Instead, they sent baskets of eggs and loaves of bread to complete strangers, all the while keeping their charity hidden, so as not to offend the pride of others. To this day, my grandmother, whom I called Nana, made it her mission to quietly help others who weren't as blessed as we were.

And, to educate her only granddaughter on how the rest of the human race lived.

My mother's family, on the other hand, came from generations of money. They'd maneuvered their way around the stock market crash of '29 and managed to happily keep the family fortune moldering in the vault. And in case no one's ever told you, there's a difference between old money and new money. A very big difference. Gigantic, you might say. And the two mix together like oil and eau de toilette water. Sometimes I'm amazed that my parents even got married. But there's no accounting for taste or attraction, and apparently they were so smitten back then that they didn't really care about things like social standing and such. I'm told that blessed state of bliss didn't last long. Once the bloom was off the rose, they put their time and energy into raising my "perfect" older brother, Benjamin, who is now a semester away from finishing law school.

As for me, well, my father adores me and my mother is pretty sure I'm not hers. I suspect she attributes our differences to a mix-up at the hospital when I was born, and my guess is she's always on the scout for her *real* daughter. Unfortunately, her theory falls apart whenever someone mentions how much I look like Nana. I've got the same caramel-colored hair that Nana once had, and according to her portrait that hangs above our drawing room mantle, I am a dead ringer for Nana in her younger years. She owns the big mansion now that my grandfather has gone to that big oil gusher in the sky, and we all live there together, just like a good, upper-crust family should.

But I would trade that cavernous mansion any old day, just to have my grandfather back. It's been a year and a half since he passed away, and not a week goes by that I don't miss him and his light-hearted outlook on life. It struck me that, if he were alive today, he'd probably even find some humor in my current situation.

If only I could do the same.

Another flash of lightning illuminated the sky before it went as dark as night. The driver pulled out the knob to turn on his headlamps, and I could see heavy raindrops hitting the pavement hard. I only hoped the train, which was known for leaving precisely on time, would be less than punctual today. Especially since it was Friday evening and I really wanted to go home.

My mother put her gloves back on and glared at me. I knew she was about to start in again. Luckily, I spotted a blurry vision of Union Station just ahead.

The next few minutes were a whir of porters and packages and people holding umbrellas while we all ran to catch the train. We boarded the *Sunbeam* at the very last second, while our mountain of baggage was rapidly stowed for us. I reached into my purse and pulled out some bills and passed them around for tips. It had taken the efforts of a small army of men to get us loaded up on time, and Nana had taught me to always tip generously. So I did just that with a smile.

I got plenty of smiles in return, and I realized the money I'd given them would probably go toward feeding their families. They bowed and waved goodbye as the train pulled away from the station. Soon the lights of the city began to flash by, along with more lightning, and I could hear the *clickety-clack* as the wheels rolled over the rails. It's funny how cozy a train can be in the middle of a thunderstorm.

I made a beeline to the washroom to check out the soft curls of my just-past-the-shoulder hairdo. A glance in the mirror told me it needed some work, so I took out the combs that held my hair back at the sides and put them back in place, a little tighter this time. Then I straightened my suit and the seams on my stockings. I pinned my hat securely back on my head, at a perfect tilt, before I rejoined my mother and we headed for the luxury of the parlor car. I loved my new navy suit, which the saleslady at the Neiman fashion show had insisted would bring out the navy in my eyes. Maybe that was true, though I wasn't sure. Mostly I liked it because it looked smart, sophisticated, and gave me some womanly curves. Ever since my fiancé, Michael, had commented that I still looked like a skinny kid, I was a little sensitive about my figure.

We found our seats in the parlor car and I ordered a Coca-Cola® while my mother ordered a champagne cocktail. I could tell from the snarl on her face that she was about to let me have it. I sighed and stared out the window. Rain slid in droplets across the glass as the storm picked up even more.

And suddenly I felt it. A strange tingling across my skin, like something mysterious, maybe even dangerous, was about to happen. My mind instantly went back to the latest Katie McClue novel I'd devoured. The mystery series had been my favorite since I was in my teens, and this newest episode, *The Case of the Mysterious Moments*, had started out on a train. And like most of the adventures of the 21-year-old detective, a massive thunderstorm had blazed and boomed in the background.

I shivered and sipped my drink through a straw. Then I glanced out from under the tilted brim of my hat and studied the people around me. Most of the passengers were men in suits and ties, and I guessed they were businessmen coming home from Dallas. Many of them were probably oilmen, like my father, or they were in some of the other businesses or professions that sprung up around the oil industry. Nearly every one of them had a fedora in their laps and a newspaper in front of their faces. There were also a few military men sitting with perfect posture and looking dapper in their uniforms. Instead of reading, they sat relaxing and enjoying their drinks. I also spotted an older couple on one end of the car and what appeared to be some newlyweds on the other. Both couples were huddled together and engaged in quiet conversation.

After I secretly gave everyone the once over, I let my eyes give them all a second going over, too, just to make sure I hadn't missed something. Though I'd never told a soul, I'd harbored the fantasy of becoming a private investigator myself, ever since Gramps had told me tales of the brief time when he was a Pinkerton Detective. Long, long ago. Before he became a wildcatter and then an inventor. And though all his lifelong stories were interesting enough, his adventures as a detective intrigued me the most. But the thought of me ever becoming a private investigator was nothing but silliness, and I was well aware that my dream would never see the light of day. Upper-crust girls like me had their whole lives mapped out for them, even before they first set foot inside a first-grade classroom. They didn't just take off and delve into the seedy underbelly of life as a P.I.

Beside me, the voice of my mother droned in my ear. "It was hardly necessary for you to create such a little drama by tipping every one of those porters. I won't stand for this common, openhanded display of charity you insist on performing in front of all. Simply to annoy me."

"Generosity is a not a crime, Mother."

"You'll never make a good wife to Michael if you don't start acting properly for someone of our set. Michael is going to be an exceptionally important man someday, most likely a United States Senator. His mother and I have discussed Michael's career at length, and believe me, she was hesitant when I suggested *you* as a prospect for his wife."

I rolled my eyes. "So kind of you to say, Mother. I can't think of anything more romantic than being thought of as a prospect. Who needs hearts and flowers when a simple business deal will do?"

My sarcasm was lost on my mother. "Young lady, I hope you appreciate how much effort it took on my part to convince *her* to convince *him* to propose to you a month ago. So I certainly will not stand for you behaving in a way that might cause him to terminate this arrangement. For instance, I will not stand for you treating the hired help like you did when we boarded. It's undignified. Someday, when you have servants in your own household, they will never respect you if you toss money around like you're feeding pigeons."

While she went on, a man near the rear door stood up and walked out, seconds before another man got up and stretched. He left through the opposite door, just as a blonde woman strolled in. For a moment, she stood by the entrance and practically posed for the whole car, jutting out one hip and then the other, all the while keeping her hands on her waist. With each movement, she sighed and shook her hair behind her. Then she sashayed down the aisle, walking slowly, like a panther on the prowl. Her vanilla-scented perfume tickled my nostrils as she went by, and I almost sneezed. Even in the dim light of the car, I could see she was the kind of woman that would be called a "bombshell," especially judging by the way several of the men had dropped their newspapers just before they'd dropped their jaws. Her entrance had certainly put some ripples in the quiet little pond of our parlor car.

She wriggled into a chair a few seats down from us on the opposite side. Oddly enough, there was something about this woman's entrance that sent a cold chill running down my spine, and made the little hairs on the back of my neck stand up. Though for the life of me, I couldn't explain why. Sure, she was putting on quite a show, but that wasn't exactly a cause for alarm. Nor was it a crime.

Yet something inside me said otherwise. And I knew Katie McClue wouldn't have questioned her instincts in a situation like this. She was an expert when it came to spotting a suspect, sometimes even before an actual crime had been committed. She was also an expert when it came to observation, as proven by her testimony at many a trial, where she would recount every last defining characteristic of a villain, from the scent of their soap to the hour when they'd last polished their shoes. Afterward, she usually received a standing ovation in the courtroom, whereby she would give credit to her keen powers of observation and her fantastic feminine intuition. Not to mention, the ability to turn her senses on full alert at just the right moment.

So I knew I'd better have my senses on full alert right now, too. I closed my lids halfway and pretended to be bored while I nonchalantly sipped my soda. All the while, I kept the blonde woman in my sights.

I watched while she sighed loudly and dropped a Neiman's hatbox at her feet. That told me she'd probably come up to Dallas to shop just like we had. She looked a little older than me, and I wondered if she might be the daughter of one of my mother's friends or someone else in my parent's social circle.

Yet the more I studied this blonde woman, the more I realized my mother and her pals would've been appalled at this woman's appearance. After all, I'd been drilled on the subject of "Style and Proper Attire" since I was four, and like it or not, I knew all their favorite fashion faux pas. I had no doubt they would've crucified the woman sitting a few chairs down.

For starters, that blonde hair had come from a bottle, and probably not a very expensive one at that. And even though the woman's fur coat must have cost an arm and a leg, it clashed with the poof of pink feathers she wore for a hat. Not that anyone would've noticed the hat when the woman flashed far too much jewelry to be considered appropriate. She had clips on her coat, and rings galore, along with a huge necklace, a brooch, dangling earrings, and several sparkly bracelets. Everything but a wedding ring. Of course, none of that jewelry was real, which would have sent my mother's clique to clucking like a bunch of hens. Nonetheless, it was still very nice costume jewelry, clearly Eisenberg, a beautifully crafted brand that looked very close to the real thing.

But all that sparkle and shine made the blonde woman look more like a beacon than a beauty. If nothing else, it certainly was eye-catching.

My mind tuned into my mother's voice again, like turning the dial on a radio. "For instance, Tracy, your choice of evening gowns was terribly inappropriate. I was in complete and utter shock when you insisted on trying on that black satin strapless evening gown! With a white lace peplum? How horrendous. I've never seen anything so low class in all my years. Women should never show their shoulders like that! Thank goodness I prevented you from purchasing such a gown."

I almost choked on my soda. Funny that my mother should choose this moment to criticize my wardrobe choices when I was secretly scrutinizing the woman across from us. Yet inwardly, I smiled. Little did my mother know, but I'd bought that black satin gown anyway. I'd used some of the money I kept stashed away in the secret drawer of my jewel case. A drawer she didn't even know existed. I'd arranged for the gown to be sent to my best friend's apartment, along with a matching pair of black satin gloves. My mother, of course, had picked out a very voluminous pink organza gown for me and insisted on buying it, even though I complained it looked like the dress worn by Glinda the Good Witch in the *Wizard of Oz*. But my words fell on deaf ears, as my mother had gushed on and on about how much Michael's mother would adore the gown.

I turned my attention back to the blonde woman. The steward had just brought her a Manhattan and she'd downed it like she'd just crossed the Sahara and was dying of thirst. She ordered a refill and then made quite a production of unbuttoning and removing her fur coat. She'd sighed and stretched and carried on in such a fashion that she soon had every eye on her. I'm sure she would've even gotten a whistle or two, had we not been in such a refined setting.

Amazingly, the woman had accomplished all that without saying a single word. Much as I hated to admit it, I was a little bit fascinated by how skillfully she'd managed to make herself the center of attention. She was a masterful manipulator, and she was working hard to lure men into her grasp. Once she'd caught their eyes, she smiled and winked at them. So who was she and why was she acting this way? I knew a call girl would never be allowed to operate in this high-class compartment. Even so, there was something unmistakably shady about this woman. In the world of Katie McClue, she was a clear-cut suspicious suspect.

Again I had to wonder about the purpose of her performance. Was she merely on the hunt for a husband? I glanced down at the huge diamond on my ring finger, a ring that had once belonged to

Michael's grandmother. At twenty-three, I'd been dangerously close to being considered a spinster. Did the woman across from me fear she'd end up as an old maid? After all, there was a lot of pressure on girls to get married by a certain cutoff date. And the blonde woman had probably passed that mark several years ago.

Much like I nearly had myself, had I not gotten that all-important proposal. Though I'd known Michael for years through my brother, we hadn't actually started dating until late last summer. If you could call it that. Our outings had mostly been formal affairs or group events. Nothing where we really got to know each other's deepest thoughts. In fact, I was pretty surprised when he popped the question in early November at a country club dance. Of course I'd said yes. What else was I going to say in front of my family's entire social circle? Especially with all the girls *ooohing* and *aaahing* over his movie star good looks, while the grownups referred to him as "a good catch." Though now I had to wonder how good a catch he really was.

Beneath my feet, I could feel the train pick up speed to its advertised mile-a-minute run. The darkness outside was punctuated by lightning flashes and the lights from an occasional farmhouse. My mother's mouth had picked up speed, too, and her gripes began to fly at a rate I couldn't keep up with. Right after the steward brought her a third champagne cocktail.

"You've got a lot to learn, Tracy, before you become Michael's bride in June. And I certainly hope the situation in France is cleared up rather quickly since I must have your wedding dress made in Paris. If Chanel isn't open by then, I suppose we'll have to settle on a design at one of the other couture houses. You simply *must* wear the dress of the season. Maybe you could put on a little weight so you'll fill out a dress properly by then . . ."

I finished my Coke® and watched as the blonde woman upped the ante, almost like she was on a mission. She had managed to make a connection with one of the soldiers, and together they flirted and laughed, though they were a few seats away from each other. Her painted red lips parted in a smile, though her eyes didn't quite seem to follow. In fact, she had the coldest blue eyes I think I'd ever seen on a person, and it reminded me of a glacier I'd once visited on a family vacation to Alaska. For some reason, I shivered.

But the woman's performance stopped when the door on the other end of the car opened up and another man walked in. He was an older man, probably near the same age as my grandfather had been before he passed away. The man was lugging a large package wrapped in tattered newspapers and tied with string. He took a seat near the door and removed his hat, which was still dripping with water, much like his crumpled trench coat. That's when I noticed his salt-and-pepper hair and dark eyes.

Shifty eyes. They darted left and then right, before he lowered his lids and glanced around, apparently taking mental inventory of the occupants of the car. As near as I could tell, he was watching people exactly like I was! He reminded me of someone, though at the moment, I couldn't quite think of whom. If nothing else, he made me think of a suspect in a Katie McClue novel, *The Case of the Shifty-eyed Stranger*.

His eyes finally settled on the blonde woman, and that's when her smile faded and she shrank back into her chair. She had gone from ostentatious to invisible, all with the appearance of this shifty-eyed guy.

Was she threatened by him? And for that matter, who was he?

Katie McClue would have made it her mission to find out.

For a second or two, my mother's voice found it's way into my consciousness. "Of course, nothing but the most expensive orchids will do for your bouquet. . ."

That's when I stood up. "Excuse me, Mother, but I've got to use the washroom."

"But you just went."

"Well, I'm going again."

Then I slowly walked toward the end of the car, glancing only occasionally at the shifty-eyed man, so it wouldn't be too obvious that I was trying to investigate him. For some reason, I felt completely compelled to find out who he was and what he was doing here. But how would I go about doing just that?

As far as I knew, my only option was to talk to the man. But what exactly would I say? In a situation like this, what would Katie McClue say?

The man raised one eyebrow as I approached him. That's when I realized who he reminded me of — Humphrey Bogart as Sam

Spade in the *Maltese Falcon*. Only, an older version of the man. I'd seen the movie when it came out a little over a month ago, and now I realized that even his newspaper-wrapped package looked a lot like the prop in the film.

Was it possible he was carrying some valuable treasure all wrapped up in that paper? And what did any of this have to do with the blonde woman?

All of a sudden, my heart began to pound like the bass drum at the start of Benny Goodman's swing song, *Sing, Sing, Sing*. And I knew I had to find out what this man was doing here.

I gulped and mustered up every ounce of courage I could find.

"Awful storm we're having, isn't it, Mister?" I said in my sweetest drawl.

For some reason, this made the man chuckle. "Well, yes it is, Miss. If you have a particular interest in electricity, it's the night for you. I almost expect to see old Ben Franklin out flying a kite."

That made me smile.

But I quickly remembered that I was here to investigate. So I made my eyes go wide and tried to act as innocent as possible. "That looks like an awfully heavy package you're carrying . . ."

He laughed again. "I bought a doll in Dallas for my niece."

I touched my lower lip with my forefinger. "Must be some doll if you had to go all the way to Dallas for it. How old is your niece?"

Now he grinned, just before his eyes darted left and right again. "You're good, kid. You've made me, like a fox hiding in the henhouse. Haven't seen too many people your age who are so smart. You've got a heckuva future ahead of you."

With those words, he stood up and nodded, right before he turned and headed out the door.

I gasped in amazement.

Who was that man?

And what had just happened here? Was it possible I had just walked into a real, live mystery?

CHAPTER 2

Bouquets and Best Friends

For a second or two, I stood planted to the spot with my mouth gaping open. The train rocked back and forth, making me sway like I was on the dance floor. But I came back to attention when a small burst of lightning lit up the sky outside the window. While the storm on the outside appeared to be on its last legs, now I wondered what kind of storm was brewing on the *inside* of the train.

Because there had to be some reason why the shifty-eyed man had suddenly bolted out the door. But what could it be? And what was in that package? Not to mention, what in the world did he mean by that comment about a fox in a henhouse and me being "good"?

None of it made any sense. At all.

I shook my head to clear the cobwebs and glanced back at the blonde woman. She'd managed to pull a newspaper from out of thin air and placed it squarely in front of her face. As near as I could tell, she was doing her very best to hide. And I had to say, her best was pretty darn good.

So why had the appearance of the Bogart look-alike brought a halt to her "notice me" routine? If she *was* threatened when he showed up on the scene, then why was *he* the one to do the disappearing act? Normally, it would have been the other way around. Though one thing was for sure — that blonde woman knew what she was doing. She was just as good at hiding as she was at getting everyone's attention. Almost like someone had trained her or something.

Right at that moment, I sure could have used some training myself, because I honestly didn't have a clue what to do next. Whatever was going on in our car was a real mystery. And if there was one thing I'd learned from reading all those Katie McClue books, it was that a good mystery should never go to waste. I also knew Katie would have gone searching for the disappearing Bogart-guy right away, so I figured that would be my best move. I only wished I'd brought my camera with me on this trip, since Katie often carried her camera. She'd managed to get mounds of incriminating evidence on film.

But for the time being, I would have to settle for finding the guy and trying to talk to him again. So I took a deep breath and strolled straight into the next car, as though I really *was* headed for the washroom. But instead of going inside, I paused daintily in front of the washroom door and leaned over to smooth my stockings. All the while, I kept my eyes up so I could scan the sea of passengers in this car. I'd been told that I had great gams, so I knew men would be watching my legs and would never notice that I was actually eyeballing every passenger up and down the aisle. It was a trick that Katie had used time and again, and it worked like a charm. The only problem was, no matter how hard I searched with my eyes, I couldn't spot the shifty-eyed man anywhere. He must have moved on to another car.

I decided to pop into the washroom anyway, just so I wouldn't blow my "cover," as it were. When I came back out, a very thin steward was standing there waiting for me. His dark, beady eyes bore into me, making me think he might be a member of some criminal gang and was now disguised as a steward.

"I beg your pardon, ma'am," he said in a surprisingly high voice, "but are you Miss Tracy Truworth?"

My heart started to pound against my ribcage. In her fifteenth book, *The Secret of the Disappearing Diamond Dealer*, Katie McClue had been approached by a steward in a very similar fashion. Of course, with her mystery-solving expertise, she'd remained calm and collected, knowing full well the man was about to pass her a piece of information that was so vital, so earth-shattering, that it would be the one clue to crack the case.

Surely that was exactly what was about to happen to me. Now I had to wonder, would the man hand me a film canister full of jewels? Or maybe even a map written in invisible ink that led to some kind of buried treasure? Or maybe he was about to pass me a message written in a secret code, one that I would have to ponder for days. Then again, it was entirely possible the Bogart-guy was using him to send me an invitation, something telling me to meet him under the third streetlamp east of the train station, and to come alone, an encounter that would prove to be nothing more than a trap. That had certainly happened to Katie a time or two. Though I never fully understood why she always walked into such situations with eyes wide open.

"Yes, I'm Tracy," I said, while I fought to keep the excitement out of my voice. I steeled myself, ready to receive whatever information he might impart.

"I'm afraid your mother sent me to find you," he said. "She would like you to return to your seat, if you please."

"Oh," was all I could mutter. "Thank you."

I sighed, feeling like a child who'd just had the air let out of her balloon. Obviously Katie McClue never had to deal with an overbearing mother.

I went back to my seat and once again tuned out my mother's nonstop griping. She finished her fourth champagne cocktail and ordered another one. In the meantime, I sank down in my seat, and alternated between secretly watching the blonde woman and checking the door to see if the Bogart look-alike would return. Much to my disappointment, absolutely nothing happened.

For a moment or two, I even thought about trying to strike up a conversation with the blonde. But with my mother right beside me, now going on and on about how inferior American fashions were, that idea quickly fizzled out with the last of the lightning.

By the time we reached Houston, the skies were clear and full of stars. But the real showstopper was a big, bright moon that was only a couple of days past the full.

The blonde bombshell barely let down her newspaper when the train pulled into Grand Central Station. She got off in front of us, and I kept my eyes on her until our driver waved to us. Then I lost her in the throng of people.

I sighed and glanced around to see if I could spot the Bogart double. I watched all the men in fedoras and trench coats race past, and finally, when the crowd cleared a little, there he was. Several car-lengths away, near the front of the train. He had his hat angled low over his brow, so I had a hard time making out his features. But I knew it was him. Especially when he looked up, shifted the package in his arms, and touched the tip of his hat. Then he gave me a grin, displaying a full set of pearly whites. I could almost picture him saying the line from the *Maltese Falcon*, "I don't mind a reasonable amount of trouble."

A group of people passed in front of him, and by the time they had moved away, he was gone. I blinked a few times, just in case my eyes were playing tricks on me.

But sure enough, once again, the man had vanished. He was as good at disappearing as the blonde was at getting noticed and then hiding.

So who in the world were these people?

If only they'd left some kind of clue for me to follow, something that could lead me to them and help me figure out what was going on. That is, if there actually *was* something going on. But sadly, I would probably never find out, since most likely, I would never see these people again.

"Don't just stand there daydreaming, Tracy," my mother commanded. "Get in."

I turned to see Hadley, our driver, had been holding the door for me. All of our packages and luggage and shopping bags had been loaded up, and I hadn't even noticed.

"A long and difficult trip, Miss Tracy?" Hadley's deep baritone sounded as melodic as usual.

Hadley was an older black man with gray hair and large glasses. He and Gramps had become friends when Hadley worked for Gramps in the oilfields. But before that, Hadley had taught Literature at a high school, and to this day, he loved the classics.

I shook my head. "No, Hadley, not bad at all. I'm afraid I had my mind somewhere else."

He smiled at me with sparkling gray-brown eyes, eyes that matched his suit. "Do not follow where the path may lead. Go instead where there is no path and leave a trail."

I blinked at him a couple of times. "I'm sorry, Hadley, what was that?"

"Ralph Waldo Emerson. You know, sometimes the journey we're on isn't the *actual* journey we're on. For the mind can take us on many a magical adventure, and there is no harm in indulging in a daydream now and then. 'They who dream by day are cognizant of many things which escape those who dream only by night.'"

"Longfellow?"

"Edgar Allan Poe."

I laughed. "I don't think Poe or Emerson or Longfellow ever anticipated a shopping spree to Neiman's."

"No," he agreed. "But I would suspect that shopping isn't the only place you've been. At least not within the confines of your own cranium. In other words, young lady, I believe you have a rather hardy imagination, one that takes you on many flights of fancy. Travels that are perhaps more interesting."

His words made me smile. "Well, after hearing about all the adventures you and Gramps had during the wildcatting days, I suppose I have high expectations."

Hadley responded with a hearty laugh. "We had some fine escapades, your grandfather and I. God rest his soul. Though I suspect the tales of our adventures became taller with time. But enough of that. Let's get you home so you can relax. Your grandmother is waiting there for you."

And sure enough, she was.

She was standing out in the yard of our huge mansion on Inwood Drive when our car rolled into the driveway. In the moonlight, I could make out the wrought iron fence surrounding the property, as well as the precisely manicured gardens. The house itself was dark, though I knew it only appeared that way from the outside. Nana made sure our blackout curtains were pulled tight every night, even when the local Air Raid Warden wasn't conducting a drill. In fact, she'd had the curtains sewn the second the Office of

Civilian Defense began broadcasting the idea last May. When it came to war preparedness, Nana took the cake. I only hoped her preparations would never have to be put to real us, and that America wouldn't become embroiled in the mess going on in the rest of the world. But only time would tell.

I stepped out of the car, and glanced up at the night sky. The darkness of the house made the stars appear even more vivid, and suddenly I felt the stirrings of the Christmas spirit. I let my eyes wander and I searched for the brightest star, trying to imagine what the Christmas star must have looked like way back then. I hoped it was going to be a beautiful Christmas this year, but with all the uncertainty in the world, who knew what our holiday season might hold?

Nana clasped her embroidered shawl tightly around her thin shoulders and ran over to join us. As always, her dark blue eyes were dancing and her bright silver hair was loosely piled atop her head. Even at her age, she remained a stylish beauty. She moved with the grace and poise of a ballet dancer.

She hugged me first and then did her best to give my mother a hug, too. "Welcome back, Eleanor. I trust you had a successful trip."

But my mother just shrugged her off. "Not in front of the help, Caroline. Isn't it enough that you've had such a horrendous influence on my daughter? You're the reason she acts so 'common' sometimes. I only wish I had raised her properly." Her words were slurred together, and she swayed as she made her way to the door.

My grandmother laughed. "Tracy has grown up to be a fine young woman."

My mother scowled at my grandmother. "According to your standards, perhaps. But thankfully I've finally got her on the right path, and soon she'll be married to Michael. The wedding will be the event of the decade. And mark my words — you'll do nothing to interfere with any of my plans!"

Nana lowered her lids and looked out from under her lashes. "Why, Eleanor, how can you say such a thing? I only have Tracy's happiness in mind."

"What on earth does happiness have to do with anything?" My mother tossed over her shoulder before wobbling into the house.

I grabbed a few shopping bags and my suitcase. "Hello, Nana. Wait till you see what I brought you."

My grandmother peeked into a bag. "Ooooh. Now you've got me intrigued. Did you find some pretty things?"

I nodded. "Tons of them. Plus I bought Christmas presents for everyone. I'll be ready to put them under the tree, just as soon as we get it up."

Nana laughed. "Well, in that case, I'll have Giles go out and find one this weekend. Then we'll put it up right away. You and I can decorate it."

"That'll be fun."

Giles was our butler, who my mother had imported straight from England, right after someone had told her the only real butlers were British. He'd been with us for years now, and even though he was an expert at the "stiff upper lip," he tended to let down his guard around Christmastime. Yet this year I noticed a distinct glint of worry in his eyes.

And of course I knew the source of his stoic struggles. Since England had been so badly bombed by the Germans during the Blitz, I guessed Giles had his friends and family in the forefront of his mind. I even thought of asking Nana if we might invite a few of his people to come over and stay with us, since we certainly had the room. But these days, with German U-boats patrolling the Atlantic, ocean travel had become even more perilous than staying put.

Yet it all seemed so far away when Giles helped Nana and me carry all my things up to my bedroom. After Giles had excused himself, Nana and I had our own little fashion show. I'd bought her a cornflower blue dress that turned out to be a perfect fit, along with a matching wool hat. Plus I'd bought her a new bathrobe and some new slippers. She pirouetted around my room and flitted from one piece of furniture to the next. She paused in front of my dresser to pluck a flower from the fresh bouquet of chrysanthemums, lilies, and roses that cascaded from a crystal vase. Apparently the flowers had been delivered just this afternoon and their perfume already filled my room.

She stuck the flower in her hat and handed me the card that had come with the bouquet. "Special delivery, my dear."

I glanced at Nana. "Are those from . . .?"

She was already nodding. "They are. Your fiancé whom you haven't seen in ages sent them over. Too bad he's been so busy working that he hasn't had time to take you out on a date."

My sentiments exactly. Supposedly, Michael was up to his eyeballs in a big case. Or at least, so he'd said, not long after we'd officially become engaged. As his future wife, I thought it would've been nice to hear more about his work. Or his day-to-day life in general.

But maybe that would come once we were married. And if nothing else, at least we were "scheduled" to attend the big Christmas dance together at our country club a week from tomorrow. Which was the main reason my mother had hurried us off to Dallas for our shopping spree, to make sure I had precisely the right gown to wear. Or, rather, a dress that my mother was sure would please Michael's mother.

I sniffed the bouquet and then pulled the card from its holder. "Best Wishes," was all it read. No poetic words of love or romance, nothing about how he wanted to while away the hours gazing into my eyes or nibbling on my earlobes. No, there wasn't even a "Love, Michael," or a "Looking forward to the Christmas dance." Just "Best Wishes," the same words our family dentist had written on a card when I graduated from high school.

My stomach suddenly took a nosedive and practically sank all the way to my ankles. I put the card on my dresser and turned to my grandmother.

Her elegant brows rose on her perfectly sculpted forehead. "Disappointing? You know you don't have to marry him, if you don't want to. There are plenty of fish in the sea. And you, my dear, are a real catch."

I laughed. "But if the men are the fish, doesn't that make me the one doing the catching?"

She smiled. "Now you've got the idea. And you know, being in love, really in love, is more wonderful than you can even imagine. I wouldn't trade what I had with your grandfather for anything in the world."

My sigh nearly sent the flowers flying. "If only I could find a guy like Gramps."

Her voice turned soft. "How do you know you can't? You

haven't looked all that hard, darlin'. You've been under your mother's thumb since the day you were born. And she started plotting this wedding right around the time your first tooth poked through your gums."

"But everyone thinks he's such a great guy. Plus the wedding is all set and everybody knows about it. Not only that, but I already told Michael that I'd marry him."

She came over and wrapped me in her arms. "But it's your life, darlin'. You can do whatever you want with it. And you can marry whomever you want. Now, let's go downstairs and I'll make us some sandwiches. I'm starving."

"Me, too. I'll be down in just a minute. I've got to call Jayne first."

"Tell her I said hello," Nana said as she headed for the door. "I like that little Jayne. She's a real sparkplug."

My best friend Jayne was an old college chum who now worked as a manager for an apartment building. She lived in a first-floor apartment of the converted Victorian mansion and, as the manager, she got her rent for free. An arrangement she hoped to continue after she and her fiancé, Tom, tied the knot.

She picked up the line after only a few rings. "So, did you buy out the entire store?"

I wondered how she happened to know the call was from me. "Close enough," I said. "I've got a dress heading to your place compliments of the United States Post Office. Mind if I run by and pick it up tomorrow?"

She laughed. "Sure. If you're shipping it my way, you must be hiding it from Eleanor. I'm guessing she didn't deem it worthy?"

Now it was my turn to laugh. "Hardly. I think the word she used was 'horrendous.'"

"Then I'll bet it's positively stunning," Jayne chirped. "Run on by around ten so we can have a cup of tea and a good chat first. My mailman gets here at eleven on the dot."

"Sounds swell. Thanks a bunch. I'll be there."

"You might even catch a glimpse of my new tenant while you're here. She moved in across the hall from my place a few weeks ago. She took Mr. Masamoto's old apartment, after he moved back home to Tokyo."

"My goodness, that was quick. Sure seems like the apartments in your building don't stay vacant for long these days."

Jayne chuckled on the other end of the line. "You can say that again. With all the people moving into town for work, she's lucky she got the place. Talk about being in the right place at the right time. She walked in the door only seconds after I learned Mr. Masamoto was leaving."

"And she's all alone? No roommate?"

"Just her and her piano. You should have seen the day they moved that beauty in. Whew."

I laughed. "Is the new tenant nice?"

Jayne went silent for a moment and I heard static crackling in my ear. "Well, I wouldn't say she's nice, exactly. She's all business around me, and I get the feeling she's avoiding me like the plague. To tell you the truth, I'm not sure what her story is."

"Maybe she's shy."

Jayne chuckled again. "No . . . she's not what you would call a shrinking violet. But you'll know what I mean when you see her. She's got bright blonde hair that stands out like a beacon, and she wears enough fake diamonds to look like a one-woman Milky Way. But her furs are real, and she's pretty popular with the fellas."

And that's when I felt a cold chill run up and down my spine. Because I'd just seen a woman who fit that very description. As a matter of fact, I'd just gotten off the train with her. Was it possible that Jayne's new tenant was the bombshell that had been sitting across from me on the *Sunbeam*? It seemed so farfetched, but then again, how many women matched that description?

I took a deep breath and managed to get out the words, "Sounds interesting. Hopefully we'll catch a glimpse of her. I'll bring some bran muffins."

Seconds later, we said our goodbyes and I put the receiver back in the cradle. Then I stood frozen to the spot, hardly believing what Jayne had told me. What were the odds that her new renter and the blonde bombshell were one and the same?

What in the world was going on?

Maybe I really had walked right into a real, live mystery. Just like Katie McClue.

CHAPTER 3

Bran Muffins and Bombshells

Early the next morning, I started to mix up a batch of muffins right after breakfast. But our cook, Matilda, or Maddie, gave me a smile and took the bowl from me. Of course, we both knew why. My mother would have a thrown a tantrum worthy of Scarlett O'Hara in *Gone With the Wind* if she were to catch me cooking, and Maddie would have been in big trouble for allowing me to so much as touch kitchen utensils.

Because, in my blue-blood world, young women did not demean themselves by baking a bunch of muffins. Or cooking an entire meal. Apparently, the bluer the blood the fewer the actual practical skills a girl was supposed to possess. Except for such time-honored talents as arranging seating charts and acting as the perfect hostess to one's rich and powerful husband. Even so, I'd always had a yearning to figure out how things worked in the kitchen. Nana, who hadn't been born rich and actually did most of the cooking for the first half of her life, even conjured up a meal or two, or baked a cake on Maddie's day off. And while I didn't dream of ever being a fantastic cook like Nana or Maddie, if I ever got stranded on a desert island, I at least wanted to know how to crack open a coconut.

Maddie's blue eyes twinkled, and her pale skin already had a rosy glow this morning, meaning she'd been hustling around cooking soup or baking bread or something for the day's meals. She had various helpers, including a young girl named Violet, who served most of meals.

I adored Maddie. She'd been with our family since I was a child and during that time her hair had gone from a rich red to a silky gray. And once, when I was young and my parents had been away on an extended vacation, she'd taught me the few elementary cooking skills that I did possess. To this day, those lessons were our little secret.

I smiled at her. "A dozen muffins would be swell."

"I'll have them ready in no time a'tall, Miss Tracy."

Sure enough, she wasn't kidding.

Because it wasn't long before I was driving Nana's 1940 Packard Super Eight Sedan and wearing my favorite forest-green wool day dress, along with a matching felt hat and gloves. I had the basketful of still-warm muffins beside me on the front seat. The sun was glaring in through the windshield and thankfully I'd remembered to bring my sunglasses. There weren't a lot of cars on the road, so it was a pretty nice day for a drive. It dawned on me that I should have invited Nana to come along. She rarely drove anymore, and she'd more or less turned the car over to me. Gramps had bought it for her, and I knew how much she loved the sleek, maroon-colored car. Especially since Packard was the first to offer air conditioning, something that was extra nice during the hot Houston summers. But besides all that, the car was one of her last connections to Gramps, the love of her life. So I made sure it got the very best of care.

Of course, I loved to drive the Packard because Katie McClue drove a Packard, though hers was an older, sportier model in bright red. But thanks to the Packard's great performance and her own superior driving skills, Katie had either outrun or chased down many a bad guy. She'd even helped the police now and then with car chases, since her car was faster than standard police cars. And just like Katie usually brought her camera with her, I had mine sitting in its leather case, right next to my purse on the floor.

I glanced at the clock and then stepped on the gas, so I could make sure I stepped into Jayne's apartment right around ten o'clock. I tuned the radio into my favorite station and sang along to Glenn Miller's *Chattanooga Choo Choo*. Loudly.

Funny, but my singing voice was the only thing my mother ever seemed to like about me, and she'd been rolling me out to entertain her guests since I was a child. Apparently she deemed it a worthwhile talent for an upper-crust daughter and the wife of a future U.S. Senator. But only as long as I sang in someone's living room or in the occasional choir. If I were ever to sing in a nightclub or with a swing band, I'm sure she'd have me locked in my room for life. The thought of such a prison made me cringe, especially when I remembered an article I'd read about the Swing Youth in Germany, who'd been brutally arrested in August. Over three hundred of them. Who knew what had happened to them all by now? I couldn't even imagine living in a world where I'd be arrested for listening and dancing to the wrong kind of music.

As for my own singing, after I graduated from high school, I didn't care to be treated like a trained poodle anymore and I quit singing for my mother's parties. Now I only sang when I wanted to. And because I enjoyed it.

Which was exactly what I did all the way to Jayne's place. Seven songs later, I pulled alongside the street in the closest parking spot I could find near her building. Then I strolled through the front door and glanced at the dainty gold watch on my wrist, which told me it was ten o'clock on the dot. The front hallway in the old mansion was always a little dark, probably since the place had been sectioned off into apartments and most of the windows were now part of someone's apartment. The only window left in the front hallway was a transom above the front door. But it didn't exactly provide much natural light, considering it was limited by a roofed-in front porch that blocked any direct sunlight. Other than that, there was one dangling bare bulb that was supposed to light up the entire hallway, until it reached a huge, well-lit staircase in the rear. The ground floor consisted of two large apartments and one public room behind the stairs. The second and third floors had more apartments, though I wasn't sure exactly how many there were.

And my friend, Jayne, was the woman who managed them all for the building's owner. Even though she was still working toward a degree in math, it was her carpentry, mechanical, and electrical skills that amazed me the most. Not to mention, her bookkeeping skills. Then again, she'd been raised on a farm where she learned to do a lot with very little, and she and her family were what you might call "self-sufficient." It didn't hurt that Jayne had worked side-by-side with her four brothers, and her father had taught her the same things he'd taught his sons. Jayne tended to run around in double-time, and her movements reminded me of a tap dancer. No wonder my grandmother called her a sparkplug.

I knocked on her door and glanced across the hall at the closed door on the other side. Seconds later I heard Jayne's footsteps on the hardwood floor.

Tap, tap, a'tappa, tap, tap.

She unlatched her door and greeted me with a huge smile. "I could smell those muffins from a mile away."

She was about four inches shorter than I was, and had soft brown eyes and auburn hair that flashed with gold and red highlights whenever she moved. Today she had on a brown A-line skirt and a pink blouse with smocking at the shoulders.

I placed the basket in her hands. "It took a lot of willpower for me to drive over here and not even take a single bite."

"I'll bet." She flipped the napkin off the top and took a good sniff of the basket contents. "Now they're really making my mouth water. I've already got the tea brewing in the pot and I've got butter on the table."

I smiled and followed my friend into her tiny, but cheerful kitchen. "Yum. Sounds good to me."

I dropped my purse and my camera case on her counter, before pulling off my gloves. Then I removed my hatpin and took my hat off, too. I set it next to my gloves.

While the hallway may have been dark, Jayne's apartment was always bright and warm. It was almost as though her place didn't belong with the rest of the building.

She poured the tea into cups. "Grab some cream, would ya? My mom dropped it off fresh yesterday."

"Sure thing," I said and looked in her icebox.

I spotted a glass bottle full of the pale yellow liquid, alongside a bigger bottle of fresh milk and a straw basket filled with eggs. One thing about being a farm girl, Jayne always had the freshest ingredients around.

I poured some of the cream into her creamer and put the rest back. Then I grabbed it and the sugar bowl, and carried them to the table.

She set out bread plates and little butter knives. "So, how are things with you and Michael? Any updates on the wedding plans?"

I sat down and shook my head. "Nothing new. The date is set for June 20th. And the church and country club are booked. But that's about it. I haven't even seen Michael for weeks now."

Jayne frowned and sat in the opposite chair. "I guess he's busy working?"

"So he says." I poured some cream into my tea and then spooned in some sugar. "Sometimes I wonder if I'm marrying a complete stranger. I mean, what do I really know about this man?"

Jayne grabbed a muffin from the basket and pulled it apart. "Well . . . honestly, you couldn't find a more handsome guy. And I guess it sounds like he's a hard worker."

I picked out a muffin and put it on my plate. "I know. He's a real dreamboat. Everyone keeps telling me how lucky I am and what a catch he is."

"Your families have known each other forever, right? So that's one way to tell if he's a good guy or not." She slathered fresh butter all over one half of her muffin and took a huge bite.

"My brother knew him in high school. And my mother, of course, thinks the sun rises and sets according to his mother's command."

Jayne raised a perfectly groomed eyebrow. "Hmmm . . . do I smell a setup? Sounds like your mother is more excited about this than you are. Are you sure he's the right guy for you?"

I took a sip of my tea. "I don't know. Everyone keeps saying we're such a good match. Whatever that means. How about you and Tom? You're sure he's the guy for you, right?"

Jayne grinned. "Are you kidding? We're so head over heels that we can't even see straight. But at least I know this — if he ever does anything wrong, he'll have to answer to my brothers. Just knowing that should keep him in line."

I couldn't help but laugh. After all, I'd met Jayne's brothers.

Even though they could be terrible teases, she could always count on them to come to her rescue if she needed them.

She finished her muffin and grabbed a second one. "We still can't decide on a date. My family is determined to see us have a big, full wedding. In their minds, that's the proper thing to do. But Tom and I want something simple. We've even joked about just going to the Justice of the Peace. So we can be married already."

I shook my head with amazement. "You are so lucky. If Michael and I went to the Justice of the Peace, my mother would probably swoop in and have it annulled. Only to see us get married all over again in some gigantic royal ceremony."

We laughed some more and each took another muffin. To be honest, I thought Jayne was even luckier in yet another way, to be head over heels for a man, and to have him feel the same way about her. So far, I'd never felt that in my life, and I wondered what it was like. Michael and I hadn't exactly declared our love from some mountaintop. In fact, the most I'd gotten from him was some mumbling about his being very "fond" of me, and saying that I was pretty. Apparently that was good enough for him to seal the deal. But now I wasn't sure if it was good enough for me, even though I'd accepted his ring. I wondered what it would be like to swoon with mad passion, and to hear a man whisper words of love and romance into my ear.

Jayne poured us each another cup of tea and started to talk about bridesmaid dresses and pew decorations. "What do you think?" she asked. "Mint green or pale yellow dresses for the girls? I've always liked yellow. It's so bright . . ." And that's when she stopped cold. Instead of finishing her sentence, her eyes went wide and her head practically swiveled in the direction of her living room.

I took the last bite of my muffin and turned to see what had suddenly caught her attention. Through the big picture window of her front room, I could see that a car had pulled up on the street outside. Even though we weren't close enough to make out the details, I could tell someone was getting out of the passenger side. Mostly because I heard very loud giggling.

"It's her!" Jayne said in a loud whisper.

"You mean . . . ?"

Jayne choked and pounded her chest. "Yes, her! My new

tenant. Hurry, let's go take a look!"

Then Jayne grabbed my hand and pulled me toward the picture window. She took us on a roundabout path, so we stayed closer to the wall and out of sight of anyone who could see in through the window. And consequently, see us.

It was a maneuver that would have made Katie McClue proud. Once we reached the edge of the window, we carefully peeked out. And sure enough, I could see a woman leaning into a car. It looked like she was saying a long, lingering goodbye to some man in a military uniform. Talk about mad passion. I was surprised the windows weren't completely steamed up.

"Is that her boyfriend? Or fiancé?" I whispered to Jayne.

"I'm not sure. He just picked her up for breakfast."

"How do you know that?"

My friend smiled. "I listened at the keyhole."

"Good job," I giggled.

It was another excellent Katie McClue move on Jayne's part.

After a full minute, the woman and her beau finally finished their goodbyes, and then she strolled to the front walk, swaying her hips so far from side to side that I feared she might injure herself. That's when I finally got a good look at her.

The hair on the back of my neck stood on end.

Because I recognized that woman. Just like I'd suspected, she was the blonde bombshell I'd seen on the train the night before.

Now I had to wonder, who was she? And why did I keep running into her?

CHAPTER 4

Bad News and Boogie Woogie

I gasped and put my hand to my mouth.

Jayne raised an eyebrow. "Do you know her?"

I shook my head. "No, but I saw her last night. She was on the train coming home from Dallas. Who is she?"

"Her name is Betty. Betty Hoffman. Get a load of all that jewelry. And that big fur coat. She's the absolute limit, isn't she?"

I nodded. "Almost like she's a character out of a movie."

Or a Katie McClue novel.

Jayne clucked her tongue. "You can say that again."

And that's when I suddenly remembered my camera. I turned on my heel and made a beeline for the kitchen counter where I'd left it. Then I quickly pulled the snaps open on the leather case and took out my Argus C2. Everyone called this camera "the brick," and let me tell you, it was the perfect nickname for it. Not only was it the size and shape of a brick, but it weighed about as much as one, too. On the other hand, it took terrific pictures.

I only hoped it wouldn't let me down now, as I slid back into position at the side of the window, until I had the perfect vantage point. As before, I could see without being seen. I focused the camera and immediately snapped off a whole bunch of shots. I remembered I'd just put in a new role of film not long ago, so I didn't hold back. By the time I was done, I was pretty sure I'd gotten several good photos of the blonde woman, and I even managed to get one of the guy who had dropped her off.

Why I was taking these pictures, well . . . I wasn't exactly sure. I also had no idea what I would do with them once they were developed. But I did know that Katie McClue took pictures of things she thought were suspicious, and I figured if it was good enough for her, it was good enough for me.

By now, the woman had moved out of our line of sight as she sashayed toward the front door.

I lowered my voice to a whisper. "Where does she get her money? She's not a . . . "

"Lady of ill repute?" Jayne finished my thought in a whisper of her own. "Nope. She seems to have lots — and I do mean lots — of male admirers. But they always drop her off out in front. She never lets any of them into her apartment. I think she must have some kind of personal rule she sticks to."

"Well, I have to give her credit for that. But the way she's dressed and the way she acts . . . she doesn't seem like the type to live in a quiet neighborhood like this. She seems more like she belongs in a hotel suite apartment, or someplace fancier. Or more exciting."

Jayne motioned for us to tiptoe to the door of her apartment. "Maybe she already gets all the excitement she needs. Because she's a nightclub singer. Mostly sings at the Polynesian Room in Galveston."

My jaw dropped open. "Really? She must be pretty good to sing down there. That could account for her income. And her many male admirers."

That, and the fact that she certainly knew how to get a man's attention. After all, I'd seen her skills firsthand on the train the night before.

"Have you talked to her much?" I asked Jayne.

Jayne shook her head as we scooted over to the door. "She steers clear of me. I've tried to strike up a conversation a time or two, but it's nothin' doin' with that girl."

We paused and listened next to the door, where we heard the

woman's high heels clacking on the hardwood floor of the hallway. As near as I could tell, Betty must have been in a big hurry all of a sudden to get to her apartment. Finally, we heard her key in the lock, just before her door creaked open and then *thunked* shut.

I sighed. So that was the end of my great investigation into the blonde bombshell. For the moment, anyway. Though when I thought about it, I wasn't sure there actually *was* much to investigate. She was a singer at a famous nightclub and lots of men adored her. On the surface, the whole situation seemed pretty cut and dried.

Even so, my feminine intuition told me there was something amiss about this woman. And more to her story. Especially when I remembered how she'd been pursuing all those guys on the train, in a very clever, clandestine sort of way. Yet why would a woman with so many admirers be so desperate for that kind of male attention? And why did the hairs on the back of my neck stand up every time I saw her?

That's when I remembered the Bogart look-alike. Was he just a lovesick fan who wouldn't leave her alone? Was the package he'd been carrying last night on the train meant for her? But if she wanted to squelch his unwanted advances, she could've simply snapped her perfectly manicured fingers and any of the guys she'd been flirting with would have come to her rescue. Instead, she turned into a shrinking violet. Why?

I moved over to the kitchen counter and stowed my camera back in its case. "Have you ever seen an older man lurking around here? Someone who is a dead ringer for Humphrey Bogart, if he was, say, about twenty years older?"

This time it was Jayne's jaw that dropped open. "As a matter of fact, I have seen a guy like that hanging around a time or two. How do you know *him*? Don't tell me he was on the train last night, too?"

"Uh-huh," I nodded. "That's right."

Jayne looked at me like I'd just told her Martians had landed in Houston. "Holy moley! I guess I need to take the train more often."

Before I could ask more, Jayne pointed to her living room window. "My goodness, is it eleven o'clock already? There's Artie, the mailman. And take a look at what he's got in his hot, little hands."

Once again, we flew back to the front window. We certainly

were getting an eyeful this morning.

Jayne leaned closer to the glass. "See that box he's carrying? That's gotta be your dress, right?"

I grinned. "Looks like it to me."

And sure enough, he was carrying the very package that I'd secretly paid a Neiman's store clerk to ship from Dallas on Thursday. I'd done it while my mother was off in a dressing room, getting fitted for an evening gown of her own. Now I could hardly wait to see my dress again.

Jayne let out a little squeal. "I'm so glad you shipped it here, so I get to see it. You're going to be real knockout. Come on! Let's go."

I followed her back into the kitchen, where she paused barely long enough to grab a huge set of keys from a drawer. Then we jumped into the hallway just as Artie, the mailman, opened the front door.

The elderly man flashed us a set of pearly whites that showed a couple of gaps in his otherwise perfect smile. "Well, if this isn't just sweet as pie! Two beautiful young ladies here to greet me at the door. Must be my lucky day."

His pale eyes sparkled with mischief, and his white hair had been combed with enough pomade to ensure every single strand stayed precisely in place. He paused near the door and let his bag slide to the ground. While he held onto my package with his left hand, he clicked his heels together and announced, "Corporal Arthur J. Lister reporting for duty." Then he gave us a snappy salute.

Jayne smiled and saluted back. "At ease, soldier."

She broke her salute and flew down the hallway with a *tappa, tap, tap, tappa* to grab Artie's heavy load. She slung it over her shoulder, linked her arm in his, and together they conducted some kind of parade march until they reached the wall of brass mailboxes, just to the right of the door to her apartment.

She dropped his bag on the floor. "Artie, this is my friend, Tracy. That package you're carrying is for her."

He glanced at the box and then at me. "Tracy Truworth? That's the name on the label, but the address is yours, Jayne. Is Tracy your new roommate?"

Jayne took the package from his hands and passed it to me. "Nope, she's just visiting."

"Well, nice to meet ya, young lady. Any friend of little Jayne's here is a friend of mine."

I gave him my brightest smile. "That goes for me, too. And it's very nice to meet you as well."

He gave me a nod. "Thank you, kindly. Now I'd best get to work and get this mail delivered."

But Jayne had already beaten him to it. She isolated a large brass key from the huge cluster on her key ring and used it to unlock the entire wall. She pulled the door to the boxes open so we could see into each of the small, individual square mailboxes for the building's residents. Most were completely empty, but a few had envelopes resting at an angle.

Then she disappeared back into her apartment and came *tapping* out with a kitchen chair in her arms. "Here you go, Artie. Why don't you take a load off for a sec or two? I'll put the mail in the boxes."

Artie shook his head. "Now, wait a minute. I don't need you girls treating me like a helpless baby."

Jayne waved him off. "Oh, nothin' doin', Artie. I just enjoy the chat, and I figure if you sit for a minute, you'll stay a little longer."

"You girls and your feminine wiles . . ." Artie chuckled and dropped into the chair.

That's when I noticed how thin he was, and that he could probably use a good, home-cooked meal. I wondered why a dear old man like him was out hauling a heavy mailbag around, instead of relaxing at home with a good book.

I smiled at him again. "I brought some homemade bran muffins with me today. Would you care for one?"

His face broke into a smile again. "Muffins? You girls are really spoiling me today. But I don't need you to go to any fuss."

"No fuss," I told him. "We've got some extras and I'd hate for them to go to waste."

"Well, in that case, young lady, I'd say yes, please. Been a long time since I've had a good bran muffin."

So I walked back into Jayne's apartment and dropped my box on her counter. I put a couple of muffins on a plate, split them in half, and slathered them with butter. Then I grabbed a napkin and took the muffins out to Artie.

In the meantime, he'd opened his bag and handed Jayne a bundle of mail that had already been sorted into smaller bundles. She began putting those smaller bundles into the right tenant's slots while he watched.

He took a bite of a muffin and closed his eyes. "Mmmm, mmmm, mmmm. Delicious. My wife, God rest her soul, used to bake these every Monday. You know, Tracy, if you can bake like this, you're going to make some man a good wife one day. If you haven't already."

I didn't have the heart to tell him that our cook had actually made the muffins. And that my husband-to-be would be mortified if I did any cooking.

"Tracy is getting married in June," Jayne piped up. "It's going to be a huge wedding."

Artie looked at me much like my grandfather had once looked at me. "Well, he's a lucky man, that's for sure."

Jayne grabbed the last stash of letters for the final box, this one located in the front, bottom corner. As she did, she raised an eyebrow in my direction. Then she held up the top envelope so I could see it. She tapped a perfectly polished fingernail right above the address line, where the name "Betty Hoffman" was written in a decidedly masculine hand. Then she moved that letter to the bottom of the pile and showed me the second letter that had obviously been penned by another hand. She kept this up until she had gone through the entire stack of letters, all with different envelopes and different handwriting. Though I had to say, the writers of those letters had probably all gotten "A's" in their penmanship classes.

"Somebody sure gets a lot of letters . . ." Jayne murmured before she stashed the envelopes into the box.

Just as she did, piano music rang out from the apartment across the hall. Betty's apartment. A snappy boogie-woogie rhythm, eight to the bar, reached our ears. This was accompanied by the voice of a woman singing — obviously Betty herself — though I didn't recognize the song. Whatever it was, she was definitely good enough for Glenn Miller's orchestra.

Jayne, Artie, and I glanced at each other before Jayne started to snap her fingers, and Artie shook his head and stared at Betty's door. My feet instantly went into a rock step ready for a swing dance.

Funny, for as much as I loved to go swing dancing, Michael insisted on going to places where the music and the dancing were much more sedate. So I usually went to the Big Band spots with my friends rather than my fiancé.

Now Jayne began to move her feet, too, while I took some twirls with an invisible partner. Right before the music stopped all of a sudden. As the saying goes, the silence was deafening. Jayne and I stopped moving, and the three of us all turned and stared at Betty's door.

"I'll bet that girl knows how to get the place jumping," Jayne sighed.

I nodded at Betty's apartment. "Maybe we should go see her at the Polynesian Room some night."

Artie sat up straight. "Only if I can be your escort, girls. Everybody's always talking about the Polynesian Room and I wouldn't mind seeing it. Especially since it's in Galveston, and that's the place everybody goes for the nightlife."

"I've heard the Polynesian Room is pretty swank," Jayne said as she swung the huge brass door of the mailboxes back into place and locked it.

Then she put her hand on Artie's shoulder. "Care for a cup of tea before you head out? One for the road, as they say?"

Artie finished off the last of his muffins. "You girls are treating me like a king. But yes, I'll have a quick cup and then I'd better get a move on. I've got lots of mail to deliver. With war coming, I can hardly keep up with it all."

"Sugar and cream?" Jayne hollered over her shoulder as she went *tap, tap, tappa* into her apartment.

"Yes, ma'am. Thank you."

I smiled at Artie. "You certainly have a crisp salute. Were you a soldier?"

Jayne re-emerged with a cup and saucer, and the tea that she'd doctored according to Artie's specifications. "In the Great War, right, Artie?"

He took a sip from his cup. "Sure was. Uncle Sam's army. Even took a bullet or two. Both of 'em went right through me and left some pretty good scars."

Jayne put her arm around his shoulders. "Artie went from Uncle

Sam's Army to Uncle Sam's Post office."

"Are you close to retirement?" I asked carefully. After all, I didn't want to insult the man by making him feel like a relic.

Artie shook his head. "Absolutely not, young lady. If I don't do this job, there won't be anybody left to do it. Because lots of our Southern boys are just itching to get into this fight, and a whole bunch of 'em have already gone to Canada to join the Royal Canadian Air Force. Then there'll be lots more of our young fellas shipping out, since you can bet we'll be at war soon. Sure wish I was going with 'em."

Jayne raised her eyebrows. "You want to go back, Artie?"

He nodded. "You'd better believe it. Still got the uniform and the gun, and I could help train the young ones comin' in. My country needs me, and I don't intend to be left out of the action."

At first I wasn't sure what to say to his "proclamation." Of course, he was well beyond the age of enlisting, but I didn't exactly want to hurt his pride by pointing that out. Especially when I had to admire his determination. If not his patriotism.

So I settled on saying, "You sound pretty sure the U.S. will get involved in this war."

He gave a little laugh before he downed the rest of his tea. "We've already been in this war a lot more than most people know. We've been shipping supplies across the Atlantic to England for a while now, and Germany hasn't taken too kindly to that. Their U-boats have been blowing our boys out of the water. Including our Navy ships guarding the shipping convoys. Plus we've been involved with the big mess of Japan invading China and Indochina."

A lump formed in my throat. Many of those "boys" Artie was talking about were probably about my age. They could have been my classmates. Or guys I knew from around the neighborhood.

Artie handed his cup and saucer back to Jayne. "Congress hasn't made it official yet, but mark my words, girls, we're going to war. Have you been hearing all the bad things that Hitler has been doing? Especially to the Jews? Believe me, I've heard the stories. From the people I deliver mail to. The lucky ones made it over here before Hitler started going after 'em. But now he won't even let them out of the country. And the Japanese soldiers aren't any better, with the way they've been raping and murdering Chinese women. So we've gotta put a stop to all this evil."

I shuddered at the thought, just as boogie-woogie music started up again in Betty's apartment. But this time I didn't feel like dancing.

Artie pulled himself up to a standing position. "These Nazis want to take over the world, girls. They've already got most of Europe, and you can bet we're next on their list. But there's only one way to stop it, and that's to fight. So, much as I hate to say it, I'll bet we're in this war by Christmas."

For once, Jayne and I were speechless. Without another word, Artie saluted us, picked up his bag and wandered out the front door.

War by Christmas. The very thought of it made my heart beat faster than the music coming from across the hall.

CHAPTER 5

Satin Gowns and Sam Spades

Artie's words of war seemed to hang in the air as Jayne and I went back into her apartment. Of course the subject was on the tip of everyone's tongue these days, so to hear him talk like that shouldn't have been any big surprise. And more and more people were absolutely chomping at the bit to stop the unspeakable horrors of Hitler and Hirohito. Even the Southern Baptists, at their Birmingham Convention in May, said "there were some things worth fighting for and worth dying for." Despite all that, there was something about the words "war" and "Christmas" being used in the same sentence that hit home a little more than usual.

Needless to say, Jayne and I were both a little silent as we opened my package. I was working hard to keep a smile on my face, and I could tell she was doing the same. So I let her unfold the tissue paper and pull the dress from the inner Neiman's box, hoping it might take her mind off all the "war talk."

Jayne gasped when she saw it. "Holy Moley! That's the most beautiful dress I've ever seen. You've got to try it on now!"

"Okay, okay," I laughed before I went to change.

Once I had it on, I realized it was even more glamorous than I had remembered. The black satin was heavy, a nice quality for an evening gown. And the lace peplum made my waist look tiny while the sweetheart neckline gave me some womanly curves. The dress was a showstopper, that was for sure. For a moment, I wished I could wear it out tonight. But I knew that wasn't likely. Michael was supposed to be working, and all my girlfriends had dates.

As I twirled in front of Jayne's full-length, cheval floor mirror, she sat on her sofa and sighed. "You look so elegant. And so ladylike. All you need is one of your necklace and earring sets and your outfit is complete. All eyes will be on you. And Michael's eyes are going to pop right out of his head when he sees you in this getup."

The image of that made me smile. Somehow I couldn't picture Michael ever showing any eye-popping emotion. The best I could hope for would be a twinkle in his eyes and maybe a straightening of his tie.

I smoothed down the black satin gloves and laughed. "Well, I'll be fine as long as neither one of the mothers sees it. According to my mother, Michael's mother would faint at the mere sight of a dress like this."

Jayne shook her head. "Heavens. That bunch of upper-crust gals sure seems like a delicate lot. Sounds like there's an awful lot of fainting going on between them."

Just then, piano music floated in from Betty's apartment. This time she was playing a song we all knew. A Glenn Miller song. I started to hum along.

Jayne's eyes went wide. "Say, in that outfit, you could be a nightclub singer, too. Here, take the stage please, madam."

She scooted a footstool over for me to stand on. I laughed as I stepped up and Jayne handed me a broom for a microphone. I put it before me and gave my vocal cords free rein. Naturally, I also added plenty of theatrics to my performance. I flung one arm wide, batted my lashes and gazed longingly upward, as though basking in the moonlight. I emphasized each stanza with more and more movements, to the point where I almost fell off the stool.

Jayne got into the melodramatics by pretending to be a member of the audience, or rather, my number one fan. She sighed and gasped, and then rolled her eyes upward before she fanned her face with a newspaper, as though she were about to faint herself. By the time the song was over, I wasn't sure who'd given the better performance — Jayne or me.

When the piano music went on to a tune that we didn't know, I stepped off the footstool. "And that, my dear friend, is the closest I will ever get to being a nightclub singer."

Jayne raised an eyebrow. "I wouldn't be so sure."

I couldn't help but laugh. "If my mother thought this dress was bad, that's nothing compared to how she would react if I ever got up on stage at a nightclub and sang. It would probably give her a heart attack. And of course, Michael would be absolutely appalled!"

Jayne placed a wrist to her forehead, mimicking an impending faint. "Oh, my goodness! The horror! You in that glamour girl dress singing at a swank club. However will you live with the shame?"

To which I broke out in giggles.

Then Jayne rolled her eyes. "Honestly, if something like that gets her so upset, what will she and her friends do if we end up going to war?"

And there it was again, the subject we couldn't avoid if we wanted to. War. It was the number one topic in every newspaper and on every newsreel at the movies. And the radio news didn't skimp on it either. It was everywhere you looked. We all feared it was coming, and anticipated it at the same time, as though we could all sense we were standing on the brink of something big.

I shook my head. "I don't know what my mother and her gang would do if we went to war. Especially if the fighting came onto our shores. Do you think Artie was right? Do you think we'll be part of the war by Christmas?"

Jayne's tone suddenly became serious. "Artie may be old and ailing, but he knows his stuff. And I'm inclined to believe him. These old timers have been in the same spot that we're in now. They've seen all this before, firsthand."

"I know what you mean. Nana's the same way. Their generation has lived through it. They know what it's like."

Jayne nodded. "Artie takes so much pride in being a veteran. I love that he always gives me a salute. But I think he's dying to salute a real commanding officer, in the Army."

I chuckled. "He's a dear, all right. Hard to picture him being our age and going off to war. But I guess he was one of the lucky ones, since he made it back."

"Yes," Jayne whispered. "He was one of the lucky ones."

I slid my gloves off. "The numbers of people who died in the Great War are staggering. Not to mention, all the people who were injured."

"Or lost loved ones," Jayne added as she took the gloves from me and carefully folded them into the dress box.

I unzipped the side zipper of my gown. "And now we're wondering if we'll be facing the same thing they faced. I don't want us to go to war . . . but still . . ."

Jayne helped me lower the gown so I could carefully step out of it. "Still?"

"Let's face it — Hitler and his Nazis are pure evil. So is Hirohito. The things they've been doing to people are atrocious."

Jayne gently folded my dress and rewrapped it in the tissue paper. "I know what you mean. Even though this isn't really *our* war, and nobody wants to go to war, how can we stand back and just watch these evil empires take over the world like that?"

I slipped back into my day dress. "Exactly."

Jayne put the lid on the dress box and retied the string. "Like being stuck between a rock and a hard place. Glad I'm not the one who has to decide what to do."

I straightened the seams on my stockings. "Me, too. But you can bet our generation will be the ones to carry out whatever decision someone else makes."

All of a sudden, Jayne's eyes welled up. Then a couple of tears slid down her cheeks, which surprised me. For as long as I'd known her, I'd hardly ever seen her cry. Jayne was usually the Rock of Gibraltar, and I'd never seen someone who could turn a frown upside down like she could.

"What is it?" I asked softly.

She grabbed a hankie and dabbed at her eyes. "Sorry to be so silly, but I can't help but think about Tom and my brothers. If we went to war, they'd probably all join up."

And I knew she was right. They were the kind of guys who wouldn't hesitate even a second to jump into the fray, especially if

America herself were threatened. They would defend our country with everything they had.

Jayne blew her nose. "I love them all so much, the big palookas. I'd be so proud of them, but I don't know what I'd do if anything ever happened to even one of them."

I put my arm around her and hugged her. "I know, I know. But these are your brothers we're talking about. And Tom. They would probably take out the Nazis single-handedly and win the war for us. That's the kind of guys they are."

Jayne sniffled. "You're right. They're all bigger and tougher than any old Nazis. If we went into this war, we would win it. I don't know why I'm being such a big baby. A few scary words from Artie and here I am spouting the waterworks. Not exactly what you'd call brave. You're probably just as worried about your brother and Michael."

I sighed. If only that were true. Because, much as I was ashamed to admit it, I wasn't sure if either one of them would sign up to fight. In one way it was sort of a blessing, and yet, in another way, it was a little embarrassing, to think the men in my life might be cowards. Sure, I didn't want anything bad to happen to them, but I knew if we ever went to war, we'd have to be all in or not in at all.

I held Jayne back at arm's length. "I'd be worried about everybody. But right now, we can't let it get us down. So let's keep our chins up, okay? We're Americans, and Texans, at that. If we go to war, Hitler's goons won't know what hit them."

Jayne laughed and wiped away her tears.

She was back to her old self by the time I had my hat and gloves back on. I insisted that she keep the rest of the muffins, before I gave her a hug and headed out of her apartment with my dress box in hand. The music had just started up again from across the hall, and I could still hear it as I strolled into the sunlight and down the front walkway.

Funny, but even though I'd succeeded in cheering her up, I suddenly wasn't feeling so cheerful myself. I could feel the blues trying their best to seep into my mindset. If only we could make the world stop spinning for a few days, and take a break from all the war talk. If only life could go back to normal, before the days when Hitler and Hirohito went on a rampage.

I guessed the people in Europe were probably thinking the same thing.

I unlocked the Packard and dropped the dress box onto the front seat. Then I slid in, keeping my unfocused gaze in the direction of Jayne's building, as I thought of her brothers and Tom, who were such a terrific bunch of men. I knew how upset she would be if one of them was killed in a war. I would be upset, too. Very upset.

I felt tears stinging my own eyes and I fought to blink them back. Then I started to put the key in the ignition when a slight movement caught my eye. I leaned forward and focused in, like Superman zeroing in with his pinpoint vision. At first I thought it might be someone's cat, or maybe a squirrel in the bushes next to Betty Hoffman's ground floor apartment window.

But then I realized the disturbance wasn't caused by anything from the animal kingdom. At least nothing at the bottom end of the food chain. Especially when I spotted the edge of a trench coat and a fedora.

It was the Humphrey Bogart guy.

And sure enough, he was sneaking around on the other side of Betty's apartment, standing just behind some tall shrubs, and doing a pretty good job of blending in with the background. Much to my amazement, it appeared he had the same newspaper-wrapped package with him that he'd had on the train.

So what was he doing there? And what was in that package? Was it supposed to be a gift for Betty? Any way I looked at it, it was hardly proper for him to be sneaking around her place, trying to get a peek inside her windows. No, a decent gentleman would walk into the hall and knock on her door. And then, if she didn't want to see him, he would take no for an answer.

But near as I could tell, this guy was about to do a great imitation of a peeping Tom. And while I had to agree with Jayne that Betty was the absolute limit, she didn't deserve some deranged guy bugging her.

Before I could give it a second thought, I jumped out of the car and made a beeline for the guy. "Hey!" I yelled in a most unladylike fashion. "What are you doing there?"

His eyes went from shifty to squinted. "Beat it, kid. This doesn't concern you."

I sauntered across the lawn and headed for the shrubbery, trying to keep the heels of my pumps from sinking into the grass. "Oh, yeah? Well, I'm making it my business."

"Take a hike, kid. You're blowing my cover."

"Somebody's gotta do it. It might as well be me." I could hardly believe the words coming out of my mouth as I moved closer.

He took a few steps back. "For the last time, kid, I'm telling you to scram."

By now my heart was pounding at least a million miles an hour. "I'm calling the police."

This made him laugh. "You're good, kid, and I have to admit, I am impressed, all right. But unless you've got a bullhorn in your pocket, I don't think the police are going to hear you from here. Never make a threat that you can't follow through on."

"Um . . . well, okay, then . . . I'll run back inside and call the police from there."

The man rolled his eyes. "And I would be long gone by the time they got here, wouldn't I? Nope, kid, you're going to have to do better than that."

I had to say, this conversation was really throwing me for a loop, because he wasn't exactly acting like the creep I thought he was. Then again, he wasn't exactly making any sense either. Especially with the way he seemed to be critiquing my actions.

So I decided to use a different tactic. "Okay, then, what is your name?"

If I thought he'd laughed before, well, it was nothing compared to the way he laughed now. "My name? Okay, I've gotta hand it to you, that's an original approach. Though I don't see where it's going to get you. The name is Sammy."

This time I rolled my eyes. "Come on. Sammy? As in Sam Spade? As in the *Maltese Falcon*?"

"Blame my mother, kid. Not me."

"And you just happen to look like Humphrey Bogart?"

"Blame my father for that one."

I stepped forward again. "Let me guess. What do you have in the package? A bird just like in the movie?"

He stepped back so that he was now completely out of the bushes. "You've been spending too much time at the movies, kid.

And by the way, what is your game plan here, coming at me like this? Have you thought this over? What if I had a gun?"

Suddenly I froze in place and my throat went dry. "*Do* you have a gun?" I managed to squeak out.

He shook his head. "Of course I have a gun. Just not with me at the moment. But maybe you should've thought of that before you came at me like gangbusters."

Much as I hated to admit it, he was probably right.

He tipped the brim of his fedora. "Well, kid, it's been swell seein' you again. Thank you for the lovely dance. I had a wonderful time."

With those words, he turned to go.

That's when it hit me — Katie McClue would've never let a guy like him just walk away like that. Obviously he was a suspect of some kind, even though the actual mystery itself was still a little hazy at the moment. Even so, Katie McClue would have demanded answers from this guy.

And clearly I needed to do the same. So when Sammy walked off, I went right after him.

He stopped and turned to face me. "For the last time, kid, I'm telling you to amscray!"

I put my hands on my hips. "No way. Not until you tell me what's going on here."

"Stay out of it. This is a dangerous business. And you don't need to get your pretty little head in deeper than you can handle."

Then he turned and took off again, picking up speed. And like a bloodhound following a scent, I *followed* him.

He walked even faster and so did I. Soon, he was almost going at a trot. I kept up, even though I was hardly wearing the kind of shoes a girl could really run in. Before long, we reached the end of the block. He turned the corner and so did I. All the while, I got my brains in gear and tried to remember if Katie McClue had ever been in a situation like this. Thankfully, a scene from *The Mystery of the Runaway Man* popped into my mind. And I knew just what to do.

I put the coals to it, ran ahead, and jumped in front of him. Then I grabbed his arm with one hand and the string of the newspaper-wrapped parcel with other.

I looked him square in the eye. "If you don't tell me what's going on right now, I'm going to scream."

He laughed even louder and shook his head. "I've gotta give you credit, kid. That is creative. I wouldn't mind having you on my team."

His team? What in the world was he talking about?

He tried to yank his arm and the package from my grasp, but I hung on like a dog with a bone. Then I tipped my head back and screamed for all I was worth.

In a matter of seconds, a very muscular man popped his head out the front door of a house. "Are you all right, Miss? Is that man bothering you?"

The man flew down the steps, letting his screen door slam behind him.

Still hanging on, I turned to my rescuer. "Yes, this man is trying to steal my package!"

Suddenly the package I'd been holding by the string became dead weight in my hand. It dropped, and I dropped to my knees along with it, refusing to let go. On reflex, I grabbed the bottom of the package with my other hand, so it wouldn't hit the ground. But that also meant I'd just let go of my quarry, and I couldn't get my footing back quickly enough to run after him.

I finally stumbled to my feet and turned just in time to see Sammy, the Bogart look-alike, jump into a black sedan and start the engine. Before I could even think of catching him, he took off and disappeared once more. But this time, he'd left his newspaper-covered parcel behind. I had it, right there in my arms.

CHAPTER 6

Fancy Footwork and Nana's Knowledge

"Are you all right, Miss?" asked the man who had run out of his house to rescue me.

"Thank you. I'm fine," I told him with the best smile I could manage.

He took the package from my hands and helped me to my feet. "Looks like that chump got away. Otherwise, I would've given him a knuckle sandwich. He had it comin', all right."

"That is terribly gallant of you," I told him as I dusted off my knees and inspected the damage. Luckily, the fall hadn't put a hole in my silk stockings.

He handed the package back to me and I wrapped my arms around it. Surprisingly, it wasn't as heavy as it looked. I detected a faint musty odor, though I spotted a recent date on one of the newspapers surrounding it. So I guessed the actual contents of the bundle must have been the source of the slight smell. That only made me more inquisitive than ever to know what was inside. If I had been a cat, my curiosity might have gotten the better of me, and who knows how that might have ended.

All that brought up another question — what should I do with this package now that I had it? In all honesty, I didn't mean to take it from him and I certainly hadn't planned to end up with it. All I really wanted was some information, so I could find out what was going on. But now that Sammy was long gone, I couldn't exactly return the package to him.

And since I couldn't see another option, I thanked my rescuer once more before I walked back to my car. All the while I kept my eyes peeled, wondering if Sammy was about to drive up. Surely he still wanted the item that I was holding, *whatever* it was that was tightly wrapped up under all that newspaper and tied up with twine.

But I didn't catch a single glimpse of him as I rounded the corner and walked the entire distance to the Packard. And I still didn't spot him when I slid into the front seat and settled the package beside me, right next to my dress box.

I glanced around once more before I started the car and pulled into the street. That's when it dawned on me — what if he'd actually *allowed* me to have the package so he had an excuse to follow me home? And if he found out who I was and where I lived, was it possible he'd start hanging around outside our mansion, lurking in the shadows and trying to peek in windows? Suddenly chills ran a road race up and down my spine. He'd warned me to "stay out of it," saying it was a dangerous business.

Now I had to wonder, what did he mean by that? Not to mention, what had I gotten myself into?

I shivered in the bright sunlight. Sure, I would have been more than happy to give this bundle back to him. But on my *own* terms, not his. Though one thing was for sure — I did not want this man following me home. And now, for all I knew, he might be idling at another corner, waiting for me to drive past. So he could tail me. I suddenly remembered a scene between Katie McClue and some very nasty gangsters in *The Case of the Terrifying Car Chase*. Of course, Katie had managed to outmaneuver several cars filled with crooks, cleverly leading them all into the Police Department parking lot and then boxing them in. But only after some very harrowing moments and some pretty fancy clutch-work in her own Packard.

I slipped my sunglasses on, so the glare of the sun bouncing off the hood wouldn't blind me. Sure, I was a pretty good driver and I'd been trained by the best — Hadley himself. But was I ready to handle a car chase?

I glanced at my rearview mirror. A couple of cars had pulled in behind me, but I didn't see any that looked like the dark sedan that Sammy had been driving. Then again, Sammy had taken off so fast that I'd only caught a quick glimpse of his car from the rear. To be honest, I couldn't really picture what his car had even looked like. It was just sort of, well . . . common. The kind of car you wouldn't look at twice or remember once you'd seen it. And of course, I hadn't been close enough to get his license plate number.

So even though I checked the traffic all around me, I knew it was possible for Sammy to be keeping enough distance so that I couldn't spot him. Meaning, he could still be following me the whole way home. That's when I decided to try a maneuver that Katie McClue used whenever she needed to lose a tail. I took a sudden left turn onto an empty street and hit the gas. Then I turned right and zigzagged through a neighborhood, taking random right and left turns. Between my clutch, gas pedal, and brake pedal, I did some pretty fancy footwork of my own. After a few minutes, I slowed down and looked in my mirror again. This time I was the only car on the street, so I was pretty sure Sammy hadn't followed me. In fact, as near as I could tell, no one had followed me. No gangsters, no nightclub singers, and certainly no Sammy.

With a huge sigh of relief, I got back on my normal route and drove west on the Boulevard to River Oaks, without spotting a suspicious dark car in my rearview mirror. Eventually, I even turned on the radio and started to sing again. I warbled through a couple of songs when I realized that I'd forgotten my camera. I'd just have to remember to pick it up the next time I was at Jayne's.

I arrived home unscathed and turned the car over to Hadley.

"So how is your dear friend Jayne?" he asked as I handed him the keys. "Still running the apartment building like an expert? That young lady has an excellent mechanical mind."

I grabbed my dress box and the newspaper-wrapped parcel from the car. "She's the best, Hadley. Wish I knew half the things that she knows."

He nodded and closed the car door behind me. "Well, now, I believe you could learn. Some things simply take time and practice. 'Education is the kindling of a flame, not the filling of a vessel.'"

"Yeats?"

"No, my child. Just plain old Socrates. Alistair was more a fan of Yeats than I."

The mention of Hadley's grandson, Alistair, or Al as we called him, made me smile. He'd gone off to college in Atlanta this year, and I missed him. Especially since he'd been spending his summers with Hadley every year since he was young, in Hadley's apartment over the garage. Hadley's wife had passed away when I was but a teen, and Al had helped his grandfather get through the worst of his grief. To this day, the two were as close as Nana and I were.

"How is Al? Is college going well?" I asked Hadley.

Hadley shook his head. "He's left Morehouse and gone to Tuskegee."

"Tuskegee? Where is that?"

"Alabama. He's in a completely new military pilot training program over there. Something Eleanor Roosevelt is supporting. In a nutshell, my grandson is going to fly airplanes."

The idea of that made me grin. Not only was Al as brainy as his grandfather, but he was one of the most fearless guys I knew. I could just picture him in a cockpit, flying loop de loops.

"He'll be home for Christmas, right? Maybe we can talk him into giving us a plane ride," I told Hadley.

He laughed. "I am certain we can. And yes, he'll be here for Christmas Eve. With the feast and festivities that your grandmother has planned for us, he wouldn't miss it for the world."

With that, I bid Hadley goodbye and tiptoed in through the back door of our mansion. Then I used my best Katie McClue stealth skills to avoid running into my mother. I didn't exactly want her to find out that I'd bought the black dress she despised so badly, and I especially didn't want to her to see me with the twine-tied package that I'd gotten from Sammy. I caught a glimpse of her reading the newspaper in the parlor as I slinked past. Clearly, she was too enraptured with some article to even notice me.

I took the back staircase up to my room and quietly shut the door. Then I laid the package on my desk, and carefully hung the dress in the back of my closet. All the while, I wondered what I should do with that bundle I'd brought home. The curiosity itself was just about to kill me. Exactly what *was* inside that parcel? Was it a present meant for Betty? Or a stash of jewels, or a rare statuette? Or a gigantic poisonous snake?

I knew Katie McClue wouldn't have hesitated for a moment to unwrap it. But oddly enough, I felt a little funny about doing just that, now that I had the package here. After all, it didn't really belong to me, and the contents weren't even mine to look at. Especially since Sammy hadn't exactly handed the bundle to me. No, I'd only ended up with it by accident.

But then another thought occurred to me. What if I accidentally put myself in danger by simply taking a peek at the contents? I remembered Katie McClue's fifth adventure, when she'd found a false bottom in a closet, one that was filled to the brim with cash. Stolen cash. From that moment on, the bad guys were after her, since *they* knew that *she* knew about their hidden stash.

I threw my hands up in the air and groaned. Katie McClue never had this much trouble making a decision. And until I figured out what to do with the package, I thought it was best to hide it in my closet. I had just finished stashing it behind some shoes when a knock sounded at my door.

Nana pushed the door open and poked her head inside. "Got a hot date tonight with Michael?"

I rolled my eyes. "I wish."

She frowned. "Well, then, darlin', how about being my date this evening? Let's go to the movies after dinner."

"Sounds swell."

"By the way, your mother is serving early. Better get changed and down there," she said with raised eyebrows.

"I'll step on it," I told her with a smile, right before she gave me a little wave and took off, probably to get dressed herself.

Dinner on a Saturday night at my house was always a formal affair. My mother insisted. So I changed into one of my long dinner dresses, a blue number with smocking at the shoulders and the waist. Then I put on my real sapphire necklace and earrings, applied just the right amount of lipstick and blotted it on a tissue, right before I swept down the stairs and headed to our huge dining room. Giles escorted me to my seat and held my chair for me. My grandmother was already there, and she smiled at me from across the table. She was seated next to my brother, who nodded to me before he glanced at his new wristwatch.

My guess was that he was in a big hurry to get somewhere, but didn't want to formally cancel out on the family dinner. Probably to avoid the third degree about where he was going tonight. Or more importantly, *whom* he was going with. He most likely had plans with his buddies or a date with some young woman whom my mother would never approve of. Benjamin's curly, toffee-colored locks and cherubic face certainly made him popular with the girls. Lots and lots of girls, of all social sets. But being the golden child that he was, he wanted to keep his less-than-high-society-plans under his hat, especially if he was going slumming in some seedy bar.

While my father sat frowning at one end of the table, my mother was in rare form at the other. It appeared the champagne cocktail she was drinking had not been her first of the evening.

"I read the most interesting story today," she gushed. "The King of the Belgians married a commoner. A commoner! Isn't that positively wonderful? I'm sure it was the most spectacular wedding ceremony ever seen."

She turned her bleary-eyed gaze straight at me, as though this announcement was supposed to bring about some kind of epiphany within my brain. Perhaps she'd now decided she'd set her sights too low in all her maneuvering to get Michael to marry me. After all, while Michael came from a prominent, well-to-do family, he was hardly heir to any thrones. And now maybe my mother had suddenly realized that nothing but royalty would do. If the King of Belgium would marry a commoner, well, there might be hope for such an arrangement with her daughter.

But only if she had a *different* daughter. Someone other than me.

Maddie's helper, Violet, brought in a soup tureen and served us all. It looked like beef consommé with vegetables tonight. I could tell from the scent wafting up from my bowl that it would be delicious.

My father took a spoonful of soup and raised his hazel eyes to my mother. "Did you read the entire article, my dear?"

She flitted her hand as though batting away a mosquito. "I caught the gist of it."

He sat up straight and ran his fingers through his cropped, silver hair. "It was hardly much of a wedding. A very low-key affair, actually. That's because he couldn't have much of a wedding since he's under house arrest in his castle."

My mother dipped her spoon into her own soup. "House arrest? He's the king. How can the king of a country be under house arrest?"

My father's brow went up. "Because the Nazis put him there when they took over the country. That was, after the Belgium army had so many bloody battles with the Germans, the King surrendered rather than see his countrymen slaughtered."

Now Benjamin jumped in. "But some say the King is a Nazi sympathizer. That he gave up too soon and that he should have continued to fight the Germans. No matter how many men were killed. Especially since he's not enduring the torture that others in the army were subjected to."

My mother gasped. "How can the two of you say such horrible things? That's hardly the kind of talk one should have during dinner! Thank goodness we don't have guests tonight. From now on, I forbid any talk of war during meals."

While Benjamin glanced at his watch again, my father shook his head. "Yes, it would be so much better if we waited until we heard the whistle of Nazi bombs dropping on us before we discussed it."

My mother downed the rest of her cocktail. "We won't be going to war. So there's no use ruining a lovely evening with such vile talk."

My father shook his head. "I wouldn't be so sure. And I, for one, plan to enlist if we do."

My mother's jaw practically hit the table. "What? How could you? You're too old to enlist, Jonathan. The military is for young men."

"Then I'll sign up instead," Benjamin piped up. "I'm ready to fight Hitler and his henchmen."

Benjamin smiled at me, and I smiled right back at him. I had to say, I was suddenly very proud of my brother. Whether he enlisted or not, I was proud of his sense of duty. And the fact that he was thinking of someone other than himself for a change.

"No, you won't!" Both my parents practically shouted in the same instance.

"Not until you finish law school," my father said firmly.

But my mother was not to be outdone. "I will not allow you to demean yourself by becoming a soldier. Not my son."

"Nonsense," my father added. "I won't have the boy being mollycoddled. And there is nothing demeaning about being a soldier. My father served in the Great War, and I regret that I didn't sign up myself. I have always found it to be a point of embarrassment at the club. Most of the fellows are veterans, and when all the veterans gather around for drinks and cigars, I'm the odd man out. And I wonder if some of the men think I was a coward, though none have had the bad manners to say so. So I will not stop my son from serving if he so chooses. As for me, I will sign up if the occasion arises. I am hardly ancient and perfectly capable of serving our military in some capacity."

I reached over and squeezed his hand. "I'm proud of you, Daddy. You'd make a great soldier."

Nana patted his arm. "Yes, you would, Johnny."

"And what about your oil company?" my mother said before she finished her champagne cocktail. "Who will run that?"

"I'm sure I can train some of the other fellows to handle it while I'm gone. Or perhaps you might step in to help, my dear."

The look of sheer horror on my mother's face brought the conversation to a screeching halt. First she turned pale and then she turned red. I feared she might explode at any moment. Instead she clenched her teeth and took in a couple of ragged breaths.

Then she said in a low voice. "Are you trying to humiliate me, Jonathan? Women of our class do not engage in employment . . ."

And so it went. On and on and on.

After dinner, I changed clothes before Nana and I headed to the movies.

"I'll get the Packard," I told her as I buttoned my coat and slipped on my gloves.

She donned her own coat. "No need. It's a beautiful night and a little fresh air would do us good. Why don't we walk?"

I smiled at her. "Sounds lovely to me."

We grabbed our purses and strolled out the door. And she was right — it was a beautiful night. We laughed and talked the entire way to the River Oaks Theater. Nana wanted to see *Sergeant York,* so I bought two tickets while she bought the popcorn. I was surprised she'd picked a war movie, but I didn't mind seeing Gary Cooper on the silver screen. I got the impression she didn't mind admiring him for a few hours, either.

We found some seats just in time to catch the newsreel that brought us up to date on the war in Europe. Right after that, there was a segment on the superiority of our Navy, and how it was second to none. At least that made me feel a bit better. It was nice to know that our Navy was so strong that nobody would dare mess with our ships.

The movie itself turned out to be pretty good, though personally, I would have preferred a whodunit. Especially since I could hardly stop thinking about that newspaper-wrapped bundle I had hidden in my closet.

When the movie had finished and the lights went up, we joined the rest of the crowd leaving the theater. A few people were picked up by chauffeurs and some drove their own cars. But most of the movie-goers walked home and enjoyed the clear night full of stars and a bright moon, just like we did.

Along the way, we ran into Mr. and Mrs. Fields, who were friends of my parents.

"I hear the wedding plans are coming along nicely," Mrs. Fields chirped.

"Why, yes," I said, stumbling over the words. "They are. Thank you for thinking of me."

That's when it struck me that other people seemed to know a whole lot more about my wedding than I did.

"Want to talk about it?" Nana asked once the Fields had turned down another block.

I sighed. "I'm not sure what there is to talk about."

"Let's start with whatever's been on your mind this whole night. Somehow I don't think you're pining away for that absentee fiancé of yours. I think something else is bothering you."

And that's when I sighed and told her about Sammy and the blonde bombshell and everything else that had happened. Everything except for my reverie about Katie McClue, of course.

Nana stopped dead in her tracks and stared at me. "Well, Jeepers Creepers! Let's get home and see what's inside that package!"

"But . . . do you think we should?"

She grinned. "Sure do. Who knows what's in that thing? It could be a ticking time bomb. Or maybe it's a rubber plant that needs watering. But as long as we've got it, we'd better be sure we know what's in it."

"All right. If you think it's best."

"Of course I do. Besides, I know how to untie a knot and retie it so no one will ever know it's been tampered with."

I felt my eyes go wide. "Nana . . . really? You do?"

She wound her arm around mine. "Sure. Your grandfather taught me how. Something he picked up when he was a Pinkerton man."

"Why did Gramps stop being a detective?"

A dreamy look came over Nana's face. "He decided that hunting desperate criminals might be too dangerous for a family man. So, instead he got into oil, and became a wildcatter, which turned out to be a whole lot more dangerous. Anyway, it's nice to see you take after him, since I can tell you've got a bit of the 'detective' coursing through your veins."

For some reason, that made me smile.

Minutes later, we were in my bedroom with the package on my desk.

"Lock the door," Nana whispered, right before she dabbed a tissue into a glass of water and then touched the tissue onto the twine knots. "This'll make them easier to pull apart."

She repeated this step several times, until the knots were all good and wet. Then she pulled a big safety pin and a can of Vasoline® Jelly from her purse.

She dipped the pointy end of the pin into the jelly and then inserted it between one of the knotted strands of the twine. She began to wiggle it and, little by little, she loosened the knot. Before long, we were able to untie that first knot. So she repeated her trick on the rest of the knots, and finally, we were able to pull all that twine off the package.

"Be careful," she instructed. "Let's make sure we keep these newspapers in the order we found them."

So we just let the newspapers fall onto the top of my desk.

To expose a beautifully crafted wooden box underneath.

"Let's open it." I said very quietly, though I wasn't sure why.

Together, we carefully lifted the latch and slowly pulled the lid upright. That's when I felt my jaw fall open, right before I gasped. Nana and I looked at each other with wide eyes, and I could tell she felt the same way that I did.

We could hardly believe what was inside that box.

CHAPTER 7

Peculiar Contents and Dire News

Obituaries. Lots of them. Clipped from what appeared to be a variety of newspapers. From all around the country. Of all the things I thought I might find inside the package I'd gotten from Sammy, this had to be the absolute last collection I ever could've imagined. I was almost too shocked to speak.

"What in the world . . .?" I finally said. My voice came out in a whisper. Maybe out of respect for the dead.

Beside me, Nana let out a low whistle. "Wow-wee. I know people who browse the Obituary Section of the newspaper, but I've never come across someone who collected the clippings. Must be some kind of morbid curiosity. But it looks like this Sammy guy has gone a bit overboard with it."

I picked up a clipping and looked it over. "My goodness, the boy who died in this one was only twenty-two. How sad."

Nana glanced at another one. "This young man was barely twenty. You're right. This *is* sad."

For some reason, learning that two of the write-ups had been about young men just seemed to spur us on. We wanted to read more. So together we glanced over clipping after clipping. As near as we could tell, they were all obituaries of men. Mostly young men. Men who died long before their time.

I shook my head. "Do you think some of these boys went to the same school or something? Or college, maybe? Or maybe some of them are related?"

Nana shrugged. "Your guess is as good as mine. Why anyone would run around with a whole collection of death notices is beyond me."

I reached in to grab another handful of obituaries, and that's when my hand bumped something at the bottom of the box. I carefully scooted some of the newspaper clippings out of the way, until I could wrap my fingers around a thin, leather-bound book. I pulled it out to find it was a high school yearbook, from Abilene, Texas. So I dug in again, until I found another yearbook, this one from Austin. Then I found another and another. Before long, I had a stack of six on my desk.

"Let's see what else is in here," I said as I moved my fingers around the bottom of the box. Seconds later, I pulled out a full-blown photo album.

Nana opened one of the yearbooks. "I'm starting to wonder if you're going to find everything but the kitchen sink in here."

I had to say, I was starting to wonder the very same thing.

To make my search easier, I pulled out a handful of obituaries and straightened them into a stack. Then I set them next to the yearbooks, before grabbing another bunch of obituaries and stacking them neatly, too. Finally, I could see the rest of the items at the bottom of the box. That's when I found baby pictures and school pictures, and a few more photo albums. I even found a locket with a lock of curly, blond hair inside. And a silver baby mug, with the name "Bobby Thompson" engraved onto it.

I shook my head as I surveyed the assorted things now on my desk. "What could all this mean?"

Nana chuckled. "I think it means you should stay away from that Sammy character. Looks like he's got a few screws loose."

"So why was he carrying all this stuff around with him? There doesn't appear to be any rhyme or reason to it."

Nana rubbed her eyes. "You've got that right."

I put my index finger to my lower lip. "Maybe that's the key.

Maybe I need to find out how all these things are connected."

Nana smiled. "If there is any connection."

Yet somehow in the back of my mind, I had a feeling there was. I remembered a scene from one of my favorite Katie McClue novels, *The Mystery at the Secondhand Store*, where Katie had been given an entire duffel bag full of odds and ends. There was a brush, a picture frame, a bandana, and a pair of pliers. And tons of other things.

They were odds and ends that didn't seem to have any connection to each other. But after Katie had examined each piece and figured out what all the items had in common — that each item started with the letter "B" or the letter "P" — she quickly realized the whole stash was nothing but a gigantic clue meant to steer her to someone with the initials "B.P." And that very clue was the final piece of the puzzle that helped her uncover the murderer, a man named Baltazar Peazance. Her deductions were brilliant as always, and she even received an accommodation from the mayor thanks to her superior detective work.

Now I wondered if I needed to do exactly what Katie had done — find out what all the things in this box had in common. Then maybe I could figure out how it fit into the scheme of things. Whatever that scheme might be.

But not tonight.

With Nana's eyes starting to droop and my own mind turning to mush, I knew it was time for a visit from the Sandman. Any more sleuthing on my part would have to wait until the next day. Right after church.

I gave Nana a kiss on the cheek and sent her off to bed. Then I packed all the picture albums, yearbooks, and obituaries back in the wooden box. I folded the newspapers in the order I'd found them, and I hid it all in my closet. I quickly changed into my pajamas and brushed out my hair before I hit the hay.

I spent the whole night in a fitful sleep, with images of Humphrey Bogart and the *Maltese Falcon* and the blonde bombshell floating in and out of my dreams. By the time my alarm clock *ding-ding-dinged* me awake, I felt more exhausted than rested.

I was still feeling the effects of it all when I half-stumbled down to breakfast, after getting dressed in my Sunday best. I downed an extra cup of coffee before I walked with Nana, Benjamin, and my father to the one-year-old St. John the Divine Church. The "Chapel in the Woods," as it was known around the city. And while I knew my mind should have been on the prayers and the sermon, I couldn't stop thinking about the contents of that box. More specifically, the fact that most of the names on those obituaries belonged to young men.

And each of them probably had a funeral in a church very much like the one I was in now.

So why had Sammy been carrying that box around, all wrapped up? Did he personally know each of those boys in every one of those obituaries? Maybe he'd been their teacher or professor. Or a headmaster. Or maybe even a camp counselor.

Yet the image of any of those scenarios almost made me laugh out loud as the minister said the closing prayer. Luckily I clapped my hand over my mouth before so much as a peep came out.

Somehow I just couldn't picture a Bogart look-alike as a high school math teacher. Or wearing shorts and boots and leading kids on a hiking trail. No, from what I had seen of Sammy, he looked more like he belonged in the seedy underbelly of some major city, while he smoked cigarettes and downed rotgut bourbon.

When the church service had ended, we said our goodbyes and headed for home.

Nana took my arm. "Say, Tracy dear, why don't we go through our closets and find some things we don't wear anymore. We need to make another donation to Bundles for Britain."

"Sounds like a good idea," I said as I leaned into her arm. "Right after lunch."

I was proud to say, the good people of my hometown had donated very generously to Bundles for Britain. Nearly everyone agreed that we needed to do all we could to help the British War Relief Society send much-needed items to the victims of the Blitz, that horrific time when the Nazis had bombed England. Relentlessly.

But this afternoon, I knew Nana had an ulterior motive for our donation as well. She wanted a "cover," of sorts, so we could secretly take another look at the loot we had uncovered the night before. Though loot was probably not the right word to use to describe a box of obituaries and old photos.

We got home to find Giles and Hadley setting up a nice, solid fir tree in the parlor. The two men always went to an earlier service at a different church, and apparently they'd gone straight from there to find us a Christmas tree. And I had to say, they'd done an excellent job.

Hadley grinned, and for once, even Giles allowed himself to smile, making his face, with his Roman nose and baldpate, look handsome. He wore a brocade vest over a white shirt and dark trousers, but no jacket. A true "dressing down" for him. Whereas Hadley had his shirtsleeves rolled up and his work pants on.

It reminded me that I'd have to change clothes myself before I helped to decorate the tree. I always looked forward to this part of Christmas, especially with the fresh scent of pine filling the air.

That was, until the fresh smell of baked bread took over, and I knew that Maddie had been busy this morning, too. We all headed to the kitchen to find she'd made homemade potato salad and set out slices of cold cuts, ready for sandwiches. Nana insisted that Giles and Hadley and Maddie all join us for Sunday lunch in the dining room. We made our sandwiches first and then carried them in. I slathered a little mayo and mustard on my bread before adding a big leaf of lettuce, a layer of tomatoes, and a slice of Havarti cheese. Then I added some thick-sliced ham.

Nana talked a mile a minute, and I could tell she was in her element, entertaining and making sure everyone got enough to eat. The conversation quickly turned to Al's flying lessons, and everyone wanted to know the details.

In the meantime, my mother sat silently and glared at Nana. I knew she did not appreciate this "fraternizing with the help," and I'd probably hear all about it later. She'd missed church this morning, saying she had a headache. With a scowl, she excused herself early to go to the parlor, saying she didn't want to miss a moment of the Philharmonic on the radio.

After lunch, I went to my room, changed into a skirt and a sweater, and began to find things in my closet to donate — a sweater here, a skirt there, and a dress or two. All the while I waited for Nana to join me. Suddenly I felt the Christmas spirit coursing through my veins, since I was playing Santa Claus, in a sense, for people I'd never even met. People who'd been through horrors that I only knew about through newspaper photos and newsreels at the movies.

Ever since the Nazis had conducted nightly bombing runs on England during the Blitz, starting in September last year, the reports had been shocking. Thirty thousand bombs had been dropped on London between that September and November, and a third of the city had been destroyed. And though the Blitz had basically ended in May of this year, the war for Britain was far from over. The impact from the devastation would go on and on for a long time. For a moment, I tried to imagine what it must be like to endure the sounds of bombers flying overhead every night, and hear the whistle of the bombs as they fell to earth, not knowing if your house or apartment was going to be hit next.

But it was the British attitude that truly amazed me. That stiff upper lip they were so famous for hadn't drooped. "We can take it," was their motto as they had fearlessly endured the torment night after night.

Funny, but my sending old clothes in a care package seemed so small in comparison. Much too small in comparison. So I pulled out an old coat that I hadn't worn in years and added it to the pile. It was the least I could do.

By now I was beginning to wonder what was keeping Nana. She had promised to join me so we could go through the things in the box I'd gotten from Sammy. Maybe she was still laughing and talking at the table, or helping with the Christmas tree. Or maybe she hadn't finished pulling clothes to donate from her own closet.

Whatever she was doing, it was hard to believe she'd gotten sidetracked. After all, I knew she was dying to study the contents of that box as much as I was.

At long last, I heard a gentle knock on my door and Nana poked her head in.

I laughed. "There you are! I was wondering where you were. Here I thought you were my partner in crime, or rather, my partner in detective work, and then you do a bunk . . ."

And that's when I noticed she wasn't smiling. In fact her face looked pale and drawn. Considering she'd been laughing and happy when I saw her just a little bit ago, I knew something was wrong.

Very wrong.

I rushed to her side. "Nana, what is it? Are you sick? Come in and lie down."

But she just shook her head and swallowed hard, as though she had a lump in her throat. "No, darlin', I'm not sick. But I think you'd better join us in the parlor."

"Um . . . okay. Is there something wrong? What's going on?"

She put her arm around me. "It was just announced over the radio a few minutes ago. We don't know all the details yet. But I think you'd better come and listen to this."

She took my hand and together we headed for the stairs.

I stopped on the landing, before we went down. "What, Nana? What's going on?"

"We've been attacked," she said breathlessly.

I glanced up at the ceiling. "We have? We, as in, our house and our family?"

She shook her head. "No, darlin'. The United States has been attacked. In Pearl Harbor. By the Japanese."

"The Japanese?"

Much as I hated to admit it, I had no idea where Pearl Harbor was.

Nana seemed to read my mind. "It's in the Territory of Hawaii. They've bombed our ships and attacked our fleet. Battleships have been blown up and sailors have been killed."

Suddenly my heart started to pound like it was going to bounce right out of my chest. Tears pricked at my eyes.

Nana took my hand. "Come down to the parlor. We're all gathered around the radio. I don't think the U.S. will be staying out of this war much longer."

And with those words, I followed her down the stairs. Somehow I was desperate for more news and details, and at the same time, I didn't want to hear another word. Because I knew, deep down, that nothing in our lives would ever be the same again.

CHAPTER 8

Radio Watching and Catty Receptionists

We spent the rest of that Sunday afternoon just sitting in the parlor, "watching" the radio, as they say. Regular programming was interrupted on a *regular* basis, to the point where there *was* no more regular programming at all. We hung on every word of every announcer. Before long, we knew that Pearl Harbor had been attacked from the air. There were over three hundred Japanese fighter planes, bombers, and torpedo planes in the sneak attack.

Hadley joined us, while Maddie and Giles brought in coffee. They served everyone and stayed, their eyes fixed on the radio, with its beautifully designed, art deco wooden exterior. For the next few hours, the rest of the household staff flitted in and out as more news and details of the attack trickled in. Emergency services were put on notice. One announcer informed us with great authority that, "Citizens are asked to remain calm to avoid all unnecessary confusion because of hysteria. There is no immediate cause for alarm, and coolness will accomplish more than anything else."

Strangely enough, we *were* calm. On the outside anyway, probably because we were all in complete shock. Hadley was strangely silent, without any of his usual quotes or words of wisdom.

In fact, not one of us said anything as we leaned closer to that radio, our only connection to any information about the disaster at the moment.

My mother asked Giles to bring her a champagne cocktail, and he left the room just long enough to mix the drink and return with it on a silver tray.

Another announcer came on with more details, saying that, "Lives have been lost. Anti-aircraft gunnery was very heavy. All lines of communication seem to be down between the various Army posts. At Pearl Harbor, three ships were attacked . . ."

Before long it seemed like the words from the different announcers just ran together, like I was dreaming them, rather than hearing them in real life. "The Oklahoma was set on fire . . . the governor proclaimed a state of emergency . . . several squadrons of Japanese planes came in from the south, dropping incendiary bombs over the city . . . After machine-gunning Ford Island, the first Japanese planes moved to Hickam field . . . There were 350 men killed in a direct bomb hit on a barracks at Hickam field . . ."

Eventually, the White house released a statement, from the President's Press Secretary, Stephen Early. "The attack was made on all naval and military activities on the Island of Oahu . . . The Japanese attack on Pearl Harbor would naturally mean war. Such an attack would naturally bring a counter attack . . . The President will ask Congress for a 'Declaration of War' . . . Japan has now cast the die."

While my mother sipped her drink and stared out the window, Nana took my hand. My father's face remained stoic as he stood up and motioned for Benjamin to join him.

"We'll head down the street and see if any papers have come out," my father said quietly.

"Very good, sir," Giles responded. "If I might be so bold, would you mind terribly if I joined you?" It was a daring question for Giles, the butler extraordinaire, whose training forbade him from making such a "brash" request of an employer.

"Not at all," my father said. "Please do."

"Thank you, sir." Giles gave him a small bow before he left to gather their hats and coats.

It seemed like the trio had barely gone out the door when they were suddenly home again. And sure enough, they returned with a special edition paper that had already been put out by the Houston Chronicle. Newsboys had been out hawking them on street corners.

My brother and father bought several of the papers, so we could each read our own copy while we listened to the latest news broadcast. My mother was the only one who didn't have a paper in her hands, probably since her hands were already full with another champagne cocktail. So while we sat reading, she sat drinking and glaring.

As always, I seemed to be her favorite subject to glare at. She downed her drink and motioned her empty glass toward Giles, who immediately raced to get her another one.

By now she was out-and-out staring at me. "This had better not interfere with your wedding," she pronounced. "Or you'll be in big trouble, young lady."

Everyone turned to stare back at her, as though we hadn't heard her correctly. Nana raised her eyebrows and turned to my mother, and my chin nearly hit the sofa cushions just as the absurdity of her words hit me. She had spoken as though Pearl Harbor being bombed was somehow my fault, and that I was only doing it to ruin my wedding day . . . for her. I didn't know whether to laugh or give her a snappy retort, though to be honest, her comment left me speechless. Amazingly, neither bombs nor war nor Hitler's taking over the world would stop her from putting on the wedding of the century for a daughter she detested.

Yet for the life of me, I couldn't understand how she could think about something so minor in comparison to the horrors we'd been listening to on the radio. The whole world was about to be at war, and making sure I had Houston's biggest and most perfect wedding was the last thing on my mind.

Instead, my thoughts immediately turned to my father and my brother, who had both said they'd sign up to fight. Then I thought of Jayne and Tom, and her brothers, and my classmates in college. And on and on and on. What would happen to us all if Congress officially declared war?

Plus there was Michael. What did he think about the attack on Pearl Harbor? Was he home listening to the radio broadcast with his family, too?

Though I knew it was considered forward for girls to call fellas — and Michael seemed to be pretty strict about following that unspoken rule — I decided this was one of those moments when protocol could be forgotten. So I went to my room, shut the door, and dialed his number. Unfortunately, I couldn't get through, since the line was busy. I only hoped that he might think of calling me. After all, he was my fiancé.

But would he?

I sat on my bed and stared at the ceiling for a few moments, saying a silent prayer. A prayer for all those who had been injured or lost loved ones. And a prayer for our nation. Then I strolled back downstairs to find several of the neighbors had stopped by. Maddie was busy serving coffee and teacakes. Her face was pale with shock and horror over the news of the attack, though she went about her duties, silently serving everyone.

While my father and Nana and the men stayed in the parlor, close to the radio, my mother held court in the dining room.

"I don't see how this should make any difference to us," I heard her say as I passed by. "Hawaii is a world away from Houston."

I didn't wait to hear how the other women responded. Hawaii may have been a long way away, but America was America, no matter what shore we were talking about. As far as I was concerned, if someone attacked even an outer territory like Hawaii, they might as well have attacked us here in Texas. This was my country, and I didn't take lightly to anyone bombing us.

I made my way back to the parlor, and that was where I stayed for pretty much the rest of the evening. My mother returned, too, with another champagne cocktail in hand. Maddie brought our dinner into us there, since by now, we all seemed to be permanently tethered to the radio. God help us if one of the tubes should burn out. Or if the thing broke down. Because that radio had become our lifeline of sorts. It was our link to the rest of the world, and what a small world it had suddenly become.

Around nine o'clock, my mother stood up and did her best to glare at me again, though she was clearly having a problem focusing. "I've had enough of this nonsense," she announced. "I'm going to bed."

There were a few murmured good-nights, but that was about it.

She went without much fanfare while the rest of us sat there until way past our usual Sunday night bedtimes. We listened and listened to the point where I wondered if my ears might fall off, while so many pictures of the mayhem and horror filled my mind's eye.

Yet we were all well aware that we were the fortunate ones. We could turn off the radio and go to bed, whereas those poor sailors serving in our Navy, and the people of that island, the ones who had survived, didn't have the luxury of just turning a knob to "Off."

The next day my father stayed home from work, and we all gathered again in the parlor to listen as President Roosevelt addressed Congress, saying that yesterday was a day that would live on in infamy. Well, he sure had *that* right. Shortly afterward, the U.S. declared war on Japan. And that evening, we read all about it in the Houston Chronicle. The front page showed a gigantic red "V" for Victory, with three dots and a dash beneath it, the Morse Code symbol for the letter "V".

Once again, thoughts of Michael crossed my mind. More than anything, I wanted to hear his voice and know that he was all right. So why hadn't he called me by now? Or stopped by, or something?

I'd had about all the waiting I could stand. I went to my room, shut the door, and tried to get him on the phone. Of course, I had to resort to calling him at work now. I tried two different times, whereby I talked to two different, very catty receptionists who told me that "Michael was busy and insisted that all calls be held."

To say that rubbed me the wrong way was the understatement of the century. I felt a sudden chill run up my spine and I headed to my closet for a button-up sweater. I'd barely walked in when I remembered the box I had gotten from Sammy. I pulled it from its hiding place and brought it out to my desk.

Then I opened it and stared at all those newspaper clippings of obituaries. Obituaries of men, mostly young. That's when it struck me as being oddly coincidental that our nation had just endured the worst attack on U.S. soil ever, whereby countless military men had been killed, and as a result, there would be many, many more obituaries in many more newspapers around the country. Yet here Sammy had been carrying around a package with obituaries of lots of other men who had been killed, too. What did it mean? And for that matter, why was Sammy carrying them around? Could one of the boys have been his son? Maybe two of the boys? Or his students?

I figured I would never know the answer to any of those questions until I found a link between all these obituaries and baby pictures and high school yearbooks. So I perused a handful of the clippings, wondering if I might find similar family names, but it soon became clear that most of the men didn't share a family name at all. So then I tried to see if they all went to the same college, but I quickly abandoned that idea when I realized most of them hadn't even gone to college. Last of all, I tried sorting them by newspapers and hometowns. That's when I finally had some luck, because I did find some clippings that came from the same papers. And I also found deceased who had come from the same towns in Texas. Still, there was such a variety of men from all over, that I could hardly call it any kind of a connection.

So what did these poor guys have in common?

Maybe the link was Sammy himself. Maybe he could be considered criminally insane and he got some sort of perverse pleasure from collecting obituaries and reading about dead people. I shuddered at the thought. Yet while I tried that theory on for size, somehow it just didn't fit. Sammy didn't exactly act like he was deranged, or like he was some kind of criminal weirdo. No, he mostly acted sort of grandfatherly.

I heaved a loud sigh and put all the clippings and photos and yearbooks back into the box. Then I hid the box in the closet once more. To be honest, I really didn't know what to think or what my next move should be. I didn't know if I should try to find Sammy and return the box, and maybe get some answers. I also wondered if I should call the police. But I figured the police probably had enough on their hands at the moment, now that we were at war. Besides that, they'd probably just label me as nothing but a hysterical female.

Especially after we listened to Roosevelt's fireside chat on Tuesday night. With all the talk of war, there were bound to be lots of people running high on hysteria.

By the time breakfast rolled around on Wednesday morning, I wondered if I might just fit that description myself. Nana slept in and was having breakfast in her room, and I soon wondered if I should have done the same. Because I was a little on edge and not feeling too terribly grownup.

My father, on the other hand, was a bundle of energy and efficiency. "Eleanor, I'll be going with a group of my friends to the Navy Recruitment Office this morning. Rather than sitting on the sidelines, we have all decided to enlist. We want to fight and win this war, so our lives can get back to normal."

My mother shrieked and dropped her etched glass full of orange juice onto the tiled floor. Glass shards and orange juice flew everywhere, and the smell of champagne filled our breakfast room. The explosion in our dining room instantly brought to mind the image of bombs being dropped onto Pearl Harbor. Not to mention, London. I shuddered while Violet rushed in to clean up the mess.

My mother put her hands to her chest and took short, shallow breaths. "What about your business? I am *not* going to run it for you. And Benjamin will not be running it either, since he is going to finish law school. Whether he likes it or not."

Benjamin grinned at me. "Maybe Tracy could run it."

My eyebrows practically shot up to the top of my hairline. "Well, I suppose I could learn . . ."

"Silence!" my mother yelled as she pounded her fist on the table. "You are going to marry Michael, and that's that."

I almost added the words, "whether I liked it or not," but thought better of it. This time I knew better than to poke the bear.

"Not to worry, Eleanor," my father said firmly. "I've asked Dashiell DuMonte to take over for me while I'm away."

"Dashiell?" my mother gasped. "That playboy? He'll run the company into the ground!"

Dashiell was the dark-haired son of one of my father's friends, David DuMonte. My father had agreed to employ Dashiell after he graduated with an engineering degree. And while Dashiell proved to be a perfect employee, his personal life was like something out of a radio drama. It didn't help that he was often confused for Howard Hughes, Jr., despite being a few years younger. Though I suspected he dressed and wore his hair just like the famous millionaire's son on purpose. Like Hughes, Dashiell was known for having a blonde on his arm and owning the latest and fanciest automobile.

I'd met him a few times when I was younger, but hadn't seen

him in years. Occasionally I'd hear about him from my father, as apparently he was doing well at work.

At least my father seemed to think so. "Eleanor, you never give the boy enough credit. He is perfectly capable of running the company. And so what if it goes under? You inherited plenty of your own money to live off for a long, long time."

By now my mother seemed to be having trouble breathing. "But what if you don't come back? Then what? Have you thought about that?"

"Of course I have. But there are some things we simply must fight for. Regardless of the consequences. And I happen to believe freedom is worth fighting for."

The idea of my father dying on some battleship in the middle of a cold ocean somewhere made my heart skip a beat. I put my hand on his arm, just to hang onto him for a moment, while he was still here. I wanted wrap my arms around him, and tell him not to go. But I knew this wasn't a time for wallowing. He was being brave, so I knew I needed to be brave, too.

My brother stiffened up. "I'm willing to help out in any way that I can. You name it, and I'll take on the job. Though honestly, I really want to enlist myself. I don't want to be left out, since most of my friends plan to enlist. I want to go fight for our country, too."

My father nodded at my brother. "And so you shall. Right after you finish law school."

With those words, my father glanced at the clock on the wall and quickly excused himself from the table. I tuned out my mother's tantrum and left the room myself. For some reason, I needed to hear from Michael now more than ever, to know what his plans were, too. *If* he had any plans. Either way, I couldn't take another minute of the silent treatment he'd been giving me. If he was going to be my husband, then I needed to talk to him about all the happenings in the world the last few days. I needed to know what he was thinking and feeling. And, well . . . I guess I just needed to hear his voice.

So I went straight to the phone and called him. At work. This time I didn't take no for an answer when the receptionist tried to put me off.

He finally picked up the phone and instantly sounded irritated. "Tracy, I told you never to call me here."

My heart sank. And all of a sudden I wasn't sure what I'd been hoping to get from him. Maybe words of encouragement, or love, or something. Maybe some connection in a world that seemed to be falling apart at the seams.

"I know," I said, holding back my own annoyance. "But under the circumstances, I thought we might make an exception. Now that our country is officially at war . . ."

"I'm well aware of that."

"And since you and I are going to be married . . . I guess I just wanted to make sure you're all right."

"Of course I'm all right. I wasn't *at* Pearl Harbor."

At that point, there was no more hiding my annoyance. "Very good then. I'm glad to hear it. Best wishes to you."

"Tracy . . ." He sighed loudly into the phone. "I realize I haven't been the best fiancé lately."

"I wouldn't know, since I'm not sure I would even recognize you at this point. I'd hate to mistake you for an enemy agent and shoot you with my father's gun if you should show up at my house one night. Especially since I'm not sure I can recall what you look like. Perhaps if I had a recent photograph?"

He sighed again, even louder this time. "Your joke about shooting me is not funny in the least. Especially not now that Roosevelt finally got us into the war. So please be mature enough to be patient a little while longer. The case I'm working on is terribly complicated and extremely important to my career. Didn't you get the flowers I sent?"

I wanted to mention how I'd had to move them to the floor in order to go through the package I'd somehow wrangled from a complete stranger who looked like Humphrey Bogart. One who was playing peeping Tom through the window of a blonde bombshell who was a nightclub singer at the Polynesian Room.

But I didn't think he'd understand. Or be interested. So I held my tongue.

He sighed once more.

If only all his sighing signaled some sort of deep-seated passion for me. Yet deep down in my heart, I had a bad feeling that it didn't.

"Tracy, we'll talk on Saturday night. At the dance. I promise you'll have my full attention."

That's when it dawned on me that the Christmas dance might be cancelled. After all, events were being cancelled all around town, out of respect and reverence for a grieving nation and for those who had lost their lives. And their loved ones. But as far as I knew, the country club dance was still on. Probably more out of spite, with the idea that we weren't about to let a Japanese attack stop us from holding our Christmas festivities.

"All right," I said quietly.

"I've got to get back to work," he told me in a voice that held almost no emotion.

And that was that. The conversation had ended. No terms of endearments. No "I love you's" or "I miss you's" or anything a young engaged couple would probably say.

Right at that moment I knew the truth that had been bouncing around inside my head. And my heart. It didn't take any great Katie McClue detective skills to know that Michael didn't love me. And for that matter, I didn't love him. Probably because I barely knew the man, and it seemed like we'd grown even farther apart and more like strangers the minute he'd put that huge diamond on my finger. Sure, lots of people got married without really being in love, and they somehow made it work. But I knew I wanted much, much more than Michael was willing to give me. I knew I wanted what Nana and Gramps had had. And if I never found that kind of enduring love, at least I wanted to know that I'd done my very best to *try* to find it.

Even if I had to search for the rest of my life, and even if I ended up with that dreaded "Old Maid" title. It was better than walking headfirst into a loveless, lonely marriage.

Now the question was, how would I break it off with Michael? Was it appropriate to end things when I saw him next, at the Christmas dance? The timing seemed sort of lousy, but if he wouldn't even take my phone calls, what other chance would I have to talk to him? For a moment or two, I toyed with the idea of writing him a letter, but that was probably a chicken's way out. No, I would just have to tell him at the dance.

Then I'd have to figure out how to break the news to my mother.

CHAPTER 9

Wedding Bells and Bad Breakups

Funny, but when it came to breaking things off with Michael, I was well aware that I wouldn't be breaking his heart. But telling my mother was another matter altogether. That, I knew, would produce at least another Scarlett O'Hara from *Gone with the Wind* scene, and maybe worse. The thought of it made my stomach turn. It didn't help that she was still upset with my father, ever since he'd announced his plans to enlist.

Before I could give it another thought, the phone rang and I nearly jumped a mile. I guessed it was probably Michael calling back. What if he wanted to apologize? Or make it up to me? Actions like that would make it a whole lot more difficult for me to break off our engagement. Especially when ending engagements to handsome and soon-to-be-powerful men simply wasn't done in our circles.

I took a deep breath and answered the phone. "Listen, we need to have a long talk . . ."

"Tracy?" I heard Jayne's voice coming through the phone line.

And for some reason, that's when I felt tears pricking at my eyes. "Oh . . . Hi, Jayne . . . I thought you were someone else."

"Jeepers, I picked up on that. Anything you want to tell me about?"

I grabbed a hanky and dabbed at my eyes while I fought to keep my voice under control. "Later. We'll talk about it later."

"Okay, but don't forget. Sounds like you're a little upset."

I sniffled. "It's the attack on Pearl Harbor. Everybody's upset here. I'll bet you are, too."

"Upset? Yup, we're upset, all right. But Tom and my brothers are just plain mad." Jayne's voice held an intensity that I'd never heard before. "They're fighting mad. So much so that Tom has decided to enlist."

"Oh . . ." was the only thing I could manage to utter.

Because all of a sudden, I was at a complete loss when it came to finding the right thing to say. I searched the farthest corners of my brain for words that would be both comforting and encouraging. But those words completely eluded me, and they refused to form on my tongue.

I finally came up with, "Tom is such a great guy. You must be very proud of him."

"I am," she sort of sighed. "Especially . . . well . . . especially since he's about to become my husband."

Once again, I fell silent for a second, while my little gray cells worked overtime to register what she'd just said. Or rather, not so much *what* she'd said, but *how* she'd said it. After all, Jayne and Tom were already engaged. They had been for a while. It was no secret that he was going to be her husband.

Yet right at that moment, I was pretty sure Jayne was trying to tell me something else. Something different.

"You mean . . ." I started.

"Uh-huh. Sure do. Tom and I are going down to the Justice of the Peace in the morning. We're going to get married before he signs up and ships out. I want you to be my Maid of Honor."

I put my hand against the wall and tried to steady myself. My emotions were already running in high gear, with the attack on Pearl Harbor, and Congress declaring war on Japan, and my father talking about signing up for the Navy. Not to mention, my decision to break off my engagement. Now Jayne's news sent me spinning, like I'd been twirled around the dance floor too many times in a row. On the one hand, I was excited that she and Tom were going to be married finally, especially since they were so crazy about each other. But on the other hand, he was about to leave and go fight in a war, one he might never come home from.

Yet even though I'd been thrown for a loop by her news, as her best friend, it was my job to boost her morale and to help her keep her chin up. Especially since I knew she was doing her very best to be brave. I could hear it in her voice. And while I knew Jayne and Tom didn't want a really big wedding, somehow I didn't think getting married in a hurry because he was headed to boot camp was exactly how she'd pictured things.

And if she could be brave, well, so could I.

"Oh, Jayne . . . Congratulations," I did my best to gush, though my words probably sounded more like I was reading them aloud for the first time in grade school.

Then I quickly added, "I'd be delighted to be your Maid of Honor. It's about time that you and Tom tied the knot, anyway."

A smile came back into her voice. "I only wish my folks would have been happy about it, because they were pretty upset at first. You know they had their hearts set on a proper wedding. But once they found out that Tom was going off to fight for our country, well, then they understood. Three of my brothers are signing up with him, and hopefully they'll all end up together. Wherever Uncle Sam sends them."

"I hope they *do* get to stick together. It would be so much better for them."

"I think so, too. They can look out for each other. Anyway, my whole family will be coming in from the farm and they'll be with us at the courthouse in the morning.

"How lovely," I told her. "But what about you? What are you planning to wear?"

She sighed again. "I don't really have anything nice enough for a wedding, so I guess I'll just wear my best church dress. I have a nice evening gown, but that's probably too fancy for a Justice of the Peace wedding."

"Then let's go shopping," I told her. "I want to make sure you have something special to get married in. So I'd like to buy you a new dress or a new suit. It'll be my gift to you and Tom. And I'm not taking no for an answer."

I heard her gasp on the other end of the line. "Tracy, it's too much. You can't do that."

I dabbed at a few tears again. "I insist. After all, you only get married once. It's one of the most important days of your life."

Jayne went silent for a moment. Since I'd met her at college and we'd become fast friends, we'd had an unspoken understanding. We'd never let my family's money and her family's lack of money come between us. I hadn't insulted her by offering her any kind of "charity" and making her feel like a poor kid. And she'd never insulted me by mocking my new clothes or jewelry or mansion home, and making me feel like a spoiled, rich brat. No, we'd always just accepted each other "as is." And now, with my determination to buy her something to wear for her wedding, I'd probably overstepped a few of our unspoken rules.

But if there was ever a time to break a few rules for the sake of a friend, this was it. Not only was Jayne my best friend, but the man she loved more than life itself was about to go to war. Memories of her wedding and letters home would be all she'd have to hang onto for a while. Maybe even for years, for all we knew. She was going to need that, especially since it was possible that Tom might not come back, like many soldiers didn't come back.

So her quick impromptu wedding had to be something special, something memorable. Something that would get her through some very long and lonely nights. With that in mind, I didn't see anything so wrong with me doing something extra nice for her, to give her a few moments of happiness. The whole world as we knew it was changing by the hour. And if I wasn't going to get my wedding, why not at least let my friend have a few special moments that brought her joy?

Still, I knew Jayne could be a tough cookie when it came to accepting something she might consider to be extravagant. Fortunately, I knew the trump card that would persuade her.

"Do it for Tom," I said softly. "Let him see you that day at your prettiest. With him going to war, he'll need your wedding photo to get him through the tough times, so he'll feel like you're near him. Let's make this moment extra special for him, too."

"All right, I know when I'm licked," she chuckled. "I'm crying

'Uncle.' You drive a hard bargain, Tracy Truworth. You can be very convincing when you want to be."

"I do my best," I laughed. "Meet me at Sakowitz in an hour. I'll see if Nana can come, too. She won't want to miss this."

"Sakowitz? But that's the most expensive place in town . . ."

Before she could protest, I said, "Oh, gotta run! I'll meet you out in front of the store! In an hour!"

"Fine. I'll be there," she agreed, right before I set the receiver back in its cradle.

Nana knocked on my door and poked her head in. "Did I overhear you mention Sakowitz? Are we going shopping?"

I laughed and gave her the full story. Of course, she was more than happy to come with me. In fact, she wouldn't have let me walk out the door without her.

"I'll have a bridal bouquet of soft pink roses sent over to her place right away," Nana said, her eyes dancing. "With Baby's Breath. And you'll need a nice corsage, too. And a boutonnière for Tom."

Then she made a beeline for my closet. "What are you going to wear?"

"I've got my new navy suit," I told her. "And hat."

She nodded. "Very smart. And perfect for the occasion. But let's see what Jayne's going to wear first. So you two girls will be coordinated. Plus, you want to make sure you don't outdress the bride."

"Don't worry," I laughed. "Tom will only have eyes for her."

Minutes later we were flying along in the Packard. The whole time, I watched for any signs of Sammy, but I didn't see even so much as a hint of the guy. Or his dark sedan. Even after I parked the Packard and we made our way to Sakowitz, located in the Gulf Oil Building.

While Dallas had Neiman-Marcus, we had Sakowitz, which I thought offered clothes that were every bit as lovely as Neiman's. My mother, of course, would have had a complete conniption if she'd found out that I'd been shopping there, since, shopping locally to her was the equivalent of drinking domestic wines.

But Nana frequented the place, and I'd bought some of my favorite dresses from Sakowitz. And I knew Jayne would be tickled pink to wear something from the store.

We waved when we spotted her standing out front. She waved back, but I could tell she wasn't her usual rock-solid self. Funny how finding out that your fiancé was about to go off to war and that your wedding date had been moved up several months could throw a girl for a loop. Still, she was determined to keep on the sunny side, despite her eyes being a little red and puffy.

I greeted her with a huge hug and then linked my arm through hers. I could tell that Nana had tuned into Jayne's frame of mind, too, since she wrapped her arm around Jayne's shoulders and together we led her into the store. For once, her steps were more faltering, and she didn't move with her normal *tap-a-tap-tappa*.

She leaned her head first onto Nana's shoulder and then onto mine. "You two are spoiling me. I really don't know if this is right for you to be buying me something like this."

Nana waved her off. "Nonsense. You're about to be a bride, and a bride has to have the right outfit. Besides, there's nothing that could make Tracy or me happier. Right, Tracy?" She peeked over and smiled at me.

I smiled back and hugged Jayne's arm a little tighter. "Right. This will be so much fun."

And so it went. We all agreed that a smart suit might be the best bet, and it wasn't long before we found one that looked absolutely stunning on her. It was made from the most luxurious wool crepe I think I've ever seen. The top of the jacket and the puffed sleeves were white, and came down in a "V" on the front and back of the jacket, and in the middle of the sleeve. The white fabric was met first with a black stripe and then a white stripe in the same "V" pattern. From that point on, the bottom part of the jacket and sleeve, as well as the A-line skirt, were all crafted from black crepe. The jacket cinched in nicely at the waist before it flared out again in a modest peplum. All in all, it gave Jayne a perfectly feminine, hourglass figure.

Once she had it on and twirled around in front of a tri-fold mirror, there was no doubt it was the suit for her.

"Black and white is so elegant," Nana sighed. "And it will look stunning next to the pink rose bouquet I've sent over."

Jayne's mouth fell open wide. "You did what? No, you can't. You've both done too much all ready."

Again, Nana waved her away. "Please. What good is the money Gramps left me if I can't use it to make someone else happy?"

And before Jayne could protest, Nana arranged for the saleslady to hem the skirt up a couple of inches so it was the perfect length. I saw Nana slip the lady an Andrew Jackson, and I knew the skirt would be ready by the time we'd finished lunch.

We added some new silk stockings and a white hat with a little veil — something that looked a little more bridal — to Jayne's ensemble, and she was all set. Of course, Nana and I each picked out a new hat ourselves and we checked our packages before we walked to a nearby restaurant for lunch.

Over soup and sandwiches, Jayne gave us the details of her conversation with Tom that led to their sudden wedding plans.

She finished it up with, "I know some people might think we're crazy, but this war has changed everything. I love the big guy, and he loves me, and we didn't want to wait until he came home again before we got married. Especially since we were only a few months from getting married anyway. I guess we just wanted to know that our hearts would be joined together. Forever. As husband and wife. No matter what happened." She blinked back a couple of tears and wiped her nose with her hankie.

Nana squeezed Jayne's hand. "I know exactly what you mean, my dear one. I was married to a soldier once, too."

Jayne turned to her with wide eyes. "You were?"

"Oh, yes," Nana nodded. "My husband and I were head over heels in love with each other. And yes, oddly enough, there is something comforting about knowing the other one is out there for you."

Jayne blinked again. "How did you . . . I mean, you got through it all, right?"

Nana smiled. "Most definitely. And we went on to have a long and lovely marriage. But it wasn't always easy when he was away. Loneliness can be a mean companion. And even when a soldier returns home, being together again takes some getting used to. On both your parts. But if you love each other, you'll work through it."

With those words, Jayne finally smiled again. "Thanks, Nana. That helps a lot."

Nana patted Jayne's hand, right before Jayne turned her attention to me. "So, how about you and Michael? Will he be signing up, too? Any thoughts about you changing your own wedding plans?"

With that, Nana choked on her soup for a moment. "Not a chance. Eleanor's nearly got that ceremony completely orchestrated and perfectly in place. She's done everything but make sure the press will be there to cover every second."

That was about the time when I suddenly took an interest in the way the noodles swirled around the spoon in my soup. It had only been a few hours since I'd made my decision to break up with Michael, and since then, I hadn't changed my mind. I knew I couldn't marry the man.

"Oh, boy, what's going on?" Jayne asked, leaning closer to me. "Is this the reason you were so upset when I called this morning?"

I took a deep breath and tried to keep my emotions in check. "Things haven't exactly been swell between Michael and me."

"You can say that again," Nana agreed softly, as she put her hand on top of mine.

"Not that they've been going badly," I went on. "But there really hasn't been enough between us these days to even *go* badly. He's been so distant, and well, he just claims he's working all the time. In the meantime, I've been nothing but a spectator watching my mother plan my own wedding to a man who is practically a stranger to me."

Jayne put her hand on my arm. "I know things haven't been going the way you planned. Do you think your love might pull you through?"

I shook my head. "I guess that's the real problem. Because I can't really say I'm madly in love with the guy. And honestly, he certainly doesn't act like he's in love with me. I feel like we're engaged in name only."

Nana was nodding furiously. "I couldn't agree with you more. He doesn't act like a man who is romancing his future bride."

"So I've decided to break it off," I said before I bit my lip.

Nana put her arm around my shoulders. "That's very brave of you, my dear. And very smart. You deserve so much better than a man who barely knows you're alive."

"I am so sorry for what you're going through," Jayne said gently. "But scout's honor, I'm not surprised. You haven't sounded happy about the whole thing at all. If only you could get out from under your mother's thumb so you could have a real romance."

Nana snickered. "More like a *thumbscrew*, I'm afraid. Eleanor had been determined you would marry Michael since you were a teen. For years now, she's been chasing away plenty of other interested young suitors who did not meet her standards."

I blinked back a few tears. "Wish I could have met some of those fellas. Because I want to meet someone special and wonderful some day. I want to be madly in love, and I want a marriage like you and Gramps had, Nana. And I want to be crazy about a guy like you are, Jayne."

Nana gave my shoulders a squeeze. "And you should find that, my darlin'. It's an important part of life, and I want you to know that joy of being in love."

Jayne found my hankie in my purse and handed it to me. "Me, too. There's nothing like it. So have you told Michael yet? And more importantly, have you told your mother?"

I let out a heavy sigh and dabbed my tears away. "No, I haven't told anyone. Except for the two of you. I plan to tell Michael on Saturday night, at the country club Christmas party dance."

"Maybe it would be a good idea to tell him in private before then," Jayne suggested.

I held up my palms. "I wish I could. But he won't take my phone calls and he claims he doesn't have time for me right now. The only chance I'll have to break it off will be on Saturday. At the dance."

"Eleanor will probably faint," Nana mused. "And then she'll be fit to be tied. So we might want to find a place for you to hide out for a few days. Until she calms down a bit."

Jayne's face brightened. "I know! You can stay at my apartment. Because Tom and I will be going out of town tomorrow for our honeymoon. We'll be gone the whole weekend. To Fredericksburg."

Nana became a little more animated. "That would be perfect. On both accounts. Your honeymoon and Tracy's hideout. Plus, Tracy and I can take care of the apartment building while you're gone."

"I can pass out the mail," I told her.

"And I'll get Hadley to help in case anyone has any problems with their apartments," Nana added with a smile.

Jayne just laughed. "What would I do without you two? And yes, I would really appreciate it if you wouldn't mind filling in for me. I was going to have one of my brothers stay in from the farm, but this will save him the trouble."

Nana smiled. "Then you can go on your honeymoon without a care in the world."

I nodded. "We'll head to your place right after lunch, so Nana and I can learn the drill and get a key. Then I'll bring a suitcase over tomorrow and plan on staying until you get back on Sunday night."

Jayne was all smiles. "Jeepers, that would be swell. And just so you know, a couple of my brothers will be pretty interested to know when you're available again . . ."

My mouth fell open wide. "That sounds lovely, but I think I'd better take things one step at a time. First I have to end things with Michael. And handle the situation with my mother. After that . . . well . . . we'll see."

Jayne nodded. "I can understand. You've got a few uphill battles in front of you. But wouldn't it be fun if we were sisters-in-law, instead of just best friends?"

"It would," I laughed. "Provided I survive that long."

Nana squeezed my hand. "Don't you worry, darlin'. We'll be with you every step of the way."

I sure hoped so. Because when my mother found out I was breaking off my engagement, she was probably going to be as explosive as any bombs that had been dropped on Pearl Harbor. Leaving me as the only casualty . . .

CHAPTER 10

A Black Cat and a Mystery Man

As soon as we'd finished lunch, we returned to Sakowitz and picked up our packages, along with Jayne's new suit. I could tell by the way she cradled it like a baby that she absolutely adored it. It was going to be perfect for her courthouse wedding, and she would look every bit as beautiful as a model on the cover of *Vogue*.

We were still talking about her wedding as we walked to the Packard. All the while, I kept a lookout for Sammy in his trench coat, or his dark sedan. But with so many cars zooming by in downtown Houston, he could have passed us twenty times while waving the Texas flag and I probably wouldn't have spotted him.

Yet I had to admit, a very big part of me fully expected to see him again, and it was starting to feel odd to me that I hadn't. After all, I figured he'd want his box full of obituaries and things back, for whatever reason he'd been carrying them around with him in the first place.

So I kept on watching for him as I shifted gears and drove us out of the downtown and in the direction of Jayne's apartment building. I had to say, I was at a loss as to what I should do next, so I tried to imagine once again how Katie McClue would have handled such a situation. The answer stood out in my mind like a neon sign. Katie would never just sit around twiddling her thumbs waiting for Sammy to show his face. No, instead, she would take the longhorn by the horns and go out searching for him.

And then she would have gotten some answers, once and for all.

Which, I had to admit, wasn't a bad idea. Maybe if I found Sammy again, then I'd have a better idea of whether or not he was on the level. Or if he really was criminally insane, and I needed to go to the police.

Either way, I had a pretty good idea where to start looking for him. After Nana and I had finished up at Jayne's apartment, I decided to pay a visit to the blonde bombshell. Maybe if I told her that a guy in a trench coat had been lurking around the place, maybe, just maybe, she could shed some light on a very dark subject.

The idea of having a plan, even if it wasn't much of a plan, made me smile. I stepped on the gas so we'd get to Jayne's place a little quicker. I found a parking spot right in front, and I was pretty happy to hear boogie-woogie music fill the hallway when we walked into the building. That meant Betty was home.

Nana immediately started to sashay from side to side. "Somebody's tickling the ivories. And doing a nice job of it, too."

"That's my new tenant, Betty," Jayne said as she unlocked the door to her apartment.

Nana raised her eyebrows to me. "The blonde bombshell?"

I grinned. "The one and only."

Jayne had barely opened her door when a sleek, black cat suddenly appeared in the hallway. It strutted right into Jayne's apartment, and if I didn't know better, I'd say it stepped in time to the music. Jayne rolled her eyes.

"Do you have a cat living here now?" I asked my friend.

"Not formally," Jayne chuckled. "But he showed up one day and Betty asked if she could keep him. Probably one of the few times she's even spoken to me. I don't usually allow cats to stay in the building, but this guy is a real charmer. And he's good about going outside to do his business. Besides that, he's fixed. So he won't be doing any Tom-catting around."

I laughed. "So he'll be true-blue to Betty."

"Except that Betty forgets to let him into her apartment and she locks him out a lot," Jayne sighed. "So he spends a lot of time at my place. As you can see, he's been making himself right at home here."

Nana bent down to pet the kitty. "My goodness, but you've got such shiny fur, Mr. Cat. All you need is a white bow tie and you're ready for a night out on the town."

To which the cat purred up at her and rubbed around her knees. If I didn't know better, I could have sworn he was flirting with her.

Jayne laid her new suit across her living room chair. "Watch out for Clark, Nana. He's a real ladies' man. And he sure knows how to win hearts."

"Clark?" I kneeled down and the cat immediately climbed into my arms.

Jayne closed her apartment door. "That's what she named him. After Clark Gable, I think."

"Clark Cat," I said seconds before the cat reached up and gave me a kiss on the nose. "So close to Clark Kent. Are you really Supercat in disguise? Do you run into a phone booth and change into a cape when people aren't looking?"

But the cat didn't say a word, and instead just grinned up at me as he stared into my eyes and purred.

"See," Nana said. "You haven't even ended things with Michael and you're already attracting the boys."

"Of the wrong species," I laughed as I put Clark down. "Okay, Jayne, let's see what I need to do to keep this joint running while you're out of town."

Jayne smiled. "For a few days, it shouldn't be too bad. I've already spoken with all the tenants to let them know I'll have a fill-in. So everyone promises to handle things themselves as best they can until I get back. And several of the tenants are going to be out of town this weekend anyway."

"That's a good start," I said with a smile.

Then she took me to the small closet that held her collection of manager's materials. She pointed to a list of phone numbers that included everyone from the police and fire department, to plumbers and electricians and more.

"I can usually handle most of the situations that come up on my own," she told me. "But if you should have an emergency, here's who you call."

Next, she gave us the keys for her door and the mailboxes. She also showed me where she locked up the duplicate keys to all the different apartments, as well as her master keys for the apartments by floor. Then she gave us a list of all the tenants and the apartments they rented. There were three stories to the old mansion, and while there were only two large apartments on the first floor, along with a sitting room that had a radio, the rest of the floors had four apartments each. And every apartment had its own bathroom and small kitchen. All in all, it was a pretty nice setup.

After that, Jayne gave me a quick description of all the tenants, so I'd have an idea who was who. And I had to say, her tenants were as different as they could be. From a husband and wife with a young son, to men working for oil companies to a few elderly people. I wondered if I would have time to meet them all.

Nana stood next to me as I learned all that I needed to know. I could see she was taking mental notes along with me. She nodded when Jayne showed us her toolbox.

"Hopefully you won't need to use any of these while I'm gone," Jayne said with a raised eyebrow.

"Not to worry," Nana assured her. "If she does, we'll just call Hadley. He worked alongside my husband in the oil patch. My husband used to tell tales about how Hadley once fixed an entire drilling rig with nothing but a pair of pliers and a role of wire and a couple of screws."

Jayne laughed. "Sounds like a good story."

I glanced at Nana. "For another time. But right now we'd better get out of your hair. I'm sure you've still got lots to do to get ready for your wedding and your family coming to town. Not to mention, packing for your honeymoon."

Jayne smiled. "You can say that again. I never dreamed I'd get married so suddenly like this. In a way, it's kind of exciting."

I gave her a quick hug. "I know. It'll be wonderful. And by this time tomorrow night, you'll be Mrs. Tom Riesling."

Nana hugged her, too. "An old, married lady."

Clark Cat started to rub around my legs again, and I realized I had the perfect reason to knock on Betty's door.

"I'll see that Clark gets out of your hair, too," I said as I picked him up and cradled him. "I'll take him home to Betty."

Jayne laughed. "Don't expect her to be terribly friendly. She may be a hot tamale when it comes to the fellas, but she's pretty icy to us gals."

"Not to worry," I told her as we walked to her door.

Nana opened it for me. "We'll see you in the morning, Jayne, my dear. You're going to make a beautiful bride."

And just as we were stepping into the hallway, Betty's door opened so forcefully that it practically suctioned the air from our side of the building. A middle-aged man stepped out and practically knocked us over before he slammed the door behind him. Thankfully, we managed to jump back in the nick of time.

Then he stood there scowling at us for a moment, his small, gray eyes peering out from metal-rimmed glasses. He slapped his gray fedora over his close-cropped blond hair, and instead of having the good manners to say, "excuse me," he turned on his heel and stepped away.

Almost like he was marching.

Clark started to growl while us girls just stood there dumbfounded, our mouths wide open.

Jayne was the first to speak. "That was strange. As far as I know, she's never let a gentleman into her place before."

I hugged the cat a little closer, to calm him down. "He looked like a nasty character. And Clark certainly didn't seem to like him one bit."

Nana clucked her tongue. "That man was no gentleman. The nerve of him, practically running us over and not stopping to make sure we were all right."

"Hope *Betty's* all right," Jayne said softly.

"We'll check on her," I told my friend. "So you can get back to your preparations."

With that, we said our goodbyes and Jayne ducked back into her apartment. I knew she had a lot on her plate, with very little time to get everything done. In the meantime, I had the perfect opportunity to ask Betty a few questions.

Now the question was, what *would* I ask her? And how would I approach her? After all, I'd never actually interviewed someone before, especially not on the sly like this.

Katie McClue, on the other hand, was an expert when it came to extracting information from just about anyone, from victims to witnesses to suspects. In fact, she'd won awards for her great techniques, and even been asked to teach her skills at police academies.

So I decided to do what she'd done a million times. I plastered a big old smile on my face while Nana rapped on Betty's door. At first, we were greeted with nothing but silence. But when Nana knocked a second time, we heard footsteps marching toward the door.

Betty opened the door just a few inches and peeked out. "Yes? What is it?"

And that was all I needed. I pushed the door open farther with one arm and handed Clark to her. That left her no choice but to release her hold on the door, so I could finally push it wide open.

Then I slid inside to a long hallway with Nana on my heels. Clark clearly wasn't happy to have Betty holding him, because he acted like he barely knew her and he immediately jumped down. Then he ran and jumped up on a baby grand piano that was just visible from where we stood.

I held out my hand to shake hers. "I guess you're Betty, and I'm Tracy Truworth, a friend of Jayne's. And this is my grandmother, Mrs. Caroline Truworth. We just wanted to bring your cat back to you and say hello. I'm going to be filling in for Jayne this weekend while she goes on her honeymoon."

Betty shook my hand, and I couldn't help but notice how cool and sweaty hers was. Yet her face was like a mask, and somehow she managed to avoid showing any kind of emotion at all. For that matter, she also managed to stay completely silent, despite my nonstop chatter.

All in all, she made it pretty clear that we weren't welcome. But I wasn't ready to leave, not without getting *some* information from her. The only problem was, I was just about running out of things to say. I caught Nana's eye, and she must have sensed what I was after.

She pointed to the black baby grand in the far corner of the room. "Oh, would you look at that gorgeous piano! Tracy, come over here and see this."

"Um, okay," I said before I followed Nana farther into the apartment, until we'd passed through the hallway and fully into her living room.

That's when I noticed the opposite wall covered in mahogany paneling, with flat decoratively carved pillars, and layers of crown molding. There were also separate square center panels set back from the main panel and finished off with half-round molding. The effect of the woodwork was absolutely stunning, a real showpiece. It appeared to be an original part of the house, since it matched the woodwork on the staircase and the fireplace that had ended up in Jayne's apartment.

Betty followed us in, practically marching in annoyance. "I'm sorry, but I must practice now."

Nana waved her hand in the air. "Oh, my dear, don't let us stop you. You go right ahead. Tracy here is quite the singer, and I'm sure she'd love to sing along to anything you'd like to play."

I picked up some sheet music that had been on the piano stand. It looked like it had been handwritten, and not completely finished.

I started to hum a few bars.

But apparently that hit a very sensitive nerve with Betty since she snatched the sheet from my hands. "That's my music and not for you to see."

"You mean," I stumbled, "you wrote that yourself?"

"It's none of your business."

I felt my eyebrows go up my forehead. "That's pretty good."

Beside me, Nana was nodding. "That *is* good. Have you been writing your music long, Betty? My, but you're a talented girl."

Betty grabbed my upper arm and started leading me toward the door. "Do you not know a thing about manners? How dare you waltz into my flat without being invited."

Nana followed as we moved ever closer toward the door. "How about a cup of tea and a nice chat? I'd be happy to make it."

"No, it is time for you to go home!" Betty announced. "I have no more tea. You must leave."

"By the way," I said as I sort of dug in my heels. "A few days ago, I saw an older gentleman outside your window. I'm not sure what he was doing there, but he looked a lot like Humphrey Bogart and I was wondering if you knew him . . ."

With those words, Betty gasped. "I know no one. I've never met any such man."

I paused and studied her face. She had suddenly gone pale, and for a moment, I was a little worried about her.

I put my hand on hers. "Betty, are you all right? Do you need to sit down? I'm so sorry, I didn't mean to upset you."

She grabbed my hand and forcibly removed it from her arm. "You must leave. You must leave now. Right now. I have much practice to do. Now."

Something in her tone told me there was no use even trying to wheedle any more information out of her. Because clearly she had clammed up, once and for all.

"Thank you for showing us your lovely apartment," Nana said sweetly as we stepped back into the hallway and Betty slammed the door in our faces.

I was pretty sure my jaw practically hit the floor, and I noticed Nana's eyes had gone as wide as saucers. She took my elbow and we walked silently from the apartment building. We headed straight for the Packard, though I glanced back once along the way. I spotted Betty's outline near the window, so I was pretty sure she'd been watching us leave.

"What in the world . . ." Nana said once we'd shut the car doors. "I've never met a young woman who was so unfriendly. What is her story?"

I started the car and pressed in the clutch with my left foot. "Beats me . . . but one thing's for sure — she's terrified of Sammy."

And that's when I wondered if I should be terrified of him, too.

CHAPTER 11

Wedding Songs and Sneaky Subs

I was still wondering about Betty and Sammy the next morning when I put on my new navy suit and hat that I'd bought at Neiman's. Nana wore her favorite dark pink suit, and I drove us to meet Jayne and Tom and their families at the courthouse. I ended up dropping Nana off in front while I searched and searched for a parking spot. I could hardly believe all the cars and traffic downtown today. By the time I had the Packard nicely nestled into a spot, I really wished I could fly like Superman to get to the courthouse on time.

Some Maid of Honor I was turning out to be.

But at least my slight tardiness didn't turn out to be a problem, since the front reception area was absolutely wall-to-wall with wedding couples and their families. To top it off, there was a long line that snaked out from the doorway to the Justice of the Peace, as couples in love waited their turn to tie the knot.

Outside of church, I don't think I'd ever seen so many people dressed in their Sunday best, as well as young women wearing elegant suits and lace dresses. Luckily, I spotted Nana almost the second I walked into the building, but then it took us a bit of jostling through the crowd to find Jayne and Tom's party.

I greeted Jayne and Tom with a hug, and then said hello to all their family members. Tom, with his football player physique and his perfectly combed dark hair, looked unusually nervous today. I guess getting married can make even the toughest guy weak at the knees.

"My goodness," I said to Jayne. "This place is packed! I wonder what's going on?"

"All these couples are doing the same thing we're doing," she said. "Everyone is getting married before their fellas sign up for the service and ship out."

Pride swelled in my chest, just knowing that all those boys were so brave, and willing to drop everything and go to war, without even being asked. I looked around me, at the wide array of men here today. I could only guess from the way they were dressed that some were businessmen, and probably lawyers and accountants. And maybe schoolteachers and factory workers. Clearly some were farmers and ranchers. And yet here they were, along with their beloveds, each and every one of them ready to sacrifice their regular incomes, and their time with their new brides, and even their very lives. All in the name of putting a stop to evil dictators who would steal freedom from the face of the earth. Nameless faces in front of me, but men who were going off to war so that the world could be free.

I said a silent prayer for them all. I asked God to watch over each of them, as well as the women they were leaving behind, who would be waiting and worrying, and no doubt shedding more than their share of tears.

For a moment, I felt tears prick at my own eyes. But this was not a day for crying. Not unless they were purely happy tears.

Thankfully, Nana knew exactly what to do in a situation like this. She held up her favorite pair of sapphire and diamond earrings that she'd brought for Jayne to wear.

Jayne's eyes went wide. "Are those for me? You've done way too much already."

But Nana just waved her off as always. "You know the old saying. Every bride is supposed to have something old, something new, something borrowed and something blue. My husband gave me these earrings a long time ago, so you can consider them as your something old, borrowed and blue."

Jayne laughed. "And the suit is something new. My goodness, if it weren't for the Truworth girls, I wouldn't be nearly so stylish today."

"And you're the most beautiful bride in the whole place," Tom murmured as he slid his arm around Jayne's back.

Of course, Nana and I both sighed.

It was past eleven o'clock when Jayne and Tom finally got their turn before the Justice of the Peace. Jayne was absolutely aglow when they said their vows. I've never seen her so nervous and yet so happy and excited at the same time.

Everyone in our party cheered when Tom and Jayne were pronounced "Man and Wife," and then kissed.

When they pulled apart, Jayne turned and smiled at me. "I want you to sing, Tracy. Sing something for my wedding."

I glanced around at the crowded room. "Right here? In the courthouse?"

"Please. It wouldn't be a wedding without a song. Every wedding is supposed to have one."

And so I sang. The only song I could think of on short notice was Glenn Miller's *Moonlight Serenade*. I started a cappella and before I knew it, two of her brothers stood beside me and sang as a backup chorus. Nana came and joined us, too. Soon all eyes turned to us and we were suddenly the center of attention.

Tom glanced down at his new bride. "May I have this first dance, please, Mrs. Riesling?"

Jayne smiled and took Tom's hand. Seconds later, they were swaying together as they danced. And before I knew it, several of the other couples joined together and danced, too. So I sang the song again, with an extra chorus.

When I had finished, the whole room broke out in applause. I gave a little bow before we all headed to Jayne's apartment for some cake and punch. While we were there, Artie showed up with the mail.

"Let me kiss the blushing bride," he announced to the room before grabbing Jayne in a big hug and planting a kiss on her cheek.

Then, while he ate a good-sized piece of buttercream-frosted cake, I helped him sort the mail, just like Jayne usually did. The mood remained festive as I finished off by putting several hand-written letters into Betty Hoffman's box. I was just locking up the door to all the boxes when Betty's apartment door swung open and out walked a middle-aged gentleman.

Yet despite the boisterous wedding reception going on across the hall, and the fact that Artie and I were just a few feet away, the man didn't even seem to notice us. His teary eyes had a faraway look to them, and his face was contorted in agony. He was wearing a worn fedora and a threadbare suit, while he clutched an envelope to his chest. An envelope much like the ones I'd just put into Betty's box. He'd barely stepped into the hall when the door was slammed behind him, loudly, as he sort of wandered toward the front entrance.

Artie and I glanced at each other with raised eyebrows.

"Think I'd better go see if he needs any help," Artie said as he put the last bite of cake in his mouth and handed the fork and plate to me. He gave me a quick salute before he grabbed his mailbag and moved surprisingly fast to catch the man outside, leaving me to wonder what was going on and who this man was. Not to mention, why he'd been in Betty's apartment.

For a girl who didn't allow men into her place, I was surprised to have seen two of them walking out her door in just two days. Though I had to say, neither one of them looked terribly happy about it. Had they both tried to get fresh with her, only to have their advances spurned? Could the same thing have happened with Sammy? Had she turned down some romantic overture on his part? I guess when a girl was a bombshell nightclub singer, she could attract all sorts of male attention — both wanted and unwanted.

But I didn't get time to think more about it, because minutes later, Jayne and Tom were ready to take off. Nana and I and the rest of the bunch threw rice as the newlyweds raced to his car. I noticed someone had painted the words "Just Married" on the back with shaving cream, as well as tied tin cans to the bumper to drag along the ground. The stunt had her brothers' names written all over it. I had no doubt that Jayne probably expected as much, as she let Tom help her in the passenger side of his blue-green Ford.

Tears stung in my eyes as I waved goodbye to my friend and her new husband. It was heartwarming to see them look so happy, and I hoped that happiness would be with them always. Especially since

Jayne would soon be saying goodbye to Tom as he went off to war, and the truth was, she might never see him again. It was a hard reality to face, and I prayed that Jayne and Tom would be some of the lucky ones, and that he would come home to her again in one piece.

Not long after that, both of the families left, with Jayne's own family wanting to get an early start back to the farm. Nana and I stayed behind and cleaned up.

It was early evening when we finally made it back to River Oaks. I had just pulled the Packard into the garage when my father rolled into the driveway in his black, Sixty Special Cadillac. Nana and I got out of the Packard as he maneuvered his car into the six-stall garage. Hadley walked over to close Nana's door.

"Ah, the wedding party returns," Hadley said with a smile. "How was the ceremony, whereby two hearts were joined as one?"

I smiled back at him. "It was wonderful, Hadley. Short and sweet, but very intimate. Tom and Jayne have already left for their honeymoon."

Hadley put his hand to his broad chest. "Keep love in your heart. A life without it is like a sunless garden when the flowers are dead."

I raised my eyebrows. "Shakespeare?"

He shook his head. "No. Oscar Wilde."

Nana smiled at him. "Truer words were never spoken."

My father got out of his car and joined us. He was definitely not smiling. In fact, he looked thoroughly irritated.

Nana frowned. "What's the matter, son? Trouble at the recruitment office?"

My father shook his head and grunted. "They turned us all down. They wouldn't take me, or any of my cohorts. They said we were all too old. In other words, there's a war going on and we're not allowed to be part of it. How utterly insulting!"

"That's ridiculous," Nana said with a gasp.

My father ran his fingers through his hair. "We were under the impression the military was in need of men and would take all the able bodies they could get. Especially now that we're officially at war with Germany."

For a moment, I wasn't sure I'd heard him correctly. "We are?

When did that happen?"

My father looked me right in the eye, and I could tell he was not about to mince words. "Yes, it's official, my dear. Germany declared war on us this morning. And then our Congress voted later to declare war on Germany."

I could hardly believe it. Tom and Jayne's wedding day was the very day when Hitler declared war on us. And we declared war right back. Ready or not. If I'd thought things were moving too fast before, it was nothing compared to now.

Hadley put his hand on my shoulder. "As a result, we're basically in a conflict against all the Axis powers. Germany, Italy, and Japan."

Nana straightened up and stood soldier straight, like she was planning to enlist herself. "Well, if there's anything we've learned from the Great War, it's that everyone must contribute in some way. In order to win, we must all give our best effort. From the homefront to the battlefield."

I linked my arm through my father's. "That's right. And I'm sure there's something you can do stateside, even if Uncle Sam won't let you enlist."

He patted my arm. "Oh, but not to worry, my dear daughter. The gents and I haven't given up. One of my cronies, Teddy, has a number of military connections. He knows of a Navy recruiter in New Orleans whom he claims will accept pretty much any man who wants to join up. And can pass the physical."

"Where there's a will there's a way," Hadley said.

"So you'll be going overseas," I said quietly.

My father shook his head. "Not necessarily. I may be a lot closer to home than you think. Teddy says he believes the men our age will most likely be put on subchasers in the Gulf."

"Subchasers?" I repeated.

Hadley turned to me. "That's correct. Many citizens claim to have seen German U-boats in the Gulf of Mexico. Though the government refuses to acknowledge it. Perhaps so people won't resort to panic."

I gulped. "You mean . . . you mean, the Germans are actually on U.S. soil?"

"More like U.S. waters," my father told me. "And now the big concern will be shipping Texas oil by tankers through the Gulf and then up the East Coast. To keep our Navy running, and to supply oil to our military and our Allies."

Hadley nodded vigorously. "Mark my words, oil will be paramount in this war. We must keep a continual supply going through, because our ships and our armies will be burning through it as fast as it can be produced."

My father pulled out his pocket watch and checked the time. "I suspect that's the reason the Japanese invaded Malaya on the same day they hit us at Pearl Harbor. Now it will be simple for them to attack the Dutch East Indies next, and take over their oil fields."

"Precisely," Hadley agreed. "Because the Japanese don't have any natural resources of their own. Of course, Germany already invaded the Soviet Union for their oil fields, as they're certainly in need of oil to fuel their own military machine."

Nana made a fist with one hand and hit the palm of her other hand. "So we can't have the Germans blowing up our oil tankers as they leave Texas, or Louisiana. Or when they're going up the coastline."

My father folded his arms across his chest. "I've heard rumors about tankers that have already gone missing. None from my company but from others. The first thought was that German U-boats may have gotten them. After all, we know U-boats have been sinking supply ships traveling from the East Coast over to England. That's why there's been the need for convoys, with our Navy ships escorting them for protection."

Hadley shook his head. "But it also puts our Navy ships in grave danger, as they make the long journey across the Atlantic. The German U-boats have been blowing them up as well."

"So lots of Americans have already died . . ." I said just above a whisper.

But it was enough for my father to hear me. "That's about the size of it, my dear. Lots of men have been taken out on our ships. That's why it's so important to spot those U-boats in the Gulf and eliminate them before they can kill again."

And that's when it hit me — the very connection I had been looking for with Sammy's collection of obituaries. Why hadn't I thought of it before? After all, I'd heard snippets of what was going on in the Atlantic on the radio, and I'd seen newsreels at the movies. Not to mention, articles in the newspaper. Why in the world hadn't I put two and two together?

Suddenly I couldn't wait even a second longer to check out my newfound theory. So I excused myself from the group and ran into the house. And straight up to my room. I closed the door behind me and made a beeline for my closet.

"Could it be?" I muttered aloud as I grabbed the box and put it onto my desk.

Had I finally figured out what all those obituaries had in common? Was it possible they'd all been on a ship together, a ship that had been blown up by German U-boats in the Atlantic? The realization made me gasp.

An hour later I had confirmed my suspicions. And I had done it by sorting the clippings into three different groups, based upon the day of death. Soon I discovered all the men had died on one of three days. That many men dying at the same time indicated some kind of mass casualty. And my best guess was they had died on a ship of some kind.

Just like Katie McClue relied on her female intuition, I relied on mine now. Because something inside me said I was right. Those men had all died at sea. They may have sailed out of the Port of Houston or Galveston. Maybe up to New York and then across the Atlantic. Not that it mattered. Being blown up at sea was a horrific way to die. And from what I'd seen in the newsreels at the movies, most of the crews of those ships that went down in the icy, cold Atlantic did not survive.

For a moment, I sat on my bed and just stared out the window in disbelief. All those young men. Wiped out in a matter of moments.

I shuddered at the thought.

But if nothing else, I might have finally figured out the connection to all those clippings. Now I had to wonder, why was Sammy carrying all that stuff around with him? Had one of his sons died on those ships? Or maybe he knew someone else who had died.

I returned my carefully sorted piles back to the box. Later, I put the box on top of my suitcases, after I'd packed all the things I wanted to take with me to Jayne's apartment this evening, right after dinner.

I was still thinking about all those poor boys when I walked into the dining room and joined my family.

I took my seat and touched my father's arm. "If you go to war as a subchaser and prevent other men from dying, Father, I don't think I could be more proud of you."

My father smiled at me. "Why, thank you, Tracy. That's very thoughtful of you to say."

Nana smiled at him. "I would be proud of you also, son. And one thing I know beyond a doubt — your father would've been very proud of you as well."

My father stiffened and blinked a few times. "If only he were still with us . . . I would have liked for my father to see me wear the uniform." He wiped his mouth with his napkin while he got his emotions under control.

Benjamin grinned at us all. "Well, if Father's going to wear a uniform, so am I. I'm told women can't resist a man in a uniform. So I'm going to sign up, too. Time for me to go see the world."

To which my mother slammed her fist on the table. "I've had it up to here with all this war talk. Must we discuss this at every single meal? And once again, Benjamin will *not* be going to any war . . ."

My brother rolled his eyes. "I know, I know . . . not until I've finished law school. But if all the other guys are going, I should be going, too. You don't want me to look like a coward, do you?"

"Your father is the real coward," my mother said with venom in her voice. "He's so quick to leave me when we have a million social engagements for the holidays. He's only determined to enlist so he can embarrass me. Subchaser, indeed. That's hardly a position one can brag about over bridge, now is it?"

"Mother!" Benjamin and I both yelled at the same time.

And so it went. Another night at the dinner table with my family. I was pretty happy to escape and run off to Jayne's place a little while later. Nana had insisted on loaning me the Packard for as long as I needed it.

She caught me just as Giles was carrying my suitcases down the stairs. "If you need anything," she said, "don't hesitate to call. Hadley and I can be there in a heartbeat."

"Thanks, Nana. But I'm sure I'll be fine. Besides, I'll be back on Saturday evening to get ready for the dance."

Nana raised an eyebrow. "And . . . your date with Michael. Or rather, your big 'moment' with Michael."

I let out a long, slow breath. "Uh-huh. That's right. He'll be picking me up here."

"Well, I'll be there Saturday night, too, in case you need me."

"Sounds good. Thanks, Nana. But I want you to have fun at the dance, too. And not spend all your time worrying about me."

She gave me a quick hug. "But worrying about you is my job, darlin'. Especially since you didn't end up with the kindest of mothers."

She certainly had *that* part right. I hugged her back and I was off. I arrived at Jayne's building and let myself into her apartment with the key she'd loaned me. Clark Cat had been waiting in the hallway again, so I let him stroll on in. I decided he could spend the night with me, since Betty's apartment was dark and quiet. I guessed that meant she was off singing at the Polynesian Room in Galveston.

That night, I studied the stacks of obituaries a little more. And the more I did, the more I was sure all those boys must have been on ships together when they died. Hard to believe so many lives had been taken all at once, by a German submarine. The idea of it was beyond tragic. Still, I had to wonder why Sammy had this stash of clippings and such, and where did this information lead me now?

For the life of me, I couldn't think of a time when Katie McClue had been in a situation like this one.

The rest of the night passed uneventfully, though I didn't exactly get much sleep. I heard every creak and crack in that building, especially whenever a tenant came home through the front door. Even so, I must have dozed off when Betty arrived, since I didn't hear her come in. I let Clark Cat cuddle up next to me all night, and to be honest, I was glad to have his company.

Things went pretty smoothly for the next few days, and I didn't have to do much at all to keep the building running. Every morning the newspapers showed the death toll at Pearl Harbor was still rising, and the names of those who had been killed were being released to bereaved family members. I showed the latest papers to Artie when he came with the mail each day.

As always, Artie greeted me with a salute, and he insisted on putting the sorted bundles of mail into the little boxes himself, as his way of helping out while Jayne was gone.

On Saturday, he tried to stash all of Betty's letters into her mail slot, but for once, there simply wasn't enough room. So he grabbed the pile of envelopes that again looked like they'd all been written in different handwriting. He knocked on Betty's door, holding the letters out before him.

A few seconds later, we could hear the sound of footsteps marching toward us, right before Betty's door opened a crack.

Artie gave her a smile. "Mail delivery, ma'am."

Without smiling in return, Betty snatched the mail from his hands and shut the door.

Artie shook his head and came back to me. "Not the friendly sort, is she? But for being so unfriendly, she sure gets a lot of letters."

I raised my eyebrows. "I'm surprised she didn't fall for you, Artie. From what I can tell, she likes a man in a uniform."

Artie puffed out his chest. "Guess she only goes for the young fellas. And she seems to go for a lot of those. Speaking of which, how's your young fella?"

"Well, I'm finally going to see him at the dance tonight," I said as brightly as I could.

Somehow I didn't have the heart to tell Artie that I was about to break up with my fiancé. Not after he'd made mention of how I was going to be a good wife someday.

He smiled and patted my shoulder. "That's good for you young kids to go out at night. Have some fun. Enjoy life while you can. Especially now that we're officially at war. The boys will all be shipping out soon. Oh, what I wouldn't give to be goin' with 'em."

I shut the facing to the mailboxes and locked it again. "My father tried to enlist and got turned down. He and his friends are headed to Louisiana to join up."

Artie grabbed his mailbag. "Wish they'd take me, too. But at my age, I'll never get in on the real action."

I linked my arm in his and walked him to the door. "Uncle Sam needs you to deliver the mail."

He nodded. "You can bet there'll be lots and lots of letters heading home from our boys. I'll be pretty busy, that's for sure."

I had a feeling he was right.

He saluted me and I saluted back, before he left the building. I'd barely put the keys away when Hadley dropped Nana off so we could go to lunch and then to our appointments at the beauty parlor.

All to get ready for the big dance.

Later, with nothing interesting going on at the apartment building, I drove the Packard home. Dark clouds were forming on the horizon and the wind had already picked up quite a bit. I saw a flash of lightning race through the sky, and I knew we were in for a humdinger of a storm. I got the Packard into the garage before the first raindrops hit.

Then I raced into the house and changed into my poofy pink dress, the one my mother had insisted on buying for this dance. Since she was so sure Michael's mother would approve of it.

Not that it really mattered anymore. Because little did my mother realize, but tonight would be the last of "Michael and me" as a couple. I hadn't changed my mind about breaking off my engagement. I only had to find the right moment and the right words to tell him.

Strangely enough, I couldn't honestly say I was going to miss the man. After all, how can you possibly miss someone you'd barely spent any time with, and didn't know terribly well?

Still, I wasn't looking forward to the repercussions of ending an engagement, especially to a man that most people would consider the biggest catch since Cary Grant.

Outside, thunder boomed and rain now pelted the windows. I only hoped the violent storm wasn't a portent of things to come. Especially since my feminine intuition was running wild and telling me to beware, as chills staged a road rally up and down my spine. Suddenly I had the sense that something ominous was about to happen, and that this night would bring about more than just my breakup with Michael.

I only prayed that I would still be in one piece by the time the dance was over and morning had rolled around.

Because something told me I was in for a pretty wild night.

CHAPTER 12

Singing and Slugging

The storm was making even more of a racket by the time Michael arrived to pick me up. The thunder was so loud that I didn't even hear his car on our driveway, and I didn't know he was there until Nana knocked softly on my door and poked her head inside my room.

She raised her eyebrows. "The man of the hour has arrived."

Of course, she didn't have to say his name. We both knew who she was talking about.

"Thanks, Nana," I murmured as I sat in front of my mahogany vanity with the huge round mirror.

The reflection I saw looking back at me appeared a little sad, and full of resignation. The beautician had put the front of my caramel-colored hair into rolls, and left the rest curled under. I was powdered and coiffed to perfection, a real glamour girl, but yet somehow the look just didn't reach my eyes.

"Still going to give the bum the old heave ho?" Nana asked.

I let out a little laugh. Michael may have been many things, but a bum he was not.

"That's my plan. I haven't changed my mind. I'm going to end this sham of a relationship and give back his grandmother's ring." I rolled another layer of my red, kiss-proof Max Factor® lipstick across my lips, even though I couldn't imagine much kissing in my immediate future.

"Stick to your guns," Nana told me. "And by the way, you look positively gorgeous, my dear."

"Even if I resemble an overgrown, upside-down rose blossom?"

Now it was her turn to laugh. "Nothing wrong with roses. And that dress truly is pretty, though it's maybe more suitable for a royal ball. Still, it is pretty. If only you had a diamond tiara to go with it."

Her words made me laugh again. "I'll be sure to pick up a couple of those next time I go to Neiman's."

She touched her elegant silver-haired updo. "I think we would look positively smashing in tiaras."

I took in her navy-blue satin dress. "You already look like a million bucks, sister," I said in my best James Cagney gangster voice.

She waltzed in and checked her own reflection in the mirror. "Your father and I will all be there if you need us. Of course, your mother will be busy with her clique, which means she'll most likely be out of your hair. But if you need any moral support, you can come to me. Hadley will be taking your mother and father and me to the country club, and we'll probably get there shortly after you and Michael do."

"I'll be fine," I lied. "I've just got to find the right moment and the right words to say."

She put her hand on my shoulder. "I know you will, darlin'. It's not easy ending a relationship, even one as distant as what you and Michael have. But you'll get through it and go on to something better. Because, Lord knows, there will be lots of nice, single boys at the dance just looking for a beautiful girl to dance with. So the night won't be a complete loss."

I nodded and put on my bravest face. Which wasn't easy, considering my insides were quivering like a Jell-O® salad, no matter how much I tried to stop them.

Nana walked me downstairs to greet Michael. We found him sitting in the parlor with Benjamin. He was leaning back in a wingchair with one foot resting atop his other knee, and a snifter of brandy in his hand. Both he and my brother were wearing brand-new, double-breasted tuxedos. At first glance, I couldn't help but notice how devastatingly handsome Michael was.

Movie-star handsome.

Yet it was like looking at someone in a movie or a still photo, rather than gazing upon someone who was truly dear to me. And it suddenly occurred to me that ending my engagement might not be as hard as I thought.

"Good evening, Tracy," he said in his smooth baritone. "You look lovely tonight."

I gave him my brightest smile. "Why, thank you . . ." And just for fun, I brazenly threw in the word, "Sweetheart." Something I knew he would never approve of.

The word hit its mark. His eyes flew wide momentarily before a frown crossed his face.

His reaction made me laugh.

Now his dark eyebrows knitted together to form one long line. "I've brought you something."

He stood up and handed me a purple and white orchid corsage. Once it was in my hot, little hands, he plopped back down in his seat. I stared at it for a moment, guessing I was supposed to pin it on myself.

Thankfully, Nana turned to me, rolled her eyes and took over. She pinned the corsage to my dress and made sure it was perfectly in place. And would stay there.

Just as my mother and father strolled in.

As usual, my mother only had eyes for Michael. Her smile lit up the room like Edison inventing the light bulb as she sat on the couch next to Michael's chair. She ordered Giles to bring her a champagne cocktail, and I could smell that she'd already had one or two.

Or three.

"Lovely corsage, Michael," she cooed. "It goes perfectly with our dress."

Our dress?

Michael returned her smile. "Well, thank you, Mrs. Truworth. But I can hardly take the credit for it, because naturally, I didn't have time for such frivolities. My mother, of course, made the arrangements and had it delivered."

My chin almost fell to the black-and-white tiled floor. It was bad enough that he couldn't be bothered with something so trivial as buying a corsage for me, but to announce it to everyone in the room was just plain rude and insulting. Now I wondered if Michael would so much as bat an eye when I told him our relationship was over. Maybe he couldn't even be bothered by what he might refer to as "frivolities." In fact, maybe his mother was the one I needed to inform instead.

"Of course you don't have time for such things," my mother agreed, nodding her head as she practically oozed charm along with the champagne that coursed through her veins. "Your work must be so terribly important."

He nodded back to her. "Most certainly. And I have a few highly important things I need to clear from my docket rather quickly."

Nana and I shared a knowing look and then wandered into the hallway. Minutes later, Michael emerged, with my mother on his arm.

"We'll follow you two lovebirds to the country club," my mother told him with a squeeze of his bicep.

For a moment I wondered who those lovebirds might be, until I realized she was talking about me and my soon-to-be-former fiancé.

Giles helped me with my coat and held an umbrella so I could get to the car without getting wet. In the meantime, Michael made a dash for the driver's side of his roadster. As I slid into the passenger seat, lightning flashed and sizzled across the sky. Seconds later, thunder boomed.

I jumped and let out a little squeal, before covering my mouth with my gloved hand.

Michael knitted his brows together again. "Haven't you outgrown the fear of thunderstorms yet, Tracy? That's rather childish, don't you think?"

I blinked a couple of times. "People get killed every year by lightning, so I suspect it's healthy to have a fear of thunderstorms."

He sighed. "Fine."

Just to ease my discomfort, I tried for a few moments of pleasant conversation. "How are things going at work? Is everything all right at the office?"

But this only brought another sigh from him. "You wouldn't

understand, Tracy. It's far above the things you're used to dealing with."

I wanted to ask, how would he know, but I fought hard to hold my tongue. Thankfully, despite the storm, we made it to the country club in no time at all. He handed his keys over to the valet, and we had barely walked in the front door when he took off to talk to a couple of his chums. It was as though he'd forgotten I was even there. Now I wasn't sure what to do, whether I should simply follow him, or if I should go off on my own. Thankfully, I spotted two of my married friends, Suzanne and Sylvie, and made a beeline for them instead.

Unfortunately, the only thing they wanted to talk about was my upcoming wedding. Somehow, I didn't think it would be right for me to tell them there wasn't going to be a wedding before I even broke the good news to Michael. Though more and more, I was beginning to wonder if I would ever have a chance to actually *talk* to my so-called fiancé. As near as I could tell, it might be necessary for me to end our relationship by telegram. Or carrier pigeon.

So I changed the subject with my friends just as a waiter came by with a tray of drinks. Sylvie grabbed a glass of Sauvignon Blanc for me, probably something from the Loire Valley, and I enjoyed every drop. Especially since I knew that even the most amply-stocked wine cellars would soon run out of French wines like this one, and wouldn't be able to get more, now that the Nazis occupied most of France.

I glanced around at how beautifully the club had been decorated for this party. The lights were low and candles illuminated tables and sideboards. A Christmas tree in the middle of the room glowed with strand after strand of strung lights. No matter how many times I saw a tree like that, I never got tired of it.

Yet something felt very different this Christmas, and even though the crowd became louder with every guest who entered, I could still feel a certain tension in the room. And I had a pretty good idea what was causing that tension. All around me, I caught bits and pieces of people talking about the war.

But it didn't stop the band from starting off with a snappy Glenn Miller tune. Before I knew it, one of Michael's friends was at my elbow and asking me to dance. I accepted with a smile. After that, I danced with a few other fellas, and then an old high school classmate, Pete Stalwart, showed up.

Pete was a sandy-haired boy with pale blue eyes who always had a smile on his face. I knew he'd had a crush on me in high school, but back then, I thought he was a little immature for me. Though I had to say, he'd certainly grown up in the years since then.

We danced one dance and kept on going around the floor for a second song. Somehow I didn't recall him being so tall. Or that his shoulders were quite that broad. Nor did I remember him being such a terrific dancer.

"What are you doing these days?" I asked, with my lips just inches from his ear.

"I've got my engineering degree now," he said as he pulled me a little closer. "I'm working for the Gulf Oil Company."

"In the Gulf Building? Downtown?"

"That's the one."

"I love that building. I like to shop at Sakowitz there."

He chuckled into my ear. "Next time you're in the neighborhood, be sure to let me know. We can have lunch."

"I'd like that," I told him as we finished dancing to a third song.

That's when he suddenly pulled back. "Say, didn't you used to sing every now and then?"

I laughed. "*Used to* is right. Mostly in my living room when my mother made me."

"I'd love to hear you sing again, Tracy."

I felt my eyes go wide. "Here? Now? People don't get up and sing at the country club. It would be unseemly. My mother would faint."

In fact, I could almost picture her complete unrestrained histrionics over the whole thing. It would be nothing short of the "melting" scene from the *Wizard of Oz*. Because even though she used to trot me out to sing at very sedate and refined home parties, the idea of her daughter crooning popular tunes with a "band" on a stage at a dance would be, in her mind, right up there with performing a half-naked can-can at a cabaret club.

But Pete wasn't about to give up. "Are you kidding? It would be swell if you sang. You're so pretty you belong in front of a band," he told me before he guided me right up to the bandstand. "I want to hear you sing 'When You Wish Upon a Star.' You know the words, right?"

"Everybody knows the words . . ." I started to say just before Pete got the attention of the bandleader.

The bandleader leaned over so Pete could talk directly into his ear. Then he looked at me and smiled back at Pete. And before I had a chance to protest, I was getting half-pulled and half-pushed up onto the stage. Seconds later, there I was, standing before the microphone in front of a big band, and trying to get the big skirts of my poofy pink dress straightened out in that small space.

And the band began to play the introduction to the song.

Which meant I had no choice but to sing. So I stood directly in front of that microphone and held onto the metal stand to steady myself. Seconds later, the music flowed into the actual melody of the song, and I did my best to find that first note. It was a good thing I had a wide range on my voice, since I didn't even get a chance to choose my key.

My first few notes rang out perfectly. Thankfully, I remembered all the words, and I just relaxed and let my voice pour from my throat. My singing filled the room and people stopped dancing and turned to watch me. Nana edged up close to the stage with a wide smile on her face. I could see several of Michael's friends turn and stare with admiration, while fury crossed Michael's own face. I was halfway through the song when I spotted my mother, who had gone deathly pale.

When I finished, I did a little curtsey as the room erupted in applause. I smiled and threw a kiss to the crowd and did another little curtsey.

Just as I felt a hand grab my arm and tug me, so that I lost my balance and started to fall off the stage. Thank goodness a few people jumped forward to catch me and help me land on my feet.

Then I turned to see who had so unceremoniously set me up to come tumbling down to the dance floor. I could hardly believe whom I saw. It was Michael, and his face was contorted in anger. In fact, I'd never seen such ire on a man's face before. My mother's face, yes, but no one else's.

And clearly Michael wasn't finished with me yet. Because he immediately grabbed my hand and pulled me across the floor and out one of the side doors to the back patio. Outside, the thunder and lightning hadn't let up one bit. Though we were under the cover of the back porch roof, the wind whipped my dress and my hair around like we were in the middle of a hurricane.

"How dare you humiliate me like that!" Michael yelled above the storm.

I hugged myself, trying to keep warm. "Humiliate you? How on earth did I humiliate you?"

"Tracy, if you had an inkling of how undignified it is for a man's fiancée to stand up on a stage like that . . . And sing like a common floozy . . ."

"Floozy? Who are you calling a floozy?"

"Look, Tracy, I just don't think you're the right woman to be my wife. I need someone who can act properly in the most formal of situations. Not someone who can't control herself."

"Properly? What's wrong with the way I act?"

He shook his head and, even though I couldn't hear it, I knew that he had just sighed again.

He ran his fingers through his hair. "Listen, I don't think you and I were meant for each other . . . I think you've got too much of your grandmother in you."

That hit a nerve, and I felt my eyebrows shoot to the top of my forehead. "Nana is one of the kindest, most wonderful people in the world!"

I could tell he had sighed again. "If only you were more like your mother. But the truth is, having you as my wife could hurt my career. And my career is much too important to let it be denigrated by an impetuous woman like you."

For some strange reason, I laughed. And I laughed hard, uncontrollably, though I could barely hear it, since the sound seemed to float away with the wind. Finally, I managed to get out the words, "What are you saying, Michael? Are you breaking off our engagement?"

He nodded. "With the way you behave, you leave me no choice. It's for the best."

Boy, he could say that again. It really *was* for the best. And oddly enough, I suddenly felt lighter than air, like I could float away at any moment. I couldn't believe the relief that washed over me, much like the rain would have if I had stepped out from under the patio roof. I no longer had to find the right words to end our relationship. Because Michael had done that for me.

"I couldn't agree more," I said with a smile.

And that was that. Before I could say another word, one of his friends opened the door and called Michael to join him.

He turned to me one last time and said, "Best wishes to you." And then he was gone. He left me shivering outside in the middle of the thunderstorm.

I stared out at the rain for a second or two before I went back inside myself. I knew my first stop needed to be the ladies' room, to see what kind of shape my hair and dress were in. The band had taken a break, and I was halfway across the empty dance floor when my mother rushed up to me.

Or wobbled was more like it. "Teresina Anne Truworth! What have you done?" she screeched. "You're a mess! You can't be a wife to Michael looking like that!"

I patted the rolls of my hair into place. "I am not *going* to be Michael's wife. We have broken up. We've ended our engagement."

Before I could say another word, my mother screamed. And she screamed some more, like she'd just seen a deadly rattlesnake or like someone was coming at her with a butcher knife. She screamed so loud that conversations everywhere came to a halt, and the room around us went silent.

"How could you?" she went on screaming. "How could you do this to me? What did you do to ruin it?"

And before I could walk away, she reached her arm back and brought it toward me. She hit me so hard that it bent me over in the other direction. Stars circled in front of my eyes as I heard everyone in the room gasp.

But I wasn't waiting around for more. Instead, I shook my head to get my bearings. Then I hiked up my skirts and ran. I made a beeline for the front door and raced through as a reluctant porter held it open for me.

I stumbled out into the storm just as another bolt of lightning lit up the sky. I kept on running and running and running. I knew it was probably the most stupid thing I could do in the middle of a thunderstorm, since I'd learned long ago in Science Class that lightning prefers to strike a moving target.

And I was one heck of a moving target.

But right at that moment, I honestly didn't care. Cold rain fell in torrents and soaked through my dress. The big, poofy skirts soon became heavy with water. All the while, warm tears fell from my eyes, making it even harder for me to see. My cheek stung, and I could tell right away that it was starting to swell. I had known my mother would be upset when she learned I was no longer Michael's fiancée, but I had never dreamed she'd be capable of such violence. And to hit me like that in front of our entire country club set made it even worse. People would be talking of nothing else right now, and the lines of gossip would be buzzing like bee hives. Of course, some people would feel bad for me, while others — probably lots and lots of others — would take her side. They'd see me as nothing but the willful daughter who had no appreciation for her family's generosity.

In other words, they'd think I was a spoiled brat.

And while I might be many things, privileged among them, I was hardly what a person could call spoiled.

So I kept on running. Soon I could see our mansion up ahead. I couldn't remember ever being happier to see my home before, though I realized it might not be my home much longer. It certainly wouldn't be my home for the night.

Once I reached the back door, I sneaked in and went straight up to my room. A glance in the mirror showed that I looked more like a drowned rat than a human being. My hair hung in wet ringlets and my mascara had run. I wiped it off only to find that my left cheek was starting to turn purple and it was about twice the size of my other cheek.

The dress, of course, was ruined.

Which oddly enough, seemed to give me some kind of strange satisfaction. That's when I ran to my closet and grabbed my black strapless gown. With every ounce of defiance I could muster, I carefully put it and the matching gloves into a suitcase, along with a good pair of black pumps and several pieces of my nice jewelry. I made a promise to myself that I would find a place to wear this gorgeous outfit.

Then I raced to the garage. Thank goodness Hadley wasn't around when I tossed my suitcase into the Packard and took off.

Straight for Jayne's place. Soon I would have a hot bath and a cold ice bag for my face, something that would make me feel a whole lot better.

But driving was treacherous, to say the least. Water ran across the road and I worked to prevent the Packard from sliding off into the ditch. With lightning that flashed with renewed fervor, and even heavier torrents of rain, I drove at practically a crawl.

At long last, I arrived.

The apartment building was quiet, and judging by the few apartments that were lit, I figured most of the tenants were gone for the weekend or out on a Saturday night. Even though it was hardly a night fit for man nor beast.

Betty's apartment lights were blazing, which I thought was pretty odd. I figured she'd be singing at the Polynesian Room or somewhere else this evening.

But to be honest, I didn't want to think about Betty or Sammy or anyone else as I pulled the front door open and stepped out of the rain and into the building. Tonight, more than ever, I noticed how terribly skimpy that one single bulb was when it came to lighting the hallway. Seconds later, I would have been grateful to have even that one single bulb. Because I'd barely shut the front door behind me when a lightning flash nearly blinded me, followed by an ear-splitting thunderclap.

The lights immediately went out and I stood there in darkness. For the first time that entire night, I felt fear course through my veins.

Then I remembered the millions of times that Katie McClue had found herself in just such a predicament. And I knew I only needed to stay calm and look for the matchbook I always kept in my purse. Then I could make my way into Jayne's apartment and find a flashlight.

And I have to say, I did stay pretty calm. I quickly dug into my purse, found the matchbook, and pulled a match from the pack. I was about to light it when I felt something furry touch my ankles. I let out a little scream and nearly jumped to the ceiling.

That was, until I heard the strangest noise. It sounded an awful lot like . . .

Purring?

"Clark, is that you?" I said into the darkness.

I received a very loud "*Meow!*" in response.

I laughed. "You nearly scared me to death, Clark Cat."

I lit a match and it gave me just enough light so I could see to unlock Jayne's door. Then I lit a second match, and with Clark at my heels, I went inside and searched the kitchen drawers for a flashlight. Sure enough, I found one in the closest drawer. That was Jayne for you. Ever the vision of efficiency.

By now the rain on the windows was nearly deafening, and I wondered if I might have to deal with some broken windows while Jayne was away. Lightning flashed again and lit up the whole room, giving me enough light to switch on the flashlight, just as more thunder rattled the entire building. Along with what sounded like a car backfiring. Though oddly enough, the sound seemed like it had come from inside the building. There was another major flash of lightning, and I heard the same noise a second time. I tried to listen through the ruckus for more unusual sounds, and for a moment, I even thought I heard something at the front door.

Had the rain broken through the small transom window above the door?

I hurried into the hallway, with Clark still running around my feet. I shined the flashlight on the front door and the window above it, and thankfully, everything looked fine.

Had the noise come from Betty's apartment?

I turned my flashlight beam to Betty's door, expecting to see that same wooden door that I always saw.

And that's when I noticed something was different. Very different.

Instead of being shut, Betty's door was wide open.

"Betty?" I cried out. "Betty, are you home?"

Clark zoomed on in ahead of me as I shined the flashlight down the little hallway at the front of her apartment.

"Betty, are you okay? Betty?"

But there was still no answer. I stepped further inside and kept calling her name. And I kept on shining the narrow beam of the flashlight the whole length of her apartment's front hallway. I could see her piano off in the corner. And when I stepped out of the hallway, I shined the light across the mahogany paneling on the opposite wall. From there, I kept on shining that flashlight around the room.

Until I shined it over a pool of liquid on the floor. A pool of liquid that was right beside her sofa. For a moment, I thought it might be rainwater that had leaked in.

But it wasn't long before I knew better. The liquid was too dark to be water. And I confirmed just that when I walked around to the other side of the sofa and saw the source of the dark liquid. As near as I could tell, it was coming from the dead body on the floor. A body that appeared to have a gunshot wound smack dab in the center of the chest.

Betty's body.

CHAPTER 13

Bad Eyesight and Bloody Knives

I knew Betty was dead the second I saw her. Don't ask me how, since I haven't exactly been around a lot of dead bodies. Other than at a funeral or two. But I couldn't say I'd ever been around a "murdered" body before.

Yet there was something about the way she was lying there, not breathing or moving, in an unladylike position that was completely unbecoming to any bombshell. Strangely enough, it all seemed so incongruous with the gorgeous evening gown she was wearing. The sequins covering the bodice, as well as her jewelry, sparkled and danced in the beam of my flashlight. Her skin, that had once been perfectly rosy, was now paler than any skin I'd ever seen. All together, it only added up to one thing — Betty was gone.

Even so, I wanted to be sure. Because a part of me didn't want to believe it was true. Sure, Betty had never been especially friendly to Jayne or me, but I still hated the horror of a young woman being violently taken from this world. So I knelt down and touched her wrist to see if she had a pulse. But all was quiet when it came to her veins, even though her body was still a little bit warm.

Was there a possibility she could be revived?

Right away I knew the answer. Judging from the puddle of blood I'd just stepped into, I knew she'd lost much too much of it. Especially after I stood up again and directed the beam from my flashlight up and down her body. That's when I noticed what appeared to be another gunshot wound on her leg.

More lightning and then thunder punctuated the moment, and all of a sudden, I felt lightheaded. I've never been the kind of girl who faints in the face of danger, but at that moment, I was pretty sure I was close to passing out. Yet I knew I could never let that happen, so I fought the feeling with everything I had. After all, Katie McClue never fainted during the many, many times she'd encountered a dead body. Which, when I thought about it, was probably pretty important, considering she was usually the one who discovered the corpse in the first place, typically under harrowing circumstances. But Katie didn't so much as break a sweat when she investigated a murder. Instead of getting shook up, Katie always focused her attention on the crime scene.

So I took a few deep breaths and closed my eyes for a moment. Then I forced myself to look at Betty's body again as more lightning flashed and thunder rattled the building.

I'd already noticed that Betty had been shot twice. The bullet through her heart was most likely what killed her. It showed that her murderer was either very lucky or very good when it came to handling a gun. Then again, maybe the shot through the leg showed the shooter *wasn't* such a deadeye, because that shot didn't quite make sense to me. Maybe the killer had shot her in the leg only to stop her from getting away. Or, maybe the lights had gone out and the shooter was now dependent on the lightning to see. Meaning, their aim was off. If that was the case, Betty must have been shot after the lights went out, and the car-backfiring sounds I'd heard earlier probably weren't the sounds of a car backfiring at all. Instead, those sounds were probably . . . gunshots. Which also meant . . .

Whoever had killed her might still be nearby. Maybe even in the building.

The very thought of it made every hair on my body stand on end, and I shivered in the darkness.

That's when it dawned on me that having a weapon of some kind might be a really good idea. Just in case I needed to defend myself. And just in case the person who had killed Betty was a homicidal maniac who simply liked to murder young women.

So I quickly shined the flashlight around the room and then into the kitchen. Right away I spotted some knives in a rack on the counter. Lightning lit up the room as I raced toward those knives. I put the flashlight in my left hand, and grabbed the handle of the biggest knife of the bunch with my right hand. A cook's knife.

Holding it before me while thunder rumbled, I flew to the little hallway that led to the door of Betty's apartment. Or, at least, I tried to fly. But every step I took felt leaden, and the door of her apartment suddenly seemed like it was a million miles away. It didn't help that I was still dragging the heavy wet skirts of my dress as I went.

My flashlight beam caught the image of Clark Cat as he raced ahead of me. Once I got to the edge of Betty's door, I shined the flashlight into the apartment building hallway and peeked out to see if the coast was clear. My plan was to jump across the hall and into Jayne's apartment. Then I could lock myself in and call the police, provided the phones were still working. Hopefully, whoever had killed Betty had run out of the building already. Or maybe they were in an upstairs apartment hiding out.

And hopefully they hadn't gone through the open door to Jayne's apartment to find a nice hiding spot. It was a chance I'd have to take, especially since I couldn't come up with a better option in the darkness.

Thank goodness the hallway was empty when I shined the flashlight around. I took a few steps forward, still holding the knife out before me. From the beam of the flashlight I could see Clark now trotting into Jayne's apartment. I figured that was a good sign, since I didn't think Clark would go running straight toward someone who had killed his owner. Now I just had to make it across the hall unscathed, so I could join him.

For a moment, I directed the beam up toward the staircase, to make sure no one was there. But it turned out I wasn't alone at all. Because two faces squinted in the light and stared back at me. I let out a little scream and nearly jumped a mile. That was, until I took a second look and realized those faces belonged to an elderly man and woman who were standing on the stairs and clinging to the railing.

Probably as they'd tried to make their way downstairs when the lights went out. I guessed they must be Mr. and Mrs. Eldridge, from apartment 2B.

I also figured it was highly unlikely that this elderly couple would have shot Betty. But in case the real killer still happened to be around, I wanted to get these seniors to safety with me in Jayne's apartment. Right away. Yet I needed to be careful how I spoke to them, so I didn't alarm or upset them, given their age.

"Hello, I'm Tracy Truworth," I called out, letting the beam of the flashlight dip, so it wasn't shining directly into their eyes. "I'm watching the place for Jayne while she's on her honeymoon. Are you Mr. and Mrs. Eldridge?"

"Oh, Tracy, dear," Mrs. Eldridge hollered back. "Yes, Jayne left us a note. She told us you were coming. So glad you're here."

"There's been a terrible accident," I said. "I want you to come down here and wait with me in Jayne's apartment. Where you'll be safe. I'm going to call the police."

Mr. Eldridge moved down a step. "The police? What exactly is the problem? What's happened?"

"It's Betty," I told them as officially as I could. "She's dead."

"Dead?" Mr. and Mrs. Eldridge both exclaimed in the same exact moment.

The very same moment when the most brilliant lightning I've ever seen flashed across the sky, lighting up the entire building for a second. Mrs. Eldridge screamed at the top of her lungs. Then she caught a breath and screamed again.

What in the world had happened? Had the murderer gotten to them, too? Were their very lives in danger?

I held my knife up even higher for protection, as more lightning flashed.

"Are you all right?" I cried up to them. "Mr. and Mrs. Eldridge! Speak to me!" I shined the flashlight in their direction, hoping I didn't see blood seeping from yet another body.

But they both appeared to be alive and well. Or *alive* anyway. Together they'd suddenly turned as white as ghosts.

Mr. Eldridge jumped up and wrapped his arms around his wife. "Don't hurt us! Please, I beg of you! We won't tell a soul what we saw!"

I'm sure my eyes must have gone pretty wide, except for my left one, which was too swollen to move much. "I don't want to hurt you. I want you to wait with me. In Jayne's apartment."

But they didn't even respond, and instead, they scuttled up the stairs like a couple of mice running for a hole to hide in. I stood there with my mouth hanging open, until I heard a door slam on the second floor. I guessed it must be them.

So much for my plans not to alarm or upset them. At least I hoped they'd be safe while they were locked up tight in their own apartment.

With them taken care of, I ran the rest of the way to Jayne's place and locked the door. Then I headed straight for the phone, which thankfully was still working. I got the operator right away and told her it was an emergency. She connected me to the police and, after telling them there'd been a murder and giving the address, the dispatcher said someone was on the way.

"You're the second party to call this in," she told me. "We just got the message from someone else. Seconds ago."

That news surprised me. Who else knew Betty had been murdered?

Unless . . .

I ran to Jayne's cheval floor mirror and shined the flashlight off to the side so I could take a good look at my appearance.

I gasped when I saw myself, because I was barely recognizable. Standing in front of me was a ghoul of a woman. Or in other words, me, with mascara that had run down my face, a huge bruise across my cheek, damp hair matted to my head, and blood all over my once poofy pink dress. Added to the picture was the huge knife I'd been wielding for self-defense. Funny, but I'd started my evening out looking like a complete glamour girl, and now I could have doubled for the creepy villainess in any horror movie.

If not the very homicidal maniac that I feared might be running around.

Which was probably how I must have appeared to Mr. and Mrs. Eldridge, since I guessed they were the ones who had called the police already, probably thinking that I'd murdered Betty.

But Betty had been shot, not stabbed. And certainly not by me. Yet what if the police didn't even bother with an investigation, not after they got the "eye witness" testimony of an innocent, elderly couple who would swear up and down that they'd seen me, and they knew I had murdered Betty? It would make things nice and easy for the police, if they could quickly pin the crime on yours truly.

"Oh, swell," I said aloud, and suddenly I realized that I could be in big trouble.

But how could I prove my innocence if I ended up dealing with a lazy detective, one who wanted to look no farther than the woman wearing the blood-stained dress in the mirror? Katie McClue herself had been in my blood-stained shoes herself a time or two. She'd dealt with more than her fair share of crooked cops and had to solve many a murder simply to prevent herself from getting sent up the river.

So how had she gotten herself off? In one of her later books, *The Case of the Crime Spree Cops*, she'd had the smarts to take plenty of pictures of a crime scene and to gather other evidence as well. Then she used all that information to prove her innocence in court.

And that's when I remembered my camera. I'd left it at Jayne's the day I'd picked up my black satin gown. So I made a beeline for the counter where I'd seen it last, only to find a perfectly neat, clean, and organized counter space.

My heart started to pound as I looked around. Jayne must have moved it. But where?

If I wanted to find my camera, I knew I had to start thinking like Jayne did. She was "a place for everything and everything in its place" kind of girl. So what place would she have deemed proper for my camera?

I knew the answer right away. It would be in her hall closet. The place where she kept all her important items.

And using the flashlight, with Clark still hovering around the bottom of my skirts, that was exactly where I found it. Then I brought it, along with its carrying case, back out to the counter. I rewound the old film, and put in a new roll of film in world record time. In fact, if film changing had been an Olympic event, I would have gotten a gold medal. Without wasting another second, I added the flash attachment to the camera and put the camera strap around my neck. Then I grabbed a couple of flashbulbs in one hand and the flashlight in other.

By now the storm was starting to let up, as I paused at the door of Jayne's apartment. I still didn't know the whereabouts of Betty's killer, and by going back to her place, I could be taking the chance of running into him or her again.

But it was another chance I was willing to take. Especially since I knew the police were already on their way, and I truly doubted the killer would have stuck around this long anyway.

So I unlocked the door and raced back to Betty's place. With my wet skirts, it felt more like I was running through an entire field of cotton batting. Finally, I made it into her living room and got in position to take the best pictures. I tried not to think about the fact that I was photographing a corpse and a crime scene as I took a few good shots. The flashes from the bulbs were almost blinding, and I had afterimages dancing in my eyes for several seconds after each picture. My camera flashes competed with the lightning flashes, which were finally showing signs of slowing down a little.

Once I was sure I'd gotten pictures from every angle, I ran back to Jayne's and locked the door again.

I could hear sirens as I returned my camera to its case, and put the case back in the closet. If nothing else, I knew I had what I needed to prove Betty had died from bullets, not a knife blade.

For a couple of seconds, I toyed with the idea of changing my dress. But I knew I was pretty much out of time when the first police car pulled up outside. Instead, I opted to wipe the mascara from my cheeks and apply a little lipstick.

Anything to improve my appearance so I wouldn't be confused with a homicidal maniac. Though with the way I looked at the moment, it was going to take a whole lot more than just lipstick to make me look better. I probably needed something more on par with the parting of the Red Sea, or turning water into wine.

I saw another police car arrive, so I ran into the hallway, opened the front door, and waved the police on in. The first two bunches of men were in uniforms and practically blinded me with flashlights aimed straight for my face.

"Are you hurt, ma'am?" one of them called out as he trotted up the walk. "Do you need an ambulance? You look like you've been in a bad accident."

I shook my head. "It's the girl across the hall. Betty. She's been murdered."

And from that moment on, my already chaotic night turned into pure mayhem. More police arrived, this time men wearing suits. Then men with very fancy cameras also showed up and took tons of pictures. I explained everything that had happened since I'd arrived this evening, including the sound of the car backfiring, and the noise at the front door. I told them everything I could about Betty, what little I knew of her. And I also explained to them that I was just filling in for Jayne.

But if I thought things were chaotic then, well, it was nothing compared to what was yet to come. Especially after a few of the uniformed police officers knocked on tenants' doors and started questioning the few that were home, shortly after the electricity came back on. That's when Mr. and Mrs. Eldridge came limping down the stairs, accompanied by one of the officers. They both looked straight through their wire-rimmed glasses and pointed directly at me, while I was standing in the middle of the hallway.

"It was her!" Mrs. Eldridge shrieked. "She did it! She's the killer. I saw her with my very own eyes!"

Weak as those eyes may have been, it certainly didn't stop her from expressing her limited view of her surroundings.

Not to be outdone by his better half, Mr. Eldridge added to the accusations with, "She had the bloody knife!"

And to think, not long ago I'd been worried about them and their safety. Yet here they were, ready to send me to the electric chair and probably even help pull the switch.

A very strong hand clamped down on my arm. I glanced up to see an extremely tall and overweight detective examining me like he had x-ray vision, as well as the capability to read my mind and determine whether I'd done it or not. Just by looking at me.

"What's this about a bloody knife?" He tilted his charcoal-gray fedora back to expose curly brown hair.

"I had it for protection. In case the real killer was still here."

"So you killed the other girl in self-defense?" He flicked my bruised cheek with his forefinger.

I let out a *yowl!* and put my hand to my cheek. "What? No! I did not kill Betty. After I found her dead, I grabbed the knife in case the killer was still around."

"Uh-huh. Judging by that shiner you've got going, I'd say you and the dead girl got into one helluva row. Looks like she hit you pretty good."

I turned to stare into the man's cold, gray eyes. "No, that's not what happened."

"How'd you get the bruise then? Let me guess, sister," he said with a laugh. "You fell down a flight of stairs."

I tried to wriggle away from the man but he was holding on tight. "Someone else hit me. Earlier tonight. At the country club dance."

"Yeah, right," he scoffed. "Honey, you don't exactly look like you belong in the country club set. Mind telling me why the knife had blood on it? And why you've got blood all over your dress?"

"I told you, I found Betty lying on the floor. I kneeled down and checked for a pulse and that's how my dress got blood on it. And my hands. So when I picked up the knife, I got blood on it, too. And to be quite frank, there was *barely* any blood on the knife at all. It wasn't exactly dripping with the stuff."

He smirked. "Boy, oh boy, you've got an answer for everything, don't you?"

I rolled my eyes. "What do you expect me to do, *not* answer your questions? Well, maybe you could answer a question for me, then. Why are you asking me about a knife when Betty was killed with a gun?"

"How do you know that?"

About that time, I was ready to pull my hair out. Trying to get through to this big palooka was like talking to a brick wall. No matter what I said, he seemed determined to put me at the top of his suspect list, a list that apparently was pretty short, considering I was the only one on it. He was exactly the kind of cop that I had feared might show up. Just like the kind of police detective that Katie McClue had wrangled with a time or two in several of her books.

So I took a deep breath and looked this guy directly in the eyes. "Because I saw her, remember? I found her after she'd been killed. I saw two round holes in her body, and gee, golly, Mr. Detective, but I'm pretty sure that indicates a gunshot. The one through the chest was probably at close range."

"Oh, a wiseguy, huh? Or maybe I should say, a 'wisegirl'? How do you know so much?"

I wanted to tell him that it was from reading every Katie McClue book that was ever written, but I figured he probably wasn't a fan of the young female detective. Fictitious though she may be.

But I didn't even get a chance to answer before he said, "I think we should finish this conversation down at the station."

And the next thing I knew, I'd been handcuffed and hauled off in the back of a police car. Minutes later I was at the police station, sitting in a plain room in front of a very plain table, getting the third degree over a murder I hadn't committed. All from the gorilla who'd packed me off to this place. At least I now knew the man's name was Detective Denton, though he seemed to fancy himself as a regular Dick Tracy and God's gift to crime solving. At any moment I fully expected him to bring out the rubber hose and shine a hot, bright light directly into my eyes. As near as I could tell, that was all that was missing to make this scene complete.

Of course, I soon "stood corrected," when the door to the little room flew open wide and in walked Michael and my mother, followed by Nana.

My mother gasped and put her hands to her cheeks. "Teresina Anne Truworth! What have you done?"

Michael's gaze went up and down my blood-stained dress, and then to my black eye and bruised cheek. His own eyes went wide with astonishment. It was as though he were looking at an oddity at the circus.

"Tracy," he cried out in the loudest voice I'd ever heard him use. "I knew you'd be upset when I broke up with you . . . But I never dreamed you'd go out and . . . and . . . and . . . kill somebody!"

That's when I was pretty much ready to scream. How was I ever going to get out of this mess?

Even Katie McClue hadn't been in a scrape as bad as this one.

CHAPTER 14

Bad Night and Bail Blues

Okay, maybe I'd exaggerated just a smidge about the part where Katie McClue hadn't been in as bad a situation as the one I was in now. After giving it a little more thought, I recalled the case where she'd been incarcerated in a foreign jail, and another case where she'd been kidnapped and held for ransom. And while it was true that my situation probably didn't compare to all that, it was still pretty lousy. Especially since my own mother, who appeared to be so drunk she could hardly sit up, and my fiancé, or rather, ex-fiancé, were not exactly helping matters. My mother took a chair at the far end of the table and Michael sat on my right. Nana slid into a chair on my left, next to the wall. I could tell she was really exhausted, and probably belonged in bed about now.

Detective Denton, of course, sat right across from me. Between his size and the wingspan of his arms, he practically took up the entire expanse of the other side of the table. He'd been grinning like a Cheshire cat ever since Michael, a well-known Houston attorney, had walked in and made such a gigantic leap to such an erroneous conclusion. Of course, it didn't help that Michael had practically announced his assumptions from a rooftop. Since then, Detective

Denton had all but thrown the book at me.

Though at least he'd removed my handcuffs.

"Soooo . . . little missy," he said in a slow drawl, one he seemed to have acquired somewhere between the apartment building and the police station. "This is all about a man, huh? And looking at your fiancé, being the handsome fella that he is, I can see why you'd want to 'fight for your man.' So when your fiancé called it quits, you headed straight for the girlfriend that he had on the side, and you got into a brawl. Only she was more of a scrapper than you thought, and the fight got more heated than you expected. And you ended up grabbing a knife and killing the little tart."

"Excuse me?" Michael jutted out his chin. "I did not know the deceased in any way, and I was not having a dalliance with some mere floozy in a low-rent apartment. As for why Tracy stabbed this woman, I cannot say."

I slammed my hands on the table and stood up. "Again, Betty was shot! She was shot, with a gun. She wasn't stabbed. A stab wound makes a cut, whereas a gunshot leaves a hole. And I did neither of those things to her."

Then I turned to Michael. "And why, pray tell, are you here? I thought our relationship was over."

As always, Michael sighed. "I am here to represent you, Tracy. Pro bono. I am your lawyer."

To which I let out a little shriek. "This is the best I can do for a lawyer?"

Now my mother glared at me. Or at least, she tried to glare at me, but no matter how hard she seemed to work at it, she could not manage to hold her gaze steady.

"Michael has a brilliant legal mind," she huffed. Just before she turned her smiling face toward my ex, while her gaze fought to catch up. "Right, Michael?"

He raised one eyebrow. "Actually, Mrs. Truworth, I am only here to represent Tracy with the hopes of getting her out on bail soon."

I gasped. "Out on bail? I haven't been arrested. There isn't going to be any need for any bail since I did nothing wrong."

Nana touched my shoulder. "Tracy is not a murderer. She wouldn't harm a fly."

My mother scrunched up her face. "Who *knows* what Tracy would do? I can't believe she actually got up on stage and sang this evening. How terribly common. And improper. And who knows what she did to ruin her engagement, though we do know it was clearly all her fault."

"Tracy was going to break up with Michael," Nana interjected. "She was planning on doing it tonight. He just did it first and saved her the trouble."

Michael turned to me. "I'm shocked by this news. Positively shocked. It seems I hardly even knew the woman I was about to marry."

I rolled my eyes. "Why would this come as a surprise? Maybe if you'd spent more time with me, we might've actually gotten to know each other."

Michael sighed. "I don't think it's possible for a man to *ever* spend enough time with you, Tracy. Because you're much too selfish and immature. And I won't be spending much time here, either, since I'm only handling things to get you released while you await your trial. After that, I simply do not have the time to take on a murder case."

I rolled my eyes again and sat down. "Of course you don't. Though once again, may I remind you, that I have not been arrested. Or charged with anything. Because I didn't kill Betty. There isn't going to be a murder trial. At least not for me, anyway."

"Tracy is innocent," Nana announced.

The detective leaned forward. "Not from where I stand. Maybe she'd like to explain that shiner she's got. I still think she and Betty got into a fight. As near as I can tell, little missy, Betty must have walloped you pretty good."

Whereby I glanced at my mother. "Betty didn't hit me. My own mother did. In public, at the dance."

"And she had better not lay a hand on you ever again!" Nana clenched her teeth and stood up.

My mother put a hand to her forehead as though she might faint. "How dare you both accuse me like that! I did no such thing!"

"And that only makes things even more interesting," Detective Denton grinned. "Your mother beats you up and then you go and take it out on an innocent girl . . ."

I shook my head. "I did not kill Betty! But maybe we should talk about why you're allowing a crowd in here while you're questioning me. Because I would like Michael and my mother to leave."

Detective Denton leaned back and grinned even wider. "Oh, please, by all means, let's let these people stay. This little Marx Brothers' routine is teaching me a lot about Tracy Truworth and why she had motivation to kill Betty Hoffman."

Michael suddenly gulped. "Betty Hoffman? Did you say Betty *Hoffman*? Betty was living in that apartment building? And now she's . . . dead?"

Detective Denton pulled out a notepad and flipped over a few pages. Then he started writing something before he raised an eyebrow to Michael. "So you *did* know the deceased, after all."

Michael tugged at his collar. "I may have met her once or twice. At the Polynesian Room."

I'm sure my eyes were about to pop out of my head when I turned to Michael. "When did you have time to go to the Polynesian Room? Or down to Galveston? I thought you were working day and night."

He sniffed. "One must occasionally entertain for business purposes."

Nana snorted and sat down again. "Business purposes! I'll bet. It sounds to me like the only kind of business you were involved in was monkey business."

"What a terribly common thing to say," my mother retorted.

All the while, Detective Denton wrote more and more notes on his notepad. "This must be my lucky day. Neglected doll. Philandering fiancé. And mother who humiliates her in public. Boy, oh boy, the jury is absolutely gonna love this one. This will probably make the front page of the paper. I'll be famous after this case."

I groaned, wondering if there was any hope at all for me to get out of this gigantic hole I'd suddenly found myself in. A hole that my mother and ex-fiancé seemed to be digging just as fast as they could make their shovels move. The more they dug, the more Detective Denton was determined to see me hang. Did the facts in this case even matter? Or was he just trying to wear me down and get me to admit to a crime that I hadn't even thought of committing? To think, all this had happened because I'd had momentary hopes of reviving Betty.

I was suddenly very thankful that I'd taken pictures of the crime scene. Because, judging by the way things were going, I might need all the evidence I could get to prove my innocence.

Detective Denton leaned forward and touched my hand. "So, Tracy, you say that Miss Hoffman was shot . . . where did you get the gun?"

"She made a comment about shooting me with her father's gun the other day," Michael added with a frown.

I let out another shriek. By now I was reaching the point where the thought of committing murder was actually starting to sound like a good idea, starting with my ex-fiancé.

I raised both eyebrows and stared at him. "What kind of a lawyer are you? Aren't you supposed to come to my defense, instead of doing your level best to incriminate me?"

He sighed. "I am hardly a criminal lawyer, Tracy. Though I am well aware that sometimes it's best to simply confess and throw yourself on the mercy of the court. Perhaps you could go for an insanity plea."

My mother touched Michael's arm. "Don't worry, Michael. Insanity does not run in our family. Tracy will not produce any heirs who would turn out to be insane."

This from a woman who was drunk and had just slapped her own daughter in front of an entire room full of people.

I shook my head in disbelief. "There won't be any heirs because Michael and I are no longer engaged. And besides that, I'm not insane and I didn't kill Betty."

Nana threw her hands up in the air. "Tracy is not a murderer. How many times must I repeat it? I'm going to call my own lawyer."

Just then the door to the already crowded room flew open wide. Speaking of insanity pleas, in strode none other than Sammy himself, a man whose hobbies included walking around with a box full of obituaries. As always, he wore his trench coat and fedora.

I stifled a moan. Of all the interrogation rooms in all the police stations in all the towns in all the world, why did this Humphrey Bogart look-alike have to walk into mine? He was all I needed to add to this group who was about to convict or commit me.

Detective Denton let out a laugh. "*Now* who do we have? Another character in this little Vaudeville Act? This is better than going to the movies." He jerked a thumb at Sammy. "Especially since this new guy is a dead ringer for Sam Spade."

That's when I dropped my head into my hands. Could this night get any more bizarre? Speaking of movies, I felt like I was smack dab in the middle of one, a real horror story. Because reality simply could not be this strange. Or maybe I was in the middle of a nightmare and about to wake up at any moment. Sort of like Dorothy in the *Wizard of Oz*.

Sammy didn't bother to remove his hat and coat, signifying that he wasn't planning to stay long.

"I understand you're giving my girl here a hard time," he said as his dark eyes practically burned into Detective Denton's skull. "I don't appreciate the rubber hose treatment. It's no way to treat a lady."

"*Your* girl?" Everyone around me asked with the same surprise at the same moment.

Now Sammy removed his hat and studied it. "Good. At least we know your hearing's working. Because obviously your brains aren't, or you never would have hauled her in here in the first place."

That seemed to get Detective Denton's hackles up. "What's it to you? And what are you doing here?"

Sammy peered out from under dark brows. "Miss Truworth is in my employ and you're wasting her time — and mine — while we're working on a very important case."

We were? I was? I tried not to show the complete and total astonishment that was swirling inside my mind.

Detective Denton scooted his chair back. "And *who* exactly are you?"

Sammy pulled a leather I.D. folder from his inside pocket and flipped it open to show a badge. "The name's Sammy Falcone. Private Investigator. Of the Falcone and Archez Detective Agency."

Falcone and Archez? I could tell Detective Denton wasn't exactly buying into Sammy's act. And for that matter, neither was I. Sammy's story was a little too close to the *Maltese Falcon* for me. I still wasn't sure if Sammy was on the level.

Though I had to say, aside from Nana, he was the only one in the room who had come to my defense.

He nodded to Nana. "How are you, Mrs. Truworth? Must be pretty lousy to see your granddaughter treated like a common thug."

Nana twinkled up at him. "You've got that right, Sammy. But I'm sure happy you showed up."

Detective Denton shook his head. "Wait a minute . . . If she's working for you, then why didn't she say something?"

Sammy snickered. "Because I instructed her not to breathe a word of this case to anyone. For any reason. And when I tell her to keep her trap shut, I can count on her not to spill the beans."

Detective Denton snickered. "Not even to the police?"

Sammy turned his attention to me, and gave me a slight smile. "Not even to the police. Right, kid?"

I wasn't quite sure what to do in that moment, so I just gave him a little smile back.

Sammy nodded to Detective Denton. "See, what'd I tell you? She may be only an Apprentice P.I., but she can clam up like an expert."

The detective scrutinized me with a squint and a snarl. Much to my amazement, he seemed to be at a loss for one of his half-baked ideas.

Sammy turned to me. "So, kid, what did you think of the package I gave you? Did you put two and two together and figure out what's what? It's all right if you talk about it in front of the police now. It's all public knowledge anyway."

Again, I didn't exactly know what to do, so I decided to play along for the moment. After all, I knew what package he was talking about.

The box I had practically taken from him. Or so I thought.

I sat up straight. "Yes, I did figure out the link. All those men, mostly young men, died at sea. In shipping convoys. Some in Navy and some in merchant ships. Their ships were headed to England, to take supplies over so the British wouldn't starve. But the Nazi U-boats have been torpedoing those ships and sinking them so the supplies can't get to England. Lots and lots of lives have been lost on those ships that have gone down."

Sammy raised his eyebrows. "Very good, kid. Like I said, you're a natural at this."

Michael shook his head. "I'm just not buying it. Tracy as a private detective? She's not that bright."

Sammy's head swiveled in Michael's direction. "Well, Junior, she's a whole lot brighter than that redheaded receptionist you've been palling around with. The one whose husband has been at sea for Uncle Sam for a few months now. I was just about to tell my young associate here all about it, but I thought you'd like to save me the trouble."

Michael stiffened while Nana shot him daggers with her eyes. "No time for Tracy, huh? But time for another woman? And plenty of time to go to the Polynesian Room? I'm glad Tracy won't be marrying you. You were never good enough for my granddaughter."

Now Sammy glanced at his wristwatch. "I hate to break up the party, but Miss Truworth and I need to get back to work on this case. She can change out of that dress and I'll have it sent over for evidence," he said with a nod to the detective.

But Denton wasn't letting me go without a fight. "Wait a minute . . . I'm not buying this. Who's your client?"

Sammy raised his voice. "Mr. and Mrs. None-of-your-Business. In other words, I can't say and I won't say."

Detective Denton snarled again. "Then tell me this much — what was she doing at Betty Hoffman's apartment?"

Sammy raised an eyebrow. "She was in the right place at the right time. We'd been tracking Miss Hoffman for a while. We thought she knew something about our case that she wouldn't tell us. Unfortunately, Miss Hoffman was murdered before we could convince her to give up the information. My young associate here walked into the scene shortly after Miss Hoffman was shot. Which in the end, turned out to be pure, dumb luck, on Miss Truworth's part. Otherwise, she might have bumped into the murderer and she might be lying in the morgue along with Miss Hoffman, instead of sitting here putting up with your nonsense. And of course, she got there too late to save Miss Hoffman. Though I know she tried. That's the kind of gal she is."

While I knew parts of Sammy's story was pure fabrication, he certainly had some things right. I really *had* wondered if I could save Betty. And yes, I probably had missed the murderer by a matter of seconds. What if I had been his or her second victim of the night? The thought of it made me shiver.

Sammy slid his hat back on his head. "Now, Denton, unless you plan to charge my associate with something, I'm taking her with me. We've got work to do."

Detective Denton lowered his lids halfway and glared at Sammy. "Fine. But this isn't over yet."

"It never is," Sammy laughed before turning to me. "You ready, kid? Let's get a move on."

For a split second, I wondered what I should do. After all, I still didn't know if Sammy was sane or not, and I had no idea if he actually was a P.I. I hadn't gotten a good look at his badge, and for all I knew, it was a fake. Maybe Sammy loved the *Maltese Falcon* so much that he tried to become Sam Spade. To the point where, somewhere in his mind, the line between fantasy and reality got a little hazy, and he started to believe he really was Sam Spade.

But if that were true, why use a name like Sammy Falcone? Why not fulfill the complete fantasy and call yourself Sam Spade?

In any case, I had a choice to make and I needed to make it in a hurry. I could either stay put and be accused of a murder I didn't commit, or I could take a chance by going off with a man who might suffer from delusions of grandeur. And right at that moment, I chose to go. Somehow, that option seemed a whole lot better than being tossed into a jail cell for what was left of the night. Especially since, if nothing else, Sammy seemed to be on my side.

I stood up and gave Nana a peck on the cheek. Then, without saying a word, I turned and followed Sammy from the room and out of the police station. He held the door of his dark sedan for me. The same sedan I'd seen days ago, right after I'd gotten the package from him that contained so many obituaries. And the very same sedan I'd been watching for when Jayne and Nana and I went shopping.

Now here I was, sliding onto the seat, and pulling my still damp, lumbering skirts in, too. Once I was safely tucked in place, Sammy shut the door and hurried around to the driver's side.

"You ready, kid?" he asked, as he pushed in the clutch with one foot, put his other foot on the brake, and started the engine.

"I guess so . . ." I sort of murmured before he backed out of his parking space.

All the while, I wondered if I'd just jumped into the car with a madman. I also had to wonder how he happened to know about the murder and that I was being interrogated at the police station.

Maybe he knew those things because he happened to be the person who had killed Betty Hoffman . . .

CHAPTER 15

It Was the Worst of Nights, It Was the Best of Nights

Katie McClue had once encountered a homicidal maniac, in the *Mystery of the Maniacal Man*. Of course, she had spotted his tendencies long before the police did, and long before any doctor might. Not only had she noticed his unblinking stare and cool indifference, but her superior female intuition told her right away that something was wrong with the man who had suddenly started appearing at garden parties and black-tie galas. She quickly realized he was dangerous and, as a result, she caught him right before he attempted to kill her best friend.

Now I tried to tune in to my own female intuition and listen to what it was telling me about Sammy, the man who was driving the dark sedan that I had so readily gotten into, without even giving it much thought.

Or, without even having a clue where we were going.

Was I in grave danger? On the surface, Sammy was certainly eccentric, but other than that, he basically seemed like a sweet, old man who was perfectly harmless. Besides, he showed absolutely none of the characteristics that Katie McClue had recognized in a homicidal maniac.

Except that he seemed to read my mind.

"Okay, kid, where should we start? I'll bet you've got lots of questions and you probably want some answers. I'd be the same way if I were waltzing in your shoes right now. The only problem is, we don't have much time for chitchat. Not when we need to get to work."

"Ummm . . . Sammy, you do realize I don't work for you, right?"

I glanced out the passenger-side window and up at the starless sky. A few remnants of the earlier storm remained, though mostly all I could see was the occasional flare of lightning in the thick clouds above us. Below, the street was still wet and leaves and small branches littered the road. Clearly the wind wasn't finished with us yet, as it swung tree branches from side to side.

Sammy grinned. "I wouldn't be so sure about that, kid. But maybe we'd better stop for a few minutes and chew this over."

Then before I could say a word, he pulled the car to the curb, right beneath a big streetlight. I had to say, I was pretty thankful for that big light. And I was also thankful the whole city wasn't in a blackout for an air raid drill at that moment. Because, if it weren't for those bright streetlights, the whole place would have been completely dark. And a lot of bad things can happen to a girl when it is late at night and dark out. Then again, a lot of bad things had already happened to me tonight. Some in the dark and some in the light. Either way, just to be on the safe side, I put one hand on the door handle, ready to make a fast getaway if I needed to.

Sammy put the car in park, turned off the engine, and nodded at me. "By the way, kid, that's quite a shiner you've got there. Hope the other guy looks worse. Who'd you tangle with anyway?"

I sighed and stared at the skirt of my sagging, blood-stained pink gown. "My very own flesh and blood. My mother. Only it wasn't exactly a 'tangle'."

"More like a sucker punch, is my guess." He made a *tsk-tsk-tsk* sound with his tongue. "I was afraid of that. Hate to see it when parents take things out on their own kids. Especially a daughter."

I raised my head and looked at him. "You mean, you've seen this kind of thing before?"

He nodded. "More times than I care to remember. I've been in this business a long time, and by now, I think I've seen it all."

His words were so kind, and, more than anything, I wanted to believe what he'd said to me. But I still needed to make sure that he was on the level, and not just leading me on for heaven knew what reason.

"Tell me, Sammy, is everything you told the police true? And would you mind if I saw that badge you flashed them? Or better yet, your P.I. license?"

He reached into his jacket and pulled his license from his inside pocket. "Those are some nice investigation skills you've got there, kid. And the answer is yes. Those things are true. My name is Sammy Falcone, and sure, I know people find some kind of connection between my name and the *Maltese Falcon* movie. Especially since everybody tells me I look like Humphrey Bogart. Though frankly, I don't see the resemblance. I think Bogey is a lot shorter than I am and he's got a smaller waistline. Either way, I was working as a detective long before the *Maltese Falcon* came out last October. Before that, nobody ever said I looked like Bogey at all."

I held his license up to see it better in the light from the streetlamp. I gave it the once over, and sure enough, as near as I could tell, it was the real deal.

I passed it back to Sammy. "Well, I *do* think you look a lot like Bogart, but you're starting to remind me of my grandfather. Gramps. He passed away not that long ago. He once worked for the Pinkerton Detectives. When he was young."

Sammy raised an eyebrow. "I know."

My mouth fell open and my chin practically hit the car seat. "How in the world could you know something like that?"

He readjusted his hat. "C'mon, kid. Since I wanted to hire you, I had to check you out first, right?"

I gasped. "But when did you have time to do that? And how did you know who I was?"

Sammy laughed. "It wasn't hard. Not after I followed you the day you wrangled that package away from me."

I shook my head. "So how did you follow me? I watched in my rearview mirror for anyone tailing me. Then I made a whole bunch of turns through a neighborhood and checked my mirror again. I didn't see a tail."

Not to mention, I'd done exactly what Katie McClue would have done.

Sammy grinned. "You did pretty good, kid, but you were a little predictable. Rookie mistake. You didn't vary your turns enough. I got your license plate right before you came out of the neighborhood. Then I had a friend check the state files and find out who the car belonged to. That's when I found your grandmother, and consequently, you, too. But you did a good enough job that I figured you were worth hiring and training."

"You were serious about that?" I sputtered. "About hiring me?"

He nodded. "I am and then some. I'm down a partner, and like I said, you're a natural. Not to mention, between the peace-time draft and men joining up to serve in the military, most of the able-bodied men will be heading off to war. But I see no reason why a woman couldn't do this kind of work. In fact, I see some real advantages to it. The guy who founded the Pinkerton Agency ninety years ago — the late, great Allan Pinkerton — did pretty well when he hired the first lady detective in the country, Kate Warne. Turns out she was one of the best detectives he ever hired, because she could go places that a man couldn't go and really get the scoop."

"That's all very . . . interesting. But what happened to the partner you had? Archez?"

Sammy rested his left arm on the steering wheel while he stared out the windshield. "Abe. Abe Archez. Best partner I ever had. A whole lot younger than me. He left a month ago to sign up for the Army."

"Oh . . ." I sort of murmured. "I guess you're probably proud of him. And sad to see him go, all at the same time."

He kept on staring out the window. "That about sums it up, kid. Lots of us knew this war was coming, since Uncle Sam had one foot in it already. Abe was antsy to go and fight for the greater good. And for Uncle Sam."

I put my hand on his arm. "Your old partner sounds like he is a good man. My father is trying to join up, too. Lots and lots of guys are."

Sammy nodded. "Don't I know it, kid. Don't I know it. Meanwhile, there are still crimes over here that need to be solved and probably fewer men to solve them. That's why I could use you in the agency. You can cut your teeth on this case and we'll go from there."

I raised an eyebrow. "But what exactly is this case? I know you've been following Betty. But why?"

Sammy wiped a speck off his windshield. "I was hired by a group of six mothers."

"Mothers?" I repeated, not sure I'd heard him correctly.

"Bereaved mothers. Turns out their sons all went down in the Atlantic, in ships that were blown up by German U-boats. The mothers met when they attended the memorial services of each other's sons, purely out of respect, after seeing a notice in the paper. And even though they didn't know one another at the time. Later, they got to talking and comparing notes and photographs, and that's when they learned an interesting tidbit — their sons all believed they were engaged to Betty."

I sort of gasped, and for a moment I couldn't speak. "So there were six fiancés in total?"

"For starters, kid. But after this group of ladies started looking into it, getting the names of more of the men on board each ship, they counted ten fiancés in all. On three different ships. And here's the interesting thing — none of the moms had ever met Betty in person. In fact, they didn't even know who she was, or where she lived, or where she was from. Just a name and maybe a photograph or a description of her."

"So their sons got engaged but didn't introduce their fiancée to their moms?"

Sammy let out a long sigh. "Seems those engagements were all quickie deals, kid. War was just on the horizon, and with the future so uncertain, things were pretty intense for many of those boys. Still are. Emotionally, anyway. And lots of young people have been getting engaged or married in a hurry, especially with boys going off to join the service."

I had to say, I'd seen it all firsthand on Thursday at the courthouse. The place was full of couples getting married before the guys shipped out. And I knew it wasn't quite the wedding that Jayne and her family had wanted. That probably went for a lot of the couples who were there. But the timing on weddings and engagements had been sped up all of a sudden, now that we were at war.

Even so, it was one thing to get married or engaged to one guy.

But ten? For the life of me, I couldn't imagine what it would be like to be engaged to that many men. Personally, I'd had enough trouble just being engaged to one. How in the world could a woman juggle all those fiancés? Maybe it helped that they'd obviously left town, so she didn't actually spend a lot of time with them. Much like Michael hadn't spent much time with me, and apparently, from what I'd learned tonight, he hadn't been true-blue either.

Still, somehow two and two did not equal four in Betty's case. I remembered the evening when I'd first spotted her on the train ride home from Dallas. I'd seen her in action as she flirted and carried on to get the attention of the men around her. Back then I'd wondered if Betty was desperate to find a husband. Yet little did I know, she'd already been engaged to ten different guys. Wouldn't she at least take a moment or two to grieve the loss of all those fiancés before she dove in again? But judging from the many letters she had in her mailbox, as well as the steamy scene outside the apartment building the morning I'd run over to pick up my dress, Betty had a whole lot of men under her spell.

Again, I had to wonder, why did she put on such a show coming home on the train? And for that matter, why did a bombshell nightclub singer even need to pursue other men, when men already hounded her?

Could it be that she hadn't met Mr. Right? Maybe she got engaged to guys in a hurry, but wasn't passionately "in love" with any of them. I had certainly been betrothed to a man whom most women would consider the catch of a lifetime. But despite the way Michael appeared on paper and in pictures, he wasn't really much of a catch. There'd never been any great mad passion between us, and no matter how hard I tried to be happy with him, I just wasn't.

But getting engaged to an entire fleet hardly seemed like the way to find true love. And if she wasn't in love with the man she'd been kissing outside the apartment building, well, you could have fooled me.

I guessed her multiple engagements also accounted for her unspoken rule, whereby she never allowed any of her suitors into her apartment. That way she'd never risk any of the men bumping into each other. Yet despite her "rule," I had seen two older gentlemen leave her apartment — one sinister and one sad. Somehow I couldn't picture them as being potential fiancés for Betty. Or even romantic interests of any kind.

Once again, I wondered about her being a prostitute, or even a very loose woman. But women like that didn't go around getting engaged en masse.

I glanced at the big diamond still on my ring finger. Funny, but in the heat of the moment, I'd forgotten to return it to Michael. Now I had to wonder, did Betty get rings from each of her suitors?

I turned to Sammy. "If she was engaged to all those guys, she must have had a whole collection of diamond rings. Probably other jewelry, too."

Sammy nodded. "She wasn't lacking when it came to the ice. Or, at least, not the fake ice."

I thought back to how Betty always wore enough jewelry for three women. Had most of that jewelry been given to her as gifts? I'd recognized the brand as being Eisenberg, and even though Eisenberg was only costume jewelry, it was the best there was. And very realistic looking.

So, if she did receive jewelry from so many men, how did she keep from getting it all mixed up?

Maybe she made it easier by telling all her guys that Eisenberg was the only brand she liked, to pretty much ensure it was what they would buy. And by only wearing Eisenberg, and lots of it, she could avoid any suspicion from the other guys. If they asked about some piece they'd given her, she'd either have it on or say she'd forgotten to wear it that day. And if they asked about the pieces she wore that they *hadn't* given her, she could say they were pieces she already owned. Since, after all, it was her brand.

If that had been how Betty operated, in a weird way, it was sort of ingenious. Even so, there were still so many things about her that didn't add up.

I rubbed my forehead. "No matter how much I try to make sense of this, the pieces just don't fit together. How did she keep everything and everyone straight? And what was going to happen when one of those guys wanted to set the date? I have to say, something really seems amiss. Aside from the obvious."

Sammy glanced out the driver's side window for a moment. "I'm with you, kid. Any way you look at it, there's more to this than meets the eye. And I've been in this business long enough to know when I smell a fish. A very big fish. Especially when I found out she'd been engaged to several guys who all happened to be on the same ships. That was just too big of a coincidence for me. And I don't exactly believe in coincidences."

"I couldn't agree with you more," I said with a nod.

"The mothers who came to me felt the same way. They thought something was really off base about the whole situation. And, in general, they wanted to know more about Betty and what she was up to. So they hired me to investigate."

I touched my finger to my lips. "It sounds like a good case to me."

Sammy nodded. "That's what I thought, too. And since they're mothers who just lost their sons, I took this case at a special rate."

I smiled at him. "That also sounds good to me. But what happens now that Betty's been murdered?"

"We're still on the case, kid. We still need to get to the bottom of this, and find some answers for the moms."

And for ourselves, I thought.

I raised an eyebrow on the uninjured side of my face. "There's one thing I don't understand. What was the idea behind the box with the pictures and obituaries?"

"Good question," Sammy said with a grin. "Not long after I agreed to take the case for this group of moms, I located Betty. Which wasn't easy, considering I couldn't find any past addresses or relatives. Or any connections at all. Then I tried to talk to Betty, to learn more about her and get some information. But she avoided me like the plague."

I turned to look outside as a gust of wind picked up leaves in the street and tossed them around. "I tried talking to her, too. But she wanted nothing to do with me, either."

"I believe you, kid. Because I think Betty had ice water running through her veins. I couldn't even appeal to her soft side, by showing her all those obituaries and pictures and things, of all those boys who had died on those ships. The mothers had put that all together for me, and I tried to approach Betty with it several times. But even that didn't melt Betty's heart, and she still backed away. As near as I could tell, she didn't have a heart. Or a soft side."

I felt a light bulb go on in my head. "That's what you were doing on the train. You were tailing Betty so you could talk to her. With that package. But why was it so mangled up, with all that paper and string?"

Sammy chuckled. "You don't miss a thing, do you, kid? It was because of the rain. I'd put the paper around it and tied it up to protect the box. But it didn't do much good after that rainstorm hit and I got soaked. It pretty much mangled the paper covering it." He leaned into his door and took a good look at me. "Wait a minute . . . don't tell me you really were thinking about the package in the *Maltese Falcon* . . . you didn't think I had some bejeweled treasure in there or something, did you?"

I shrugged and was pretty glad he couldn't see the color rising in my cheeks. "I had no idea. But I could sure tell you were hauling around something that was pretty important to you."

He chuckled and rubbed his chin. "You got that right. And yes, I did follow Betty to Dallas, and then I caught her again when she was heading home. I wanted to keep an eye on her in case she was trying to do a bunk and run out of town. Before I got the whole story from her."

I shook my head. "I wish you could have seen her flirting for all she was worth in the parlor car, before you showed up on the scene. How could a woman have that many fiancés and not care one bit that they'd died? All of them?"

Sammy raised an eyebrow. "Your guess is as good as mine. But I suspected right away that little old Betty was up to her bottle-blonde hair in something. What her scheme was, I'm not sure. And I have a feeling we'll need to figure out who murdered her before we can find out what she was up to."

"And that's why you want my help."

"Yup, kid. That's where you come in. All those grieving mothers deserve some answers. And I intend to find those answers. Which brings me to the deal I'd like to offer you. I'd like you to start working as my apprentice for a few years. Until you've got enough time and training under your belt to get your own P.I. license. Then we can talk about a partnership. In the meantime, I'll pay you a fair salary. Plus expenses. And we'll start by solving the murder of one Betty Hoffman."

Suddenly I felt a little dizzy. I didn't know if it was a lack of sleep, or the fact that I'd found my first dead body tonight, only moments after the murder. Or, maybe my mother had hit me so hard that I now had a concussion. Then again, maybe the gigantic emotional roller coaster I was on was the cause of my lightheadedness. Because I'd just gone from the *worst* night of my life to the *best* night of my life. One where my dream of being a private detective was about to come true.

Just like Katie McClue.

Well, almost like Katie McClue. Unlike her, I had to start out as an apprentice and work my way up to being a full-fledged private eye. Still, it all sounded pretty swell to me!

Of course, it also meant that I'd have to prove myself and earn my keep. For starters, I'd have to play a big role in solving Betty's murder.

Could I do it?

I would never know until I tried.

I held out my hand to shake Sammy's. "You've got a deal, boss. Where do we start?"

He shook my hand in return before he started the engine again. "The same place you should always start — the scene of the crime."

CHAPTER 16

Expensive Art and Black Widows

Sammy turned his dark sedan in the direction of Jayne's apartment building. "This is gonna be touchy, kid. Because we don't have jurisdiction when it comes to looking at the scene of the crime. And the police will still be working the scene. So I say we go into the building under the guise of you wanting to change out of that dress. To turn it over to the police. Then while you're changing, I'll chat with whoever's in charge and try to get a good look inside Betty's apartment."

"Sounds like a plan," I agreed.

"In the meantime, let's start by having you tell me everything you saw. In detail."

I sat up straight and tall. "I can do even better than that. I took pictures."

Sammy sort of sputtered before he put a hand to his chest. "Pictures? Be still, my beating heart. Kid, I gotta hand it to you, you've got some great instincts."

For the first time in a long time, I let a big smile cross my face, even though it hurt. Thanks to the bruise on my cheek.

"I also took pictures of her a week ago," I told my new boss.

"When she was strolling up the sidewalk." Though I knew "strolling" was hardly the word to describe the way her hips swayed from side to side with enough motion to cause a tidal wave.

Sammy chuckled. "I spotted a good apprentice in you, that's for sure. Now where is this film? I'm guessing you didn't have time to develop it."

"It's at Jayne's place. The apartment right across the hall from Betty's. In case you didn't know, Jayne is the apartment manager and I'm filling in for her while she's on her honeymoon."

Sammy held up his hand. "Thanks for trying to catch me up to speed, but I know all about it."

I crinkled my brow. "You do . . .?"

"Yup, kid," he told me. "Now let's get that film so we can go and develop it. But do us a favor. Don't let on that you've got it, so keep the canisters in your purse until we get out of there. Let the boys in blue take their own pictures. I'll keep the cops busy and try to take a gander at the crime scene while you head into your friend's place."

"Aye, aye," I said with a little salute.

Once we got back to the apartment building, we entered through the rear door and slid past the police who were still there.

I was just inches from Jayne's door when a police detective in a double-breasted suit grabbed my arm. "We still need that dress of yours for evidence."

"If you'll get your paws off me, I'll go change out of it right now," I told him. "After that, as far as I'm concerned, it's all yours. You can have it. I never want to see it again."

So, while Sammy stayed in the hall and jumped into what sounded like a tense conversation with the detective and a few other uniformed officers, I went to change out of the big, pink monstrosity that had once been my dress. A glance in the mirror showed that I was a complete and total wreck. I had gone from beauty to beast in the span of one very long night.

I put on my navy suit and quickly reapplied my makeup. Then I brushed out my hair, pulled it back with a couple of combs, and pinned on my navy hat. I set it at a severe tilt, hoping to shadow my poor black eye. My mother had hit me awfully hard to create a shiner the likes of the one I had now. I could feel that blow all over again, just thinking about it.

And yet she'd denied it at the police station. How could a woman hit her own daughter like that in public, and then turn around and pretend it never happened just a few hours later? Sure, I knew she'd blow a gasket when she got the news that Michael and I were through, but smacking me with the force of a prizefighter was extreme. Even for her.

Now I had to wonder, could I ever go home again? She hadn't even bothered with any kind of an apology. Not that I expected it from her. But if she'd hit me once, would she do it again?

Unfortunately, I had a pretty good idea what the answer would be. Especially since I really wasn't much use to her now, when her dreams of my wedding had been snatched away from her for good. I slid Michael's grandmother's ring from my finger, and dropped it into my suitcase. I didn't have time to think about my mother at the moment. Instead, I had a case to help solve.

As a brand-new Apprentice P.I.

The very idea of it gave me a little thrill.

I was just about to head for the door when I heard a sleepy meow coming from Jayne's living room. It was Clark.

"Oh, you poor kitty," I soothed. "You've been through a rough time, haven't you? Losing Betty tonight. But don't worry, you can stay here with me."

It seemed as though he understood every word I'd said, because he came running straight for me. I picked him up and gave him a quick hug. He immediately started to purr. Then I poured him a saucer of milk and left a side window slightly open, so he could go in and out. In case he needed to do his business.

"I'll be back soon," I said to him with one last pet.

Or at least, I hoped I'd be back soon. Frankly, I didn't have any idea what the rest of the night held for me. Yet oddly enough, even though it was the wee hours of the morning, I wasn't the least bit tired.

So I hid my camera case inside my purse, grabbed my ruined dress, and left the apartment, locking the door behind me. And I joined Sammy in the hallway.

One of the large, uniformed men jabbed a finger at Sammy's chest. "Just remember pal, we got jurisdiction. So don't be interfering with our investigation."

"What's the matter, slick?" Sammy laughed. "You afraid of a little competition? Afraid I'm going to solve this crime before you boys ever do?"

Yet as the officer took out his frustrations on my new boss, Sammy didn't even seem rattled. In fact, he almost acted like he was enjoying the whole encounter.

Sammy nodded at me. "Ready, kid?"

I handed my dress to the police officer. "Ready."

"Then let's get a move on," Sammy said as he motioned toward the back door.

I followed him out to his car. "That officer you were talking to sounded pretty nasty. Should we be worried?"

Sammy laughed out loud. "*We* shouldn't be, but *he* should. He accidentally spilled the beans on what they found tonight."

I'm sure my eyes went wide. "He did?"

"Yup, kid, he did," Sammy said as he held the car door for me. "Turns out only three of the building's tenants were home tonight. Two of 'em didn't hear a thing, probably because of all the thunder and lightning. Only an older couple heard something. Right around 10:30. That's when they came downstairs and spotted you. They're sure you're some kind of crazed killer." He chuckled at that.

I slid into the passenger seat. "Must be the Eldridges."

"You got it, kid," Sammy said right before he shut my door.

Seconds later, he was back in the driver's seat. "We'll need to talk to them, and the other tenants, too. It'll give you a chance to learn how to interview people."

"I'm not sure the Eldridges will ever speak to me again. But I'm more than willing to give it a try. In any case, I don't think Betty's killer was a tenant."

Sammy's right eyebrow went up. "Why's that?"

"Because I heard two sounds that I first thought was a car backfiring. Now I'm pretty sure they were gunshots. Right after that I heard a noise at the front door."

Sammy was already nodding. "Probably the killer leaving. Odd that he or she went out the front, instead of the back. But the front was probably the quickest. And nobody saw them because the whole place was pitch black."

Once again I realized just how close I must have been to Betty's killer.

"Wish I'd gotten there a little sooner. I got a tip about the crime from a buddy, and I showed up just as you were being hauled away. I managed to get enough tidbits from the guys standing guard to put two and two together. Right before I went down to the station and rescued you."

I turned to stare at him. "So that's how you just happened to show up when you did."

He put his key in the ignition and turned the engine over. "Yup, kid. But right now we'd better get to the office and develop that film. My gut tells me we're going to find some pretty important clues in those photographs."

I gasped. "We have an office?"

To which Sammy just smiled.

A few minutes later, we arrived at the six-story Binz Building, downtown on the corner of Main Street and Texas Avenue. The building was famous for being Houston's first skyscraper, having been built before the turn of the century. Of course, lots of much, much bigger buildings had gone up since then. Even so, the Binz Building was still a nice place and most definitely well kept. I soon learned the Private Investigative Firm of Falcone and Archez was located on the top floor.

To be honest, I'd pictured Sammy's office being in some seedy building, with barely enough lighting and questionable characters lurking around the corner. Yet as we got off the elevator, I was a little disappointed to see the place was as neat as a pin, and perfectly clean, with several thriving plants in the corners and on top of bookshelves. Apparently my new boss not only solved crimes, but he had a green thumb as well.

In the front area, I saw a beautifully carved Victorian desk with a sign that read, *Mildred Paninsky, Secretary.* I wondered when I'd get to meet her.

Sammy led me through the door to the main office.

I gasped when I noticed a stunning framed painting on the wall. "Is that a . . .?"

"Monet?" he finished for me as he hung his hat and trench coat on a corner coat rack. "Good eye, kid. And over there is a Picasso, though I'm not as fond of that one."

I turned to see the other painting and was instantly in awe. It seemed there was a lot I didn't know about Sammy. Starting with the fact that he must have been making millions to afford that kind of artwork. I was surprised the business paid so well. And I also had to wonder what my salary would be, since we hadn't talked about exact dollar amounts.

Sammy slid his double-breasted suit jacket off and put it on the back of a desk chair. "I know what you're thinking, kid. No, I did not make enough money to buy those things. They were given to me in lieu of payment. I recovered a big cache of stolen loot, and the owner was so grateful, she gave me both of those paintings. Can't say as they're exactly my style, but I leave them up for her sake. Sort of like the ugly wedding gift you keep around the house because the in-laws gave it to you and you never know when they're going to show up for a visit."

I laughed at that. "Well, I look forward to meeting this client. And I can hardly wait to hear the rest of the story."

Sammy grinned. "You'll be meeting her soon, kid. She's a Jewish woman who made it out of Germany in one piece. She and her family both. Before Kristallnacht. But since Hitler had more or less confiscated any valuables owned by the Jewish, getting her valuables out and back to her was another ballgame. Let's just say that I ended up with a few German stamps on my passport."

Under normal circumstances, I might have asked for more details right away. But since I was now eye-to-eye with a Picasso, or at least one of the oddly-placed eyes on the painting, well, I was amazed to the point of being speechless.

Sammy rolled up his white shirtsleeves and nodded to a room just to the side of the office. "Let's talk about your salary while we develop this film."

I unpinned my hat and set it on a desk. Then I pulled my camera case from my purse and followed him into what was once probably a large supply room that had been turned into, of all things, a well-stocked darkroom. Once we were inside, Sammy shut the door and hit the switch for the red light. My eyes quickly adjusted to the dimness.

Sammy pointed to my camera case. "May I, kid? Let's see what those crime scene photos can tell us."

I opened the case, and pulled out the film canister with the photos I'd taken of Betty on the day I'd gone to pick up my dress at Jayne's place. Then I rewound the film in my camera and removed it. I handed both canisters to Sammy.

"Have you ever developed film before?" he asked me. "This would be something good for you to learn."

I nodded. "I have done a little bit of developing. I know the basics anyway."

Of course, Katie McClue was an expert when it came to developing her own film. Her skills had come in handy many times, so naturally, I wanted to learn the techniques, too.

I watched carefully as Sammy took the lead and I assisted. It wasn't long before we had those negatives in the enlarger, and from there, into the pans with the developer, fixer, and water bath. Then I hung all the newly developed pictures up to dry on the twine that was strung high across the length of the room.

Right away, Sammy grabbed a magnifying glass from a drawer and started to examine the pictures closely. I had to say, I was pretty pleased with my photography, since all my pictures turned out in focus and with perfect clarity. Which surprised me, considering I was shooting them in the dark with only a flashbulb for lighting. Not to mention, trying to time them between lightning flashes.

"These are great, kid," Sammy said with a smile. "You've really got a knack for this. Here, take a look."

He passed me his magnifying glass and pulled a second one from another drawer.

"Let's start with the pictures of Betty herself," he said. "Anything about her stand out as unusual?"

I inched my magnifying glass closer to the first photo, the one where Betty had been strolling up the walk. "Well . . . I'm not sure what I'm supposed to be looking for."

"C'mon, kid. Forget about anything you're *supposed* to be looking for. And just tell me what you see. Tell me what stands out to you."

So I blinked a few times and stared at Betty's pictures. "Well, for starters, she was overdressed for any morning events. And, to tell you the truth, she doesn't exactly look like anyone I've ever met.

Except . . ."

"Give it to me straight, kid. Don't hold back."

I shrugged. "She dresses like a character who stepped right off a Hollywood set. Her attire and her attitude . . . it's as though it's all an act. Like she's not who she pretends to be."

Sammy nodded. "I think you've nailed it, kid. Betty was playing a role of some kind. Which means Betty Hoffman might not have been her real name."

And that's when I suddenly felt a chill run up and down my spine. I remembered I'd had the same reaction around her the first few times I'd seen her. Why?

"So, I wonder what her real name was?" I sort of whispered, though I wasn't sure why.

"Good question. And if it's true, that Betty wasn't who she said she was, that leads us to a very important question — why was she pretending to be someone else?"

I moved on to the next picture. "Hmmm . . . maybe she was hiding from someone. Maybe she'd escaped a bad situation and didn't want anyone to find her."

Sammy cleaned the lens of his magnifying glass with his handkerchief. "People in hiding usually keep a pretty low profile. But everything about Betty screamed for attention."

I paused for a minute and stared at the wall. "Yes . . . and no. She only wanted attention from men. Younger men. But she couldn't have been more unfriendly to women. Or older men."

"So she was targeting young men. And getting engaged to lots of them. I dunno, kid. She's starting to sound like a black widow to me."

"A black widow?" I instantly shuddered, thinking of a very creepy black spider I'd seen near our swimming pool when I was young.

Sammy moved to another picture of Betty and put his magnifying glass close to the paper. "A woman who really hates men, though she pretends to be the opposite. Black widows are homicidal maniacs, and they either prefer to kill men or enjoy seeing them dead. The only difference is, they usually marry their victims. Then they bump them off and move on to the next one."

I'm sure my eyes went wide right at that moment. "What in the world would possess a woman to do something like that?"

Sammy chuckled under his breath. "Partly because they like it. It gives them power over their victims. Like a female black widow spider who eats her mate when she's done with him."

"What's the other part?"

Sammy squinted and kept on looking at the picture. "For the insurance. Lots of these women collect the insurance money from their victims. But that only works if they marry the man first."

I tried to picture this in Betty's case. "Maybe Betty didn't have that chance. Maybe all her fiancés shipped out before she could walk down the aisle with any of them."

"Could be, kid," Sammy sighed. "That could explain why she didn't show any remorse at their loss. Those boys would have been nothing but a waste of time, if they died before she had a chance to marry them. As for why Betty might be in hiding and pretending to be someone else . . . could be she's running from the law. Black widows may be a rare breed, but they don't usually stop murdering people."

"So if she really was a black widow killer, she might have murdered men in some other town."

"Could be, kid," Sammy said again as he pointed to the photos at the end of the line. "Time to take a look at the crime scene pictures. Looks like those are dry enough to take out into the light."

So we did just that. We each grabbed a few photos carefully by the edges of the paper and took them out to the office. Sammy turned off the red light as soon as I'd opened the door.

I blinked a few times as my eyes adjusted to the light of the office. I glanced toward a window·and noticed it was still dark outside. I wasn't sure what time it was, but I guessed it would probably be daylight soon.

Sammy put his bunch of pictures onto his desk. So I did the same. He took his desk chair, and I sat in the chair across from him. Then we both used our magnifying glasses to examine the photos. Very, very closely.

For a second or two, the lightheadedness I'd felt earlier, when I'd first seen Betty's dead body, came back in full force. Looking at her picture, even though it was in black and white, made me feel like I was right back in her apartment, with the thunder making a big racket while the lightning flashed and sizzled. Especially since the pool of blood seemed much more prominent in the pictures than I'd noticed when I was at the scene.

"Okay, tell me what you've got," Sammy said with his head down.

I took a deep breath and fought against the dizziness. I knew Katie McClue never felt the least bit dizzy when she was examining a crime scene photo. So I took another breath and closed my eyes for a second, while I worked to get myself under control.

"You okay, kid?" Sammy asked gently.

"Uh-huh," I murmured.

"These things can be pretty shocking. And they might take a little getting used to. Why don't I get us started on this?"

"Okay," I said as I took yet another deep breath.

He pointed to Betty's body. "As near as I can see, we've got two gun shot wounds here. One to the leg and one to the chest. We can only see the one to the leg because her long, evening gown was hiked up to her knees when she landed."

I nodded. "Probably because she was running from someone. My guess is she had grabbed her skirt and lifted it up to free her legs." It was a sensation I was much too familiar with, considering I'd had a lot of experience running in an evening gown lately.

Sammy looked impressed. "Good call. That could account for why the shot on her leg looks like it was from a distance. And not much of a shot, for that matter."

By now, the dizziness had passed and my head was starting to clear. "That means the shooter only managed to hit her leg with the first shot and slowed her down. But then, once he had her down, he went in for the kill with the second shot to the chest. Which, according to these pictures, was a pretty close range shot. So we don't know if our killer is an expert. Or an amateur."

"That's about the size of it, kid. Anyone with a gun could've killed Betty Hoffman. Or anyone who knew where to get a gun."

I looked at the pictures some more. "Something else stands out to me. Why wasn't Betty singing at the Polynesian Room that night? In Galveston? After all, it was a Saturday night."

"Good question," Sammy agreed. "Maybe we need to take a little trip to the Polynesian Room and check things out. Maybe there is more to that place than meets the eye. But we'd have to do it inconspicuously."

I stood up straight and looked him in the eye. "You mean . . . undercover work? In disguise? Incognito?"

He laughed for a moment. "Nothing quite so elaborate, kid. I was thinking it would be best if we went as a foursome. You get a date and I get a date. Then we just appear to be a group of people going out to dinner some night."

I sighed. "I'm afraid I might have a little trouble getting a date. Considering I am currently without a fiancé or a boyfriend of any kind."

"That won't last long," he said with a grin. "As for me, I think I'll see if your grandmother might be available for an evening of dinner and dancing."

My mouth fell open and, for a moment or two, I was completely speechless. "Nana? You're going to ask Nana out? On a date?"

Sammy chuckled. "Don't panic, kid. I'm just going to ask her out to dinner. Not to walk down the aisle. For the sake of this case. A man with a doll on his arm won't stand out. Besides, people never suspect us older folks of doing anything out of the ordinary. If I get caught investigating, I'll pretend I got lost. And they'll brush it off like I'm some doddering old geezer."

That's when I smiled. "In that case, I think Nana might enjoy being your partner in crime."

"Thought she might, kid. Now, back to this case. Let's finish up with these photos so we can move on."

So we did just that.

I focused in on another photo. "It looks to me like Betty was busy with something. See her desk? I think she was working on something there. The cap is off her fountain pen."

Sammy moved his own magnifying glass around to get a closer look. "But she's also got a spike receipt holder on her desk. Stacked with papers of some kind . . ."

I moved to yet another photo for a better view. "I see it. I think they're letters! They're all about the same size — the size of a piece of stationery. And I know from helping the mailman sort the mail that Betty received all kinds of handwritten letters. My guess is that they were probably from guys."

"Love letters," Sammy murmured. "Lots of them."

I glanced at a window again, and this time I noticed the sun was coming up. "Which means she must have had a whole bunch of other guys on the hook."

Sammy let out a low, slow whistle. "That would be my guess, too, kid. And then she just stacked them up like a bunch of sales receipts. Business as usual."

I raised my eyebrows. "I don't think that's all she did. Take a closer look over here. It looks like she circled a few sections in the top letters."

Sammy scrunched up his nose. "That's odd. And for once, I have to say, it's something I've never seen before. In any case, as near as we can tell, Betty was sitting at her desk working."

"And not planning to head to Galveston to sing at the Polynesian Room," I added. "When someone either broke into her apartment or knocked on the door."

Sammy glanced at the door to the office. "I'll bet they knocked on the door. Maybe she was even expecting this person to come over. Then she probably let him, or her, into the apartment . . . maybe they even had a conversation. Or an argument."

I looked up at the light fixture. "And then the lights went out."

Sammy rubbed his chin, now with a five-o'clock-shadow. "But before that, I'm guessing the other person pulled a gun in the heat of the moment."

"Or maybe that person was there to rob her," it suddenly occurred to me. "Maybe she had something they wanted."

"And Betty refused to give it to them," Sammy added, raising one finger. "Instead she tried to run and the shooter got her in the leg. It wasn't much of a shot, but Betty was a moving target. In the dark. Once the shooter had her down, he finished her off with a second shot to the chest. And ran out the front door, probably the way he came in."

"Or . . . maybe Betty was the one with the gun. Maybe the person who was there got it away from her and then shot her."

Sammy nodded. "Good guesses either way, kid. But any way you look at it, it gives us something to go on."

"So now what do we do?" I yawned, feeling tired for the first time.

"We need to get a look in Betty's apartment," Sammy said, with a glance at the clock. "And see if anything pops out at us. Whenever the police are finished and we can get in."

"And we need to check out the Polynesian Room," I added.

Sammy rolled down his shirtsleeves and buttoned the cuffs back into place. "Plus, let's see if we can check out Betty's mail. Whatever is left in her box. Before it gets forwarded to her next of kin. Because my guess is we'll find some good clues in those letters. And don't worry, I'll steam them open and reseal them so nobody'll be the wiser."

I had to smile at that. Sammy knew how to steam open a letter and Nana knew how to break into a package. Without leaving a trace. Did everyone from their generation grow up with these skills?

Sammy grabbed his fedora and coat. "But first, let's get you home. Back to that apartment building, where you can get a little shut-eye. You're looking pretty dead on your feet, kid."

He could say that again. Not that he needed to tell me twice. Because, honestly, I could barely keep my eyes open much longer.

I grabbed my hat and pinned it on the best I could. Then I ran back into the darkroom and retrieved my camera. I barely managed to stay awake as Sammy drove me back to Jayne's place. The sun had risen in the sky, and I realized that normally I would've been headed for church about now, with my family.

For a moment, I wondered if I would ever do that again. Or if I'd ever go back home. Though at my age, it was probably time for me to be on my own anyway.

Sammy parked his car on the street and walked me inside. A couple of police officers were still finishing up in Betty's apartment, but none were in the hallway.

Even so, the hallway wasn't empty. Because apparently I had someone waiting there for me. He was sitting on the floor next to Jayne's door, and it looked like he'd been sound asleep. But his light blue eyes popped open wide and his face creased with concern when I walked up with Jayne's key.

It was Pete.

What in the world was he doing here?

CHAPTER 17

Subterfuge, and Shipping Out

When I saw Pete sitting on the hardwood floor of the hallway and leaning against the wall, I did a double take. Was it really Pete sitting there? Or had my eyes deceived me? Maybe I was so exhausted by now that I was seeing things.

But apparently I wasn't.

Pete wiped his bloodshot eyes and struggled to his feet. "Tracy! I've been looking all over for you. I've been so worried. I finally found your grandmother and she told me where you were staying. Are you all right?"

His tuxedo was wrinkled and damp, and the hems of his pant legs were splattered with mud. His bow tie was askew and his hair was plastered down on one side, probably from where he'd fallen asleep against the wall.

I laughed. "Pete, what are you doing here? You look like you've already been to war."

He stared at my black eye and bruised cheek. "You look like you've been through some battles yourself. I mean . . . you look beautiful, of course. But your eye looks a little tough."

I groaned and cringed. "So I guess you heard all about it."

I took a glance behind me and noticed that Sammy had hung back. He was leaning into Betty's apartment and talking to the police who were working inside. I wasn't sure if he was trying to get an up close and personal look at her place, or if he was just giving Pete and me a little privacy.

Or both.

"Everybody heard about it," Pete said gently. "I am so sorry. I sure didn't mean to get you in trouble with your mother. By asking you to get up and sing like that. I had no idea she'd get so violent about it all." He didn't take his eyes off my face.

I gave him the best smile I could conjure up at that moment, but it hurt even worse to move my cheek by now. "It's not your fault, Pete. I don't blame you. I blame my mother."

He moved closer and put his hand on my arm. "That was a lousy thing she did. She had no business hitting you like that. Is there anything I can do to help?"

For the first time since I'd gone running out of the country club and into the storm, I felt like crying all over again.

He must have noticed, because he slid his strong arm around my waist and pulled me close to him. I leaned my head against his shoulder, and that's when a few hot tears slid down my cheeks. I fought with everything I had to turn off the waterworks.

He pulled his hanky from his pocket and handed it to me, while he still kept me in his embrace.

Before I knew it, Sammy was right there. "Say, you big lug. What did you do to make our girl here cry?"

Pete pulled back. "Nothing, sir. Honest. I was just trying to make her feel better."

"Uh-huh," Sammy muttered. "I'll just bet."

"Really, I wasn't trying to get fresh. I just felt bad because I asked her to get up and sing, and that's what made her mother so mad."

"I see," Sammy said with a nod. "Well, if you want to put a smile back on her face, you could start by asking her out. On a proper date. And not to some cheap gin joint, either. No, you'd better take her to some swank place. Where you can both dress to the nines. The Polynesian Room would do nicely. In Galveston."

I rolled my eyes at Sammy. I wanted to let out a laugh, but by

now, I was just too tired. Sure, I knew we wanted to go to the
Polynesian Room to investigate, but coercing Pete to take me like
this was crossing a line. A thin one, maybe, but still . . . it was a line.

Pete stood up soldier straight. "Sure, mister. Whatever you say.
The Polynesian Room it is. Sound good to you, Tracy?"

I dabbed at my eyes. "I would like that, Pete."

Pete put on his usual smile. "How about Tuesday night? I'll
pick you up at six? I've got my new Cadillac and she's a real dream.
It'll be a breeze to drive down to Galveston. We'll have a wonderful
dinner, and dance as much as you like."

I smiled and handed his hanky back to him. "That sounds swell,
Pete. Now, if you don't mind, I've had a long night and I'd probably
better get some sleep."

"I'll see you then," he said, before he leaned over and shyly gave
me a peck on my good cheek. "I'm glad to see you're okay. I really
was worried about you."

"Thanks, Pete. You're a good Joe." Without thinking, I reached
up and gave him a peck on the cheek, too.

His face lit up just before he turned and strolled to the back
door. Funny, but he'd never even asked who Sammy was, and I was
so tired that I'd forgotten my manners and hadn't even made proper
introductions. Yet the only thing Pete seemed to care about was
whether I was okay or not. To top it off, he hadn't even asked about
the police and the goings on across the hall. Then again, maybe he'd
already talked to them.

Any way you looked at it, it was comforting to have a guy show
some care and concern for me. Unlike Michael, who was ready to
lock me up and throw away the key.

I honestly had to wonder what I'd ever seen in Michael in the
first place. Sure, he was movie star debonair and had a career that
would take him to the top, but aside from that, there wasn't much to
him. And he didn't treat me well at all.

Sammy kept his eyes on Pete as he walked out. "I gotta say, kid,
that is one nice young man. The kind of guy I'd want my daughter
to date. If I had a daughter. Or a granddaughter."

I took out my key to Jayne's place and unlocked the door. "But
you don't even know him. And I forgot to introduce you."

He pushed the door open for me. "I've gotten to be a pretty

good judge of character, kid. Right off the bat. It comes with the job."

"That's good to know," I said as I leaned down to pick up the Sunday paper that had been slipped under the door.

It was hard to believe that Pearl Harbor had been attacked only a week ago. So much had happened since then. Reports of the damage and death toll from Hawaii were still coming in. And still in the headlines.

What a world we lived in. Funny how life can turn on a dime. Mine certainly had.

Sammy followed me into the apartment. "This might be a good time for you to get that mailbox master key and see if Betty had any mail. But don't make a big production of it. We don't need the boys in blue across the hall catching wind of what you're doing."

"Got it," I said with a salute.

Oddly enough, I felt a little exhilarated that Sammy had given me this small task. Here I'd barely become an Apprentice P.I. and I was already doing something that involved subterfuge. Maybe even something borderline illegal, if not completely illegal. Of course, Katie McClue had made many such maneuvers in almost every single one of her episodes. So I knew exactly what to do. The trick, as she always mentioned when she taught fledgling detectives, was to make your moves swiftly, smoothly, and with purpose. Hesitation was a dead giveaway that you were doing something you weren't supposed to be doing.

So I grabbed the master key and quietly stepped into the hallway. Then I inserted the key into the slot and opened the main door to all the boxes, without so much as making a squeak. As always, Betty's box was full of letters. I pulled them out with my left hand, before I shut and locked the door again with my right. Then I checked to make sure no one had seen me. Thankfully, the coast was clear.

I walked back into Jayne's apartment and handed the letters to Sammy. "You didn't tell me . . . do you have a daughter? A wife? Or a family?"

Sammy flinched. It was barely perceptible, but it was there. "Did have, kid. Did have. Wife and daughter. They died a long, long time ago. Back in October, 1918. From the Spanish Flu. The city ordered the shutdown of schools and theaters and churches. But by then it was too late. They both got sick and went in a hurry."

"I'm so sorry . . ." I managed to murmur.

He shook it off with a smile. "Like I said, it was a long time ago. Now, why don't you get a few hours of shut-eye, and I'll go take a look at these letters. I'll check in with you later tonight."

I had to say, that certainly sounded like a good idea to me. Especially since it seemed like the Sandman was about to pay me a visit.

"One last question," I said to Sammy. "Did you learn anything interesting from the police just now? Do they have any suspects yet?"

Sammy chuckled. "They're going with a spurned lover. Though it didn't sound like they had much to go on. Considering they hadn't found any worthwhile prints or evidence."

I shook my head. "Just a few short hours ago, they thought I was the killer."

He put his hand on the doorknob. "They're looking to pin this on somebody and quick. Guess they've got a lot of guys ready to sign up and ship out. The police are about to find themselves shorthanded."

The idea of that scared me. "That will make it a whole lot easier for criminals to get away with all kinds of crimes."

Sammy grinned once more. "Not with us here to pick up the slack. Just think about it, kid. You'll be doing a vital service for your country, by filling a job that needs to be filled."

His words sort of took me by surprise. I was still pondering them as I let him out and locked the door behind me. With fewer men around to carry on the regular work of the nation, would it be necessary for women to step into their shoes? And, in essence, was that exactly what I was doing now?

It was something I would have to think about later. I changed into my pajamas and finally, at long last, fell into bed. I couldn't remember the last time I had truly gotten some sound sleep. I was barely aware of Clark Cat crawling onto the bed and cuddling up next to me. He started to purr and it was enough to send me off to dreamland.

The next thing I knew, Jayne was shaking me awake. Judging

from the low light coming in through the blinds, I guessed it must be around dinnertime. She was back a little earlier than I expected.

"Wake up, sleepyhead," she said. "My goodness, I go away for a weekend and look what happens. There's a murder across the hall. The police over there told me all about it. Asked me lots of questions, too. I can hardly believe it. Right here in my apartment building. I knew there was something odd about that Betty the minute I laid eyes on her. But this . . . murder . . . is the last thing I would've figured."

She flitted around the room, pulling clothes from drawers and her closet. Then she lifted her suitcase and set it on the end of the bed. She opened the latches on either side and lifted the lid. Funny, but it seemed to me that she was putting more clothes into that suitcase, instead of taking clothes out.

I yawned and tried to force myself to get out of bed. But my body wasn't having it. Some apprentice detective I was turning out to be, sleeping the day away. Katie McClue almost never slept until after she'd solved a case. In fact, she could easily go for days without so much as a nap.

Finally, I let my feet slide to the floor and sat up. "Welcome home, Mrs. Riesling. How was your honeymoon?"

Jayne's eyes twinkled as though they actually were full of stars. "Wonderful . . ." she sighed. "Just wonderful. I love being married. And I love that man so much. He is so wonderful."

Her happiness made me smile, which brought instant pain to my cheek. "Ouch!"

And that's when Jayne looked right at me and her eyes went wide. "What in the world? How did you get that shiner? Here I come back to find that one of my tenants was murdered and my best friend has a black eye. Jeepers, and all in one short weekend! What happened here?"

I got up and grabbed my bathrobe. "It's a long, long story."

She pulled a few things from her dresser and set them next to her suitcase. "Well, tell me everything. And you'd better make it quick. Because I have a really big favor to ask you and I don't have a lot of time."

So I gave her the whole scoop, from the singing to the slug to the thunderstorm. And from finding Betty's body to get hauled off to the police station to suddenly becoming an Apprentice P.I."

Jayne stood at the end of the bed and just stared at me with fascination. "And I thought getting married was big news. Looks like your weekend was nothing but non-stop action. Do you think we should be scared about staying here now? Do you think one of my tenants is a murderer?"

I shook my head. "Sammy, my boss, and I don't think he, or she, lives here. Because I heard the killer go out the front door."

This was when Jayne, who absolutely never panics about anything, suddenly shivered. "How terrifying! To think, you were just a few feet and a few seconds away from a murderer!"

I felt a little shiver myself. "I'm trying not to think about it. Now, what was that favor you wanted to ask me? And by the way, just where is Mr. Wonderful, anyway?"

Jayne sighed again. "That's part of the favor I have to ask you. Tom is headed to Abilene with some of the other new husbands. And I drove back home with some of the other new wives."

I rubbed the sleep out of my eyes. "Wait a minute, he went to Abilene? And what other husbands? What other wives?"

Jayne sat on the bed and stared at her dresser. "Well, for starters, the Hill Country was full of honeymooners. I guess lots of couples tied the knot before the guys planned to go into the service. We met a whole bunch of them up there. Nice folks. And a bunch of the boys were headed to Camp Barkeley, outside of Abilene. They're all taking off together so they'll be there tomorrow morning. Tom included."

"Oh, Jayne . . ." I murmured. "That was awfully fast."

She nodded. "I know. But not to worry. Because a bunch of the wives drove home with me. We came back to pack up a few things, and then we're headed to Abilene ourselves. We're going to rent a place together, so we can be there and see our guys for a while longer, before Uncle Sam sends them somewhere. And, for as long as we can afford it."

"Well . . . at least you'll get to see him," I said softly, hoping to help her keep up her morale.

She stared at her shoes. "Uh-huh. Hopefully. But he'll have to stay in the barracks, so we won't really be together."

I scooted over and put my hand on top of hers. "We're going to get through this. All of us. We're going to get Hitler and Hirohito, and we're going to win this war. And then Tom will be home before you know it."

She blinked back a few tears. "I feel so lost without him already. Did I mention how much I love that man?"

"And he feels the same way about you. Now, what was that favor you wanted to ask me? How can I help?"

She started to sniffle. "I really hate to ask you, because you've done so much already . . . But I was wondering if you could fill in for me here at the apartment building and watch things for a while. I'll call as soon as I get to Abilene and give you my number. And I can help over the phone if you have any problems. Honestly, I didn't want to burden you, but well, I really want to see my husband for as long as I can . . ."

I put my arm around her shoulders and hugged her. "I would be happy to fill in. I'll get Nana and Hadley in on it, too, if I need them. Because I understand completely. It's pretty rough, considering you barely got married and now he's taken off."

Jayne dabbed at her eyes. "It is. But no waterworks. We all knew it was going to be like this, and we're all making sacrifices. We have to, to win this war."

Just then Clark Cat jumped onto the bed and scooted in between us, with his front paws firmly placed on Jayne's leg. He let out a loud and commanding "*Meeorrow!*"

It was enough to make us both laugh.

"Looks like Clark's ready to fight, too," Jayne smiled as she dabbed at her eyes again.

I leaned back and petted him on his head. "I think you're right. And if we all have his attitude, we will definitely win. Now, how can I help you pack up and get ready to go? You've got a long trip ahead of you."

Jayne blinked back the last of her tears. "I know, but us girls will all take turns driving. And my brothers are following us up, so they can enlist, too. We'll be fine."

"I'm sure you will. Plus you'll have each other to lean on. So you won't be alone in this. I hope to meet all the wives when everyone comes back to town."

That brought a smile to her face. "You'd like them. They're a great bunch of gals. But before I take off, I need to run over and talk to the police. Would you mind coming with me? I need to find out what's what with Betty's apartment. There are so many people in town looking for a place to live, and murder or no murder, I don't want to deny someone a place to stay."

Especially, I thought, since she might be in those very shoes herself, considering she was headed to Abilene to look for temporary living quarters herself. Jayne and who knew how many other wives. Maybe even children. And probably at military bases all over the country.

All of a sudden, just thinking of all those sweethearts and displaced families, I found myself fighting back tears, too.

But it wouldn't do Jayne or anyone else any good if I started blubbering.

So I jumped up and went to my own suitcase. "I'll get dressed and then we can run across the hall. We'll get things sorted out."

And minutes later, there we were. I couldn't say I looked my loveliest, but at least the swelling had gone down in my cheek a little.

We found the door to Betty's apartment closed, so we knocked. Detective Denton himself answered.

Jayne held out her hand. "I'm Mrs. Jayne Riesling, the manager for this apartment building. While I spoke with some officers earlier, I'm afraid I haven't met you yet, Detective . . ."

"Denton," he said and reluctantly shook her hand.

Then Jayne went *tappa-tap-tap-tappa* right on past Detective Denton and into Betty's apartment. I followed on her heel while Detective Denton stared at her like she was a Martian who had just landed on this planet and was making herself right at home.

Jayne didn't seem to notice. "Of course, I realize that you boys need to do your job. But I hope you also realize that there's a housing shortage in Houston right now. And with Uncle Sam getting into the war, there'll be even more people moving into town. So, if you don't mind, I'd like to have this apartment available as soon as possible to rent again. I hate the thought of some person living on a street corner when a perfectly good apartment might be waiting for them."

Detective Denton's mouth fell wide open. "So sorry that our little murder investigation here is interfering with the apartment owner making some dough."

Jayne wheeled on her petite frame and took two steps toward the man. "I won't have any of your lip, Detective. You know as well as I do that this apartment will be rented out as soon as you gather the information you need. So I'd prefer to make it sooner than later. Don't you know there's a war going on? And we all need to join together and help each other out. And if people need a place to live, then, by all means, we'll do our part and give them a place to live. Do I make myself clear?"

Much to my amazement, Detective Denton sputtered for a few moments, as though he couldn't figure out what to say. "Yes, ma'am," he finally responded. "But first, where were you when this murder took place?"

Jayne put her hands on her hips. "In Fredericksburg, on my honeymoon. With plenty of witnesses and receipts to prove it."

He blinked a few times. "Um, all right. And do you know anyone who might want to murder Betty?"

Jayne shook her head. "Your boys already asked me these questions. And no, right off the top of my head, I can't think of anyone who would want to murder her. But there was something strange about the way she kept to herself. Very strange. Except where the fellas were concerned. Though she never allowed suitors into her apartment."

Detective Denton took out his notepad. "I see. And would you happen to know if she had family, or any forwarding address? We haven't been able to locate any next of kin."

Jayne sighed and crossed her arms. "I'm afraid I can't help you there. I don't know where she came from, or what her family situation was. She just showed up one day and happened to be at the right place at the right time. So I rented this apartment to her. After that I hardly got two words out of her. Like I said, it was very strange, and I suppose I always knew something was a little off when it came to Betty."

Detective Denton jotted down a few notes. "All right, then. Don't leave town, in case I need to question you again."

That got Jayne's dander up. "Excuse me? I most certainly *will* be leaving town. My new husband will be at Camp Barkeley . . ."

"Near Abilene," Detective Denton finished for her. "So he's

already enlisted."

Much to my amazement, his entire face softened, and he almost looked . . . well, fatherly. Funny, but I didn't even know the man had a softer side.

Jayne took a deep breath, and I could tell she was steadying her nerves. "That's right. And I'll be staying nearby. I'm leaving tonight and Tracy will be taking care of things here at the apartment building for me. If you need to reach me, she'll have my number by tomorrow."

He put his notepad back in his pocket. "That will be fine. You drive carefully, okay? And we'll vacate this place by Wednesday morning."

I touched Jayne's arm. "And I'll get it cleaned up. We'll have it rented in no time."

"Thank you," Jayne said in a voice that suddenly sounded shaky. "Thank you both."

About a half hour later, I helped Jayne carry the last of her things to her car. We stowed them in the trunk, pushing everything to one side and making sure to leave room for the other women's suitcases.

Then I gave her a long hug goodbye. "Give my best to Tom. And be sure to take lots of breaks along the way. Let the other wives drive, too."

"Yes, Mother," she laughed. "I'll call you tomorrow and let you know where we're staying."

"Sounds good," I told her. "I'll be praying for you both."

"We're going to need it," she said as she slid in behind the wheel. "We're all going to need it."

And with that, she was off.

I watched while her car disappeared down the street, and right then, I did say a silent prayer.

Just as another car pulled up and parked in front of the apartment building.

It was Nana and Hadley, in my mother's car.

CHAPTER 18

Chicken Dinner and First Interviews

Nana jumped out of the car and walked as quickly as she could to me. Hadley wasn't far behind. They were both still wearing their church clothes, with Hadley in a gray suit and fedora, and Nana in a pale green dress with matching hat and gloves.

Yet her face was wrinkled with worry. At first she enveloped me in a big hug, and then she leaned back. She put one hand on my good cheek and stared at the other one.

"Oh, darlin'," she gushed. "I've been so upset since last night. I never dreamed your mother would be so violent like that! She and I have been having a shouting match ever since you took off with Sammy. But I had to put my foot down in that house. After all, I do own it. So either she treats you right or she gets out."

Hadley joined us. "Your mother and father have been in a state of perpetual dispute as well. That house has turned into a war zone in and of itself. It has been most uncomfortable. Thankfully, your mother has retired to her room, so we can enjoy some silence once more."

I shook my head. "Glad I'm not there. But it's good to see you both."

Nana wound her thin arm around mine. "Well, thank God you're alive and well. That nice boy, Pete Stalwart, called this morning, trying to find you. I told him where you were staying, and he called again later to tell me that he'd finally met up with you. He said you were all right, but he figured you'd be getting some sleep for a while. It was very thoughtful of him to keep us informed like that."

Hadley held up a large picnic basket. "So we brought dinner, packed specially by Maddie herself. It's a near feast. A complete roasted chicken, mashed potatoes and gravy, and more. 'One cannot think well, love well, sleep well, if one has not dined well.'"

"Hmmm . . ." I murmured as I tried to place Hadley's quote. "Thoreau? Wadsworth?"

He smiled. "None other than Virginia Woolf, my dear girl."

I laughed. "Either way, the food sounds delicious. Thanks so much for bringing it. I'm starving."

"We brought enough for Jayne and Tom, too," Nana gushed as I led them toward the building. "If they're home yet."

I shook my head. "You just missed Jayne. I'll tell you all about her and Tom after dinner."

"Good," Nana said. "And I also want to hear the details about how Sammy thinks you're working for him."

I held the front door for them. "Well, as of late last night, I *really* am working for him. As an Apprentice Private Investigator. It's official now. I'll work for him for a while and then get my license someday."

Nana's eyes went wide. "How exciting! I'm so proud of you, darlin'!"

Hadley patted me on the back. "I can hardly wait to pass the news onto Alistair. He will be absolutely thrilled. Soon he'll have his pilot's license and you'll have your private investigator's license. You children have truly done well for yourselves."

"Thank you, Hadley," I said, feeling instantly warmed by his words. As well-educated and scholarly as Hadley was, his praise meant a lot to me.

Nana paused in front of Betty's old apartment and nodded at the door. "So was that the girl who was murdered? The one who was so unfriendly to us?"

I opened the door to Jayne's apartment. "That's the one. She was shot last night. And I found her a few minutes later."

Hadley put his hand to his chest. "How horrifying."

I gulped, remembering it all over again. "It sure was."

Nana's eyebrows came down. "I could hardly believe that Michael and your mother assumed you had committed the murder. And that they said so in front of that detective, no less. I wanted to hit them both over the head with my pocketbook."

"You and me both," I told her.

We all wandered into Jayne's apartment and Hadley put the picnic basket on the counter. That's when my stomach started to do the Rumba, and I tried to remember the last time I'd even eaten. I was surprised that I was still up and moving around, with as little food as I'd had lately.

Nana opened a cabinet and reached for some plates. "Remember when we saw that surly man come out of Betty's apartment? I wonder if he's the one who killed her."

I grabbed silverware and napkins and took them to the table. "The thought has crossed my mind."

Hadley started to put the food out. "I'll be sure to check the locks on your door before I leave again. And make sure you're safe here."

I grabbed a pitcher of sweet tea from the icebox. "Thanks, Hadley. That would be swell."

Nana set some glasses on the table and we all sat down for dinner. Hadley said grace in his usual eloquent manner, and we all dug in as Clark Cat strolled in, obviously half-asleep. He yawned and stretched, right before I gave him a little piece of chicken. He gobbled it down right away.

"Now," Nana said as she patted my hand. "Let's get caught up. Tell me everything. And I do mean everything. Starting with leaving for the dance to finding the body to going to the police station."

Hadley poured gravy over his potatoes. "Don't leave out a single detail."

So I gave them the full story, except for the specific clues and crime scene details that Sammy and I had seen. After all, I knew that Katie McClue might tell people bits and pieces about a case she was working on, but she would *never* spill the beans on anything pertinent that could jeopardize an investigation.

Nana smiled. "Oh, this is going to be such fun. Solving crimes and murders and such."

I smiled back, wondering if now might be a good time to mention an outing to the Polynesian Room. But I didn't get the chance, since someone knocked on the door. I jumped up and opened it to find Sammy on the other side.

"Pardon me for barging in like this, kid, but I found a few things that you'll want to see," Sammy said before he peered into the apartment, and immediately blushed just a little. "Oh, my apologies. I didn't realize you were eating dinner. I'll come back later."

But Nana was already on her feet. "Nonsense. You'll come right on in and join us. We've got more than enough here."

Sammy touched the bill of his hat. "Why, thank you, Mrs. Truworth. That's terribly kind of you. It's nice to see you again."

Nana took his arm and pulled him into the room. "Please, call me Caroline."

Sammy wasn't wearing his trench coat this time, but instead had on a very nice double-breasted brown suit. I wondered if he'd been dressed up for church. Or maybe he'd been *hoping* to run into Nana.

Hadley was already up and getting another plate for Sammy. He put it on the table and pulled a chair out for him, too.

"I don't believe we've been properly introduced," he said to Sammy, holding his hand out to shake. "I'm Hadley Hartswell. Very pleased to meet you."

Sammy pulled his hat off and shook Hadley's hand in return. "The pleasure's all mine. And I sure appreciate the offer of a good, hot meal. I haven't eaten much today."

Nana motioned toward the empty chair, with one graceful flourish of her arm. "Then take a load off, Sammy. And help yourself to some chicken."

I shut the door and took my own seat again.

Sammy grinned and put his hat on the counter. "This is pretty darn swell of you all. I'm not sure what I did to deserve the Rockefeller treatment here. It must be my lucky day. Remind me to return the favor sometime."

Nana picked up the bowl of mashed potatoes and passed it to him. "You can start by telling us all about you and this case you're working on. And how you had the good intelligence to hire my granddaughter to work for you."

And from that moment on, dinner was an especially happy affair. Sammy and Hadley and Nana all jumped in and talked about the "good old days" and some of their most rollicking adventures. That brought laughter from us all, and I had to wonder, would there come a day when I talked about the good old days? Would I have hilarious adventures to tell grandchildren of my own?

Dinner was finished off with apple pie topped with whipped cream. It was all delicious, but to tell you the truth, I had so much fun listening to everyone's stories that I enjoyed the company just as much as I enjoyed the food.

I put coffee on to percolate and cleared the table. Nana got up and found Jayne's creamer and sugar bowl, and some teaspoons. She put everything in the center of the table while I served the coffee.

Not long after that, Hadley pulled out his pocket watch. "We should probably be getting back," he said to Nana.

"I suppose so," she said with a yawn. "I'll leave the leftovers here with Tracy. So she'll have dinner for tomorrow night."

I got up and started to put the food away. Nana joined me in the kitchen while the men talked.

She put her arm around my waist and leaned into me. "Are you ever coming back home again, darlin'?"

I shook my head. "I told Jayne I'd keep an eye on the apartment building while she was gone."

"I thought she was coming back tonight."

And that's when I told Nana all about Jayne's situation, and how she'd taken off again.

"Good for her," Nana said. "She'll be glad she did. After Tom ships out, she'll be happy to know she spent every minute she could with him. I like that little Jayne. She's a real sparkplug."

I hugged Nana tightly. "Reminds me of someone I know."

Nana laughed before her tone turned more serious. "Well, I hope you'll consider coming home again after that. Because I miss you. And I promise, if your mother ever tries to hit you again, I'll toss her out on her hind end."

That image of that made me laugh, because somehow I just couldn't picture my dignified, blue-blood mother being tossed out of anything. "We'll talk about it later, Nana."

Because I had to say, while it was probably high time that I got out on my own, I had no idea where I'd go. After all, Jayne was going to want her apartment back when she got home. And other than that, it would be hard to find a place to live, considering there were already so many people around town who were desperate for some kind of quarters. The only place I knew that would be available soon was across the hall.

Where a murder had taken place.

And it was going to be ready right around the time when I needed a home.

Even so, I knew I could never bring myself to live in that apartment. Not after what I'd seen. No matter what, I would always remember the image of Betty's bleeding body, lying on the floor there.

Nope, I'd just have to find another place to live.

Hadley said good night and excused himself to go start the car while Nana hung back and gave me another goodbye hug.

"Mind if I walk you to the door, Mrs. Truworth? Caroline?" Sammy asked with surprising shyness. Funny, but all of a sudden he reminded me more of a schoolboy rather than a successful private eye.

Nana took the arm he offered and flashed him her loveliest smile. "I'd be delighted."

Something told me I'd be a third wheel if I walked out with them, so I stayed put. Unfortunately, it also meant I didn't get to hear the rest of the conversation. Though I already had a sneaking suspicion what Sammy was up to — he wanted to ask her out to the Polynesian Room.

And if Nana knew it was part of our murder investigation, she would be all in. Not to mention, pretty excited, too.

Whatever they were talking about, it sure took them a long time. Because I had the dishes completely washed and stacked in the dish rack before Sammy returned. He looked a little flushed.

"Did she say yes?" I asked with a grin.

"She did," he said with a little smile. "Your grandmother is quite a classy gal, and she's a pretty good sport. We're going to join you and Pete on Tuesday night. But we're going down in my car, so you and Pete can be alone."

Now it was my turn to blush. Oh swell. Here we were, supposed to be big, tough P.I.'s, solving a brutal murder, and all we could do was blush about our upcoming dates.

Somehow I didn't remember Katie McClue ever blushing about a date. Or acting like a schoolgirl in the middle of an investigation. Though one thing was for sure — I needed to get my ducks in a row if I planned to help Sammy on my very first case.

"So, did you find anything enlightening in the letters you took home?" I asked, trying to focus on work again.

He nodded. "That I did, kid. But first, I think we'd better do some 'knock and talks.'"

I raised an eyebrow. "Knock and talks?"

Sammy grinned. "Yup, kid. We'll knock on the doors of the folks who were home last night and have a little chat with them. To find out if they know anything that might help us. And, to rule them out as our killers. It'll give you a chance to learn some interviewing skills."

I glanced at the clock. 8:20. "It's a little late, isn't it? I mean, wouldn't it be rude to stop in now?"

"Nope, kid. The timing is perfect. We'll have better luck getting them to talk, because people won't want us to stay long. Showing up late on a Sunday night is just more motivation for them to tell us what they know and send us on our way."

I rolled my head from side to side. "Hmmm . . . I never thought of it like that. But it does make sense."

I had also never realized that a detective might have trouble "getting someone to talk," as Sammy had put it. After all, Katie McClue never had a problem getting people to open up. In fact, people were usually falling all over themselves to give her information. The only problem she had was that sometimes she was forced to be rude and limit what witnesses wanted to tell her.

Sammy moved toward the door. "Besides getting information from people, kid, you never know what kind of evidence we might see lying around."

I followed him as he opened the door and stepped into the hallway. "Like a smoking gun?"

He chuckled. "Probably not in this case. Then again, I *have* seen stranger things."

"How do we know who was home last night?"

Sammy pulled a little hardbound notepad from his breast pocket and flipped it open. "The police accidentally let me in on these little details. We have Mr. and Mrs. Eldridge in 2B, as you know. And we have a couple with a baby in 2C, Mr. and Mrs. Westover. Then we have an elderly man who lives alone in 3B. But I suggest we start with the Eldridges, and rule them out. Since we're pretty sure they're not the killers."

I cringed. "Great. I'm sure they'll be looking forward to seeing me again."

Sammy glanced toward the staircase and chuckled. "I never said this job was going to be all hidden clues and perfect fingerprints. Every job has its down side."

He pulled another notepad and pen from his side pocket and handed it to me. "Here you go, kid. You're going to need this. Knock yourself out."

I suddenly felt giddy, like a child on Christmas morning. I could hardly believe it. Here I was, getting my very first detective's notebook. I flipped through the blank pages and took in the smell of the new paper. Katie McClue must have gone through a million such notepads, and now I was about to start on one of my own. I couldn't stop the smile that insisted on spreading across my face.

Seconds later, we climbed the stairs to the second floor. All the while, I tried to take in the advice that Sammy sent flooding into my brain. "Act casual, kid. Ask them open-ended questions, never questions where they can answer 'yes' or 'no'. Make them feel comfortable. Like you're their friend . . ." And on and on it went.

Now I wondered if I could even remember an ounce of what he'd told me about conducting my very first interview with a potential witness or suspect. More than anything, I wanted to do a good job right off the bat. And I wanted to show Sammy that I would be an asset to the agency.

So, when he knocked on the door to 2B, I stood up straight and tall, and plastered a smile on my face. I had all of his techniques in mind and I was ready to take on the Eldridges. I planned to perform the interview of all interviews. Just like Katie McClue had done in every one of her books. I would eke out some minute detail that would turn out to be the one major clue to help us crack this case, and lead us to Betty Hoffman's murderer.

And best of all, by the time I had finished, my new boss would pat me on the back, and tell me what a great job I had done.

"Ready, kid?" Sammy asked, as we heard the doorknob turn.

I took a deep breath. "Ready."

Then the door opened and Mrs. Eldridge peeked out.

Right before she screamed bloody murder.

So much for my first interview as an Apprentice P.I.

CHAPTER 19

Rough Starts and Wrong Turns

Okay, much as I hated to admit it, my first interview got off to a rough start. A very rough start. Rocky even. Having your witness or suspect let out such a blood-curdling scream that it brought other tenants rushing from their apartments was not exactly the kind of result I was hoping for.

"What's wrong? Is someone hurt?" asked the frantic man who had jumped into the hallway from apartment 2C. I knew him as Mr. Westover, who, along with his wife, were next on our list to be interviewed.

I quickly waved him off while Sammy helped Mr. Eldridge get Mrs. Eldridge under control. Together they walked her back into the apartment while I stayed in the hallway and spoke to the tenants who'd come to the rescue of what probably sounded like a damsel in distress. Or another woman being murdered.

"Nope, nothing wrong," I told the tenants. "I'm Tracy Truworth, and I'm still filling in for Jayne. And Mrs. Eldridge just thought she saw a mouse. Luckily, we've got a cat on the payroll, too. Clark is a black cat, and he'll be taking care of any rodent problems we might have."

"I've seen that cat," said the tiny, middle-aged woman from 2D, whom I knew was Mrs. Tynesdale, a widow and a local public librarian. "He's a friendly guy. He comes over here and stays with me in my apartment sometimes. I don't mind the company, especially now, after I got home and found out the girl who lived downstairs was murdered. I heard it was a gang of escaped convicts who got her. That's what my friend who lives upstairs said she heard."

Mr. Westover shook his headful of curly, red hair. "Well, my wife and I were home last night, and we overheard the police say it was a jealous lover. My wife said she'd seen that girl with lots of different men. Outside anyway. She never let them come in. So I guess some guy found out about one of the other guys, and well, it was enough to drive him mad. But I doubt we'll ever see the killer again."

With that, I told Mr. Westover that I'd be over shortly to talk to him and his wife. Then I left the two tenants in the hallway to discuss the murder that had taken place in this very building. I noticed that Clark Cat had appeared from out of nowhere, and seconds later, he was in Mrs. Tynesdale's arms. Talk about playing the field. That cat certainly got around.

Which suddenly made me wonder — if Betty had played the field, and if she didn't allow her "dates" into her apartment, then how could one of her fellas have been in her place last night? If it was a boyfriend who had killed her, he must not have respected her "no suitors inside" rule. And he would've been taking quite a chance to come inside, since apparently people were familiar with Betty's rule, and someone might have seen him.

Except the building was practically empty last night. There were tenants home in only three apartments, and I was out, too. Meaning, the odds of someone from the outside running into a tenant were pretty slim. It had been the perfect time to commit the perfect crime. Almost like someone had timed it that way. But how could any of her beaus have known the place would practically be empty? It just didn't add up.

I was still pondering it all when I walked into the Eldridge's apartment. There I saw white-haired Mrs. Eldridge sitting on her sofa, with a bald-headed Mr. Eldridge cuddled up beside her, holding her hand. The entire room was covered in things that had been knitted, crocheted, or tatted. Blankets, afghans, pillows and doilies were everywhere, and all were beautifully-crafted. Clearly Mrs. Eldridge was not one who believed in having "idle hands." I pointed to a doily on the arm of the chair, amazed how the tiny knots of the tatting were so tight and perfectly uniform.

"My goodness. Your work is truly exquisite," I said, hoping to calm her down by turning the conversation toward something safe and innocuous. "It must have taken you a long time to create all these lovely things."

"I've been doing these things since I was a little girl," she said in a shaky voice. "Do you knit, or sew, or crochet?"

I shook my head. "I do a little knitting, but I'm afraid that's about it." I spotted a Singer treadle sewing machine table in the corner, so I knew she was a seamstress, too.

"Oh," was all she uttered as she continued to stare at me with wide, startled eyes. And even though I didn't think it was physically possible, I could have sworn she scooted even farther back on her sofa.

So I tried a different tactic to get her to relax and open up. This time I tried apologizing for scaring them the night before. And I explained what I'd really been doing and what had actually happened when it came to finding Betty's body. Then I assured them over and over that I was not a homicidal maniac.

But amazingly, Mrs. Eldridge appeared to be even more upset and terrified after I explained things. So much for tactic number two.

Mr. Eldridge frowned and motioned for Sammy and me to take a seat. I followed his lead and sat in a chair across from the sofa. All the while, I noticed Sammy was acting very casual about the whole thing, so I did my best to do the same.

Sammy offered them a friendly smile. "So sorry to barge in on you folks like this tonight. But we're trying to get to the bottom of this nasty business that took place last night."

Mrs. Eldridge was still trembling. "We already told the police everything we know."

"I'm sure you did, ma'am," Sammy said gently. "And no doubt, you did a mighty fine job of it, too. But until Betty's killer is caught, we still need to be on the lookout. I'd sure appreciate it if you told me what you saw or heard last night."

Mrs. Eldridge closed her eyes. "I don't even want to think about it."

Luckily, Mr. Eldridge jumped in right then. "We didn't actually see much. Heard, is more like it. I served in the Great War, and let me tell you, I know gunshots when I hear 'em. And even though the thunder was really loud last night, I still heard gunshots. I was sure of it. After all, the girl's apartment is right below us. I looked at the clock before we went downstairs to see what was going on. I'll admit, it probably wasn't the smartest thing to do, but we were afraid somebody was hurt. Besides, I was pretty sure I heard the front door slam and I knew somebody had gone outside. But when we got halfway down the stairs, we saw this girl here leaving the apartment with a bloody knife."

He pointed an accusing finger right at me.

I did my best to smile. "Like we've already discussed, Betty was shot and not stabbed. I had blood on me because I tried to revive Betty, and I had the knife to protect myself in case the killer was still around."

Neither of the Eldridges said a word.

I put on my very brightest smile. "What did you know about Betty, the girl who lived there?"

"Never even met her," Mrs. Eldridge said, shaking her head. "I saw her a few times, but she wasn't very neighborly."

Mr. Eldridge looked at his wife. "The only way we knew anything about her was because we asked Jayne. Otherwise, we wouldn't have known a thing."

Sammy leaned forward. "Is there anything else you'd like to tell us?"

Mrs. Eldridge stiffened up. "Only that I hope they catch the killer and soon." Again she stared at me.

I fought the urge to roll my eyes.

Her husband hugged her even tighter. "Until then, I've got my gun. I didn't get to keep my pistol from the war, but I have one that I inherited from my daddy. That one works better than what Uncle Sam issued me."

With that, Sammy smiled and nodded. "Some of these

newfangled guns just aren't as good as the ones we had in the old days."

For the first time, Mr. Eldridge smiled, too. "You've got that right."

Sammy slid forward in his chair and stood up. "Well, then, we'd better get out of your hair. Miss Truworth and I appreciate your help."

"Yes, we certainly do," I said with all the sweetness I could muster, still hoping to win them over. "And if you remember anything else that might be important, please be sure to let me know. I'll be staying in Jayne's apartment."

Mrs. Eldridge's eyebrows shot up her forehead. "When will Jayne be back?"

I quickly gave her the whole story about how Jayne had left to be with Tom.

"I'll be happy when she takes over again," Mrs. Eldridge informed me in a very matter-of-fact tone.

Well, if that wasn't just swell. Apparently the woman was holding her breath until the second that Jayne returned and I was long gone. Preferably, I'm sure, in her mind, up the river and solidly locked away in the big house. Because, as near as I could tell, no matter how many times I told her I wasn't a murderer, she was never going to shake the image she'd seen of me last night in my matted down, blood-stained, poofy pink dress with a bloody knife in my hand.

Then again, it might not be the easiest image to forget.

Somehow, I didn't recall Katie McClue ever having to deal with a situation like this one. Then again, her newest book was due out any day now, and who knew what the daring detective would be up against? I hoped I might find her latest installment under the Christmas tree.

I smiled once more as I stood up to go, and Sammy and I said our good-nights before we stepped back out into the hallway. I pulled the door shut behind us and let out a very long sigh. Obviously I had a lot to learn when it came to interviewing people. Katie McClue would not have been impressed. And now I had to wonder if my boss was impressed or not.

For some reason, he just laughed. "Don't sweat it, kid. These things take practice. You'll learn how to draw information out of people. Remember, you're still an apprentice, and you haven't even been on the job a full day. You'll learn the ropes."

Well, suddenly the idea of "learning the ropes" didn't seem all that appealing. I didn't exactly enjoy floundering when I had dreams of being an expert. Immediately.

Sammy pointed to the Westovers' door, so we headed there next. We'd barely knocked when Mr. and Mrs. Westover flung the door open wide and invited us in without an ounce of hesitation. I guessed they were probably hoping for a break from their very cranky infant. Because the minute I sat down, a very exhausted Mrs. Westover, or Peg as she told me to call her, plopped their red-haired, red-faced screaming baby boy in my lap.

"Isn't he adorable?" she said with a half-crazed smile.

"Adorable," I agreed over his screams.

Turns out little Timmy, who had inherited his hair color from both parents, had been teething and having a very rough go of it. Funny, but here he was cutting his teeth and in a strange way, so was I. As an Apprentice P.I.

But screaming and crying was hardly an option for me. As for Timmy, it seemed that no matter how I held him or rocked him or rubbed his back, that baby simply would not quit crying.

Which meant I could barely hear a word of what was being said between the rest of the grownups in the room. And as near as I could tell, it was probably the same reason this couple in their late twenties hadn't heard anything odd the night of the murder. They were too busy and nearly deaf from trying to calm a very miserable child who'd also been very scared during the massive thunderstorm.

I had to say, my heart went out to them, and well, to be honest, to little Timmy, too.

Yet strangely enough, out of everyone there, Sammy seemed to be the only one of us who knew what to do.

"Do you have a small carrot in your icebox?" he asked the dead-on-their-feet couple.

Neither one of them answered, mostly because they looked too tired to even talk anymore. Instead, Peg headed straight for the refrigerator. She produced a thin, cold carrot, and let Timmy put the pointy end in his mouth. Seconds later he was gnawing away at that orange-colored vegetable, and soon his screaming was reduced to nothing but tears rolling down his cheeks.

And that seemed to make the Westovers more than grateful to Sammy. And to me, too, as Timmy stayed on my lap, gumming that carrot like nobody's business.

Then, thanks to Sammy's skillful questioning, we learned that Mr. Westover, or Timothy, worked as an engineer for the Humble Oil Company. They had moved to Houston from West Texas about a year and a half ago.

"Did you know Betty at all?" I finally got to ask, adding my two cents to the interview.

They glanced at each other, holding each other's gaze for several seconds, in some unspoken communication.

Timothy was the first to speak. "We ran into her once or twice. She was extremely rude to my wife. And to me, at first. But then all of a sudden she started to flirt with me. In fact, she got to be so blatant about it that it was shocking. Even when Peg and I were out walking little Timmy."

Peg rolled her eyes. "She was unbelievable. Trying to steal a man away right out from under his wife's nose. But the very first time I met her, I could tell there was something odd about her. Something really odd. Almost like she wasn't from here, or something. She sure didn't know how to act properly."

I raised my eyebrows. "Not from here? You mean, not from Texas?"

Peg shook her head. "It was more than that. More like she was from a different country or something."

"She sure didn't act like a lady," Timothy added. "So we just stayed away. I always came in through the back door and straight up the staircase. So I didn't run into her much when I came home from work. Even so, I did see her out in front a few times, getting dropped off by different men. Some of them were getting pretty hot and heavy with her."

Peg gave me a knowing look. "I can't say I'm too surprised that someone killed her. It looked to me like she probably had a lot of guys going at once. And it sounds like someone got jealous."

But she'd barely gotten the words out when it happened — one of those "aha" moments that Katie McClue always talked about in her books. A moment when my female intuition started to tug at my sleeve. Hard.

I turned little Timmy forward so he could see his parents. "I've got a question. It sounds like Betty wasn't flirting with Timothy in the beginning. But that changed. And you said the change was pretty sudden. What was going on when you first noticed this change?"

Timothy put his forefinger to his cheek and looked at the ceiling. "Well . . . let me see if I can remember. I had just gotten home from work. I was really tired."

Peg pointed to her husband. "It was the day when the car overheated. And somebody pulled over with some water and helped you fill the radiator."

"Uh-huh, that's right. He was a lifesaver," Timothy nodded to his wife. "But I was late getting home. I got inside and ran down the hallway to pick up the mail from our box. That blonde girl was there and she was pretty rude. As usual."

I crinkled my eyebrows. "So if she was rude then, when did she start being so forward?"

"Well . . ." Timothy started. "It wasn't until I'd gotten my mail. Because I remember standing there, going through my letters. Then all of a sudden, she starts talking to me. In fact, she put her hand around my arm and rubbed my shoulder. She'd *never* done anything like that before. It was such a shock, coming from her, when she'd been such a cold fish before."

Peg's eyebrows came down in an angry line. "And what exactly did you do, Mr. Popular?"

He raised his hands. "I jumped away. To tell you the truth, she sort of scared me. To go from cold to hot like that . . . it sure seemed like something was wrong with her."

I tried to picture what he was saying. "So . . . you were standing there reading your mail, and she sneaks up beside you."

He was nodding. "That's about the size of it."

I repositioned the baby. "So she might have read your mail over your shoulder."

He rolled his head from side to side. "Could be."

"Do you remember what mail you got that day?" I asked.

"Hmmm . . . Let's see . . ." he started. "There were some bills and a letter from Peg's sister . . . oh, and a letter from my company."

I leaned forward. "The Humble Oil Company?"

"Yes, that's it," Timothy said. "And as soon as I looked at that envelope . . ."

"She was there beside you," I finished.

And just as I spoke, little Timmy suddenly burped and spit up all across my arm, which brought the conversation to a screeching halt. After I was led to the kitchen and did my best to wash up, Sammy and I said our good-nights.

Once we were out in the hallway again, he pointed to the staircase. "What do you think, kid? Did you buy their story? The one about Betty flirting with him and him avoiding her?"

I followed him up the stairs. "I do. I mean, Timothy wasn't exactly Clark Gable, and I'm guessing that Betty was only flirting with him to 'get something.' Though who knows what, exactly. As for him, well, I think he's probably been too exhausted to care about any woman flirting with him."

Sammy stepped up to the third floor landing. "Sounds about right. Though they did both pick up on the fact that something was pretty odd about Betty. And they both knew to stay away from her."

"Gut instincts," I said while we walked to apartment 3B.

Sammy paused in front of the door. There was only one interview left, and I hoped and prayed this one would go well. I tried to remember everything Sammy had told me, as well as Katie McClue's many techniques that she had applied when conducting her interviews. That's when I suddenly remembered one of her later books, *The Case of the Uncooperative Witness*. To get a witness to open up, she'd pretty much reworded everything they'd said or expressed, and then she'd fed their own words right back to them. And let me tell you, it had worked. And worked well.

So, as Mr. Karl Schmidt, a retired and widowed schoolteacher answered the door, I tried my best to read his expression. As near as I could tell, he looked tired but vigilant, judging from the way he poked his head in the hallway and glanced from side to side.

Sammy gave our names and held out his hand to shake. "Would you mind if we stopped in and talked to you for a few minutes? I promise we won't take up much of your time."

Mr. Schmidt started to shut the door. "No. I am very busy.

Please go away."

I immediately picked up on the panic in his voice. And I knew Mr. Schmidt wasn't giving us the brush off because he was rude or busy, but because he was scared.

I jumped in front of Sammy. "Mr. Schmidt, I know this may be alarming, us showing up here like this. But please don't be frightened — we're not here to hurt you. I'm Tracy, the girl who's filling in for Jayne while she's gone. She just got married and she's off to be with her new husband while he's in training."

Suddenly his brown eyes lit up. I guessed his full head of salt-and-pepper hair had once been dark brown, too.

He smiled at me. "Oh, yes, most certainly. Tracy. Please forgive my bad manners. And please call me Karl. I didn't realize who you were. Yes, please, come in." He spoke with a slight accent, though I couldn't quite place it.

"Thank you," I replied with a smile.

"Please hurry," Karl now insisted, as he practically pulled us into the small apartment.

Then he peeked into the hallway again, before looking both ways and shutting the door. Very, very quietly.

Sammy raised an eyebrow and darted a fleeting glance at me from the corner of his eye. I shrugged just slightly, to let him know I'd caught his drift. After all, it was pretty strange that this man who hadn't even wanted us to enter his apartment was suddenly in a huge hurry to get us inside.

"Please," Karl said, motioning toward the living room portion of the apartment. "Sit down. Be comfortable. May I get you something to drink? I have some nice whisky."

Sammy grinned. "Sure, don't mind if I do. I could use a nightcap after the night we had last night." Then he looked at me and nodded, as though instructing me to do the same.

But I wasn't exactly a whisky drinker. Especially not straight up.

Before I could say a word, Sammy answered for me. "Tracy is being a little shy about it, but she'd like a nightcap herself."

"Very nice," Karl smiled, as though he was happy to have made his guests happy. "Whiskey's all around. Would you like some soda with it?"

Sammy quickly answered with, "No, thanks."

But I gulped and said, "Yes, please. Soda would be wonderful. Lots of soda, please."

Karl nodded. "Very good. Please have a seat by the windows." Then he moved over to his liquor cabinet bar, a stunning piece of art deco furniture. He lifted the lid and went to work making our drinks.

Sammy and I walked into the living room. The apartment held just the necessities, with a minimum of wall paintings and décor items, and absolutely nothing frilly about the place. Except that every piece of furniture was uniquely designed and extremely well made. In fact, each piece looked like it belonged in a museum. But what interested me the most was the placement of the pieces, since each one was lined up with precision, exactly so many inches from the next one and then so many inches from the one next to it. It was as though the entire apartment had been measured and then divided by the number of pieces of furniture. And the entire place was neat as a pin and without so much as a single particle of dust.

Besides that, the positioning of the furniture truly emphasized the room's best feature — the huge double windows that looked right out to the front yard and the street.

Sammy slid onto the sofa, and I dropped into a chair that was next to a small table decorated with stunning scrollwork. A few minutes later, Karl brought us our drinks, along with coasters.

He smiled and sat on the chair nearest to me. "You must be Jayne's dear friend. How is she? She and her beau went to the town where I used to live, Fredericksburg, for their honeymoon."

I smiled back at him. "She's doing well. And they really had a nice honeymoon."

I took a sip of my drink and suddenly my throat felt like it was on fire. I coughed and choked while my eyes started to water. Clearly Karl had been a little less than generous with the soda in my whiskey.

And clearly I was not going to be the type of P.I. who drank hard liquor.

I could tell that Sammy was fighting the urge to chuckle. "As you know Karl, there was a murder here last night. A girl named Betty Hoffman."

And that was when Karl became as stiff as the drink I was trying to down. "I already told the police all I know. I am an American citizen, even though my family came from Germany long ago. I know nothing about anything."

Then he drank his own whiskey in one big gulp. I was amazed that anyone could even *drink* that awful stuff, let alone drink it so quickly. And it wasn't until his eyes met mine that I understood his action.

Once again, he was afraid. Something had frightened him. Badly.

I put my own drink down on the coaster and spoke in the softest, gentlest voice I could muster. "Karl, we're not here to hurt you. We're here to help. I can tell something's got you very frightened, and that worries me. Can you please tell me what has you so scared?"

He shook his head, looking more nervous by the minute. "I can't. I know nothing. I told them I wouldn't join. And I don't like Hitler, and I don't like what he's doing. He's got so many Germans fooled. But I can't talk or they would kill me, too. I know they must have killed Betty."

Right at that moment, a very big part of me wanted to gasp. Not to mention, fall down on the floor in amazement. Especially since the little bit of whiskey I'd ingested felt like it had gone straight to my head, making me feel slightly dizzy.

But I forced myself to stay sitting upright in my seat. And I forced myself to concentrate on what I was doing. After all, I knew I'd been given the perfect opportunity to draw some important information from this poor scared man. If I stopped now, he would probably clam up again and wouldn't utter another word. Across from me, Sammy raised his eyebrows and was motioning with his head.

So I had to keep going.

It was exactly what Katie McClue would do.

And it was exactly what I, Tracy Truworth, Apprentice P.I., was going to do, too.

So I took a deep breath and went on. "Karl, I'm very worried about you, and I don't want anyone to hurt you. Who is it you think killed Betty? And who do you think might hurt you?"

He shook his head and started to wring his hands. "I don't want to say more. People get in trouble for talking."

I scooted forward in my chair. "Please, Karl. This is very important. We want to help. We want to catch Betty's killer so they can't hurt anyone else."

"You don't understand," Karl sort of whimpered while Sammy picked up his glass and went to the bar to fix him another drink. "If you catch one killer, more will take his place. You can't stop them all."

I was starting to think the whiskey must have affected my hearing. "Can't stop whom?"

Sammy was back with another drink for the man in a matter of seconds. He put it in front of Karl, on top of his coaster.

Karl took the drink and, once again, swallowed it down in a couple of gulps. "Them. You can't stop them. Because I saw that man. Right out there in front of the building. Last night. He was leaving, and I saw him when the lightning flashed. I could make him out clearly."

"Who?" I asked gently. "Who did you see?"

He shook his head. "Helmut. I've seen him here before. He was here to see Betty."

"How do you know him?" Sammy sort of murmured.

He glanced toward the front door. "I've been approached. Lots of Germans who are now living in America have been approached. We know who he is."

I crinkled my brow. "You've been approached?"

He nodded. "Yes. But I said no. I didn't want to join. Where I come from in Fredericksburg, the people whose families came here years ago won't even speak German anymore. We speak only English. All the time now. Because we are Americans. And we don't like Hitler. Or the horrible things the Nazis are doing."

I leaned forward and took his hand. "What were you asked to join?"

Sweat beaded across his forehead and he spoke in a low voice. "The Bund, Miss Tracy. The Bund."

I glanced toward Sammy, who sat back and rubbed his chin. "The Bund. The German American Bund."

I lifted my shoulders as Karl nodded.

Then Sammy looked me right in the eyes. "The German

American Bund. Better known as the American Nazi Party."

This time I couldn't help but gasp, right before I downed the rest of my drink.

CHAPTER 20

Jumpy, Jittery, and Just Plain Nervous

For a moment or two, I feared for Karl's health. Because the very instant he'd uttered the word "Bund," his eyes had gone wide and his skin had turned terrifyingly pale.

I patted his hand. "Karl, it will be all right. You're safe here. We won't let anything happen to you."

But he was clearly not convinced. "You can't stop them. The Nazis are taking over Europe. And they'll take over this country, too. They're already here. They've got many tentacles, in many groups. America First Committee. Friends of Progress. They're supporting them all."

Sammy raised an eyebrow. "Roosevelt shut down most of the German groups in the country a while back. So I'm guessing these Nazi players have gone underground."

"Yes, yes," Karl agreed, as his eyes shifted once more toward the door. "It's all very secret. They threaten people with their very lives for talking. I would be threatened now, if they could hear what I was saying."

I couldn't help but glance at the door myself, suddenly wondering if someone was out there listening. "And Helmut is a part of this? The one you think killed Betty?"

I fought to keep my voice as soothing as possible, which wasn't exactly easy, considering I was so terrified myself. My heart was beating like it wanted to try out for the drum section of a big band. For the first time tonight, I became aware of how dark it was outside, and noticed the shadows in the apartment seemed to have grown.

Tears formed in the edges of Karl's eyes. "Yes, Miss Tracy. Helmut is the one who goes around and tries to scare people into joining."

Sammy leaned forward in his chair. "I know you're convinced Helmut did the girl in. But did you actually see him kill Betty? Or do you have any proof of it?"

Karl shook his head. "No."

Now I even saw Sammy's dark eyes dart toward the door. "Can you give us a description of Helmut?"

Karl squeezed his eyes shut and shuddered. "He has cold, gray eyes. Eyes as cold as ice. With glasses. And short blond hair. Very short. He's younger than I am. He never smiles and he walks like a soldier on parade."

And that's when I shuddered, too. Because I knew exactly who Karl was describing. It was the very same man that Nana and I had seen leaving Betty's apartment the day we'd bought Jayne's wedding suit.

"What time did you say you saw this man leaving the building?" Sammy asked.

Karl glanced at his watch. "It was thirty minutes after nine o'clock. On the dot. Helmut is always on the dot."

Sammy frowned. "Nazis are funny about being punctual. You said that Helmut approached you. When was that, and did he tell you how to get in touch with him? You know, just in case you changed your mind? And wanted to join the cause?"

"Yes, yes," Karl nodded. "He did. I'll tell you, but you can't tell anyone that you heard it from me. There is a small bookstore. On the edge of town. Bruning's Books. If you want to be in contact with Helmut, you pull out a copy of *War and Peace*. On the back wall. And leave a message inside the book."

Sammy snickered. "War and Peace. How fitting. Except for

the Peace part."

"These Nazis are bad. Very bad," Karl emphasized, as though we might not know this. Then again, if Karl had been approached by the group, and if he happened to have relatives in Germany, it was possible he had firsthand knowledge of the horrors of the Nazis. Unlike the rest of us, who only read about such things in newspapers or saw them on a newsreel.

Sammy gave the man a slight smile filled with sympathy, before he went silent, as though he were mulling things over. Then he got to his feet and motioned for me to do the same. I guessed he must have figured Karl had been through enough for one night.

I stood up as Sammy held his hand out to shake. "Karl, you've been very helpful. I can't tell you how much I appreciate it. Now Miss Truworth and I are going to do our best to get to the bottom of this."

Karl shook Sammy's hand in return and then took my hand and kissed it. "Be careful, Miss Tracy. Please, I beg of you. Be very, very careful. These men are dangerous. They're not afraid to kill, because they believe Germany will take over America, too. They're planning on it."

"We will be careful," I assured him. "Now, you be sure to lock your door tonight. Don't open it for anyone, unless it's me. In the morning, I'm going to see what else we can do about the security around here. Maybe I can have locks put on the front and back doors. So everyone is safer."

"Thank you, thank you," he said.

We headed for the door and thanked him for the drinks, before we said our good-nights. As we left, I noticed Karl was still pale and his pupils were huge, so I could tell he was still afraid. Even so, I saw what I thought was the hint of a smile. Maybe he felt a little bit of relief just talking about things and knowing someone was on the case.

If only I felt that same kind of relief. Because my nerves were in high gear with the gas pedal to the floor as I walked down the stairs with Sammy. If Helmut had gotten into our building so easily, and possibly killed Betty, what was to stop him from lurking here now?

Nothing at all, I thought.

And I didn't like being scared, and I knew the others probably wouldn't like it either.

"I'm going to call Hadley in the morning," I told Sammy as I peeked into the shadows of every corner that we passed by. "I'm going to ask him to install locks on the main doors to the building."

"Good plan, kid," Sammy said, his dark eyes darting around as he took in every inch of our surroundings. "You can have keys made for everyone."

"I'll ask Jayne about it when she calls tomorrow."

"Might be best if you got the locks put in and told her about it later," Sammy suggested. "No use worrying her when she's got enough on her mind already."

I nodded. "True. And I know she'd say yes anyway. Did you believe his story? That Helmut killed Betty?"

We reached the main level, and the hardwood floor let out a loud creak as we stepped down from the staircase. I nearly jumped to the ceiling.

Sammy grinned at me but didn't say a word about my scaredy-cat antics. "A lot of it adds up. But I'm not sure the guy was our killer. The timing is off."

I glanced to the other side of the hallway as we moved toward Jayne's apartment. The door to Betty's apartment had been pulled shut and roped off. There was a sign on the door that said "Do Not Enter." I guessed that meant the police weren't finished with it yet.

I was about to open Jayne's door when Sammy held up his hand, giving me the signal to stop. Then he drew his revolver from a side holster under his jacket. Funny, but all this time I hadn't even realized he'd been carrying a gun, though I probably should have.

"Let me go in first, kid," he murmured quietly with his hand on the knob. "No need to take unnecessary chances."

Then he threw the door open and hit the push button for the light. He swiveled left and then right, with his gun pointed in front of him, before he stepped into the apartment. While he checked the place out, I moved inside and waited for him.

"All clear," he hollered as he strolled back into the room, holstering his gun again.

And that's when we heard scratching at the window. I nearly jumped to the ceiling once more while he commanded me to "get down." He dropped behind a chair and drew his gun again.

Until I realized what was making the noise.

Clark Cat.

I sighed and went to the window to let him in. "I guess we're both a little bit jumpy. Ever since we heard about Nazis operating here in town."

Sammy re-holstered his gun. "You can say that again, kid. But being jumpy can be good for your health, especially if you want to live a nice, long life. Sometimes it pays to be a little over-cautious. So I want that window shut and locked when you let that cat in and out."

I picked up Clark and cuddled him. "Aye, aye. By the way, Sammy, meet Clark. Betty's cat."

Sammy rubbed him behind the ears. "Funny that a girl like Betty should have a pet. Wonder why she named him Clark."

"Jayne thought she named him after Clark Gable."

Sammy returned to the door, then shut and locked it in one swift movement. He leaned his ear against the wood and listened for a few seconds, before he moved away from the door and joined me in the kitchen. Obviously he must have been satisfied with what he'd heard, or rather, with what he hadn't heard.

Sammy smiled at Clark. "That would make sense, naming her cat after a movie star. After all, she was a dame who tried to look like a movie star herself."

"Well, Clark certainly gets around like one. Because the last we saw of him, he was on the second floor, loving up to Mrs. Tynesdale."

I put a saucer of milk on the kitchen floor for Clark, along with some more leftover chicken. Then I grabbed a pitcher of sweet tea from the refrigerator and a couple of glasses, and took them to the table.

Sammy hung his suit jacket on the back of a chair. "Let's do a quick rehash, kid, before we call it a night. I have to say, I'm pretty impressed with all the specifics we got from talking to those tenants. Near as I can tell, we learned much more than the boys in blue did."

I felt my eyes go wide. "We did?" I poured us each a glass of tea and took a seat.

Sammy sat down opposite me and took a drink of his tea. "Yup, kid. You're off to a roaring good start when it comes to pumping people for information. In fact, I'd say you're a natural. Because we sure ended up with some good pieces to the puzzle. Now we have to see how those pieces fit in with the rest of them. For starters, we know Betty must have seen something she liked in Tim's mail. Not sure what it was, though, or how she planned to use him."

I took a sip of my own tea, which tasted a whole lot better than the whiskey I'd downed at Karl's place. The compliments I'd gotten from Sammy made me smile, even though I didn't think I'd done such a great job on my first interviews. Still, it was nice to know that my new boss thought I had. And even if I stumbled a little here and there, as long as we ended up with the right information, that was all that really mattered.

I stared at the table, and tried to replay our visit with the Westovers in my mind, like I was watching a movie.

And that's when something dawned on me. "I think Betty was interested in Timothy after she spotted the letter he'd gotten from his employer. The oil company. Humble Oil."

Sammy raised an eyebrow in my direction. "Could be, kid. Because that would fit in with some of the stuff that Karl told us. I believed him when he said he saw that Helmut character walk out of the building. But the question is, was Helmut looking for Betty? Or was Helmut looking for Karl? Or both? Wish there was a way to tie Helmut to Betty."

I glanced at the door. "I think I can help you there. He sounds like the guy that Nana and I saw walking out of Betty's apartment one afternoon. If fact, he sounds *just* like him. Now I wonder if Helmut killed Betty last night."

"Good question, kid, because he'd make a good suspect, except the timing is off. After all, you heard the gunshots and found her body. It was still warm, so we know she'd just been killed. I don't think you were wearing your watch, but the Eldridges heard those same gunshots and looked at their clock. So they gave us an exact time of death. And if Karl is right, and I believe he is, that means he saw Helmut leave the building about an hour before Betty was killed."

"So unless Helmut came back and nobody saw him, we're back to the drawing board." I sighed and held the cold glass up to my black eye. The coolness made it feel much better.

Sammy shook his head. "Not necessarily, kid. Because if Betty was associating with the Bund, that could account for her having so many fiancés."

"You mean . . ."

"Yup, kid, you got it. Betty was probably luring all those men in to get information from them. That could be why she suddenly got so interested in our friend Timothy, when she figured out that he worked for an oil company. Having a good fuel supply is pretty important when you're trying to win a war. And tampering with that fuel supply is pretty high on the list of any enemy who's trying to take over the world. So Betty could have been passing along any information she gathered to the Bund."

I choked on my tea. "That means Betty was a . . . a spy? A Nazi spy?"

"That would be my guess, kid. Though if she was working for them, I'm not sure why they'd kill her. But who knows with those Nazis. I've heard they're a pretty touchy bunch. And we've been warned about the Fifth Column for some time now."

I'd read bits and pieces about that very subject in the papers. "You mean Nazis who may already be here. They're supposed to be ready to rise up and fight for Hitler if and when he invades our borders."

Sammy's mouth tightened into a straight line. "That's about the size of it. This stuff we learned tonight only confirms it. It lets us know they're here. Roosevelt shut down the German embassies — including the one in Galveston — and all the other open Nazi activities a while back. So now they've probably got some kind of covert network going. I don't have to tell you that I don't like the sounds of this."

"Me, either," I nodded. It was bad enough that we had to fight against Nazi fascism overseas. But having to fight it in our own country was even worse.

"We've got to get to the bottom of this, kid. And I think our best bet will be to attend one of these Bund meetings and see what's going on. And who is there."

I gulped. "Won't that be dangerous?"

Sammy chuckled. "It's always dangerous, kid, in this business. And for that matter, in the whole world right now. But just remember one thing. We've got it easy. We're investigating Nazis here on U.S. soil, and not in the heart of France. Or Poland. Where the Nazis have taken over. Meaning, right now, this is still our country and not theirs."

Funny, but his words didn't sound nearly as comforting as they should have.

Sammy downed the last of his tea. "Let's start by leaving a note in that book at Bruner's Books. Just like Karl told us. But I'd better do that part by myself."

I shook my head. "That wouldn't be right. What kind of a partner would I be if I let you go alone?"

He looked me straight in the eyes. "One who could be recognized, kid. Since Helmut's already seen you."

"Oh," was all I could say, until something dawned on me. "I could wear a disguise. After all, Betty was in disguise. There's no reason I couldn't do the same."

Sammy raised an eyebrow. "You know, that just might work. And it gives me another idea. Those Bund boys could probably use another girl like Betty. If you took her place, then we could really find out what they were up to."

My heart started to pound. "You mean, you want me to . . . sort of become the new Betty? Step into her shoes, in a sense?"

Sammy put a finger to his chin, and I could practically see the gears turning in his head. "I need to give it a little more thought first and figure out how we could work this angle. But judging from the way you handled yourself with those interviews, I think you could handle yourself undercover. Especially if I'm nearby. And since you offered up a disguise, how do you feel about dying your hair light blonde? Like Betty's. Temporarily, anyway."

I touched the side of my hair. "Well, I guess I could. I'll make a beauty shop appointment in the morning."

He nodded. "You know, this is where having a woman on the job could really come in handy. Because you can step into a role that I could never step into. That no man could step into."

His words made me smile. "Don't forget my female intuition."

"Which also comes in handy. But can you sing, kid? I'm told that Betty was a songbird."

"Sure, I can sing. Though the last time I did, I ended up with a black eye."

He stared at my cheek. "Let's not hope for a repeat performance. In any case, why don't you stop by the office tomorrow afternoon and get acquainted with Mildred. Then I'll get her to write a note for us in German, since she knows the language. Afterward, I'll put it in the book at that bookstore and see if we can find out where this meeting is. Once I figure that out, we'll talk about sending you in. As long as I can work my way in, too."

"Um, okay . . ." I sort of murmured. "But exactly what is this undercover operation you've got in mind?"

Sammy got up to go. "First things first, kid. We'll sort out the details after I see if I can even get past the front door. In the meantime, I want you to take a look at these letters tonight. See if you pick up on anything. We can talk about this undercover operation more tomorrow, after I've had a chance to mull it over."

He pulled a bunch of letters from his pocket and dropped them on the table, the very letters I'd taken from Betty's mailbox.

"I'm on it," I told him.

Sammy slid his suit jacket over his shoulders and plopped his hat back on his head. "You did good tonight, kid. You're going to make a great P.I." He grabbed our empty tea glasses and set them next to the kitchen sink, before he headed for the door.

"Thanks," I murmured as I stood up to see him out.

He stopped and put his ear against the door for a moment, listening carefully before he pulled it wide open. Then he glanced up and down the hallway. "Remember, keep everything locked up tight."

"Believe me, I will." I nodded in the direction of Betty's apartment. "Especially since it looks like the police have gone. I wonder if they still think I'm a suspect."

Sammy shook his head. "I doubt it. Near as I can tell, they've moved beyond you. Especially after I convinced them that you were working for me."

"Which wasn't entirely true," I laughed.

"Sure it was, kid. Just retroactively. I hadn't quite gotten around to hiring you yet." Sammy grinned and tipped his hat to me.

And with that, he was gone. So I did exactly as he'd suggested, and shut the door and locked it. Then I turned around and faced the apartment that suddenly felt a whole lot bigger and emptier than it had before, with lots of hiding places for Nazis and other killers. I reminded myself that Sammy had checked out the entire place, and that Clark Cat and I were the only two creatures stirring here. But that didn't stop my imagination from running wild, and at full speed, like it was trying to set a world record of some kind. Because I heard every squeak, creak, and rustle like I had the hearing of Superman.

So I tried to put my mind onto something else, and rather than going to bed, I decided to take a good look at the letters Sammy had left. After reading several, a few things became crystal clear — the guys writing these letters were lonely, off on their own for the first time, and had spent time in Galveston. Of course, Galveston, with its various nightclubs and taverns, was known for its revelry. To put it politely. It was a hot spot for sailors and servicemen alike, as well as oilmen from Houston. Anyone who wanted a night out on the town. And in that carousing-type atmosphere, these boys had all met and fallen madly in love with Betty. They were also clearly convinced that she felt the same way about them.

Now, as I read their letters, I could just picture them on their big ships, obviously in port somewhere, pining away with pen poised above paper. To tell you the truth, I could see it so well, and with what were probably unintended subtleties in their letters, I could almost tell when they'd shipped out. Or were about to ship out. Especially when I read such sentiments as, "My darling, I won't be able to write for a while, but know that my heart beats for you every second of every day, even when you don't hear from me for a time." Or, as I read in another letter, "Don't go falling for another guy just because my letters seem to dry up. Because I'll write you every single day, though you might get a bunch of those letters all at once."

So as long as I read between the lines, I could pick up enough hints and clues to let me know quite a lot. And I guessed Betty had probably done the same thing that I was doing now, especially if she had been a Nazi spy — and certainly all road signs were pointing in that direction. Now the question was, what did she do with the information she'd gleamed from those letters? My guess was that she must have passed it on to someone else. If so, then who? And how?

Maybe Sammy and I would find answers to those questions when we went through with his undercover plan. Whatever that might be. All I knew was that he wanted me to step into Betty's shoes somehow.

My first undercover assignment.

It was hard to believe, since I had barely become an Apprentice P.I. So was I really up to the task of going undercover already? Could I pull off whatever it was that I was supposed to pull off? Sammy seemed pretty pleased with the job I'd done so far, even though I felt more like Laurel and Hardy than Katie McClue.

I silently vowed to be more professional in the future.

Provided I was going to *have* a future. Because first I had to make it through the night while Nazis were out there running around. They may or may not have been the ones who killed Betty, which meant Nazis weren't the only things I had to worry about. For all I knew, there might be a homicidal killer in the vicinity, too.

I heard a loud creak and nearly jumped a mile. I turned to see that it was only Clark Cat, who'd leaped up onto the kitchen counter. I walked over to put him down on the floor, hoping my heart didn't pound right out of my chest along the way. Yet one thing was for sure, I had to calm down if I was going to be a full-fledged private eye someday. Katie McClue never got a bad case of the nerves. Instead, she practically thrived on pulse-pounding suspense, and she usually went undercover three or four times a book. In fact, in the *Case of the Mistaken Identity*, she spent the entire episode pretending to be a Swedish nanny, having learned Swedish in her summer abroad. So she was an old pro when it came to going undercover.

As for me, well, I guess you could say that I wasn't quite up to her speed. For that matter, I hadn't even gotten out of the starting block, compared to her. Because, right at that moment, I only hoped my teeth would stop chattering long enough for me to brush them.

CHAPTER 21

Heroes and Hitchcock

That night, I barely slept a wink. Every time I closed my eyes, I could picture Betty's lifeless body on the floor of her apartment, while lightning lit up the room and thunder boomed in the background. And when I finally did start to doze off, images of swastika flags went on parade through my dreams, and every horror story I'd ever read in the papers or seen on newsreels came to life in my nightmares. Luckily, they didn't last long, since every creak and groan in that old house made me jump, and at one point I was just sure someone tried to turn the doorknob to the apartment door. All the while, I couldn't help but think of the very short distance between where I was lying now and where a dead girl had been lying the night before.

Thank goodness Clark had decided to curl up next to me. Obviously he wasn't tormented by any of the mental pictures haunting my vivid imagination, because, as I lay awake, staring into the darkness, he rolled onto his back and started to snore.

The next morning, I drank extra coffee and made a phone call to Hadley, and talked to him about putting locks on the apartment building. He thought it was an intelligent idea, considering one woman had already been murdered there. He quoted Benjamin Franklin, saying, "An ounce of prevention is worth a pound of cure," and promised to show up that very afternoon. Then I called and made an appointment with my hairdresser, who luckily had time for me right away.

So at half past ten, I walked out of the salon and into the bright sunshine as a whole new me. A much, much blonder version of me. My beautician had done an excellent job, and my new, very blonde hair certainly didn't look like it had come from a cheap bottle. In fact, I had to admit, it looked pretty good. My hairdresser had also sold me some pancake makeup that covered my black eye almost completely, and she'd given me a new tube of red lipstick. I hated to be so full of myself, but I couldn't stop staring at my reflection in every storefront window that I passed as I walked back to the Packard. I even got a few whistles when I stopped and bought a newspaper from a boy who'd set up shop on the corner. I figured I'd better enjoy my new blonde bombshell hair while it lasted, since I planned to go back to my regular color once this case was over.

The newspaper boy looked up at me with wide, brown eyes. "Are you a movie star, Miss?"

That made me laugh. "I'm afraid not. But how about you? Are you a movie star?"

"Nope," he said with great seriousness. "I'm a businessman."

"And a great one you are," I told him with a smile, right before I tipped him an extra dime.

His whole face lit up. "Gee, thanks lady. I'd go to see you in the pictures if you ever make it to Hollywood."

"No, thanks, I think I'll stay right here in Texas," I told him. "But I hope you make a million dollars with your business."

"Me, too, lady. I'm working on it."

I had a feeling he just might reach that goal someday, as hard as he was working at his young age. I waved goodbye and perused the headlines as I strolled to my car. The front page was filled with stories about the war, and the death toll from Pearl Harbor was still trickling in. And rising. The tales of those who had suffered and tried to fend off the enemy were heartbreaking. Yet despite the horrors, I couldn't help but be proud at the bravery of our American military members. They may have gone down, but they went down fighting.

Betty's murder had not made the front page, and in fact, I couldn't find anything about her death until several pages back. Even then I had to read it twice before I was sure it was hers, since it said, "Name of the victim has been withheld pending notification of next of kin."

That's when it hit me — if Betty was a Nazi spy, where were her next of kin? Here, or in Germany? Was she from a German-America family and had been recruited by the Nazis over here? Or was she actually from Germany, maybe someone who'd spent some time abroad and spoke the language? I had to say, I hadn't noticed Betty speaking with any kind of an accent, at least nothing that sounded foreign. As near as I could tell, she spoke perfect English. What little she did speak. She'd done her best to avoid speaking to women, and she stuck to conversing mostly with men.

But judging from the reactions I was getting on the street, I guessed that men hadn't really been listening to the *way* she spoke. No, instead I had a hunch that most men were in too much of a haze thanks to the way she *looked*. And it was a look that seemed to be taken straight out of the movies, probably the reason the young paperboy had asked me if I had been in the movies myself. Maybe Betty had copied that appearance, thinking it would help lure men into her clutches, so she could get information from them.

Information that had sent many men to the bottom of the ocean.

I got into my car, pushed in the clutch and turned over the engine. I took a quick glance at my hair in the mirror, and suddenly I was even more curious about Sammy's plan. Oddly enough, I had a hunch I was going to be doing exactly what Betty had done. Except, where she'd infiltrated the Americans in order to get information, I might be infiltrating the Germans to get information from them.

Germans on American soil, that was.

I only hoped Betty and I didn't share the same fate. I shuddered at the thought, even though the sun was shining brightly in through the windshield. I put on my sunglasses, and suddenly I looked even more like a movie star.

I got back to the apartment building just as Artie was walking through the front door. His eyes turned to me and he practically jumped a mile, dropping his pack along the way. Then he *thunked* a hand to his chest and leaned over. He took a few deep breaths as I ran to him.

"Artie, what is it? Are you okay?" For a moment, I feared the poor dear man was having a heart attack.

Thankfully he stood up and shook his head. "I'm fine, just fine. Don't worry about me. For a moment there, I thought I'd seen a ghost. All anyone has been talking about this morning is that girl who got murdered, and for a second there, I thought you were her. You gave me quite a start."

To tell you the truth, I wasn't sure whether I should be insulted or flattered. I didn't like the idea that someone might think I looked as "cheap" as Betty had, but on the other hand, I must have had a pretty good knack when it came to going undercover, since even Artie hadn't recognized me at first. Still, I hadn't meant to shake him up like that.

"Hold on a sec, Artie," I said before I quickly ran into Jayne's place and brought out a kitchen chair for him. "I want you to sit for a minute or two, so I can make sure you're all right."

He took the seat while I unlocked and opened up the mailbox wall. Then he passed the smaller bundles of mail to me, so I could distribute them, just like Jayne did.

He nodded as he kept an eye on what I was doing. "Now, now, young lady, don't go treating me like a helpless old man. I've still got plenty of fight left in me, and let me tell ya, I'd be happy to go back over and fight alongside those young fellas. And I could do it, too," he added with emphasis, as he sat up straight and coughed. "If Uncle Sam would let me."

"I believe you, Artie," I said, hoping to humor him. And so that I wouldn't insult a man who had served our country like he had.

I stuck the Westovers' mail in the 2C box, and noticed Timothy had gotten another letter from his employer, the Humble Oil Company. The final bundle of mail was meant for Betty's box. Again, I could see that she'd gotten a whole bunch of different letters, each penned by a different hand. But this time I recognized the writing on some of the envelopes, since it matched the handwriting in the letters that Sammy had asked me to read the night before.

I held the stack of letters up for Artie to see. "What shall I do with these?"

Secretly I hoped he might want me to put them in Betty's box, so Sammy and I could scour the letters later for clues. Yet I didn't exactly want to advertise that activity, since it probably fit into a very gray legal area. Very gray. And well, it was up to Artie and the Post Office to determine the fate of her mail.

Artie shook his head and sighed. "Not much we can do. Just put them in the box for now, until we figure out something later. That girl doesn't have an old address. Or a forwarding address. I already checked."

I had to admit, that news didn't exactly surprise me. For all I knew, her old address might have been somewhere in Berlin. And I had a pretty good hunch she hadn't exactly put that information in big, bold letters on any government forms.

Artie nodded at the stack of envelopes as I put them into Betty's mailbox. "That girl sure got her share of letters," he said. "I wonder if she wrote as many as she got. Soldiers count on letters from home you know. Helps keep up the morale. Guys describe a letter as being like a ten-minute vacation."

"And now the people who wrote to Betty won't be hearing from her at all," I responded quietly. "They'll probably wonder what happened to her."

"Maybe it's for the best," Artie said under his breath, right before his eyes lit up and he pulled something from his pocket. "Say, I almost forgot . . . I brought something for Jayne."

Then he held up a small flag for me to see. It was a little bigger than a sheet of paper, with a wide red border and a white center. Right smack dab in the center was a blue star. The top had a wooden dowel through it, with a piece of gold string attached for hanging. I knew what it was even before Artie said the words.

He smiled. "It's a blue star banner. For family members of those serving in the military, to hang in the window. With pride," he added as he handed it to me.

A lump formed in my throat and my eyes misted over. "Thank you," was all I could manage to say. I knew Jayne would be very proud to display her flag.

"You may already know," he went on, "the star is for the person who serves. Some families have more members serving, so they have more stars. One for each military member."

Now I fought back the full-fledged tears that were threatening to form in my eyes. "Jayne will appreciate this very much. Very, very much. Thank you again, Artie."

He gave me a small smile and stood up to go. "That new husband of hers is a great guy, signing up so soon like he did."

I nodded. "He sure is."

Then I forced a smile onto my face as I walked Artie to the door. He saluted me and I saluted him back. He'd barely walked out when Hadley showed up. He had locks, keys, and tools in hand, all ready to install front and backdoor locks on the building.

This time the smile on my face was for real. "Hadley, you're a lifesaver!"

His eyes went wide for a moment. "My, my, young lady, I barely recognized you."

I knew he was obviously referring to my new blonde hair color. "Do you like it, Hadley?"

He stood back and looked at me for a moment. "It is rather striking. But I'm afraid I prefer your hair to be the very color that God gave you. You've always had a natural, wholesome beauty about you. Much like your grandmother."

"Thanks, Hadley. But don't worry, this hair color is only temporary. It's for a case that Sammy and I are working on."

"I'll look forward to hearing about it some day, when you're at liberty to relay the entire tale." Then he held up some keys. "'Prayer: the key of the day and the lock of the night.'"

This time I recognized the quote. "Thomas Fuller, right?"

He smiled and nodded. "Right you are, my child."

That's when it dawned on me, that with Hadley's pursuit of all things academic, he might be able to fill in a few pieces for me. "Hadley, have you heard much about something called the 'Fifth Column'? Like where the name comes from and what it means exactly?"

His face clouded over. "Most certainly. The term came about a few years ago, during the Spanish Civil War. A general told a journalist that he had four columns of troops approaching Madrid. But the Fifth Column, he claimed, was already in the city and would rise up from within. Hemingway got hold of the term later, but since then, the Fifth Column usually refers to the enemy operating from within. Spies and saboteurs and such, who have infiltrated a place, with plans to join an army about to invade and take over a place."

His words gave me the shivers. If Betty and the Bund were considered to be part of a Fifth Column, and were ready to rise up when the rest of the Nazi Army invaded, that meant Hitler really did have plans to attack America. The thought of it made me feel like I'd just been plunged into icy water.

Hadley furrowed his brow, just as Clark Cat strolled down the hallway to join us. "Why do you ask, my child? There has been a lot of talk about the Fifth Column in America. Have you come across anything that concerns you?"

"Nope," I lied, so I wouldn't worry Hadley. "Just curious, that's all."

He gave me a skeptical look while he kneeled down to pet Clark. "I'm always here should you have more questions."

"Thanks, Hadley. I appreciate it."

After that, Hadley went to work, while I went from door to door to pass out the new keys and explain our new security measures. I found several people at home, including Mr. Schmidt.

"Very good, Miss Tracy," he told me. "A fine idea. At least the Bund can't reach me in my home."

"And I'm just downstairs if you need something," I told him.

He raised an eyebrow and stared at my hair. I got the impression he wanted to say something, but instead remembered his good manners and held his tongue. Though I guessed he was probably comparing my hair to Betty's, and I'm sure it upset him. His skin was a dangerous shade of gray, and I could see the fear on his face. I suddenly realized how important it was for Sammy and me to get to the bottom of Betty's murder, for the sake of lots of people, if not the country.

I gave him a smile and patted his hand reassuringly. "Don't worry, Karl. We'll make sure you're safe and sound."

Then I went back to the first floor and reopened the mailbox wall. I put keys in the boxes of the tenants who hadn't been home. Then I wrote a notice and tacked it next to the mailboxes, just to notify everyone of the new security change. After that, I hung

Jayne's Blue Star Banner in the window. Oddly enough, the flag seemed strangely comforting. It let people walking by know that someone who lived here had a loved one off fighting the tyranny of the Axis Powers.

I had just finished hanging the flag when Nana called and asked me to go to the movies. I had to say, I was really looking forward to a night out, where I wasn't thinking about murdered girls or the Fifth Column or homicidal killers. Having a chance to get my mind off things would do me a world of good.

Shortly after that, Hadley poked his head in and said he'd finished with the locks. I thanked him once again and walked him out. Apparently he knew all about Nana's plans to take me to the pictures. He said he'd drop her off at Jayne's place, if I would drive her to the movies and then home. Sounded just fine to me.

Once he was gone, I downed a quick sandwich, changed into a teal-green suit, and drove over to Sammy's office. Or I guess I should say, *my* office.

I had barely walked in when an older, very round woman with curly, gray hair smiled and jumped up from behind her desk to greet me. I knew even before she clasped my hand in both of hers that I'd just met Mildred Paninsky, our secretary.

The idea of having a secretary felt so odd to me, though I knew Katie McClue had a secretary of her own. Yet that was as far as the similarities went. Where my secretary was very well-dressed and sparkling with ruby-and-pearl jewelry, Katie's secretary, Rahul, was a middle-aged man with an eye patch and several visible scars, from his left cheek to his right arm. He hailed from somewhere deep in the Orient, and while he spoke seven different languages, he'd also taught Katie fifteen different types of self-defense, one that involved disabling a grown man with a common drinking straw. And of course, he guarded the sanctity of her office with an iron karate chop.

Somehow I guessed Mildred probably wasn't the drinking-straw-defense or iron-karate-chop kind of secretary.

She smiled, and the smooth skin of her face practically glowed. "Ah, yes, my dear one. You would be Tracy. I knew who you were the very moment you walked in. Sammy described you so well. I'm Mildred. So lovely to meet you." Her accent was similar to Mr. Schmidt's, though quite a bit stronger.

Was Mildred from Germany?

And that's when it clicked. The Jewish woman Sammy had told me about, the one he helped to escape from Germany. The one who gave him the Monet and the Picasso.

"Mildred . . . so lovely to meet you, too," I said, before I chose my next words carefully. "If you don't mind my asking, how did you come to work for Sammy?"

Her round face bobbed up and down. "Oh, but I must tell you the whole story some day. Sammy helped me and my family get out of Germany before Hitler took over everything. Thank the good Lord for Sammy. He is a saver of the lives."

And speaking of my boss, he walked in and joined us. "A lifesaver, Mildred. The term is lifesaver."

"Here's our hero now," Mildred announced.

Sammy shook his head. "Only doin' my job, ma'am. That's all. Wish I'd had the chance to get more of your folks out."

Much as Mildred had been beaming one minute, darkness now clouded her face. "Oh, it is so awful. What those Nazis do. I no longer hear from friends and neighbors. I fear the worst."

Sammy raised an eyebrow. "Now that Uncle Sam's in the war, we're going to put a stop to those rotten bums. Starting right here in Houston."

"Oh, good, good," Mildred gushed. "Did you get a letter back from those men at the bookstore?"

"I did," Sammy said to both Mildred and me. "But first, let's bring Tracy up to speed. Mildred here wrote a letter for me in German this morning, one that said we wanted to join the Bund. So I took it to the bookstore, and put it right in the middle of *War and Peace*. Like I was supposed to. Then I checked back just a little while ago. Turns out these Krauts are an efficient lot. That, or they're desperate for people to join up. Because they already responded. The only problem is, it's in German, too. So I can't read it."

He handed a note to Mildred. I could see the writing was very precise and every line was perfectly straight, almost like the author had used a ruler to guide their pen.

Mildred reached for a pair of glasses on her desk and put the cheaters on her nose. "Let me see . . . it says, meeting Wednesday night. Seven o'clock. Looks like the meeting is near the Houston Ship Channel." She moved back to her desk and wrote down the address. "And you'll need to answer a few questions first before they'll let you in."

I'm sure my eyes went pretty wide right about then. "Answer a few questions? In German, probably?"

"Not to worry, my dear one," Mildred piped up. "I'm going with you. I'll answer all the questions."

I turned to Sammy. "So what is our plan for this? Did you have something in mind?"

He nodded. "Yup, kid. Mildred will be posing as your mother, and I'm playing the step-father. Our story will be that Mildred came from Germany, and married me over here. You were born here but your real father died when you were still in diapers. And even though I'm an American, Mildred here used all her charms to convince us both that the Nazi way is the only way. So now we all want to join up. As a family. And, since these Nazi boys lost their singer in Betty, we're going to offer you up to take her place. As their new singer. That way we'll find out exactly what Betty's job was at the Polynesian Room. Somehow I think she was doing more there than just looking pretty and singing pretty."

"But I don't speak German," I started to protest.

"Never you mind," said Mildred. "Because we'll just say that you never learned to speak German, since you were born here and grew up here."

Sammy was already nodding. "And whatever you do, kid, it's best to play dumb. Don't over-explain things, and don't let on how smart you are. Nazis look for people who aren't too bright, because it's easier to control people who don't think about things too much. Thinking about things can lead to arguing, and the Nazis don't tolerate anyone who doesn't agree with them."

"Got it," I said. "I can play a dumb blonde. After all, my ex-fiancé always treated me like I was stupid, so I think I've got an idea how to act the part."

Sammy rubbed his chin. "Good. And while we're sneaking into this Bund meeting anyway, let's try to figure out what kind of an operation these Nazis have going on here. But we can talk more about that on the way over."

Mildred chuckled softly. "This will take some great acting on my part, pretending to be in favor of the Nazis. And pretending that I don't hate them so much. Especially after all they've done to Germany, and the Jewish people."

I put my arm around Mildred's shoulders and gave her a squeeze. She was several inches shorter than I was. "It must have been horrible, Mildred."

Sammy answered for her. "Horrors you can't even imagine, kid. So if things take a turn for the worse at this meeting, or if that female intuition of yours tells you to run, let's get out of there. Just because these Nazis are operating on U.S. soil, doesn't mean they're not still Nazis. They're just as evil here as they are over there. Got it?"

"Got it," Mildred and I both said at once.

Then Sammy pulled a folded piece of paper from the front pocket of his suit and handed it to me. "By the way, kid, we never did talk about your salary. Will this work for you?"

My eyes almost bugged out when I opened it and read it. I had no idea he planned to pay me so much. Especially as an apprentice.

"This will do," I choked. Now, more than ever, I knew I had to do a good job and live up to his expectations.

He grinned. "Good. I'll have a desk set up for you in the main office tomorrow. And speaking of tomorrow, I've got a table reserved for four at the Polynesian Room. At seven o'clock tomorrow night. It's under the name Nicholas Charles. We'll meet you and Pete down there."

"Nicholas . . . Nick Charles?" I laughed. "As in the character from the *Thin Man*?"

Sammy raised an eyebrow. "Good job, kid. You got it. And by the way, I like the hair. Looks great. People might even mistake you for Betty."

"Yes, you look beautiful, young one," Mildred chirruped. "You will surely have no trouble convincing the Nazis to let you have the singing job. When we go to the Bund meeting. But now I must get home and make supper for my husband."

"And I'm heading to the pictures with Nana tonight," I told them.

Sammy glanced at his wristwatch. "And I'm meeting an old

buddy for drinks. To get some background information on the Polynesian Room."

With that, we all said some quick goodbyes and took off. I got back to Jayne's apartment just as the phone was ringing. I picked up the receiver to find it was Jayne herself calling.

"I'm scared to ask," she chuckled across the line. "But has anything else happened in the twenty-four hours since I've been gone? Please tell me you haven't had any more murders."

I laughed in return. "No more murders, but lots to tell you about. Let's wait till you get home and then we can get caught up."

"It's a deal. So how is everything there?"

I filled her in on how Hadley had put locks on the front and back doors, and how I'd left keys for all the tenants. Of course, I didn't tell her about the Bund and the part about Betty probably being a Nazi spy. I figured that was something I could save for later.

"Locks sound like a great idea," Jayne said. "Especially since Betty's killer hasn't been caught yet. And, because there's a war going on. We've got to make sure everyone feels safe and protected."

"I agree. So how's everything there?"

That's when I could hear the disappointment in her voice, and I could also hear her trying to fight that disappointment, just like she always did. "It's not going as well as we'd hoped. We didn't get a wink of sleep last night, and we had a hard time finding a place to stay. There wasn't a hotel room or an apartment available anywhere. Believe me, we looked. Finally, we ran into an older lady whose two sons enlisted last week. She took pity on us, and she's letting us rent her sons' old rooms. It may not be exactly what we had in mind, but at least we've got a roof over our heads."

"Have you seen Tom?"

Jayne sighed. "No, I haven't. And I'm finding out that we may not get much chance at all to see our fellas. That's the hard part."

"I'm so sorry. But at least he knows you're there. Nearby."

"He does," she agreed. "And even if I get a glimpse of him now and then, it'll be worth it. But I'd better run, since this long distance costs a fortune."

So I took down the phone number to the place where she was staying, as well as the address. Then we said our so-longs, and that was that.

I let Clark Cat outside, boiled some eggs for my dinner and made a nice salad. I finished eating only seconds before Hadley dropped Nana off.

"Wooo-weee, darlin'," she gushed after I'd let her into Jayne's apartment. "Aren't you the glamour puss? I love the new hair color. It looks wonderful on you." She gave me a nice, warm hug.

"Thanks, Nana. But I won't be keeping it. It's only for this case, and I'll be going back to my natural color when it's over."

"Either way, you look lovely. But I'm curious — do you have any plans to come home any time soon? I want to be around when your mother sees your new hair color. After all, she's bound to shoot straight to the moon when she sees it. And I want to make sure she doesn't try to haul off and hit you again."

I sighed and grabbed my purse. "I don't know, Nana. It's only been a few days and the whole thing is still pretty fresh in my mind. I'm not sure if I'm ready to face her, especially since I doubt if she's even sorry. She sure didn't sound sorry when I saw her at the police station."

Nana shook her head. "No, she certainly did not. She pretended it never even happened. And she's still going around the house acting like you and Michael are going to get married. Though at least she hasn't been going forward with any more wedding plans."

"I'm not sure she even remembers hitting me. But any way you look at it, I've had enough of her nastiness. Besides, it's way past time for me to be on my own."

"Well, I miss you," Nana said. "And your father misses you, too. He wanted to stop by, but it seems he's in the middle of the whole mess — torn between his duty as a husband and his love for his daughter. Besides, he's been spending all his time trying to get into the service. With no luck."

I pinned my hat to my head. "Poor Father. And my brother? Does he miss me at all?" I asked with a laugh.

"He probably misses you most of all," Nana explained. "That's because your mother just found out that he's been seeing some waitress from a working-class family. So now she's determined to break them up. So he's the one in the hot seat these days."

Somehow, I didn't feel too sorry for Benjamin. He'd always been the "golden child," and he'd never once stood up for me like a big brother should, not when it came to the way my mother treated me. Though to be honest, thinking about my family was the last thing I wanted to do at the moment, mostly because I couldn't imagine any kind of happy ending between my mother and me. Plus, I had to say, I was truly enjoying being out on my own. My entire life had changed within a matter of days, and oddly enough, I hadn't even thought about Michael, or our broken engagement. Funny, but I didn't miss him or being his fiancée one bit. Though it did dawn on me that I still needed to return his grandmother's ring.

Nana and I stepped into the hallway and I carefully locked the door behind us.

"What movie are we going to see?" I asked her.

"I've got a great one picked out. It's playing at a downtown theater, and it's got Cary Grant and Joan Fontaine in it."

"Sounds good," I said as we walked down the hallway and out the front door. "What's the name of it?"

"*Suspicion*," she said as she slid into the passenger seat of the Packard. "It's a Hitchcock film, and supposed to be a real thriller."

So much for a night away from all the havoc in my life.

CHAPTER 22

Undercover Assignments and Mystery Men

After a few hours of watching Joan Fontaine wonder whether Cary Grant was a cold-blooded killer or not, I was more wound up than ever.

Nana walked out in a daze, and just kept muttering over and over, "I never saw that coming. I didn't think it would end like that." I had to say, neither did I. Funny, but I despised the Cary Grant character in the movie, mostly because I believed pretty early on that he was pretending to be someone he wasn't. Yet here I was, about to take on my first undercover role, where I would pretend to be someone that I wasn't, too.

Under normal circumstances, I would consider someone who was such a phony to be despicable. But in this case, I was doing it for the sake of solving Betty's murder and trying to uncover a Nazi operation. Now I had to wonder, could I do it? Could I pretend to be a dumb blonde who was the daughter of two Nazi sympathizers? What if those Nazis saw right through my act? I was going to be dealing with people who were dangerous. Very dangerous. And it was going to take some real courage on my part to go waltzing right into their lair. Even with Sammy and Mildred at my side.

Nana was still talking about Cary Grant when I pulled into the driveway of our mansion in River Oaks. That's when I finally felt a few twinges of homesickness. Especially since it was so close to Christmas. Though it barely even felt like Christmas at all this year, not after the attack on Pearl Harbor. Of course, Jayne hadn't had a chance to put up her usual festive decorations at her apartment, and lots of people had scaled back on celebrating the holiday. And for all the men going off to fight this year, it wouldn't be much of a Christmas either.

"Are you coming in?" Nana asked softly as she opened the passenger-side door.

I shook my head. "Not tonight. My mother is probably good and drunk by now. And I'm really not interested in another big bang-up."

Nana squeezed my shoulder. "I understand. But I'll see you tomorrow night. I'm looking forward to dinner and dancing at the Polynesian Room. I'll be pulling my sequined-dress from my closet."

"You'll look smashing," I told her.

She shut the door and blew me a kiss. I waited until she was safely inside before I drove off.

But I had barely gotten back on the road when a fog rose up, making driving a little treacherous. Especially since my eyelids now felt like they were made of lead, and I had to fight to keep them open. But I shook myself awake, slowed down, and turned on my headlamps. Not that it helped much. It seemed like an hour had passed before I finally parked the Packard and hurried toward the apartment building. I had just taken the first few steps up the walkway when I spotted a man standing by the front door. He was half-hidden in the shadows, and the hairs on the back of my neck suddenly stood on end. I stopped dead in my tracks and then took a few steps backwards, to put more distance between him and me.

He lit a cigarette and blew smoke to the side. "Hello there, little lady." Now I could see he was wearing a dark overcoat and a dark hat.

He stepped out from the shadows and I recognized him. In fact, I had a photo of the guy. I'd taken it the day when I stopped by Jayne's to pick up my black dress. He was the man who'd been getting pretty hot and heavy with Betty, right before she turned and sashayed up the walk. And now I could see he was wearing a military uniform under his overcoat, just like he had the last time I'd seen him.

"Hello," I said in the firmest voice that I could muster. "Can I help you? I'm filling in for the apartment manager."

He took another drag from his cigarette, lowered his lids halfway, but kept his eyes fixed on me. "I'm here to check on Betty. She was supposed to meet me for dinner this evening, but she never showed up and she won't take my phone calls. Then when I came by, I found the front door to the building locked."

For some reason, I wasn't buying his story. And if he was lying to me, then what was he really doing here? Katie McClue always preached that criminals returned to the scene of the crime. Had he been the one to shoot Betty? Was I staring right into the cool, green eyes of a killer?

"Maybe she doesn't want to talk to you," I said, well aware that I was telling a gigantic fib, considering Betty's body had taken up residence at the morgue.

The man continued to study my face. "I think we both know better than that, now don't we?"

"I'm afraid you'll have to be more specific," I told him, while I mentally calculated the best escape route if I needed one. My female intuition was practically screaming at me, telling me there was something very wrong here, and there was something very odd about this man. Especially since he seemed to be one very cool customer.

"We both know Betty is dead," he said in a deep voice.

Chills ran a road race up and down my spine. "Then why didn't you say so in the first place?"

"I have my reasons. Maybe you can tell me what happened to Betty."

I tried to think of how Sammy might react in this situation. "You'll have to ask the police," I answered as nonchalantly as I could. "Now maybe you can tell me what it is you want?"

He blew out rings of smoke. "Just here for sentimental reasons. I wanted to see her apartment one last time."

I put my right hand in my coat pocket, searching for something I might use as a weapon. Luckily, my fingers found a pointy nail file, so I grabbed it firmly. Just like Katie McClue had done in one of her earlier episodes.

"Oh, you did, did you?" I said in a low voice. "I don't believe Betty ever let you into her apartment."

"All right, fine," he snarled. "She had something of mine that I'd like to get back."

I slid the end of the nail file up my sleeve, but kept the sharp end in my palm, just in case I needed it. "I'm afraid no one is allowed into the apartment until the police have finished with their investigation. They still have it roped off."

He brought his dark brows down in a firm line across his forehead. "That's going to make things very uncomfortable for me."

I pulled my hand out of my pocket, still hanging onto my nail file. "And why is that?"

His eyes darted to the side and then back again. "Because I accidentally gave Betty some jewelry."

My jaw dropped open. "Okay, this one I've got to hear. How does a man *accidentally* give someone some jewelry?"

He snorted. "You probably wouldn't understand, since you're obviously Little Miss Perfect."

"Try me."

He took another puff from his cigarette. "All right. Here's what happened. I bought two brooches. One made with real rubies and sapphires, and one that was just costume jewelry. They looked a lot alike, to tell you the truth. That's how I mixed them up and accidentally gave Betty the real one, instead of the one that was costume jewelry."

Now I rolled my eyes. "And who, pray tell, was the real one meant for?"

The corners of his mouth turned down. "My fiancée."

"Well, doesn't that just figure," I said with a slight laugh. "Okay, write down your name, address, and phone number. And draw me a little picture of what the brooch looked like. The minute the police are finished, I'll see if I can find it for you."

A light bulb went on in the back of my mind. I'd only seen Betty wear Eisenberg costume jewelry, and according to my theory, that was what she asked guys to buy her, making it "her" brand so to speak. To help her juggle all those men without having to account for accidentally wearing jewelry she'd gotten from someone else. Yet

I guessed she probably knew right away that the piece she'd gotten from this man contained real stones. What had been her reaction? Would she have been thrilled to get the piece? Or surprised to get something other than a nice fake?

The man let out a sigh that could have doubled as a gale. Then he dropped his cigarette to the cement stoop and squashed it with the ball of his foot, rubbing it out with more force than was necessary.

"Thank you," he grumbled. "If Sheila ever found out about this, I'd be dead. She'd kill me, and my mother would kill me, and *her* mother would kill me. You're a good egg for helping me out. Say, you look a little like Betty yourself. Are you related?" He flashed me a smile.

"No!" I said, wanting to squelch this line of thinking before it went any farther. Because I knew his next words were going to be something like, "How'd you like to get together sometime?"

Thankfully, he must have realized that "no" meant no. That, and he wanted me to get his jewelry back for him. Because he pulled out a little tablet from his chest pocket and wrote his information down in a hurry. Then he drew the illustration I'd asked for. Surprisingly, he was a pretty good artist.

"If you have to phone me and someone else answers," he commanded, "just say you're calling from the jewelry store. Say it's a surprise for someone and that you're not allowed to say more."

"Aye, aye," I said, amazed at how easily I'd just gotten this man to hand me all his vital information. Information that might come in handy when it came to solving our case, considering I'd instantly added him to our suspect list. But as suspects went, I had to say, this guy wasn't an especially bright one.

"I'll be in touch," I told him.

"That would be swell," he said with a nod, as he handed me the paper.

I took it in my left hand but still kept my nail file ready in my right. "By the way," I asked him. "How did you and Betty meet?"

His eyes went wide for a moment, and he almost lost his balance. "I met her on a train. The attraction was undeniable."

I laughed. "I see. From Dallas to Houston, by chance?"

He looked at me like I had performed some kind of magic trick.

"Yeah, how did you know?"

"Lucky guess," I told him as I scooted off the walk to let him pass by. "Were you in love with Betty?"

He started to choke. "Betty had a hundred guys after her. So I knew she would never settle down anytime soon. But, yes, I was very fond of her."

I turned my back to the front door. "What about your fiancée? Did you think of ending it with her, so you could be with Betty?"

"Good heavens, no," he smirked. "Why would I do something that stupid? Sheila is absolutely beautiful and she's going to make a great wife. Plus, she comes from money. A lot of money."

I took a step backward, moving ever closer to the front door. "When's the wedding?"

"In February." He sounded annoyed that I was prying into his business.

I raised an eyebrow. "I see. So Betty was just a sideline girlfriend. Did you plan to keep seeing her, or did you plan to end it once you got married?"

Now he snarled at me. "It doesn't really matter now, does it? Because Betty is dead."

And she can't interfere with your plans to marry a very wealthy woman, I thought.

"She's dead, all right," I said. "And how exactly did you happen to know that?"

He sighed and stared at the ground. "Some of the fellas told me. They'd read about it in the papers. That she'd been murdered on Saturday night. Rough way to go."

By now I realized I'd gotten this guy on the hook and I only needed to reel him in. "And while she was being murdered, where exactly were you?"

That's when I must have pushed him just a little too far. Because he jumped towards me and swung his fist at my face. But after being hit once in the past few days, I was a little smarter than I was before. Because this time I ducked. And as I did, I caught him off guard by planting my nail file firmly into his other hand. I pulled it out a split second after I'd stabbed him. It was a move that would have made Katie McClue proud.

The uniformed man hollered and stepped away. "Hey, what did

you do *that* for?"

"Didn't your mother ever tell you not to hit a girl? You had it coming." I said in my best Humphrey Bogart voice.

He pulled his hankie from his pocket and put it over his wounded hand. "Okay, okay. I was out with my fiancée last Saturday night. But it's none of your business, and I don't want you to go snooping around her."

"All right," I told him. "I'll keep your secret safe. And I'll let you know if I find the brooch. If I do, I'll send it right over."

"I'd be obliged."

And with those words, he turned on his heel and practically flew down the walkway. I blinked once and he was gone, having disappeared into the fog. I couldn't see him anywhere in the night. Even so, I kept up my vigilance as I unlocked the front door. I'd barely opened it when I heard a car engine turn over from somewhere down the street.

I jumped inside the building, and shut and locked the door behind me. Then I made a beeline to Jayne's apartment, got inside and locked that door behind me, too. I hit the button for the lights and went to the window to let Clark Cat in.

He'd been waiting on the sill and, judging from his very demanding meow, I could tell he was pretty annoyed. He didn't like the fog any better than I did. I found something for him to eat and then looked over the information the uniformed man had given me.

According to what he'd written down, his name was William — probably Bill — Marlowe. Though I had to wonder, if he had on a military uniform, how was it that he had so much free time to run around Houston?

I put the paper in my purse, and, after another sleepless, guarded night, I called Sammy first thing in the morning and told him all about my encounter will Bill Marlowe.

"Did you believe him, kid?" Sammy asked through the receiver. "That he was only after the jewelry? And he was somewhere else when Betty was killed?"

"I'm not sure. Because my questions most definitely got his dander up. He was pretty quick to take a swing at me. But he backed down when I nailed him with my nail file."

Sammy chuckled. "No pun intended, huh, kid? So you think he

had it in him to murder Betty?"

"I'm still wondering about that," I told him. "Because he didn't have a problem hitting a girl. And he had a lot to lose if his fiancée found out about Betty. So maybe he killed Betty so she couldn't talk. And maybe he wants the jewelry back to make sure all the loose ends are tied up. That, and the brooch might be worth a lot of money."

"Like I keep sayin', kid, you're a natural. You're thinking like a detective. I guess we'll know more after we have a chance to look over Betty's apartment. And see if that brooch is really there. If the police haven't confiscated it."

"The police are over at Betty's place now. They were knocking on the front door of the building early this morning." I pulled the phone and the cord closer to the door of Jayne's apartment, and tried to pick up on any stray sounds coming from across the hall. "Guess they didn't know that I'd had locks put on the front and back doors." I smiled, sort of enjoying the idea that I'd inadvertently pulled one over on Detective Denton, especially after the way he'd treated me.

"Guess they found out," Sammy said with another chuckle. "Let's talk about it more tonight. Keep up the good work. I'll see you later."

And with that, we got off the phone.

I let Clark Cat outside and then left the apartment and moseyed on over to Betty's door.

Detective Denton glared at me when I stood in the doorway and watched for a moment. "You really don't need to be bothering us," he said. "Like I told your friend, we'll be finishing up tonight. The place will be all yours tomorrow."

I thanked him and gave him a salute, before heading back to Jayne's apartment. The rest of the day was filled with helping tenants, reading more letters and taking care of Clark. Then before I knew it, it was time to get ready for my date.

Even though I knew I was going out mostly for work purposes, I still felt a fluttering in my stomach at the idea of seeing Pete again. Funny, but this was the first date I'd had in a long time that I was actually looking forward to.

It seemed like I had barely taken a bath and donned my new black satin dress, along with the matching gloves, and swiped a nice coat of red lipstick over my lips when he knocked on the door. I quickly snapped a sparkly bracelet and ring over the gloves, then I added a simple diamond pendant and drop earrings. I raced to the door, glancing at the clock along the way.

Pete was right on the dot. Not early, not late, but right on time. I opened the door to find him just a little bit out of breath, but with a smile on his face and a rosy glow in his cheeks.

His eyes went wide when he saw me. "Tracy, you look absolutely beautiful!"

It was a nice compliment to hear, considering I was wearing the very dress my mother had once deemed horrendous. I had to admit, when I'd put it on, I did have a momentary twinge or two of self-consciousness. What if other people thought it was dreadful? What if I really didn't have any fashion sense?

But Pete's face said it all.

Of course, I quit thinking about myself when I noticed the smoothness and coordination of his every move, as well as the way his shoulders filled out his perfectly tailored, double-breasted tuxedo. Pete had become so manly in the last few years, and now I really had to wonder, why, all those years ago when he had a crush on me, hadn't I noticed what a good-looking guy he'd been?

Apparently, I also hadn't noticed the corsage he held in his hand. "I forgot to ask you what you would be wearing tonight, but I hoped red roses would go well with your dress. I wanted to get you something different, since everybody gets orchids. Frankly, I think roses stand out more. Like you do, Tracy."

It was such a thoughtful thing to say. I smiled while he expertly pinned the corsage to the top of my dress.

"Thank you, Pete," I told him. "I love red roses. And they're perfect with my gown."

"I noticed you changed your hair color," he said. "I like it, but then again, I liked your regular color, too."

Funny, but *I* seemed to like just about every single word that came out of this man's mouth. I smiled brightly up at him as he helped me place my wrap around my bare shoulders. Then he offered me his arm and we were off. I locked the doors behind us and let him escort me to his new Cadillac. He helped me get my long gown into the passenger side, before he gently shut the door behind me. Then he jumped into the driver's seat, turned over the engine, and that Caddy started to purr. The next thing I knew, we were headed down to Galveston.

For my first visit and investigation at the Polynesian Room.

And, my first date with Pete.

CHAPTER 23

Swing Dancing and Dire Straits

It was a beautiful evening for a drive, and Pete skillfully handled the Caddy, motoring us down old US Route 75, which had partially been renumbered to State Highway 6. The sun had just started to set, giving us the most stunning display of pink, purple and orange clouds I had seen in a long time.

Along the way, Pete and I talked easily, and comfortably, and we laughed often like the two old friends that we were. Even so, I clearly noticed that something had changed between us. Sure, I could tell that the crush he'd had on me had never completely gone away. But now I began to feel something different toward Pete, an attraction that I hadn't felt years before. And somewhere along the drive, I became aware that I'd edged a little closer to him as I swiveled in my seat to face him. His hand often wandered over to mine. Yet despite wearing my gloves, it felt electric every single time his fingers touched my fingers, and I could feel a pleasant, happy glow rising in my cheeks.

After all the time I'd spent as Michael's fiancée, and after being completely ignored by the man, Pete's attention was like a salve to a sore wound. Besides that, I couldn't stop noticing his broad shoulders. And, how dashing he looked in his black fedora.

Even so, I felt it was only right that I tell him the truth about why Sammy had goaded him into asking me out to the Polynesian Room. I certainly didn't want him to find out later and feel like he'd been misled. Or used. Yet oddly enough, I had a hard time finding the right words to explain it all, since I was still afraid he might feel like he was merely a means to an end.

But more than that, I really didn't want to ruin this magical feeling between us.

So I was careful with my explanation, telling him as much as I could about the investigation, without giving away the pertinent details.

I finished my story by saying, "So now I'm working as an Apprentice P.I. And my boss, Sammy, and my grandmother, who is his date, will be meeting us down there. I hope you don't mind sharing a table. Nana is a real doll, and I think you'll find Sammy to be pretty interesting. I don't know what I'll need to investigate exactly, but I promise you, I won't be gone too long."

His face fell and his lighthearted tone disappeared. "So, you're going out with me as part of your cover?"

"Well . . . yes, it's partly for my cover . . . but . . ." I paused and took a deep breath. "The truth is, it was also a good excuse."

He wrinkled his brow. "How's that?"

"Well, it turns out it was also a good way to get you to ask me out." I was surprised by the little tremor in my voice.

This brought a smile to Pete's face. "You don't need an excuse to get me to ask you out. Tracy, I would be happy to ask you out anytime."

"I think I'd like that."

The smile never left his face. Not until he took my gloved hand in his and lifted it to his lips. He planted a soft kiss on the tips of my fingers before he returned my hand to the bench seat. I thought I was going to swoon and melt right on down to the floorboard.

He grinned even wider. "Though I have to say, I've never been part of an investigation before. And I think it's pretty swell that you're an Apprentice P.I. You'll make a terrific Private Investigator some day."

Now I was the one who was grinning. "Well, thanks, Pete. I'm looking forward to the day I get my license. But I've got a few years to go before then."

"Just so you know, I'm always available anytime you need a fella as part of your cover. I could be the muscle," he said with a laugh as he flexed his right bicep.

"I'll keep that in mind."

Which had to be the biggest understatement around. Because there was something about his muscles and his shoulders that I was going to have a hard time getting *out* of my mind.

Minutes later, we crossed the bridge to the island, and then found a parking place right along the Seawall, as though it had been waiting there for us. It was only a short walk to the Polynesian Room, which was housed at the end of a 700-foot covered pier, one that extended far beyond the beach and right out into the Gulf of Mexico. While the main room held a restaurant, dance floor, and bandstand, rumor had it there was another back room not accessible to the public, where illegal gambling took place. From the stories I'd heard, I suspected that rumor was probably true. Either way, it was well-known that, during Prohibition, rumrunners would drop off their wares at the very end of the pier under the cover of darkness. Then they would turn their boats and head right back out into the Gulf, where they rarely got caught.

I took Pete's arm as we walked up the steps toward the big double doors. I could smell the salt air of the Gulf, and overhead, seagulls floated and dipped toward the water. Pete held a door for me, and the two hostesses stationed at the front counter immediately gasped and stared at me with wide eyes.

One of them even grabbed a hankie and sniffled a little. "Sorry," she said to me. "For a moment there, I thought you were someone else."

I had a pretty good idea who she thought I was, with my light blonde hair.

Betty.

It had to be. Just to be sure, I decided to push the issue a little bit and try to find out more.

I offered the girl a gentle smile. "I'm so sorry to upset you," I said softly. "Something very bad must've happened to the girl you're talking about. For the sight of me to shake you up so much."

"It did," the young woman said, patting her brunette hair into place. "Betty died just a few days ago. She was murdered."

I put my hand to my chest. "Oh my goodness! How horrible! Were you both pretty close to her?"

"Well . . ." The other girl, a redhead, blinked eyelids that were loaded with blue eye shadow and outlined in black. "Nobody ever *really* got close to Betty. She was nice enough, but sort of kept to herself in a way."

The first girl was already nodding. "But she really *was* very nice to us, and she seemed to get along with everyone. She was very popular."

"Especially with the gentlemen," the second girl added. "Though it was funny, I don't think she said a lot . . ."

"She was mostly a very good listener," the first one finished for her. "Everyone always said she was very easy to talk to."

I'll just bet, I thought. *I'll bet she listened and listened and got all the information she wanted. As well as starting lots and lots of relationships to get more information later.*

The first hostess took a few steps toward a long hallway that I guessed must lead to the dining room. "Betty took the train down from Houston every night that she sang here, but someone always gave her a ride home."

"She was a wonderful singer," the eye-shadowed hostess said. Then she directed her attention to Pete. "By the way, do you have a reservation for tonight?"

Pete smiled. "We'll be joining another party at their table."

"Yes," I jumped in. "We'll be joining a table reserved for Nicholas Charles."

"Excellent," the first hostess said with a smile. "They're already here. Golly, that man looks an awful lot like Humphrey Bogart."

I raised my eyebrows in surprise. "Does he? I hadn't noticed," I said with my straightest face, before I turned and gave Pete a wink.

"Nicholas Charles?" Pete whispered in my ear as the first hostess directed us to the hatcheck room. "As in Nick Charles and the *Thin Man*? You and your boss are really playing up all this cloak-and-dagger stuff."

I gave him a knowing smile when we dropped off my wrap and Pete's hat with the hatcheck girl. We were then led down the hallway and up a small flight of stairs to the main dining room. I'd heard the place was swanky, and I'd certainly seen more than my share of opulent restaurants, but even then, I wasn't prepared for the sheer elegance of the place. While it had a South Seas sort of theme, it still had gleaming white tablecloths, and shining silverware and china. Not to mention, the sparkling crystal and glassware. There were gold and pearl adornments everywhere, and a giant clamshell sitting open to the side of the stage, with a large golden pearl placed right smack dab in the center of it. A large Christmas tree covered in lights and ornaments was off in one corner. And while the lights were dim in the rest of the room, candles illuminated every table, and stage lights showed off the bandstand.

Nana spotted us the second we walked in and gave us a little wave. "My what a handsome couple you make," she gushed as she gave me a hug, and Pete and Sammy shook hands. "And the dress is divine! You look like a Hollywood movie star."

"Thanks, Nana," I told her as I took in her midnight-blue gown, ornamented with sequins. "You could pass for a star on the silver screen yourself. But don't forget, I'm here on a case."

She raised an eyebrow and glanced at Pete. "Are you sure?"

Pete held my chair for me and then took his own, before we ordered cocktails all around. Sammy gave me a little salute, and I had to say, he looked pretty dapper in his double-breasted white jacket with a shawl collar, along with a black bow tie.

I leaned in to talk to him. "I told Pete a little about what we're doing here tonight."

"And I'm here to help out any way I can," Pete told him. Then he smiled at Nana.

She smiled in return, obviously very taken with Pete. "I'm in on this, too."

Sammy glanced around the room. "Let's not get too carried away here. We're just looking for a little information, that's all. So let's relax and make it look like we're having some fun. Later on, I'm going to pretend I've had too much to drink and stumble into the backroom. So I can see what's really going on in there."

"I've already gotten an earful about Betty," I told Sammy. "Sounds like she was pretty popular with the fellas whenever she worked here."

Sammy grinned. "Gosh, what a surprise. Wait a minute, let me guess, kid . . . I'll bet she was a *really* good listener."

"That's what they told me," I said with a nod as the tuxedoed waiter reappeared and brought us menus.

"Welcome to the Polynesian Room," he told us. "We just reopened last night. We were closed for a week out of respect for the attack on Pearl Harbor. Boss's orders. His son is in the Navy, but thankfully he was nowhere near the Hawaiian Islands. But the rest of those boys had it pretty rough."

"You can say that again," Nana agreed. "My husband served in the Great War."

The waiter's eyes went wide and he stood soldier straight. Then he saluted Sammy, obviously thinking Sammy was Nana's husband. Of course, we all had the good manners not to publically correct him. Instead, Nana and Sammy shared a small smile while the waiter went on to tell us the specials of the day.

After a little discussion, we decided on shrimp cocktails for starters, and shrimp and artichoke hors d'oeuvres on toast points. Then Nana and I had lobster tails while the guys both ordered nice medium-rare rib-eyes (from a nearby Texas ranch, of course), and baked potatoes. An hour later, we were halfway through our entrees when the band started to play. After a few songs, it became very apparent they were missing their lead singer. Maybe they hadn't been able to replace Betty just yet.

The waiter returned to take my empty plate when Pete leaned into me. "Care to dance?"

I put my gloves back on. "I'd love to. Thank you, kind sir."

And off we went to cut a rug. One song later, the bandleader announced, "Time for a little swing, don't you think?"

The next thing I knew, the band was playing Glenn Miller's "In the Mood" and nearly everyone jumped to the floor. The brass section stood and gave it their all, while the wind section got up, too, and swung from side to side. Pete immediately led me into a high-energy rock step and I followed along. Then he twirled me around, first left and then right. Then behind his back, before we put our arms up and turned together. Honestly, I had no idea that Pete was such a great swing dancer. But I found myself laughing and having the time of my life as we moved right up to the front, next to the band. The song ended much too soon, and everyone applauded and cheered loudly.

Pete was laughing and breathing hard. He wrapped his arms around me, and continued to sway us back and forth, as though some song was still playing in his head.

In front of us, the bandleader grinned broadly and turned to applaud his own band. Clearly he was enjoying it as much as the crowd. But his tone suddenly became serious as he turned back to address the audience.

"We'd like to continue with more Glenn Miller music," he announced. "But I'm afraid our singer is no longer with us, so this one will be instrumental only. I'm sure you all know 'Moonlight Serenade.'"

And that's when Pete raised his hand. "Excuse me, sir. But my girl here can sing 'Moonlight Serenade.'" He smiled and nodded at me. "Right, Tracy?"

"Sure, I guess so," I told him.

And then I remembered I was supposed to be undercover in a sense tonight, and what better way to get information about Betty than to step right into her spot on the stage? Especially since the bandleader was looking at me like I was God's gift to the nightclub world.

So I stood up straight and looked him right in the eye. "I can sing 'Moonlight Serenade.' I'd be happy to."

"Fantastic," the bandleader said. "And you're even dressed the part. Come on up here, beautiful."

With that, Pete helped me onto the stage. I gave my key to the bandleader and scooted over so I was directly in front of the microphone. I waited while the introduction was played, and then I let my first few notes sail out loud and clear. I took a deep breath and continued to sing. It was one of my favorite songs.

The whole room echoed with my voice as Pete leaned against the wall on the edge of the stage. He had his arms crossed while he looked up at me with a huge grin on his face. Obviously proud. Had he really just called me "his girl?" Not that I'd exactly *agreed* to be his girl. But not that I minded, either. In fact, the thought of being his girl made my heart beat just a little faster. Was I starting to have the same kind of feelings that Nana and Gramps had had toward each other? And that Jayne and Tom had? Or maybe it was just the excitement of realizing that I was actually singing right there at the Polynesian Room. It was the second time I'd gotten up to sing in front of a microphone and in front of a band in so many days. It was all so hard to believe.

The lights of the stage caught the gems in my bracelet, and it flashed and sparkled like a beacon. All the while, I sang my heart out, concentrating and hitting each note just perfectly. I saw Nana at our table, smiling, and then I noticed Sammy. He gave me a nod, right before he excused himself to Nana. I knew that meant he was going to make his move. And, he was using my singing as a distraction while he went off to investigate. So I did my level best to be as distracting as I could, putting my arms into it, and letting that bracelet flash away. By now, nearly every couple in the place was on the dance floor, clinging to each other, as they swayed and stepped to the song.

I had barely finished when the whole place erupted into applause. The restaurant's photographer moved to the dance floor, directly in front of me. Then his camera flashed while he took my picture, and I was temporarily blinded while everyone kept on clapping. Thankfully, I felt Pete's hand take mine.

"That was swell, Tracy. Absolutely swell," he murmured. "I'll help you off the stage."

I had barely followed him down and my vision had finally returned to normal, when the photographer appeared before us.

"Smile for the camera," he said.

Pete slid his arm around my waist and we did just that. The camera flashed again in the darkness, and once more I couldn't see anything but leftover light flashes.

"That's a keeper," the photographer announced. "And so is she. You two make a stunning couple."

"Thanks," Pete told him as he pulled me a little closer.

He walked me back to our table and held my chair for me. I sat down for a moment while Nana congratulated me on my singing. All the while, I scanned the place, looking for Sammy.

I squeezed Nana's hand. "Did you see which way Sammy went?"

She pointed toward a side door. "He went that-a-way," she laughed. "I've always wanted to say that."

I leaned closer to her ear. "Would you mind keeping Pete company while I go and see if Sammy needs me?"

"Sure thing, darlin'."

So I blew Pete a kiss and got to my feet. He raised one eyebrow and looked directly into my eyes for a moment, as though he knew I was about to do something related to my new job. A slight smile crossed his lips. Funny, but Michael would have had a complete conniption at the mere idea of me taking a job like this. Pete, on the other hand, seemed rather impressed by my newfound employment.

I walked quickly to the door that Nana had pointed to, and waltzed on through like I owned the place. If anyone asked me what I was doing, I planned to say I was in search of a ladies' room. But nobody even questioned me at all, probably because there wasn't a soul around.

The doorway led to a dark, narrow staircase with a very low ceiling. Since I'd come this far without anyone trying to stop me, I decided to keep going. So I carefully stepped down each step, until I got to the bottom landing. Then I tiptoed down a little hallway, until I came to two more doors. One in front of me and one to my left. From where I stood, I could hear muffled sounds of the band upstairs, and I was pretty sure I could also hear ocean waves. As near as I could tell, I was on the side of the building, and just below the main room upstairs.

I put my ear to the door in front of me, and that's when I picked up even more muffled sounds. This time I heard laughter and the occasional shouts of joy, as well as a few "Oooohs," as though people were disappointed about something. Then I heard kind of a fast *tick-tick-tick-tick* sound that went on for a while before it stopped. It started up again and stopped once more. After a few rounds of this *ticking* noise, I finally realized what it was — a roulette wheel.

Apparently I'd found the infamous but supposedly secret backroom where illegal gambling took place. Though I had to say, it certainly seemed odd to me that I was able to get this far without being stopped or turned away. If an establishment was involved in this kind of unlawful activity, I would think they'd be pretty selective about whom they allowed downstairs. I even tried the doorknob and found it was unlocked.

That's when I felt someone turning it from the other side. I flattened myself against the wall just in the nick of time, because seconds later, someone shoved that door wide open, right in front of me. A man and a woman emerged, and they were both laughing and talking so loudly that they didn't even notice I was there hiding behind the open door. They staggered up the stairs as I grabbed the edge of the door and held it open. I quickly peeked around it and into the huge room in front of me. That's when I saw lots of tables where people were either playing blackjack or craps, or betting at a big roulette wheel. Then there was an entire wall of slot machines. Women in furs and finery were busy pulling the handles of those one-armed bandits and watching the wheels spin, while the craps tables were mostly surrounded by men. I had to say, I was a little astounded by the full-scale gambling operation going on here. Especially when I spotted lots of busy cocktail waitresses, too, as I let the door slowly fall shut. I could absolutely picture lots of sailors and military men being drawn to a place like this. And if Betty had wanted to cavort with plenty of available men, well, this was probably the best place to go.

Yet with all that I had seen, there was one thing that I *hadn't* seen — my boss. Where in the world had Sammy gone?

That question, along with the question of why nobody appeared to be minding the store was quickly answered when the other door slowly opened up.

"Toss him in the brink," I heard a baritone voice command.

"See if he can swim," another man said. "If he lives, it'll teach him not to snoop. If he doesn't make it, that's just the luck of the draw."

Those very words made the hairs on the back of my neck stand at attention. Because I had a pretty good idea who they were talking about.

And my suspicions were quickly confirmed when the door opened the entire way, and I could see into what looked like a very large office. For there was Sammy, being escorted, or rather, half-lifted and half-drug out by two big goons. His tie was askew and his jacket was on crooked. And he was bending over and cringing like somebody had socked him in the stomach.

A dark-haired man sat at the desk, laughing loudly, while the goons laughed, too.

That was, until everyone spotted me standing there. That's when they all fell silent and glared at me with cold, dark eyes. And that was also when I recognized the man sitting behind the desk, for I'd seen his picture in the paper a couple of times.

It was Vito Vicchialli, a man believed to be a Galveston mob boss. A man who'd had a few run-ins with the Texas Rangers, though from what I'd read in news reports, it seemed that no one could ever pin anything on him.

And it also looked like he was not happy that Sammy and I had both been snooping around. Not only did I not like the sounds of what they planned to do to Sammy, and maybe even me, but now I had to wonder — had Betty been killed by the Galveston mob? And were we about to be killed by them, too?

Sammy lifted his head and darted his eyes back and forth, like he was trying to tell me to scram. Maybe run for help. I could tell he was in pain, though he didn't appear to be bleeding.

The thought of them being violent toward him made me sick. Yet right at that moment, I knew it was up to me, and only me, to do something. Since he was in their clutches and I was free. So I gulped and tried to take a deep breath, all the while wondering how I was going to get us out of this mess.

And with every ounce of brainpower that I had, I tried to think what Katie McClue would do in a moment like this.

CHAPTER 24

Goons, Gambling, and A Dead Girl's Apartment

Funny, but even though I'd always heard rumors of illegal gambling in Galveston, I'd never connected the dots and realized it was being run by mobster, Vito Vicchialli. Probably because the Polynesian Room was so well known for its dinner and dancing, and lots of people drove down from Houston for an elegant evening out. Yet I'd never heard any details on the gambling side of things, or about the huge hidden room. My guess was that Vito's "gambling" customers were checked out pretty thoroughly before they were allowed to join some kind of club. Even then, those customers most likely knew to keep their mouths shut, not only because this Vito could obviously be a very terrifying guy, but if he got arrested, their gambling fun would go away.

Vito, no doubt, didn't much like the idea of going to jail, either, so if he and his bunch were doing something illegal, of course they'd want to keep it hush-hush. And mob bosses weren't exactly known for being understanding when it came to someone nosing around in their business.

Now clearly Vito intended to silence Sammy, since he obviously saw him as a threat. That meant I had to think on my feet and think fast if I had any hopes of saving my boss. Not to mention, my own skin.

And the first thing that popped into my mind was something the waiter had said to us. About the place being closed in honor of those who had been killed at Pearl Harbor. That's when I suddenly knew what to do.

I plastered the biggest smile on my face that I could manage at the moment. "Gramps!" I practically yelled at Sammy. "Have you been wandering around again?"

I kept on smiling and looked straight at Vito. "You'll have to excuse my grandfather. He's a veteran of the Great War, and he gets a little confused and forgetful sometimes. Well . . . actually, a *lot* of the time. He has his good days and his bad days, but sometimes he loses track of where he is. We have to watch him like a hawk. My Nana says he has never been the same since he got that plate in his head. Apparently he was shot while taking out a whole platoon of Germans."

Sammy did his best to straighten up. "These dang Gerries! They captured me and they've been holding me here for questioning. Giving me the regular third degree. Wait till the rest of my Marine buddies find out about this."

"And oh, yes," I said with a sigh, "I'm afraid he often goes back to the time when he was captured behind enemy lines. Sometimes he seems to think he's back in Germany."

Vito's mouth fell open wide and his jaw practically hit his desktop. "Let the man go!" he commanded the two goons who were holding Sammy.

They released him immediately as Vito ran from behind his desk and started to straighten Sammy's jacket and dust him off. "Sir, I am awfully sorry. I thought you were an undercover cop. With Texas law enforcement somehow. I had no idea you were one of our distinguished military veterans. My own son is in the Navy."

"Well," Sammy said. "I'm glad to hear you're on our side. For a moment there, I thought you were one of them dirty Germans."

"Oh no, not at all. I am a true-blue American, even though my family came from Sicily. But we're all Americans now and we love this country through and through," Vito gushed. "Again, I sure hope you accept my apologies. I'm really sorry about the rough stuff.

Your dinner is on the house. I'll have a dessert sent to your table right away. And another round of drinks, of course."

I sighed again. "Poor, poor Gramps. He doesn't mean any harm. He just gets confused. I'd better take him back to our table now. My grandmother was getting worried. Once he wandered off at a carnival. He was so sure we were under attack."

One of the goons nodded. "My father was the same way. Shell-shocked. But sometimes he could get a little nasty."

I shook my head. "Gramps is usually pretty nice. Unless he thinks you're a German. Or if he believes he's just raided an enemy encampment. Then he can get a little vicious."

"Understandable," Vito added. "By the way, young lady, you handled yourself really well at the microphone tonight. You're a terrific songbird."

I gave him my brightest smile. "Why, thank you. It was easy with such a fantastic band. They're as good as Glenn Miller or Tommy Dorsey."

The compliment seemed to please Vito greatly. "They sure are. Nothing but the best at our place. But we lost our favorite canary on Saturday. So if you ever need a job singing, you're welcome to work here. After all, you were heard all over the Island, and we're still getting phone calls from folks, asking us to book you."

"You are?" I sort of gasped.

Vito raised his dark eyebrows. "That's right, sweetheart. We've got a remote radio broadcast for all our shows. Everybody in Galveston can listen in if they like. And tonight lots of them did, and they liked you. A lot."

I kept my smile plastered on my face as I took Sammy by the arm and led him out of Vito's office. "That is really swell. And I'll think about it. What happened to your other singer?"

Vito moaned and shook his head. "Betty. Hard to believe it, but she's dead. God rest her soul." He made the sign of the cross.

"God rest her soul," the two goons repeated and crossed themselves.

"Loved that girl," the taller of the two said.

"Everybody loved Betty," the other one added.

"Betty was a real doll," Vito told me, wiping a few tears from his eyes. "Why somebody would want to kill her, I will never know.

But they'd better hope the police get to them first. Because, if I find them, they'll be really sorry. It won't be pretty." His dark eyes turned sinister once more, and I could tell he was not a man to mess with.

Though I had to wonder how he would react if he ever learned he'd had a Nazi spy operating under his roof.

"I'm so sorry for your loss," I said quietly. "But I'll get my Gramps out of your hair, and I promise we'll keep a better eye on him. Sorry he bothered you."

"Not at all," Vito said.

"Sorry if we roughed you up, old timer," one of the goons said to Sammy.

Sammy blinked a couple of times, like he wasn't sure where he was. "You boys are all right. Always good to have a few Marines like you around. If you see my platoon, be sure to let me know."

"Sure, pal," the other goon said. "We'll do that. You go and enjoy your dessert now."

"You've earned it," Vito added.

I gave them another smile and a nod, before I took Sammy's arm and led him down the hall to the stairs. "Come on now, Gramps. Let's get you back to your seat."

"Nice job, kid," Sammy murmured under his breath as we climbed the stairs.

A few minutes later, we were back at our table. We'd barely returned to our seats when the waiter brought over chocolate cake with raspberry sauce for all.

Nana's eyes went wide. "Did you order this?" she asked Sammy.

"In a way," he said with an eyebrow raised in my direction. "I promise I'll fill in the blanks later."

So we ate our dessert, and Pete and I did a little more dancing. Then we quietly got out of there, after the waiter came by and, with a puzzled look, told us our bill had been taken care of.

"I'll explain later," I said to the group.

Even so, we tipped the waiter very nicely, before we walked out, and stood on the sidewalk near our cars. That's when Sammy explained how I had shown up in the nick of time and "saved him." Both Nana and Pete seemed impressed.

"Do you think they killed Betty?" I quietly asked Sammy.

He folded his arms and leaned against his sedan. "I don't know, kid. I've been wondering the same thing. They were capable of killing her."

I nodded. "They most definitely were. But somehow I find it hard to believe they'd hurt her. Because it sounds like everyone here really liked her."

"I agree," Sammy told me. "When it comes to finding our killer, I'm not sure those boys are a good fit. Sure, they've got a pretty successful gambling operation going on, and they want to keep it quiet. But I get the feeling they don't harm people who don't interfere with their business. In fact, it seems to me they might want to encourage high rollers to spend their hard-earned cash."

I noticed Sammy had grabbed his side and was rubbing his ribs.

I wrinkled my brow in concern. "Are you all right? Do you need medical attention?"

Sammy waved me off. "Nothin' I can't handle. It's not the first time I've taken a punch. But thanks to you riding to my rescue, it didn't go any farther than that."

For some strange reason, his words made me smile. I'd never exactly rescued anyone before, and I had to say, I kind of enjoyed being a heroine. Katie McClue was no stranger to that role, and I could suddenly understand why she constantly risked her life for the sake of others.

Nana slipped her arm through Sammy's. "Don't worry, I'll keep an eye on the guy. If there's any problem, I'll call my doctor."

Sammy rolled his eyes and laughed before we all said our goodnights. "Be sure to check in with me tomorrow, kid," he said to me as he helped Nana into his car.

"You got it," I told him, right before Pete and I headed for his Caddy.

While Sammy and Nana planned to take a drive around the Island before heading home, Pete had to work early in the morning, so we decided to drive back to the city right away.

Pete let out a low whistle once we were both inside his car. "Wow, Tracy. You really are good at this. I am truly impressed." He touched my hand once again, though this time he wrapped his fingers in mine and didn't let go for a few minutes.

"Thanks, Pete."

And from there our conversation came naturally, just like it had on the way down to Galveston. We talked about everything from the Polynesian Room to Nana and Sammy. And, of course, the war. It seemed like we could talk all night and never run out of things to say. The stars were bright in the night sky, and I was pretty sure I could even make out the Milky Way as we drove through the more rural areas between Galveston and Houston. There were very few cars on the road tonight, and it felt like we had the place to ourselves.

We were halfway home when we passed a yard in the country that was full of Christmas decorations and lights. Clearly there was no air raid drill tonight, at least not here, and Uncle Sam being at war certainly hadn't stopped the homeowner from decorating.

Pete slowed the car, turned around, and drove back by the place. Then he parked across the road from the yard and house. He shut the car and headlights off, but kept the key turned in the ignition. Then he fiddled with the knob on the radio and found a station playing Christmas carols.

Pete turned to me and smiled, right before he put his arm around my shoulders and pulled me close to him. I scooted in tight and rested my head on his shoulder, while he leaned his head onto mine. Together we just sat there, enjoying the familiar comfort of the Christmas carols we had known our entire lives, while being mesmerized by all those Christmas decorations. There were trees wrapped with lights, and rafters strung with lights, too. Plus there were big wooden, painted cutouts of Santa and his reindeer in the yard. As well as a Nativity Scene and a little Christmas merry-go-round. Whoever had made all those decorations had gone to a lot of work.

"I don't think I've ever seen so many lights before," I murmured. "Except in the Christmas window at Sears every year."

"Me, either. I can't decide if it's pretty or just one big fire hazard," Pete said with a laugh.

I laughed, too, though the idea of a fire was hardly a laughing matter. Still, there was something so uplifting about the carefree way the people at this house had put on an enormous display for all to enjoy, despite the horrors and changes in our world. I finally felt the Christmas spirit, something that I had been missing, ever since Uncle Sam had joined in the war. And with so many of our generation going off to fight. There would be a lot of empty seats at the table this Christmas.

Of course, hanging onto Pete made me feel so much safer, like the war was nothing but a distant nightmare. It was the first time he'd ever held me like this, and I couldn't remember ever feeling such warmth before. I wished this moment could last a lifetime.

"Kind of puts you in the Christmas mood, doesn't it?" he murmured into my hair.

"It's beautiful," I whispered back.

"So are you, Tracy. But not just beautiful on the outside. You're beautiful on the inside, too. In fact, that's what makes you so beautiful. You're good and kind and caring. And you have so much passion for everything you do."

He gently grasped my chin in his hand and tilted my face up to his. Then he put his lips firmly onto mine, slowly, with the most tender kiss I had ever known. The sensation was almost overwhelming, and went from my lips to my toes and back up again. Time and space stood still as I could have sworn my heart melted right into his.

Just before we heard a sharp "*knock-knock-knock*" on the window. I nearly jumped to the roof of the car.

"You kids having car trouble?" came the voice of a man about my father's age.

We pulled apart to see him standing there with a pipe in his mouth and a smoking jacket on.

Pete waved and rolled down his window. "No, sir, no problem. Just admiring your Christmas lights."

"Glad you enjoy them, sonny," the man chuckled. "But maybe next time you could enjoy them with a different shade of lipstick on."

That's when Pete looked up into the rearview mirror. And sure enough, my red lipstick was now spread all across his lips. He took out his hankie and wiped it off.

"Ummm . . . thank you, sir," Pete said with a laugh. "I believe we'll be going now."

And with that, we said good night to the man while Pete started the engine again. We laughed about it the whole way back to Jayne's apartment, where he walked me to the door, and gave me a quick kiss and a very snug embrace. With a promise to call soon, he left when I was safely into the apartment.

I let Clark Cat in through the window, and listened to his annoyed meows as I got him something to eat.

"Ha! For a change, you're not the only fella in my life," I told him as I petted his head.

He purred and then followed me to bed shortly afterward. For the first time since Betty's murder, I slept in a dreamy, floaty state. The entire night, I relived the sensation of being in Pete's arms, and how safe and happy that had made me feel.

I woke up in an unusually cheerful mood, and started singing as I got ready for the day. I had barely finished getting dressed and tying a ribbon in my hair when Detective Denton knocked on my door.

"It's all yours," he growled. Then he stared at me, rudely, as though he had Superman's x-ray vision and was hoping to read my thoughts somehow.

To throw him off, I leaned my head from side to side. "All mine? I assume you mean the apartment where Betty used to live."

"What else would I mean?" he snarled. "And don't think I haven't got my eye on you still. Especially since I noticed you've dyed your hair to look like the deceased." He jabbed a stubby finger at me, coming from within inches of my chest. "Just because you're not at the top of the heap of suspects, doesn't mean you're not still in the pack somewhere."

This time, I rolled my eyes. "I thought you believed the killer was one of Betty's beaus." But I had barely spoken the words when I remembered that Sammy had garnered lots of valuable information by goading the police on the night of the murder. Maybe this was my chance to do the same.

Especially since it was going to be so easy to get Detective Denton to talk. The man didn't seem to have a shortage of arrogance, and he tended to get carried away when someone challenged his authority.

So I started with mocking laughter. "Wow, you mean you haven't located all Betty's beaus? Especially the one who killed her? It's been days since the murder."

I got just the reaction I was hoping for. He squinted his eyes and chomped on his words. "Let me tell you something, sister. We've interviewed plenty of guys, everyone she dated, as near as we can tell. And believe me, it's a long list. But they've all got alibis. Indisputable alibis. But that's real police work for you. Not the two-bit, phony P.I. kind of work that you and your boss do. Oh, wait a minute . . . I forgot, you're not even a real P.I., are you? You're still an apprentice, right? And you're a woman." With that, he gave me a little snort.

I shook my head and laughed again, to push him a little more. "Oh, come on, Detective, stop trying to act so smart. You probably didn't even check out any girlfriends of these boys, did you? Or, perhaps even some wives? Somebody might have gotten jealous and wanted Betty killed."

Now his face started to turn red. "What do you take us for, idiots? Of course we checked out all the dames. But most of the boys who fell for Betty didn't have girlfriends or wives. All in all, they were a pretty lonely bunch."

And the perfect targets for a bombshell Nazi spy, I thought. With the exception of Bill Marlowe, the engaged man I'd encountered on the front stoop of the building a few nights ago. I wondered if he'd been interviewed by the police, though somehow I doubted it. I also wondered if the police had found the ruby and sapphire brooch that Bill had been looking for.

This time I folded my arms and leaned against the doorframe of Jayne's apartment. "So, you think the killer was one of Betty's boyfriends. But you don't have a shred of evidence on anybody. You boys too busy playing poker down at the station?"

"You keep talking like that and I'll keep Betty's apartment tied up for months," he said in a voice that got louder and louder. "For your information, we've been working day and night on this case. Those of us who are left, anyway. We've got boys in the department going off to fight, just like everybody else. But you mark my word, the killer was a jilted lover. I can feel it in my gut." Whereby he pointed to his substantial middle.

Then he turned and stomped away. All the while, I just shook my head. Because I knew a jilted lover hadn't murdered Betty. That's because she didn't *have* any jilted lovers. As a spy, she wanted to keep all those boys on the line. And she'd figured out a fantastic way to do just that.

Though honestly, much as I wanted to, I couldn't fault Detective

Denton. I knew he was right — the police were short-handed just like everybody else was starting to be. Men were going off to war, and maybe that's why it was even more important for a girl like me to step into a role usually held by a man.

And if I wanted to do a good job as a detective, I needed to finally step into Betty's apartment and see if I could find any clues left behind. So I grabbed Jayne's keys, along with a mop and bucket and other cleaning supplies. Then I walked across the hall and unlocked the door.

I fought my every instinct to call out her name, much like I had on the night she'd been murdered. I left the door open as I ventured farther inside, down the little hallway to her living room, right after I found a light switch. I couldn't remember ever being so jumpy in my life. To be honest, I didn't really believe in ghosts, but I half expected to see Betty's silhouette appear at any moment.

I stepped carefully, slowly, moving deeper and deeper into the apartment. By now I could see the stunning mahogany paneling on the wall, and then her couch, right next to the spot where she had died. The blood was dried up and caked now, as obviously the police hadn't cleaned a thing.

In fact, the apartment didn't really look all that different from the night when I'd found Betty's body. Yet as far as I was concerned, any way you looked at it, blood was blood, whether it was wet or dried. And the sight of it made me feel like I'd suddenly been dunked into cold water. Especially when images from scary movies popped into my mind, and for some reason, thoughts of a skeletal hand reaching out of a grave flooded my imagination. All the while, I moved farther and farther into the apartment.

That was, until I heard a scratching sound. I froze mid-step, right up until the moment when something touched my leg. Then I went straight into the air, in a silent scream, just sure the hand of Betty's spirit had reached up to grab me.

CHAPTER 25

Cleanup and Clues

Of course, my apparition turned out to be none other than Clark Cat. I'd let him outside through the window earlier, but he must have found his way back into the building when some of the tenants took off for work this morning.

I *thunked* my hand to my chest, hoping I really wasn't having a heart attack, considering the way my heart was practically pounding against my ribcage.

Clark rubbed up against my legs and I leaned down to pet him. Honestly, at that moment I didn't know whether to be angry that he'd scared me so badly or just happy because it was only him. He gave my hand a rub and then jumped up on the piano and made himself at home. Like it was a spot where he always sat.

Funny, but now that I'd almost died of fright, I felt a whole lot less scared. And I dove in and got to work right away. Within an hour, I had the floor cleaned up and Betty's meager kitchen things packed into a box. I was surprised by how few things she really had. It was more like she was a person living in a hotel room, rather than an apartment. I was also surprised by how perfectly clean she'd kept the entire place. There wasn't an ounce of dust or speck of dirt anywhere.

From the kitchen, I strode past the paneled wall of the living room and into her bedroom. I found a couple of suitcases in the closet, and easily packed up her clothes. Most of her attire seemed to be geared toward nightclub wear, and probably for her singing act. She didn't have much in the way of regular day dresses.

Next I moved onto the vanity and her jewel case. Or rather, I should say, jewel cases. For a girl who didn't have much, she certainly had a lot of jewelry. And just like I'd suspected, it was all Eisenberg. Gorgeous stuff. It looked as close to real as any costume jewelry could.

Yet amazingly, the brooch that Bill Marlowe had described wasn't there. Had his story about the two brooches been nothing but a tall tale? If so, he'd certainly come up with an awfully elaborate description to hide his real intentions. Whatever they may have been.

I put some tissues in the jewel cases to hold everything in place. Then I closed them up and stacked them next to the suitcases. I went back to the living room to continue packing, and that's when I realized there wasn't much of anything in the room that seemed to belong to Betty. No pictures of family or friends. No art objects or paintings on the wall. There was really nothing personal about the place at all. Except for Clark Cat, Betty's pet, who watched me from atop the piano while I headed for her desk.

Almost immediately, I was bowled over by the way she had everything organized and stacked. Her efficiency and orderliness were perfection itself. On the left side, she had a stack of letters in the same handwriting on the same stationery, which appeared to be letters that she'd written. On the right side, she had letters that she'd obviously received, that were pierced and stacked on a spike receipt holder. When I examined each of those letters a little closer, I could see she'd actually circled certain words and phrases in each one.

Words and phrases that could possibly be hints and clues about departure times and shipping locations. Though the wording in the letters weren't out-and-out obvious, if a person read between the lines, they might pick up on a few things. And one thing I could see for sure — Betty certainly had the ability to read between the lines.

"So she'd been perusing each of these letters to garner any information she could," I said just under my breath.

Anger welled in my throat as I thought of how she'd most likely used that very information to get our boys killed. It was amazing how deadly one woman could be.

Now I had to wonder, were there more "Bettys" out there in the city? Maybe even around the country?

I took some deep breaths and turned to the stack of letters on the left. The letters she'd been writing. I flipped through them quickly and I soon realized — every single letter had almost the exact same words. They were nearly identical, and the names were the main difference between them all. When it came to writing letters, this girl practically had a production line. They were all scripted on the same pale violet stationery, and probably spritzed with the vanilla perfume in the atomizer bottle sitting between the two stacks. It smelled like the same perfume she'd been wearing on the train the first time I saw her.

But more importantly, the letters all contained what might be considered leading questions. Things like, when will I hear from you again? And, how soon till you ship out? Or, do you know when you'll be back in the country again? Not to mention, my personal favorite, what kind of accommodations do you have? Meaning, she might get her fiancés to mention whether they were on a ship in port or still living on land somewhere.

Yet the worst part about it all was the idea that these boys were giving away this information innocently, thinking the things they were writing were harmless. They were only revealing meaningless tidbits to a woman they believed they would marry one day.

I shook my head, becoming more and more amazed at Betty's "system." But now the question remained — what did she do with the information she gathered? Obviously, she must have passed it along somehow.

But how?

And how did she keep track of everything? Surely she didn't have it all committed to memory. There would have been too much to remember. Was it possible she kept files somewhere? If so, where? I checked the drawers of her desk, but I found nothing but writing supplies.

Disappointed, I put everything from her desk into another box. Once I had her desk cleared out, I pulled out drawers and looked under them, just in case she'd hidden something there. But clearly she'd been much too smart to hide something in so obvious a place.

I paused for a minute and thought of some of the Katie McClue novels I'd read. In her books, the bad guys often hid things under a loose floorboard. Could Betty have done the same? I jumped up and started stomping around the room, listening for a board that might squeak or feel loose. But after a few minutes of searching, I found nothing. Absolutely nothing.

Then I tried looking in the piano, inside and out. From top to bottom. And all I found was a collection of sheet music, of mostly popular songs. But there was also some music that appeared to have been written by Betty herself.

All the while, Clark Cat moved over to the piano bench and purred at me as I kept on looking. Finally, I sat beside him and hit a few keys. Right at that moment, I truly wished Clark could talk. Because he'd been a witness to everything, and he would have known more about Betty's clandestine practices than anyone.

But since Clark wasn't talking, I left him when I heard Artie at the front door. I let him in and he saluted me as always.

"You're a good soldier to fill in for your friend like this," he told me. "How long do you think she'll be away?"

I smiled at him as I took his arm and walked him down the hall. "As long as she likes. Once Tom ships out, she may not see him for a long, long time."

He nodded somberly. "That is, if she ever *does* see him again. These Germans are a lousy bunch, killing people right and left. Sure wish I was in there fighting against those Nazis. To save some of these young fellas so they can come home to their wives and kids. Especially with all these 'citizen soldiers' signing up faster than the recruiters can get them in. Lots of these men are giving up good jobs to go off to fight. They're risking everything they've got in the name of freedom. What I wouldn't give to be one of 'em. Oh, how I'd love to wear the uniform again."

I smiled at him. "I'll bet you were quite the soldier."

He straightened his back. "I was, and I still could be. I'd blast those Nazis from here to breakfast. Once you become a soldier, you never forget it."

"I've heard talk about women enlisting, too. In their own branches of the Services."

"Some of 'em are Army Nurses," he told me. "They'll be needing a bunch of them now. Navy nurses, too. And don't think for a minute that those nurses aren't in danger, just like the rest of the soldiers."

"They're a brave bunch," I said quietly.

Suddenly I thought about enlisting myself. But I didn't have an ounce of training to be a nurse, and I'd already agreed to work for Sammy. In a strange way, I relished the chance to be a career woman for a while. Not to mention, a full-fledged, licensed private investigator someday.

Of course, figuring out where Betty might have hidden any information she'd gathered would have been a definite career boost.

I was still thinking about it when I opened up the wall of mailboxes for Artie. And that's when it hit me. Like a lightning bolt. Suddenly I knew exactly where Betty's hiding place might be. And I could hardly wait to get back to her apartment to check it out for sure. So even though Artie must have thought I was being incredibly rude, I finished sorting the mail in a hurry and practically ushered him out the door with a quick salute. Then I returned to Betty's apartment and went straight to the paneled wall in the living room.

Right away, I started pounding on the paneling, and I heard the same "*thunk-thunk-thunk*" as my fist hit the wood while I moved along the wall. Pretty soon I was starting to think I'd been wrong and that this would prove to be nothing but another dead end. But I wasn't going to give up until I had checked the entire wall. So I kept on pounding that paneling as I inched my way from one side to the other. I was two-thirds of the way through when I heard it — a change in the tone as I hit my fist against the wood.

And I knew I had found what I was looking for — a hollow spot.

I started to push on a square section of the paneling, until I felt it move. Seconds later, I managed to slide it out of the way. And that's when I found them. Carefully stacked inside a hidden, hollowed-out compartment. Files and files on various men. Probably all the guys she was supposedly engaged to. When I looked through them, I could hardly believe all the information Betty had gotten on each one. She'd even included what jewelry each man had given her.

Standing on its side next to the files was a notebook full of words and phrases that looked familiar. After I perused them for a moment, I finally understood why. They were a collection of the hints and tidbits that Betty had picked up from the various letters she'd gotten. Plus there were more phrases that I hadn't seen in the letters. I guessed that was probably information she'd gotten from some of her guys face-to-face. Especially after a night of drinking and gambling.

So again I had to ask, what had she done with this information? She must have passed it along somehow. But how? And to whom?

I put the notebook and the files into the same box where I'd packed all the things from her desk. Then I checked the hollowed out hiding place one last time. Something sharp stuck my finger, and for a moment, I thought I'd been bitten by a spider. But I used the edge of a file to be sure, and much to my amazement, instead of a big bug, I managed to push out a small object wrapped in tissue, one that must have been shoved into the corner. I immediately unwrapped it and almost had to laugh. It was the brooch that Bill Marlowe had described. Or, at least, what was left of the brooch. It must have been a real stunner at one time, and probably very expensive. That was, until some of the stones had been removed. Judging from the design of the piece, I'm guessing those very stones were probably the largest.

And the most valuable.

Betty must have pulled them out and cashed them in. Maybe she needed money to continue her spy operation. Or maybe she just wanted some cash. Whatever her reason, she sure didn't waste any time. And Bill was not going to be happy when he saw what she'd done. I rewrapped it and dropped it into my pocket.

Funny how I'd learned so much about Betty, yet there was one vital piece to the puzzle that was still missing.

I glanced over at the black cat who was still sitting on the piano bench. "So tell me, Clark Cat, how did your old owner pass along her information?"

And as if he understood what I'd said, he meowed to me, stood up, and made his way to the piano keys. He gingerly walked across them.

"That's not much of an answer," I told him.

Then I remembered one of Katie McClue's episodes that involved an exceptionally intelligent cat, *The Case of the Crime-Solving Cat.* The cat in the story was always leading Katie toward the right clue at the right time. If only I could get my new pal, Clark, to do the same.

But I didn't even get a chance to try, since I heard someone knocking at the front door. I went to answer it, and much to my surprise, I found my father standing on the front stoop.

I noticed he wasn't exactly smiling. "Have you had lunch?" he asked as I opened the door for him. He held up a large brown paper bag.

"Not yet," I answered.

"Maddie made us some sandwiches," he told me matter-of-factly.

Though my father was usually a down-to-business kind of guy, he seemed a little more stoic today than usual. Upset even. I could only guess that it had something to do with my mother. And the way she had treated me the night of the country club Christmas dance.

"Just a minute," I told him as I led him down the hallway. "Let me shut up this other apartment."

I glanced inside Betty's place and saw Clark Cat still sitting on the piano. Apparently he was right at home and wasn't going anywhere. So I pulled the door closed while I took my father over to Jayne's apartment.

"Your hair," my father said. "You changed the color."

I swiped at the strands that hung over my eyes. "I did. Do you like it?"

"It's pretty," he answered in a cautious way. "But to tell you the truth, I always thought your natural color was pretty. It's the same color that your grandmother's hair once was. In any case, you look like you've been working," he added with a smile.

"I have." And while I grabbed plates, napkins and utensils, I told him how I'd been cleaning up Betty's old apartment since her murder. That led into the story about how I found her and then became an Apprentice P.I. At first I wasn't sure how he'd take it. After all, I'd essentially been raised to be nothing but a socialite who would one day marry a rich man and host tons of parties to help boost my husband's career. And working as an Apprentice P.I., not to mention all the other things I'd been up to, probably wasn't in keeping with being a good blue-blooded daughter.

But to my amazement, my father beamed at me. "Your grandmother told me about your new employment, Tracy. And I have to say, I'm proud of you. Very proud. I think it's very industrious and innovative of you. You know, my father had that same side to him, and I think that's where you got it. He made a lot of money by using his brains as an inventor, and then working very, very hard to see that invention come to fruition. My mother worked very hard, too. We weren't always on easy street, you know."

Pride swelled up in my throat. I liked having my father compare me to Gramps. And, telling me he was proud of me.

I poured us each a glass of sweet tea. "I know you weren't always wealthy. But there's nothing wrong with hard work. I'm finding there's something very satisfying about working for my own paycheck."

He pulled ham sandwiches from the bag, along with a bowl of potato salad and a jar of homemade pickles. All in all, it was a feast of a lunch.

"I apologize for not being there during your ordeal with the police," he told me as we started divvying up the food. "I didn't hear about it until after the fact. From your grandmother. Otherwise I would have been there, too. I'm still pretty annoyed that your mother and Michael didn't say a word to me, and still haven't. Of course, I know you are innocent, and you wouldn't hurt a fly. But you're not under suspicion any longer, are you? Do you need any *real* legal help?"

"Nope," I said, right before I bit into my sandwich. "Instead, my new boss, Sammy, and I are hot on the trail of the person or persons who killed Betty."

This brought a frown to his face. "That doesn't exactly sound safe. Do you need one of my guns?"

"Well," I started. "That would be nice. I'll get one from you later."

"I have a pearl-handled revolver that would work well for you. If you're going to be a private investigator someday, you're going to need it." He took a huge bite out of his own sandwich.

He was right, of course. Though I hoped I'd never have to use it. Still, a girl couldn't be too careful.

He took a gulp of the tea and then cleared his throat. "That brings me to the reason for my visit. Other than to see you." He smiled quickly before continuing. "As you know, your mother is not well. I understand she even got violent toward you the other night, and as far as I'm concerned, that's the last straw when it comes to her behavior. You and I both know she hasn't been well for a long time, Tracy. And since she's come to realize that you and Michael will not be getting married, in the last two days, she's taken to her bed and refused to get up. Of course, she's also been drinking most of that time."

I sighed. "I didn't mean to cause any trouble by not marrying Michael. But honestly, I couldn't go through with it. We weren't in love. We had nothing in common. And we certainly weren't right for each other. We both knew it."

He nodded. "Yes, yes, my dear daughter. I understand. And you're right. Personally, I'm quite relieved that you and Michael have broken it off. The more I got to know him, the more I didn't care for him. And well, after my marriage didn't turn out like I thought it would, I wouldn't wish that kind of misery on anyone."

I touched his arm. "Father, I am so sorry."

He heaved a huge sigh. "Nonetheless, I believe I have no choice but to commit your mother to a hospital. I've discussed it with her doctor, and he's currently looking for a place where she might receive the proper treatment. He knew of a few places that treated people with alcohol problems. It sounded like a good idea to me, though I'm terribly concerned about how your mother will react to the news."

To be honest, I had to wonder how she'd react myself. Somehow I envisioned another huge, Scarlett O'Hara temper tantrum on her part. Maybe even more lashing out at people.

But I didn't want to discourage my father. "Well . . . that does sound promising," I murmured. "It would be nice if she got some help."

"The doctor said she could be gone a long time," he continued. "And that brings me to what I have to ask you."

Suddenly my stomach felt like it had dropped on a roller coaster ride. Just the thought of having to deal with my abusive mother right now made me sick. I sincerely hoped he wasn't going to ask me to come home and battle things out with her, to get her to go to a hospital. Because I had a very good idea that I'd be on the losing end of that one. I put my hand to my swollen cheek, remembering her slap on my face all over again.

He took a deep breath and looked me in the eye, the same look he always gave me when he was not about to mince words. "Tracy, I'm going to be gone quite a bit myself."

"Oh?" I felt my eyes go wide. "Were you accepted into the Navy as a subchaser?"

He shook his head. "Regrettably, no. I wasn't. I went to New Orleans with my cohorts, and while they got in, I was the only one who was turned away."

"Oh, Father . . ."

He gave me a small smile. "It was quite the humiliation, for a man who's been in the position of running a company for a long time. Albeit, my father's company. Worst of all, my chums spent the whole day trying to cheer me up. So I became a charity case."

Something I knew he would hate. "Did they give you a reason why they wouldn't accept you?" I grabbed a forkful of potato salad.

He was already nodding. "Yes, they did. They consider my position and company to be essential. Meaning, they're too important to the war effort already. So the government refused to let me leave my company and go off and fight."

I beamed at him. "Well, that's nothing to feel humiliated about."

He gave me a half smile. "It's not what I had in mind, but I understood what they were saying. This war will be fought on many different levels, and what we do stateside will be every bit as important as the things that will be done overseas. Supplying enough petroleum to win this war is going to be vital, and since Texas is rich in oil, our state will be playing a very significant role. And so will I."

I took a sip of my tea. "I've heard about how important oil is to this war. But what exactly will you be doing?"

"What I'm going to tell you is something that I want you to keep confidential. I've been contacted by Harold Ickes himself, the Petroleum Coordinator for War. He wants me to be a consultant. And I have agreed. So I'll be doing some work for the government and spending quite a bit of time in Washington, D.C."

"That's fantastic. You'll be an important part of this war effort after all."

He took another bite of his sandwich and nodded. "While I may not be out there fighting on the front lines with my friends, it's nice to know that I still have a purpose, and that I will still be useful. I can help fight this war, only in a different way."

"I'm very happy for you," I said just before I finished up my sandwich.

"Which brings me again to what I wanted to ask you," he said as he cleaned up his own plate. "This role also means I'll be traveling back and forth quite a bit. And since I'll be gone so much and your mother will most likely be in the hospital, I was wondering if you'd be willing to move back home. Just to be there for your grandmother. I know the two of you are very close. And though I think Benjamin will be an excellent lawyer some day, he just isn't as sensitive and thoughtful to her as you are."

The idea of being under the same roof as Nana again made me smile. "As long as I'm safe there, without my mother trying to hit me, I'd be happy to move back. To be there for Nana. And . . ." I added, "as soon as Jayne doesn't need me to fill in for her anymore. But you must understand, I have no intention of quitting my job."

He put his hand on my shoulder. "I wouldn't dream of asking you to quit. I want you to stay in your job."

With that, we drank the last of our tea and cleaned up the lunch things. I had mixed emotions about going home again. Though one thing was for sure, with the housing crisis that was going on in Houston right now, if I wanted to be out on my own, I'd have a hard time finding a place to live after Jayne got back. The only place that I knew would soon be available was the apartment across the hall. And there was no way I was about to stay in the apartment where Betty had once lived.

And died.

I walked my father to the door. "I still can't believe the world is in such a mess. I don't remember the Great War, since I was born the year before it ended."

He nodded. "I know. My own father served then, but I didn't. Not with a wife and two young children."

"Now here we are. History repeating itself. New dictators trying to take over the world again."

My father pulled the door open. "Hitler should have been stopped in his tracks. If it weren't for that huge display at the 1936 Olympics, he probably would have been."

I shook my head. "He put on quite a display, didn't he? Then suddenly people thought the Nazis might not be so bad after all."

"But the Nazis were merely lying and deceiving the world," my father said with a sigh. "It's the same old song and dance routine for all these ruthless fascists. And a lot of people die because of it."

After that, we said our goodbyes. I had to say, it was good to see my father again. And it was good to sort of clear the air, in a way. If only things were that easy when it came to my mother. Maybe she would get the help that she needed. And maybe she would turn into a nice mother after all. Yet even if she did, there was a lot of water under the bridge, where the two of us were concerned. I had never been the daughter that she wanted, and she'd let me know that early on. And much as I wanted to feel hopeful that she might be willing to get some help, a little voice inside me said that she would never agree. Even if my father actually tried to have her committed, she would never let that happen. Her own family had too many lawyers who could easily put a stop to the whole thing.

I walked back to Betty's apartment and sighed. "Like my father said, 'It's the same old song and dance routine.'"

And with those words, I stopped dead in my tracks. I suddenly had an idea of how Betty had been passing along her information.

I pushed the door to her apartment open. Clark Cat was still sitting on the piano, clearly annoyed, as though he had been waiting for me.

I stared at that baby grand and my jaw dropped open.

Could it be?

CHAPTER 26

Notebook Clues and Nasty Nazis

Back inside Betty's apartment, I made a beeline for the notebook where she'd compiled all the notes and tidbits she'd taken from the many letters she'd received. Thankfully she'd kept her notes in English, probably to make it easier for her to pass her information along in English as well. So things wouldn't get lost in translation and so nobody would suspect her if her wording came out a little odd.

With notebook in hand, I went straight to the piano and sat next to Clark on the bench. He gave me another annoyed meow, as though letting me know he was every bit as good a crime solver as any cat in any Katie McClue novel.

"I'm sorry I didn't realize where you were trying to lead me," I told him and gave him a quick kiss on top of his head.

Then I started thumbing through the sheet music on her piano, until I found what I was looking for — some of Betty's own compositions. I found two. The first was on top of the stack, and appeared to be a song that she was working on and hadn't finished yet. She was probably still composing it right before she was killed.

I found the second song in the middle of her stack of music. In fact, it was in a folder that was shoved into a larger book of songs. I could only guess she must have stashed it there in a hurry, because it was at an odd angle, rather than being neatly placed like most of Betty's things. The folder included a finished song, as well as arrangements for the entire band. I had to say, Betty certainly was a talented girl. It took a lot to write the lyrics and come up with the parts for the whole orchestra, so that everything fit together and harmonized. Then again, judging from some of the other music she had around, I wondered if she had very cleverly copied bits and pieces here and there.

I put the pages from this second song onto the music holder and tapped it out on the piano. Though I'm not much of a pianist, it was enough for me to sing the lyrics of this piece she had titled, "Saying So Long."

"Oh, how I long for you, every night at nine, the time we used to dine . . . How I wish I'd catch a sight, of the one I hold so dear, on a Friday night near the dock in Boston. Just know that you're my only love, my one and only love, at midnight and every night . . . "

When I finished singing the entire song, I had to laugh. While the melody was beautiful and just a little bit familiar, the lyrics were, well, what you might call . . . unusual.

And I had a pretty good idea why. I started perusing Betty's notebook until I found some phrases and words that matched up with some of the things in her song. I not only found "Boston," but I also found mention of "nine o'clock," and "midnight." While I didn't completely understand how it all added up, I had a good idea what was going on. Betty was transmitting her information via her songs.

Which meant it was also being transmitted all across the island of Galveston, via the remote radio broadcast set up at the Polynesian Room. That meant anyone within hearing distance could have picked it up. So whoever her contact or contacts were, they didn't even have to be in the same room when she sang out this information.

"Quite the clever girl," I murmured to Clark Cat.

I grabbed the music and the notebook, and put it into the box where I'd packed up the files. Then I grabbed the box, called to Clark, and left Betty's apartment once I was sure he'd followed me out. He stood next to me in the hallway while I locked the door to Betty's apartment. Clearly, he was a cat on the case by now.

He kept following me to Jayne's place, where I gave him a few pieces of ham that I'd saved from lunch, before letting him out the window. For a second or two, I was a little stunned to find the window unlocked. It left me feeling uneasy, though I was pretty sure I must have been the one who had unlocked it. And forgotten to lock it up again. Probably when I'd let Clark out first thing in the morning. I watched the cat dash off into the bushes and vowed to keep the window locked from this moment on.

And I made sure I locked it this time, too.

Then I went straight to the phone and dialed Sammy. After talking to Mildred for a minute, I filled Sammy in on everything I'd learned at Betty's apartment. Especially my discovery of how she'd been transmitting her information.

He chuckled across the line and gave me a "Good job, kid. Like I always say, 'You're a natural.'"

Yet no matter how many times he said it, those words always hit home, and they made me feel pretty good.

Good enough to offer to drive to the Bund meeting this evening. Sammy liked the idea, saying it would free him up to defend us. If necessary. I assumed that defense might involve a firearm of some kind, though I couldn't be sure. In any case, I agreed to pull up in front of the building at six, to pick up both Sammy and Mildred. Then, after we discussed our plans for the evening a little more, I got off the phone and headed straight for the tub. After all, I'd been cleaning the entire morning and I needed to be shiny and clean myself in order to play my part tonight.

Once I was out and dried off, I headed for my suitcase. For my next amazing feat, I had to figure out what to wear. I was supposed to be in the role of a dutiful German daughter who'd been raised in America. That meant I should probably wear something less ostentatious and more practical. However, I was also supposed to convince them to let me take Betty's place as a singer at the Polynesian Room. And that type of role called for a dress that was more showy and alluring.

After going through every dress in my entire suitcase, I was ready to spout off that very phrase that women say so often: "I don't have a thing to wear." That was, until I remembered some dresses that were right across the hall from me.

Much as I hated the idea of wearing a dress that had belonged to a German spy, well, there was a war going on and I didn't have the luxury of being squeamish. So I ran back across the hall, grabbed Betty's suitcases and brought them over to Jayne's. After trying on a couple of dresses, I settled for a long, blue dinner dress embellished with a single strand of sequins, sewn into flower designs on each side of the bodice, near the shoulders. Not only was it the smaller of her dresses and a better fit for me, but I even borrowed a pair of Betty's gloves and some of her jewels. I finished by putting my hair back with combs and applying a nice coat of red lipstick.

Then I ran to Jayne's full-length mirror for a thorough inspection. The instant I saw the image staring back at me, I let out a little shriek. Because I looked a whole lot more like Betty than I cared for, and just the mere sight of myself made me jumpy.

Especially when I heard a scratching noise at the window. But this time I knew it was only Clark Cat, wanting to come back inside. So I let him in. Right away I noticed his tummy looked pretty round and full, so I assumed he'd caught a mouse or a bird somewhere. I gave him a bowl of water, and he had a good drink before dragging himself over to one of the chairs in Jayne's living room. Apparently ready for a nice, long nap.

Just as I was ready for a nice, long undercover assignment, by playing Mildred and Sammy's daughter, one who wanted to sing in Betty's place. My name was supposed to be Greta, and our family's last name was supposed to be Reynolds. I only hoped I could be convincing in my role.

I grabbed my wrap and my purse, and the keys to the Packard. I tucked my driver's license into my brassiere, since Sammy had instructed me to hide it. In fact, we were all supposed to hide any kind of identification.

Finally, I stepped into the hallway and nearly ran right into Karl.

"How are you this evening?" I asked him as I pulled the apartment door shut and locked it.

"Fine. I am fine," he said with a frown. "But you? Where are you going tonight? In that dress? It looks like the one that girl used to wear. The girl that was murdered."

Well, wasn't that just swell? I'd barely borrowed the dress of a dead girl and somebody had already recognized it. That didn't take long.

Even so, it wasn't exactly the kind of thing I wanted to admit to. So I merely gave Karl my nicest smile. "Oh, this old thing? I've had it for a while. You know, a lot of dresses look alike."

But he was already shaking his head. "No, I know that dress. I saw that girl wearing it many times. And you changed your hair to look like her, didn't you?"

"Well, yes, it's for a case I'm working on," I started to say.

But he wasn't going to let me finish. "You're taking the place of the one they killed. You're working with them, aren't you? You're one of them!"

I put my hands up like the hero in a Western, showing that I was unarmed. "No, Karl. I'm an American and have nothing to do with the Nazis. I'm trying to stop them. Truly, I am. This is all part of my cover, and I really can't tell you any more."

Karl started to back away, taking slow steps. "You're working with Helmut, aren't you? Everything I told you the other night . . . you've already told him what I said, haven't you? I thought I could trust you!"

I shook my head. "No, Karl, you've got it wrong. You're safe here."

By now the older gentleman was starting to shake. "I see it all now. You and your partner wanted information about those meetings because you wanted to go to one. So you could join them. And so you could pull me into it, too. Helmut will stop at nothing! He'll either force me to join up or he'll kill me."

Which, I knew, was the way the Nazis operated. In Germany, anyway. But Karl was on American soil.

So I tried again to reassure him. "No, Karl, I'm not working with Helmut."

But no matter what I said, I couldn't seem to get through to the elderly gentleman. He had deemed me to be one of the enemy, and his mind was closed off to anything else. Before I could say another word, he stormed out the front door and took off for who knew where.

All I could do was stand there with my mouth hanging open.

How would I ever convince him that I was on his side, the side of the Allies? The poor man was so terrified he was becoming paranoid.

But it was something I would have to deal with later. Because I was due to pick up Sammy and Mildred outside our office building. So I jumped in the Packard and headed straight downtown. As promised, the two were outside waiting by the curb for me.

Sammy got into the front passenger side and Mildred took the backseat. Then I headed for Clinton Drive, to take us toward the Houston Ship Channel. And the address Mildred had been given by the Bund. It was already getting dark, and I was thankful for the bright headlamps on the Packard.

Along the way, Sammy talked to us about playing our roles. "Keep it low key and simple, ladies. Don't offer up too much information, because sometimes you can talk yourself into a corner. Once you give them some song and dance, you've got to remember the whole story."

"Got it," I told Sammy.

"Me, too," Mildred piped up before she read the address aloud again.

I took a few more turns and found the place where we were supposed to go. Or rather, the address we'd been given. But instead of a building or a meeting place, there was nothing there but an empty lot. So I pulled over to the side of the road and put the car in neutral. I set the brake, but kept my foot on the clutch, and I didn't kill the engine.

"I don't like this, ladies," Sammy said quietly. "But let's keep calm. Either they sent us on a wild goose chase, or it could be a trap. Or they gave us a phony address so they could keep their real address under their hats. It's very possible they plan to blindfold us and drive us to the real meeting place. One they want to keep secret."

But the mere idea of being blindfolded by a bunch of Nazis made my skin crawl. Even if we were only going along with it to learn more about the Bund. And Betty's murder. Katie McClue had gone through something similar once when she went undercover and tried to locate the secret den of some bank robbers in the *Case of the Hidden Hideout*. The only way they would take her to their liar was to put a sack over her head so she couldn't see where she was going.

But through a series of calculations, she'd figured out exactly where they'd gone. Later, after she led the police to that hideout, the whole gang went to jail. Katie, of course, hadn't so much as broken a sweat when she faced such a dangerous situation.

But Katie McClue wasn't dealing with Nazis.

"What should we do?" I asked Sammy.

Mildred had a tremor in her voice when she spoke up from the backseat. "I'm sorry, Sammy, but I don't think I could let them blindfold me. Tonight I thought we were going to a meeting, of our own free will. Free to come and go as we please." She drew in a ragged breath. "But to be under their control, well, that is different. Even for a short time. Who knows if they'd really be taking us to a meeting? You don't know what these people can do. I already escaped them once."

"That settles it, then," Sammy announced. "Let's not wait around to see what happens. We'll find their meeting place some other way. Let's head back to the office and call it a night."

"Sounds good to me," I said in my most cheerful voice, hoping to calm Mildred. "At least we had a nice drive."

I had to say, I could certainly understand Mildred's feelings. Or, at least, I thought I could. But I'd never been forced to escape my own country and a murderous government before. And while I knew she'd bravely volunteered to come tonight, everything changed the minute we saw that empty lot. To be honest, going back suited me just fine, too. While I knew that being a P.I. called for courage, the idea of running into Fifth Column folks on a dark road was using up my quota for the day.

I released the parking brake, put one foot on the clutch and the other on the floor brake. Then I put the car in gear and started to turn back onto the road. That's when I spotted two dark cars suddenly approaching us from behind. I probably hadn't seen them earlier since they were driving along at a pretty good clip with their headlamps off. I had to say, it was a dangerous thing to do on a dark night like tonight. I only hoped they would spot the Packard before they hit us.

Though I couldn't say I was all that relieved when, seconds later, one car pulled in front of us and the second pulled in behind. Two men in dark suits and dark hats jumped out from each vehicle. From the Packard's lights, I could see they were carrying burlap feed sacks. And pistols.

They strode up to our car so fast that I barely had time to react. Suddenly I wished I'd gotten that gun from my father, instead of waiting another day.

"Looks like the party is about to start," Sammy muttered. "Whether we like it or not. Have this bucket ready to roll, okay, kid?"

"Ready," I mumbled as I gave him a slight nod.

He quietly pulled his own revolver from its holster. Then he cocked it and hid his hand near his knee before he rolled the window down with his other hand.

Two men approached on my side of the car; one stood next to Mildred's window and the other one stood next to mine. Then the other two stopped right beside Sammy's door.

Sammy tipped his hat. "Evening, gentlemen. We were just out for a little drive. Beautiful night, isn't it?"

"Come with us," one of the men on Sammy's side of the car said with a thick accent, as he held up his burlap bag.

The man beside my door made a circling motion, indicating that he wanted me to roll down the window. I gave him a little smile and did so. All the while, I kept my feet firmly planted on the clutch and the brake.

"Good evening," I said as sweetly as I could.

The man held up a sack for me, too. "You will come with us. One of our men will take your automobile."

I gave him my best look of surprise. "But we haven't even been properly introduced. I would never go running off with a strange man. My Mom and Pop here would never hear of it."

I tried to get a good look at the man's face, but with his hat pulled low over his forehead and the darkness outside, his features were hidden in shadow.

Behind me, I heard Mildred push the lock down on her door. Then I heard her window come down slightly. She said something in German, and the man beside her door responded in an angry tone and an even thicker accent. Though I didn't speak the language, Mildred's tone told me she'd just tried to give the man the brush-off.

"Don't waste any more time," the man with the sack next to

Sammy's window hollered into the car.

I saw Sammy wave him off, only seconds before I spotted the beam of a flashlight in my side mirror. It appeared that another man had gotten out of the car behind us and was headed our way. Seconds later, he was next to Sammy's door and shining the flashlight right into his face. This new man didn't even bother to hide his identity.

It was Helmut.

Chills were running Olympic time trials up and down my spine. Especially when he shined the flashlight right at me.

He let out a little laugh, the same kind of laugh that evil villains in horror movies always laugh. "So, who do we have here? A lovely little family wanting to join the Bund, eh? Too bad you won't be going to the meeting. Because we already know who you are. Sammy Falcone, Private Investigator, and his new apprentice, who just happens to live across the hall from where Fraulein Hoffman lived. And look at that — she's even wearing the Fraulein's dress. One that we supplied for her."

While we all sat silently, Helmut now turned the flashlight to the backseat. "And, now who do we have? Why, I believe it's Mr. Falcone's secretary. Mildred Paninsky, citizen of Germany."

"I'm sorry, but I don't know who you're talking about," Mildred shouted to him. "My name is Ingrid. Ingrid Reynolds. This is my husband and daughter."

To which Helmut merely laughed again. "I'm afraid not. Because we have a complete dossier on you, Mildred Paninsky. Particularly since you escaped with some very valuable artwork. Some the Führer would like back."

"Those belonged to my family. They never belonged to the Third Reich!" Mildred now screamed.

"Easy there, Mildred," Sammy said under his breath.

Then Helmut pulled out a gun and aimed it first at Sammy, then at me, and finally at Mildred. "We'll find out when we get you all back to Germany. Don't expect to be treated well, as enemies of the Reich."

Sammy chuckled like the whole thing was nothing but a big joke. "Sorry, pal, but you happen to be on U.S. soil. I hate to break it to you, but you're a long, long way from Germany. And if anybody is an enemy of anybody else, well, it's you, buddy."

Helmut clenched his teeth. "Ah, you Americans. Always so superior. But I assure you, you'll come to regret that statement. Right after we get whatever information we need and want from you first. Then, if there's anything left of you, we'll put you in a concentration camp. We've got a boat waiting for us at the dock. It will take you out to a U-boat in the Gulf. And I assure you, it will not be a pleasant trip."

By now I was so chilled I felt like I'd been dunked in ice water. How was it possible that we were being kidnapped right here in America? In the Great State of Texas, even? Soon to be transported a world away. How could any of this be happening? If these Nazis got away with their plan, no one would ever know what happened to us. I would never see Nana, or Pete, or Jayne, or any of my family or friends again. I couldn't envision a more horrible fate.

Now the man on my side of the Packard reached for me, and I heard Mildred scream in the backseat.

Of all the things I thought might happen tonight, being kidnapped and shipped to Germany was a nightmare that I could have never imagined.

CHAPTER 27

Fast Cars and Bad Guys

Tears pricked at my eyes while the man beside me grabbed my left hand and brought the burlap sack closer to my head. Behind me, I could hear Mildred yelling and putting up a fuss as the second man reached in through my window to unlock her door. I couldn't see what Sammy was doing. But there was one thing I did know — I was not going to be kidnapped by a bunch of Nazis. Especially not on Uncle Sam's soil. And I wasn't going to let Mildred or Sammy be taken either.

So, while the man holding my left wrist in a vice-like grip was trying to wrestle me toward him, I clenched my right hand into a fist, swung back, and socked him right square in the jaw. He stumbled back just as the other guy gave up on going for Mildred and tried to come after me.

In a split-second move, Sammy pushed Helmut's gun out of the way and pointed his own gun at the Nazi. "Call off your dogs. If your baboons lay another hand on either of these gals, I'll plug you."

A smile slid across Helmut's round face. "It doesn't matter. I'm prepared to die for the Reich. And if you kill me, there will be another one to take my place. And another one. You can't kill us all. Soon the New Order will take over the world."

"Fat chance," Sammy laughed.

"You won't find torture to be very amusing," Helmut said in return.

"Ready, kid?" Sammy said out of the side of his mouth.

"Ready," I murmured back.

"Then hit it."

He didn't have to tell me twice. With Nazis there ready to abduct us and take us out of the country, I didn't care to wait around and see how that scene played out. Especially since the guy who wanted to kidnap me was back on his feet. But not for long. Because I let out the clutch, hit the gas and turned the Packard hard back onto the road, sending gravel and dirt flying. The move surprised them all. The man beside me fell into the grass, and the guy near Mildred was "*thwacked*!" by the bumper when the Packard's rear end fishtailed before the tires caught the road. But I'd turned the wheel so hard that the car almost went flying into the ditch on the other side. Thankfully I was able to correct it just in the nick of time, exactly like Hadley had taught me. I pushed the gas pedal to the floor, and we went racing away, just as gunshots rang through the night.

But there was no stopping to check the damage. Instead I kept the car steady as we flew like a racecar down the road. In the rearview mirror I could see a man sitting on the ground, and since he wasn't wearing a hat, I guessed he must be Helmut.

"Anybody hit?" Sammy hollered above the roar of the Packard's engine that was working for all it was worth.

"All fine here," Mildred said.

"Me, too," I hollered as I rolled up my window, and Sammy and Mildred did the same.

"Good job, kid. That was some pretty fancy footwork back there," Sammy told me.

"Thanks," I told him, almost feeling a little giddy.

My heart was pounding so hard that I thought it might bounce right out of my chest. Yet despite the fact that we had men shooting at us and we'd been mere minutes from being kidnapped and shipped to Germany, I couldn't help but smile.

"Now for the bad news," Sammy said with more seriousness. "I think the car may have taken a bullet. As long as they didn't hit the gas tank, we should be all right."

That's when I saw headlights in my rearview mirror. "Uh-oh. I don't think we're out of the woods just yet."

I hugged a slight curve and spotted a second set of headlamps behind the first, and I knew both cars were after us. At least Helmut and his gang had turned on their headlamps this time, making it a little easier to keep track of them.

But not easier to outrun them. So I kept my speed up and a good grip on the steering wheel. Every now and then I caught the sound of a squeal from the Packard's tires.

Sammy glanced out the back window. "Looks like we've got company. Anybody know where this road comes out?"

"It's a dead end. On the ship channel," Mildred piped up. "We're going to have to turn around."

That idea made my skin crawl. If we had to turn around, that meant we'd have to go right past the two cars driven by those Nazis. And I could think of a hundred things I'd rather do than that.

"What should we do?" I asked Sammy.

He nodded at the road ahead of me. "Let's see if we can lose them long enough to get headed back the right way."

"Got it," I told him.

By now we were starting to pass shipyards and warehouses. And parking lots. All places where I could momentarily hide the Packard. Just long enough for both cars to pass me and give me a head start going back the way we came.

So I downshifted and hit the gas again. I tried to run over all the loose gravel and rocks that I could. Anything to kick up a spray and some dust. And while it might have helped keep the cars behind me at bay, it also made the Packard steer like it was on a skating rink. Eventually I was making good headway, and the cars chasing us were falling farther behind. Probably because they couldn't catch the Packard.

That's when Sammy told me to kill the lights. "Take a sharp right up there, kid. At that bend. Then slide down in next to that big warehouse."

And I did just that. Right at that moment, I certainly could have used Superman's eyesight. Because without headlights, it wasn't easy to see in the dark like that. But I went straight down a little hill and behind the building. I made such a sharp turn that I think the Packard practically went up on two wheels. I could hear Mildred sliding around in the backseat. Finally I saw something dark looming up ahead, so I hit the brakes and came to a quick stop. With the way the Packard was performing, I was pretty sure I'd be buying them for the rest of my life.

I only hoped I hadn't kicked up a trail of dust that would make it easy for Helmut and his men to follow. Sammy and I both rolled down our windows and listened for the hum of their engines. Sure enough, we heard first one and then the next one fly on by.

"You did good, Tracy," Mildred whispered.

"Sure did, kid," Sammy said. "Now let's get out of here before they come looking for us."

"Okay, but hang on. I'm not slowing down till we're out of here!" I announced as I turned the headlamps back on.

That's when I gasped. Because, not five feet in front of me was a telephone pole. One we would have hit head on, if I hadn't stopped where I had.

But I didn't have time to worry about that now. Instead, I shifted into reverse and backed around. Then I shifted into gear and hit the gas. I turned back onto that road and drove us along until we were on the outskirts of town. I drove much faster than I ever would've driven at night, but I figured the biggest danger wasn't in driving after dark, but rather the two cars coming after us. I didn't see those two cars again for quite a while, but I finally spotted some headlights a long, long way behind me.

Sammy pointed to a gas station that was closed. "Pull in here for a moment, kid. Around the side. And be ready to go again in a hurry."

"But won't those guys see us?" I asked him.

"Nope," Sammy said. "We'll see them instead. We're going to tail them."

"We are?" My heart skipped a beat and my eyes went wide. "I'd never tailed a car before. As an Apprentice P.I., this night was full of "firsts" for me.

I drove into the gas station and around the corner, just like he'd instructed me. The Packard made a pretty nice turn and I stopped it right at the edge of the building.

"Kill the lights, kid," Sammy murmured.

I'd barely turned them off when I saw the two dark cars come roaring by, one after the next.

"Okay, kid," Sammy said quietly. "I've got my eyes on 'em. Take your time and pull out slowly. Like you're just out for a Sunday drive."

I turned the lights back on and did exactly what he'd told me to do. I kept far enough back so we could still see them, but hopefully they didn't even have a clue we were there. We followed them for about five blocks, at which point they started driving at a normal pace and blended in with the rest of the traffic.

"Let's see where this bunch goes," Sammy said quietly.

The two cars kept on driving down the same street, though I guessed they were probably looking for our car. They finally made a turn into a diner.

"Pull in across the street, kid," Sammy told me. "Nice and normal like."

So I made a very casual turn into the business parking lot across the street and a door down. I could see all five men jump out of their cars and, as near as I could tell, it looked like Helmut's four goons were having quite an argument. But Helmut made a beeline for a pay phone just inside the restaurant entryway. He picked up the receiver while the other four men went into the diner itself.

Sammy grinned and adjusted his fedora. "You girls stay in the car. I'll be right back."

"Where are you going?" I asked him.

"I thought we were headed back to the office," Mildred added. I could tell from her voice that she was still shaking.

"In a minute," Sammy answered us. "But first I need to get some license plate numbers. Then we'll let J. Edgar Hoover's boys know about these Nazis. And let them handle this little gang."

Before I knew it, Sammy was out of the car. He bent over so he could sneak behind the back of the vehicles, going from car to car, until he made it to the street. Then he pulled his collar up and trotted across. He moved so swiftly that he blended in with all the other people and all the other goings on in the city. Like he was just another guy out and about and crossing the street. Once he got to the other parking lot, he bent over again. Within seconds, he'd snuck up to the back of each of the black cars.

My heart felt like it was racing just as fast as the Packard had been when those Nazis were chasing us. It seemed like Sammy was gone for an hour, but in reality, he was back across the street in under five minutes. But instead of getting in the car, he went to the phone booth near the business. He put a dime in and dialed. The conversation he had seemed to take forever, but he finally joined Mildred and me once more. Minutes later, police cars and plain dark cars pulled into the parking lot of the diner.

"We can go now," Sammy said with a smile. "We'll have to make a statement to the G-men later. But they'll have those Nazi boys rounded up and in jail tonight."

"So . . . we caught the Nazis then," I said with a smile.

"Correction," Sammy said. "We caught *some* of the Nazis. At least those guys in the diner who were out to get us back there. But don't forget, there's a whole Bund meeting going on somewhere tonight, with a whole bunch of these boys. And we have no idea where that meeting is even being held."

The thought of it made me shiver.

"That brings up a question," Sammy went on. "How did those guys know who we were? I was careful not to be tailed when I left that note in the bookstore."

"And no one knows I'm here in Texas," Mildred added. "Though the Germans would know about the artwork that was taken out of the country. Because all Jewish people had to register their artwork with the German government. Later on, Nazi government claimed anything valuable for their own."

"Lousy Nazis," Sammy growled. "Well, we may not have the answers yet, but I think we're safe for the night. Let's all head home and get some shut-eye. We'll tie up the loose ends in the morning."

Mildred and I both agreed. Getting some sleep sounded like the perfect plan. I dropped Mildred and Sammy off at the office, being careful to drive around the block a few times. Just to make sure I didn't have a tail of my own, as Sammy put it.

Right before he shut the car door, he said, "By the way, kid. You've got a bullet hole in your rear fender. Good thing it didn't hit the gas tank. But don't sweat it. We'll get it fixed courtesy of the

Agency."

My eyebrows practically shot up to the top of my forehead. Having a bullet in my fender was a first for me. I wondered how I was going to explain that to Nana. Though deep down, I knew she'd probably just see the whole thing as something wildly adventurous. A badge of honor maybe. And she'd want to hear the story of me outrunning the Nazis again and again.

I got home just as Peg and Timothy Westover were coming in. They told me how they'd gotten a babysitter and gone to the movies.

"We saw *Confessions of a Nazi Spy*," Peg said with wide eyes.

"You really should go see it," her husband added. "It's a very enlightening movie. Hard to believe the Nazis are already operating over here. But it's important for every citizen to be aware."

Boy, he could say that again. I thanked them with the best smile that I could muster. But I didn't have the heart to tell them that wild horses couldn't drag me to that movie. And the last thing I'd find entertaining at the moment was any movie about Nazi spies.

While they headed upstairs, I let myself into Jayne's apartment and locked the door behind me. Clark Cat was sitting next to the window, swishing his tail back and forth and waiting impatiently to be let outside. So I opened the window for him, and suddenly I had a full-blown case of the willies. Somehow I'd forgotten to lock that window . . . again. Katie McClue would never make a mistake like that. Maybe I needed to start tying a string around my finger to remind me to lock it, so I'd be safe. Though with Helmut and his gang behind bars tonight, I should have felt a whole lot safer than I did before.

So why didn't I? What was nagging at my brain, and sending me a mental SOS? I checked out the apartment to make sure all was well and then I practically fell into bed. Yet I still couldn't rest.

Then I realized what was niggling at the back of my brain — I'd never seen Helmut go into the restaurant. Sure I'd seen him in the phone booth. And right before Sammy got across the street, I noticed he was no longer in that phone booth. But I never saw him go inside the diner. I only assumed he did.

But did he? And for that matter, who had he been calling the very second he found a pay phone.

On top of all that, how exactly did he know so much about us?

Yet there was one person who knew a lot about Helmut, including the dead drop at the bookstore. He was the same person who also knew I was wearing Betty's dress tonight.

The very person who had led us to the Bund in the first place.

Karl Schmidt.

CHAPTER 28

Singing and Setting the Trap

Bright and early the next morning, the "*rrriiiing, rrriiiing, rrriiiing*" of the telephone woke me up and sent me bouncing out of bed. Though to be honest, to say that I'd actually been "woken up" was a pretty big exaggeration. Because I wasn't sure if I'd even gotten any sleep at all. If I had, it wasn't much. Too many thoughts had floated through my mind the entire night. Mostly thoughts of Helmut and Karl. I couldn't help but wonder if Karl had somehow played a role when it came to Helmut finding out about Sammy and Mildred and me. And I also couldn't help but wonder if one of them had killed Betty.

I hadn't seen Karl since he'd stormed out yesterday evening. And when I got back to the apartment building last night, the lights in his place had been off. Now I wondered if he had even come home at all. If not, then where was he? What had happened to him?

I picked up the phone and heard Sammy's voice on the other end. He didn't waste any time with hello, but went straight to the point. "Helmut got away. He wasn't in the diner when the police and the FBI showed up." Sammy's tone was tense, uneasy, something I'd never heard in him before.

It was enough to send my pulse rate soaring. "He wasn't? Maybe he snuck out the back door."

"Nope, kid," Sammy said. "They had the place surrounded before they even went in. If anyone matching Helmut's description had gone out any door, they would've nabbed him right away."

"Did they get the other guys?"

"They got 'em. And those gorillas have clammed up like real pros. If I didn't know better, I'd say they'd done this before."

I leaned on the kitchen counter and tried to steady myself. "What about the boat that was going to take us out into the Gulf? To the U-boat that was supposed to be waiting out there?"

"The government boys are working on it. But they want our help with this. Well, *your* help, mostly. "

"My help? What can I do?"

"It's like this, kid. I told the FBI boys what you'd figured out about Betty and her songs. And how they got broadcast all over Galveston. Now the G-men are trying to figure out who was listening for Betty's messages. We're guessing some of the Bund members were tuned in, but there was probably a bigger fish somewhere, one who was looking to pass that information on to someone else. There may have been a U-boat out in the Gulf that picked it up, too. So we want you to sing one of Betty's old songs at the Polynesian Room. To smoke 'em out."

I tried to make my little gray cells move fast enough to keep up with him. "And you think the Fifth Column folks will recognize the song as it's being broadcast? And wonder what's going on? Since I will essentially be transmitting an "old message" with that song, one they've already heard before."

"You got it. My guess is they all know about Betty, and her death. So they'll wonder *who* is singing the song, and *why*. We think it'll be enough to make those Nazi guys real jittery real quick, and send them into action. Of some kind or another. And the FBI will set a wide net to catch them. Hopefully we'll get Helmut in the bunch."

For the first time that morning, I had to smile. "Sounds like a good plan to me."

"It's a bit of a long shot, kid. But it might just work. And maybe we'll get lucky and catch a few guys who are willing to rat out the rest."

My smile grew even wider. "That would be good. Then we can put those Nazis out of commission."

Sammy chuckled on the other end of the line. "It's a start. But we still don't know how big their operation is."

"And Helmut told us they'd just keep sending more," I said with a sigh. Much as I hated to admit it, somehow I believed him.

"So, what do you say, kid? Are you ready to sing at the Polynesian Room again? Vito invited you to sing anytime."

"He sure did. I'll give him a call. If he says yes, I'll make sure one of Betty's old songs gets put on the song list for tonight. I'll tell Vito it's a tribute to her. Since they adored her so much."

"Good job," Sammy said, finally sounding a little more optimistic. "You're thinking like a real detective."

Which spurred me on to tell him my theory about Karl.

I could almost picture Sammy shaking his head. "I can't see the guy spilling the beans like that," he said. "Not unless he was under duress. Or tortured. It's hard to fake the kind of paranoia he has about those Nazis. Unless he said something purely by accident. As for killing Betty, somehow it doesn't quite add up."

"I know," I agreed. "It seems a little off to me, too. But as upset as he was with me yesterday, and as rashly as he behaved, I'm not sure he's always got himself under control. And he was certainly terrified of Helmut and gang. Then he seemed terrified of us, too, when he suddenly thought we were part of the Bund ourselves."

"That's how those Nazis operate," Sammy said. "They keep people scared stiff, so they won't act rationally. And when people don't act rationally, who knows what they'll do. But let's just keep our eyes open for the time being. Until we find out the whole story."

"Will do," I told my boss.

And with that, we got off the phone and I started making arrangements for the night. When I called the Polynesian Room, Vito couldn't have been happier to have me sing, since they hadn't found someone to fill Betty's spot yet. He asked me to come down in the afternoon, to practice with the band. I gladly agreed. Especially since that meant we'd all have a chance to practice Betty's music beforehand.

I made myself some coffee and a piece of toast, right after I let Clark Cat in. Then I went off to the closet to make sure my black satin gown was in good enough shape to wear tonight. It only needed a little pressing, so I got it ready and packed it into a garment bag. Then I stashed all my accessories into another small bag, so I could change clothes at the Polynesian Room before dinner tonight.

All the while, I couldn't stop thinking about Karl. What Sammy had said rang true. But the mere thought of Karl being tortured by Helmut and friends made my heart sink clear down to my knees. Judging from the way those men had treated us last night, I didn't think they'd have any problem torturing poor Karl. Or even killing him.

Suddenly I was very worried about the elderly man. What if something had happened to him after he'd gone rushing out like that? Or what if he *had* been tortured, and was sitting up in his apartment injured right now? Or even worse, what if he'd come home in bad shape and hadn't survived the night?

Clark Cat appeared at my ankles and meowed up to me.

I reached down to pet him. "I'll bet you know something about 'curiosity' and how dangerous it can be. Only, in your case, if curiosity killed the cat, you'd have eight more lives to spare. I'm a little different."

He rubbed my legs, as if he understood what I'd just said. And if that was true, I had a hunch he wouldn't like it if I told him what I was going to do next. Because I'd decided to do something that was against my better judgment, and to make matters worse, I was going to do it alone. Though maybe not entirely alone, since clearly Clark planned to come with me. He was waiting for me by the door as I grabbed Jayne's keys. Then together we walked to Karl's apartment, and I knocked softly on the door a few times. When he didn't answer, I tried again. Finally, I used Jayne's keys to let myself in.

At first, I wasn't sure what I'd find. After all, I'd already stumbled over one dead body this week. Was I about to come across another? The whole place was dark, until I hit the light switch. That's when I found the apartment looked exactly like it had the last time I was there. Everything was perfectly in order and so neat that it felt more like a museum than a place where someone lived.

"Karl?" I called out, hoping he might answer.

But the only thing I heard was the wind rattling against the windowpanes. Clark and I quickly checked out the entire place, including the bedroom and bathroom. The bed was made, and the bathroom sink and tub were completely dry. So either Karl hadn't come home last night, or he'd gotten up and left very early this morning. Both were thoughts that made my stomach churn with worry.

Since there was nothing I could do at the moment, Clark and I left the apartment, locked it, and went back downstairs to do a few chores. We finished up just in time to let Artie in and unlock the mailboxes for him. He saluted me as always. I quickly distributed the bundles of mail, until I got to the last stack for Betty's box.

"What should we do with these?" I asked him. "Can we mark them 'Return to Sender?'"

Artie shook his head. "Naw, I wouldn't worry about it. Those military boys will think she lost interest and moved on. It's better that way. Rather than having them think she was alive and returning their mail for some rotten reason."

I sighed. "Well, the box is overflowing and Jayne will be renting out that apartment sometime soon. So I'll just keep all Betty's letters at Jayne's place. In case the police want to look at them."

"It's the only thing you can do. Doesn't sound like the police have taken much interest in her letters so far."

I shook my head. "Nope. They haven't."

"It doesn't surprise me. Pretty soon everybody is going to be shorthanded. We're losing postmen left and right, with all the fellas going off to war. Sure wish I was going with them."

His words made me smile. If he'd said it once, he'd said it a million times. I knew Artie was a true-blue American, and it was practically killing him that he couldn't go off and fight against the horrors that were happening in our world. My father had been the same way. Thank goodness he'd been given an important role in this war effort.

"We need you here," I said to Artie as I linked my arm in his and walked him to the door. "Just think of all the letters being sent home. And how important it will be to get the right mail to the right people. Why, Jayne herself will be anxious every day for a letter from Tom. And her brothers. You'll practically be a hero for delivering all that mail."

"I'll do my best," Artie said with his usual salute, before he headed out the front door.

Once he was gone, I ran back to Jayne's apartment. I let Clark Cat out the window, grabbed some lunch, and got ready to go. Not long after that, Sammy was driving us back down to Galveston.

Practice with the band that afternoon went smoothly, and the whole bunch made me feel right at home. They even remembered Betty's most recent composition, though I'd brought the music with me.

"We're going to miss Betty's songs," a red-haired trumpet player told me. "The melodies were always swell, but her lyrics were a little . . . well . . . unusual."

"They were artistic," a clarinet player corrected him with a laugh.

I didn't have the heart to tell them what those songs really were — coded messages that passed information on to the Nazis.

When practice had ended, I met Sammy for a hamburger and a glass of sweet tea at a food stand on the Seawall. That's when Sammy told me there would be FBI men in the audience and around town, ready to move in if anyone reacted strangely once I started to sing Betty's old song.

"What kinds of things will they be looking for?" I asked my boss.

"They've got it down to a science, kid," he told me as we found a bench where we could sit and eat. "They might look for a bunch of people who suddenly gather together and start whispering in a corner. Or someone who jumps up and makes a sudden phone call. Or someone who runs for their car and tries to get out of town. Basically anybody who has an instant reaction to your singing that song. We'll just have to wait and see what shakes out."

I raised my eyebrows. "They've got a lot of territory to cover."

Sammy nodded. "Yup, kid, they do. But if they can catch some of those guys and get them to talk, then they can catch even more later. And like I said before, we have no idea how big this operation is."

I stared at the ocean waves as they hit the beach. "It's strange, but I wonder if these Bund members might be more afraid of the Nazis than they are of our FBI agents."

Sammy raised his eyebrows. "Could be. We'll know more after

tonight, if we manage to nab some of these guys. But these Nazis are pretty cool customers. For all we know, they might just keep a lid on it and not react much at all."

"What about Vito and his gambling operation? Do you think the Feds will figure that out?"

Sammy chuckled. "Can't say for sure, kid. But right now they're only interested in catching Helmut. And uncovering any Fifth Column activity. So keep your eyes peeled for anything that looks suspicious."

"Will do," I told him.

And that was exactly what I did after I'd changed into my black satin gown and finished getting ready. Vito had let me use a room just off his office to change. As I left, I noticed his "gambling room" had been turned into a tea parlor of sorts. I guessed someone must have tipped him off about the G-men being on the prowl tonight. I only hoped no one had tipped off Helmut and his guys, too.

I went straight upstairs and stood to the back of the dinner area, scanning the crowd and trying not to look too obvious about it. I did notice there seemed to be a lot more men in the audience tonight. Mostly men with broad shoulders and perfectly chiseled chins. Very handsome men.

Including the one who slid up beside me now.

Michael.

He grabbed my arm and yanked me into the hallway. "Tracy, what on earth are you doing in a place like this? And what have you done to your hair? Have you completely lost all sense and class?"

"Let go of me, Michael," I said in a low voice. "I'm no longer that mouse of a girl you were engaged to. I've had enough adventures in less than a week than I would've had with you in a whole lifetime."

His mouth dropped open for a moment. "I'm getting you out of here. You don't belong in a place like this. You'll just make a fool of yourself."

"What I do is none of your business," I told him as I fought to keep my anger under wraps. "You're not my fiancé or my keeper. You're not even in my life anymore." I pulled my arm away from him.

He had the nerve to grab it again and pull me farther down the hall. "I'm sending you home in a cab to your mother."

I latched onto the side railing with my free arm and held on. "I don't think so, Michael. Though it's so terribly thoughtful of you to try to send me to the one person who hit me. And in front of our entire country club crowd, no less. So, while we're on the subject, why don't you tell me something? Why weren't you ever around when I needed you? And why were you ready to have me sent to jail for a murder I didn't commit? Besides all that, how many other girls did you date while we were supposed to be engaged?"

Michael tugged even harder. "Your mother was right about you. You're just too selfish for your own good."

I fought against him, but he was so much stronger than I was. "Well, I guess you would know, considering you're probably the most selfish guy on the planet. Tell me, Michael — do you plan to enlist and go off to fight like all the other boys our age? Do you even want to fight against these dark forces that are trying to take over the whole world right now? And make freedom a thing of the past?"

He scoffed at me. "Why would I? There are plenty of men out there to do that. I'm too important," he said, before he caught himself and quickly corrected his words with, "I mean, my work is too important."

"Yes, Michael, I think that pretty much sums it up. Everyone else in the country is talking about making sacrifices to save the free world. You, on the other hand, are only concerned about yourself. You know what? I never could have married you. You're simply not noble enough for me. I'd rather marry a man who has courage. A man who thinks there are more important things in life than himself. Especially since our entire world has been turned upside down, and everybody will have to play a part to save us now."

"I believe the lady told you to let go of her arm," I heard Sammy call out from the end of the hallway.

"Stay out of this, old man," Michael hollered back.

And that was about all I could take of this horrible man whom I'd almost married. He might have been movie star handsome, but inside his chest beat the heart of a very spoiled and very self-centered brat.

That's when I took a page from one of Katie McClue's earliest episodes, *The Case of the Pushy Paramour*, where she'd dealt with the unwanted advances of a former beau. Seems the man had a solid grasp on her arm, too, and wasn't willing to release her. So I did exactly what she did. I hiked up my skirt with my free hand and firmly planted the toe of my shoe right smack dab in the middle of Michael's shin. I kicked him with enough force to make him cry out in pain. As he let go of my arm and bent over, I hit him with a double-handed karate chop to the side of the neck. It was enough to send him sprawling onto the floor.

Just then Vito popped his head around the corner and glanced at Michael on the ground. "Is that guy bugging you, Miss Truworth?"

"Not anymore," I told him as I wiped my hands.

"Let me know if he gives you any trouble, and I'll have him kicked out. We don't take kindly to men ruffling our canaries," Vito said before he disappeared again.

Sammy chuckled as I walked toward him, leaving Michael moaning on the floor. "Kid, I don't know where you learned all this stuff . . . But any way you look at it, you're a natural. I've honestly never seen anyone so suited for detective work as you are."

I didn't know if this was a good time to tell him about Katie McClue. Or if there would *ever* be a good time. In any case, I figured it could wait for later.

Sammy offered me his arm and spoke to me in a low, quiet voice. "What do you say, kid? Ready to go help catch some Nazis?"

"Sounds like a plan to me," I murmured in return, as I allowed him to escort me back to the dining room. Minutes later, I was on the stage singing "Sentimental Journey." Near the end of the song, I spotted Michael limping back in. He took a chair next to a pouty redhead who plastered herself against his arm. I got the distinct impression this wasn't the first time they'd been together at the Polynesian Room. She gave me the evil eye while he sat there brooding. It almost made me laugh before I'd finished my song. Thankfully, I managed to keep my composure, though I did let out a chuckle or two after the song had ended, when the rest of the audience clapped wildly for me.

Honestly, I had to wonder what I'd ever seen in that man. Or why I'd gotten engaged to him in the first place. But one thing I did know beyond a doubt — I wanted to see Pete again. I even wished he was here tonight.

I went on to sing more songs, and before long, I started to feel like an old pro up there on stage, in front of everyone. I had to say, I was really enjoying myself tonight. Even so, I knew that being a nightclub singer probably wasn't my real calling. It just didn't have the same thrill as outrunning the bad guys in the Packard or putting the pieces of a mystery together. Or by contributing to the war effort on my own turf and in my own way, by making sure the local Nazis couldn't pass along information that got our guys killed.

Speaking of which, the time had come for me to make my move and sing Betty's song. The band members turned their sheet music over and the bandleader held up his baton.

"We'd like to play this one for someone who is gone but not forgotten," he announced into the microphone, right before he got the band started.

The wind section started and then the brass joined in, creating a spectacular intro, until the brass toned down and the piano and a few clarinets flowed into the melody.

I took a deep breath and stepped up to the microphone, knowing every word I sang would be broadcast over the entire island of Galveston.

My notes came out perfectly as I started to sing, "Oh, how I long for you, every night at nine, the time we used to dine . . . How I wish I'd catch a sight, of the one I hold so dear, on a Friday night near the dock in Boston. Just know you're my only love, my one and only love, at midnight and every night . . . "

The very second I started, the whole mood in the room changed. Men quit eating and drinking and I saw eyes scanning the crowd. I also saw a couple of men jump up from their table, with a look of sheer rage stretched across their features. They barely made it to the hallway when they were instantly pulled aside by other men that I could only assume were FBI agents.

When the song had ended and the clapping had died down, I could hear the squealing of tires off in the distance, and I had an idea that someone was being rounded up. I hoped that meant our plan had worked.

But I didn't get to find out for sure until later that evening, not until after I had finished singing for the night. As the band was breaking down and the last of the customers were leaving, Sammy introduced me to an FBI agent named David Stafford. We all sat together at a back table and had a cocktail.

David was probably ten years older than me, with auburn hair and blue eyes. His jaw was so square it practically looked like it had been sculpted by an artist.

"You handled yourself perfectly tonight," he informed me with great authority. "Thanks to you and your mentor here, we rounded up a nice group of likely subversives."

"Did you catch Helmut?" I asked.

Sammy frowned and took another sip of his drink. "Helmut is the only one we *didn't* catch. He was spotted by a couple of guys, but he's pretty slippery. He managed to get through the net."

The idea of Helmut still being out there on the loose made me shudder. It was not the news I'd been hoping to hear.

"We'll be on the lookout for him," Special Agent Stafford assured me. "In any case, Uncle Sam would like to thank you for your cooperation."

"Happy to help," I said solemnly. "After all, we're all going to be fighting this war together."

"You've got that right." He rubbed his eyes, and blinked a few times, showing his fatigue.

He stood and shook Sammy's hand and then mine. "We might need your help another time, Miss Truworth. If so, we'll get in touch with your boss. Or your father."

I crinkled my brow. "My father?"

"Yes, ma'am. I'm sure you're well aware that he'll be working for Uncle Sam, too, and I'm sure we'll see him as he's in and out of Washington. You should be proud of him. He'll be playing an important role in the war effort."

"Yes. Yes, he will," I agreed as the gears in my head started to turn, slowly at first, and then picked up speed. "I am proud of him. He tried so hard to find a way to serve his country and fight against Hitler and Hirohito. He only wanted to contribute."

With that, the FBI agent plopped his fedora on his head and tilted it just so. "Looks like his daughter is a chip off the old block." Then he winked at me before he strode from the room.

And suddenly I knew exactly who had killed Betty Hoffman.

CHAPTER 29

Mayhem and Murderers

"What makes you so sure, kid," Sammy asked me again, as we sat at Jayne's kitchen table, both on our second cup of coffee. I'd left the door to the apartment open, so we could hear any activity in the hallway. I was still wearing my black satin gown and the gloves and the whole works. We'd finally made it back from Galveston, where we'd hung around for the rest of the night to keep tabs on the roundup of the underground Bund members. As far as we knew, twenty people had been taken in. None of them, unfortunately, was Helmut.

I took another good sip of my coffee before I explained my theory to Sammy for a second time. As theories go, it was a pretty good one, and I could tell Sammy was impressed. Even so, he was the kind of detective who wanted to make sure all the i's had been dotted and all the t's had been crossed.

Funny, but here it was broad daylight and past ten o'clock in the morning. Yet I didn't feel the least bit tired, despite not having had a wink of sleep the night before. Instead I felt like I'd been charged with the same serum that transformed Steve Rogers into Captain America. I'd never solved a murder before, and I had to say, it was truly stimulating stuff. I could understand why Katie McClue would walk headlong into case after case after case. There was just something about putting all the pieces of the puzzle together that made a girl pretty happy.

With that said, there was one angle that I wasn't entirely happy about. Much like the saying goes about not being able to pick your relatives, it's also true when it comes to crime solving. You can't pick your murderer. At least, you can't pick the person you would rather see as the killer in a case.

Sammy added a little more cream to his coffee. "We'll get all the loose ends tied up first. Then we'll take him down easy, kid. Without any fuss."

I nodded. "I think that's best. Let the guy keep his dignity. But what if *he* puts up a fuss?"

Sammy leaned back in his chair. "Like pulling a gun on us?"

"*Just* like that," I responded, feeling my pulse quicken.

"I can't see it, kid. I just don't think it'll happen."

I only hoped he was right. Yet I didn't get a chance to say more, because someone was pounding loudly on the front door. I opened it with a smile, only to have a small, shiny steel revolver pointed directly at my chest. I guess that meant the man holding the revolver wanted to come inside.

I raised my hands. "Good morning to you, too, Mr. Marlowe."

He wore his overcoat on top of his uniform. "Where is it? You called earlier to say you'd found my brooch. And I want it now."

"It's in Jayne's apartment," I told him, sounding so cool that I hardly even recognized myself. "I thought you'd be here an hour ago."

"Well, it wasn't exactly easy to get away at a moment's notice." He motioned the gun toward the hallway. "Now let's make this snappy, since I've got to get back."

I led him into Jayne's apartment, where Sammy was still sitting at the table, drinking his cup of coffee. Though I noticed he was now drinking left-handed, and his right hand appeared to be under the table.

I plastered a smile onto my face and spoke directly to Sammy. "Here's Mr. Bill Marlowe, and he's brought his gun. He's pointing it at me now."

"Loose end number one," Sammy said to me, before he addressed Bill. "For your sake, son, I'd put that gun away."

"It doesn't hurt to have it ready," Bill squinted and pointed the gun at Sammy.

Sammy sat up a little straighter. "I couldn't agree more."

With Bill now looking at Sammy, I thought about making a fast grab for Bill's gun. But wouldn't you know it? Clark Cat chose that very moment to race into the room and plant himself firmly in front of my feet. I'd let him in when we got back this morning, and as near as I could tell, Clark didn't think highly of Mr. Marlowe, since apparently Clark was trying to protect me from the man.

For a second or two, Bill pointed the gun at Clark. "Never could stand that cat. I told Betty it was bad luck to keep a black cat around. Turns out I was right."

"So you *were* in Betty's apartment?" I said with a little snicker. "I thought Betty never let men into her apartment."

"She didn't let me in. I let myself in," he said quietly. "Now give me my brooch and I'll be out of here."

"You're welcome to it," Sammy told him. "Though we all know, son, it was never yours in the first place."

He choked and coughed. "What do you mean? How did you know?"

I nodded in Sammy's direction. "I told my boss just what you'd told me the night I ran into you on the front porch. I gave him the whole sob story. About how you claimed you'd gotten the two brooches mixed up."

Sammy chuckled. "And let me say, we didn't exactly believe your story. But we did believe the big rubies and sapphires that had been in that brooch at one time."

I played along with Sammy, keeping everything calm, even letting out a little chuckle myself. "That sounds an awful lot like a line from the *Maltese Falcon*."

He gave me a grin. "Thanks, kid. I try. After all, everyone tells me I look just like Humphrey Bogart."

"Quit messing around!" Bill stomped his foot. "And give me the brooch."

Sammy used his left hand to pull the brooch from his pocket, and then he slid the pin across the table to Bill. "I don't think you'll be too pleased."

Bill made a sound that reminded me of a wild animal. "Where are the rest of the stones? The big rubies and sapphires?"

Sammy scooted his chair back slightly, ready to spring to his feet. "You mean the high-dollar ones? The payday gems? Seems your so-called girlfriend already hocked them. And why shouldn't she? She probably got the brooch from some other guy. Even though, when it came to jewelry, she usually veered away from the real stuff. But my guess is you saw her wearing it one day and waited for your moment to steal it from her. So you could make a bundle off those big stones. After all, the larger ones would have been worth a small fortune."

That's when Bill started to say words that I cannot repeat. Not in polite company, anyway.

Though I soon forgot all about that when all eyes turned to a commotion in the hallway. We heard the front door slam, followed by thumping footsteps heading our way. Seconds later, Karl Schmidt's heaving form filled the doorway to Jayne's apartment. His face was bruised and bleeding, and he was holding his side, as though he were in great pain.

By now, Bill didn't know who to point his gun at. He went from Karl to me to Sammy and back again.

But Karl hardly seemed to notice. "Miss Tracy . . . Mr. Sammy, please . . . run!" He managed to blurt out as he gasped for air. "Run for your lives. Helmut is on the way. He'll be here any second. I just escaped from him. He is a very bad man. He plans to kidnap you and ship us all to Germany."

I pulled a chair out for Karl, and Bill pointed his gun at me, with his finger on the trigger.

I gave Bill a nasty look as I took Karl's arm. "Here, Karl, please take a seat. It looks like you're hurt."

Karl's eyes went wide when he noticed Bill and his revolver. Without saying a word, he allowed me to help him to a chair.

Sammy raised an eyebrow. "And here we have loose end number two. This is turning into quite a party. Nice to see you again, Karl, and thanks for the warning. But as you can see, we're a bit tied up at the moment."

"This is all my fault," Karl moaned.

Bill pointed the gun at him. "You took the gems?"

Karl blinked a few times. "Gems? What gems? What are you talking about?"

Sammy rolled his eyes. "Of course, Karl didn't take the gems. But I believe he has something else he'd like to confess."

Karl nodded, and heaved out another ragged breath. "I am so terribly sorry. So, so sorry. For a moment, I lost my mind. I saw Tracy wearing that dress and I thought she was with the Bund. And I thought you were too, Sammy."

Bill waved his hands in the air. "The Bund? What Bund?"

"The German Bund. Nazis," I supplied.

Bill gasped. "Nazis? You're Nazis?"

Now I rolled my eyes. "No, *we're* not Nazis. But Betty was."

Bill's mouth fell open. "What? Betty was a Nazi?"

I gave him a slight smile. "That's right. You were running around with a Nazi spy."

He sucked in air and started to cough. "I can't believe it. She was a Nazi spy? I was cheating on my fiancée with a Nazi spy? I could get kicked out of the military for this. I could be court-martialed." Bill dropped his head to his chest and his whole body drooped.

It was just the moment I'd been waiting for. In a flash, I grabbed his gun from his hand and pointed it at him.

He threw his hands in the air and flopped into one of the kitchen chairs. He seemed to be completely oblivious to the fact that I had a gun trained on him and Sammy had just pulled his own gun up from the table.

"I will be a disgrace. A laughingstock," Bill whined and went on as though he were the only person in the room. "Sheila will never marry me now. Not only am I flat broke, but I'll go to prison."

Sammy darted a glance at Karl. "You were saying, Mr. Schmidt? You thought Tracy and I were Bund members?"

I noticed Karl's jaw was hanging open and his eyes were wide. "Yes, yes. I went to Helmut that night, to tell him to leave me alone. I asked him why he sent you two, and Betty, to keep an eye on me. But he didn't know who you were. That's when I knew I'd made the mistake. I tried to leave, and he and the other men beat me, until I told them the whole story."

Sammy raised an eyebrow in my direction. "Well, that accounts for our little welcoming party the other night."

I nodded at Sammy and pointed the gun to the floor. "Then how did you get away, Karl?"

He grabbed his side again. "A lady who works for them brought me some food this morning. She was alone for the first time. And that's when I escaped. There were no guards this time."

"Probably because they were rounded up last night," Sammy said under his breath as he kept his eyes trained on Bill, who now had his head in his hands.

"So, we saved Karl, too?" I asked my boss. "Indirectly? Accidentally?"

"Looks like it, kid. What do you say we wrap up this little drama? Before the real show begins?"

No sooner had he spoken those words when I heard a sound that made my heart stand still. The front door had opened again and footsteps echoed down the hallway. Footsteps that I recognized. Because they sounded a lot like *tappa, tap, tap, tappa.*

Then I heard Jayne's voice cry out, "Hello! I'm home!"

I tried to rush to the hallway and warn her about what was happening in her apartment, but Jayne moves almost faster than a speeding bullet. She was already stepping inside her place before I even got up and made it halfway to the door.

And that's when things went haywire. Jayne took one look at Sammy with his gun and me with my gun and Karl with his injured face. Then she screamed bloody murder, and Karl let out what I can only describe as a combination of a shriek and a loud moan.

This, in turn, caused Bill to jump to his feet and start yelling, "You won't take me alive."

Clark Cat decided it was time for him to jump into the action, too, and he catapulted himself from the couch and landed right smack dab on Bill's back. He dug his claws in tight, which probably didn't hurt Bill, since he was wearing both his uniform and his overcoat.

But Bill started yelling, "I've been attacked! I've been attacked!"

Meanwhile, Jayne screamed again and I waved to her, trying to calm her down, while Karl *thunked* a hand to his chest.

Then Clark Cat made a flying leap from Bill's back and landed square in the middle of the kitchen table. Coffee cups and cream went flying, and there was more screaming, until a gunshot rang through the apartment. Everyone suddenly went silent as I looked at my gun and Sammy looked at his, and right away we all realized the gunshot hadn't come from either of our guns.

Sammy sprang up, did some kind of fancy roll across the floor, and then crouched behind the sofa, with his gun pointing toward the man who had silently joined us during the commotion.

Helmut.

And after I spotted the wide-open window on the other side of the room, I guessed that was how he'd gotten in. I'd probably forgotten to lock it again when I let Clark Cat into the room this morning.

Jayne and Karl immediately put their hands in the air, and Sammy bobbed up and down from behind the couch, since he was having trouble getting a bead on Helmut. That's because Bill was now spinning and weaving while he squeaked out the words, "I've been shot . . . I've been shot . . ."

I took a good look at the man, and, sure enough, he was right. Though at most, he'd probably just been grazed, as there was only a small tear in the outer arm of his jacket.

Still, it was enough to send him lurching forward onto the back of the couch, hitting him in the waist, which bent him in two and sent him tumbling over in a dead faint.

Right onto Sammy.

And judging from the swearing I heard coming from my boss — not to mention, the sound of his gun clattering to the floor — I figured the dead-weight of Bill's unconscious body must have knocked Sammy's gun from his hand.

That meant I was the only one left in the room with a firearm, aside from the Nazi who wanted to kidnap or kill us. And neither of those options sounded especially good to me.

I raised the gun in my hand and pointed it at Helmut, while he in turn pointed his gun directly at me. And there we were, at a standoff, of sorts.

Helmut spoke to Sammy out of the corner of his mouth, in a voice as cold as ice. "Don't bother going for your gun, Mr. Falcone. If you do, the Fraulein gets it. Then they all get it. So put your hands up and come out from behind the sofa. Move into the kitchen with everyone else."

Sammy slowly pulled himself to his feet, and sort of limped toward the rest of us, which gave me time to think. I was the only one holding a gun, so I was the only one who could shoot Helmut and save everyone else. Because Sammy couldn't go after his own firearm, and he was too far away to grab Helmut's gun from him. Karl and Bill weren't going to be any help, either, and while Jayne stood trembling with her hands in the air, I could see her glancing around the room, probably searching for something that could serve as a weapon. That idea in itself was scary, since Helmut might shoot her as she tried to grab something.

So that left me as the only one who could defend the whole bunch. Now the question was, should I shoot Helmut and hope I could hit him before he hit me? The only problem was, I didn't even know if the gun I had in my hand — the one I had taken from Bill — was loaded. For all I knew, he'd come in with an unloaded gun, with the idea of scaring me, and not shooting me. It was a possibility. Then again, the odds were good that the gun *was* loaded and I could fire it at Helmut and hit him.

Either way, it was a gamble. If I shot Helmut and missed, you could bet that he wouldn't miss when he shot back. And I certainly wouldn't be the only one he shot at.

Suddenly I remembered when Katie McClue had been in a similar situation in *The Mystery of the Armed Militant*. That's when Katie had so cleverly and persuasively convinced an armed man, who had held her and an entire group at gunpoint, to give up his gun. I remembered how Katie had started out by acting like a snotty, little brat to the gunman, to shock him. And I decided to do the same.

Helmut glared at me. "If you please, Fraulein. Put your gun on the table. Slowly."

I raised my eyebrows and put my finger on the trigger. "No," I said in the tone of a two-year-old having a temper tantrum. "No, no, no, no!"

Helmut's eyes nearly bugged out of his head. Apparently no one had ever spoken to him like that before.

Sammy choked. "Don't be stupid, kid. Put the gun down. Otherwise he'll shoot the lot of us."

"No," I said again. "Because this is America. In America, we believe in freedom. We have the freedom of religion and the freedom of speech. We are not controlled by a ruthless dictator, but instead we elect our officials to represent us in government. Abraham Lincoln said it best at Gettysburg, when he said we have a government 'of the people, by the people, and for the people. One that shall not perish from the earth.'"

Sammy raised an eyebrow and shook his head. Though he didn't try to stop me.

Jayne put her hands on her hips. "That's right, Tracy. In America, we have the right to choose for ourselves. Nobody tells us what to do."

I nodded, still pointing my revolver at Helmut, who was clearly stunned and almost frozen in shock.

And I kept on talking. "In America, we can live and travel and do as we wish. Right now I am exercising my freedom to say 'no' to being taken prisoner by a Nazi who wants to kidnap us and take us all back to Germany. But you, Helmut, you need to put your gun down. You need to think about your life, and how much better it would be if you turned yourself over to the authorities, and joined our side. Think of how happy you would be if you were free."

A sick smile crossed his face. "You must forgive me, Fraulein, but I have misjudged you. You are not a woman, but a spoiled, petulant child."

"You're the spoiled child," Jayne said. "You want to push the Third Reich's New Order on everyone. You believe people should be slaves to some government that tells them how to think and what to do."

Helmut was clearly getting annoyed by now. "It is a better way. Citizens are ignorant and most are rather stupid. They need intelligent leaders to instruct them and guide them."

"Force them, is more like it," Jayne went on.

I was nodding. "That's right, Helmut. What makes the people in the German government think they're so smart? What makes them think they have the right to rule the world? Americans believe everyone has the right to make their own choices."

"Just as I'll be making a choice of my own," Helmut said as he raised his gun and put me in his sights.

A split second before someone shot him.

CHAPTER 30

Final Farewells and New Adventures

The shot had come from somewhere in the hallway, and it had hit Helmut in the left arm. He bent over, and Sammy made a beeline for his own gun while Jayne and I ducked. That's when the real shooter came rushing in.

Artie. He'd shown up at the same time he always did to deliver the mail. And Jayne must have left the front door unlocked, since she didn't have a key yet. So Artie must have come in, just in time to catch the scene unfolding inside Jayne's place.

"I guess you didn't hear what these young gals said about America," Artie hollered as he held his gun before him and slowly approached Helmut. "Because I've had just about enough of you Nazis, hurting and killing people like you do. You should be wiped off the face of the earth. And soldiers like me are just the guys to do it."

Helmut gave him a snide smile. "It doesn't matter if you catch me or even kill me. Because there will be more coming. More to take my place. Many, many more. Soon we will take over America, just like we've taken over most of Europe. You needn't bother to fight us. We're too mighty for you."

He'd barely gotten the words out when he suddenly straightened up and aimed his gun right at Artie. To this day, I'm not sure whose gun went off first. Because it seemed to me that both Artie and Helmut shot at the same time. Artie hit Helmut right in the heart, and he was gone within seconds. But Helmut hit Artie a little lower, though I knew it was probably a fatal shot. Sammy stood over Helmut and picked up his gun, while I slid Bill's gun onto the kitchen table. Then Jayne and I rushed over to take care of Artie, and Karl moved past us to check on Bill.

Jayne held Artie's head in her lap and fought back tears. "You hang on, Artie. We'll get help. Don't you die on me!"

Sammy rushed to the phone to call the police and an ambulance.

Artie gasped and cringed, but even so, he forced a smile onto his face. "I served my country well, girls. Even though everyone thought I was too old. But I shot those Nazis. They won't take away our freedom. I saved lots of our boys from being killed, including your new husband, Tom."

"You did great, Artie," Jayne murmured. "Taking out Helmut. A Nazi."

But I shook my head. "But you did more than that, right, Artie? When you killed Betty?"

"You got it. I could tell that girl was a spy. By all the letters she got. Then when I talked to that man coming out of her apartment on the day of your wedding, Jayne . . . and I walked him outside. He was the father of a boy who had died at sea. A boy who thought he was engaged to Betty. That's when I knew for sure. And I couldn't let her kill any more of our boys."

"So you took things into your own hands, the night of the thunderstorm," I said softly.

"Yup," he said in a whisper. "I knew you'd be out, Tracy. And Jayne wasn't here. I knew no one would ever see me. I did it for Uncle Sam." He gave us a wobbly salute.

Jayne and I saluted back. "You're a good soldier, Artie," I whispered as tears started to flow down my cheeks.

Artie's arm fell and he closed his eyes. Forever.

Sammy brought a blanket from the sofa and covered Artie, while Jayne and I clung to each other and cried.

Soon, the police and the FBI arrived, and they handled things from there.

Sammy pulled me aside. "You did good back there, kid. You showed you've got a backbone, that's for sure. I'm impressed by the way you handled that Nazi."

"Really? I kept wondering if I should have shot him."

Sammy grinned. "Probably would've been a bad idea," he said and showed me the bullet chamber on Bill's gun.

It was empty.

My mouth fell open in shock.

Later, after Jayne and I had calmed down a little, I finally had a chance to talk to her.

Jayne glanced at her door. "I still don't understand why all those people were in my apartment. Or what was going on. But I realized the guy who was threatening you was a Nazi. And Betty was a Nazi spy? I feel like I came in on the tail end of a story."

I nodded. "And it's a very long story at that. How about if I tell you all about it next week? Over lunch one day. Because I've been up all night and I'm about ready to drop."

"Me, too. Next week will be fine. And by the way, I like your new hair color."

I laughed. "Well, that's a shame, because I can hardly wait to get it dyed back to my normal color."

She raised her eyebrows. "Good. Because even though it's pretty, it looks too much like Betty. And I want to see my old friend again."

I hugged her tightly. "I had no idea you were coming back so soon."

She sighed. "Well, I tried to call, but I couldn't get through. And Tom and I agreed that I should probably come back and get to work. We were afraid we'd taken advantage of you for too long. Plus Tom will come home on leave before he ships out, and we'll spend some time together then." I could tell she was fighting back tears.

As though sensing he was needed, Clark Cat came over and rubbed us both around the legs.

"In case you haven't figured it out," I told Jayne. "Clark pretty much lives here now. Do you mind taking care of him?"

Jayne picked him up and kissed him on the head. "Not one bit.

After all, with Tom gone, I could use a man around the place."

Clark purred almost as loud as the Packard.

With Jayne back, I knew it was time for me to go home and face the music. After all, I hadn't heard any more from my father. And I didn't know if he'd had my mother committed or not. Plus, I was missing Nana, and I'd told my father I would come home and take care of her.

So I returned to River Oaks, and walked in the back door of our mansion with my suitcases. All the while, I steeled myself mentally, so I'd be ready to deal with whatever drama might hit me in the face. Hopefully not literally this time.

But instead, I entered to find the kitchen warm and friendly, with Maddie and Violet actually smiling and laughing. Apparently they were right in the middle of baking Christmas cookies and having a pretty swell time of it.

I got hugs and helloes from everyone, right before Nana danced in. That's when I got the warmest hug of all.

"So happy to have you back, darlin'." She had flour on her cheek and her apron, so I knew she must have been baking right along with Maddie.

"It's good to be home," I told her. "Ummm . . . is my mother around? Or . . ."

"Did she go to the hospital?" Nana finished for me. "Yes, and no. Your father gave her an ultimatum. He said either she got help or he was going to have her committed. He really put his foot down this time, saying she would never be allowed to treat you badly again."

I raised my eyebrows. "Well, that's a relief. Let's see if she sticks to it. So what hospital is she in?"

Nana shook her head. "She's not. This all happened last night. She had Hadley drive her to the hospital but she never checked in. Instead, she telephoned her brother who took her home and called his lawyers. This morning we heard from them, and your mother has decided to live in her family's mansion with her brother and his family. She has also decided to divorce your father. She sent for her things this morning."

I had to admit, *that* was an unexpected turn. "Oh . . . and how is he taking it?"

"A little sad, I guess," Nana said. "But more than anything, in a strange way, he mostly seems relieved. He also said there are far more important things going on in the world at the moment than a marriage that went wrong. And he's right about that."

He certainly was.

Before I could say another word, Giles marched in with the most gigantic bouquet of red roses that I have ever seen. "Ah, there you are, Miss Tracy. These just arrived for you."

"My goodness," Maddie said. "It's good to have you home, Tracy. Things just haven't been the same here without you."

"Who are they from?" Violet wanted to know. "Michael?"

Oh, *how* I hoped not. I quickly pulled the card from the holder and read it aloud. "Dreaming of your sultry voice. Would you come out dancing with me on Friday night? Your Not-So-Secret Admirer, Pete."

Nana beamed with pure happiness while Violet and Maddie stared at each other with wide eyes.

"Who's Pete?" Maddie asked.

"What happened to Michael?" Violet wanted to know.

Nana waved me off. "You go call Pete. I'll fill these two in on the details."

The next night, I wore a pale purple evening gown with sequined trim, while Pete wore his tuxedo. Together we danced everything from a waltz to a foxtrot, as well as plenty of swing. We laughed lots, and conversation was as comfortable as always.

Eventually, he wove us through the crowd to some open French doors. Then he took me by the hand and led me across a huge stone patio. We sat on a stone railing under the evergreen branches of a Live Oak. The night sky was full of stars and, I had to say, it was absolutely magical. I shivered in the cool air, and before I could even wrap my arms around myself, Pete had his tux jacket off and draped across my shoulders. I could feel his warmth still in the fabric.

I turned my face to his and smiled, and he smiled right back. Before I could say a word, he planted his lips firmly onto mine, and our kiss suddenly made me feel warm all over.

He pulled away and slid his arm around me. "Tracy, there's something I need to talk to you about."

His voice sounded serious, and it made my heart start to pound.

Was something wrong? Or was something right? Was it possible that Pete was about to pop the question? In a way I was hopeful that he would, but then again, we'd barely even started to date. I didn't want to ruin everything by rushing into an engagement too soon.

I looked into his face, but he was staring at a faraway wall. "What is it, Pete?"

"Well, Tracy, as you know, the whole world is in turmoil. And Uncle Sam has gotten into this military conflict. It's a very ugly business."

"I know. The world is a different place now."

Pete kept on. "You know, if Hitler or Hirohito should succeed in taking over the world, well, it would be horrific. For other countries as well as ours. And our American freedoms would be gone for good."

I leaned closer to him. "It's true." Tears suddenly pricked at my eyes.

Pete gulped. "Here's the deal, though, it's up to us to fight this. To stop this. All of us. Us regular Joes. And Josephines," he added.

The first tear trickled down my cheek and I quickly wiped it away. I didn't want Pete to see me like this. This wasn't a time to think about myself. This was a time for courage.

Pete squeezed me tight and planted a kiss on top of my head. "Tracy, I feel like it's my duty to join up and go fight alongside everyone else. I don't want to go, and I sure don't want to leave you when we're just getting to be close. But I believe I should go and fight. I've got to. It's the right thing to do."

I turned my face upright, and by now I couldn't stop the tears that had escaped, despite my best efforts. "I know, Pete. And I know you are the kind of guy who will always do the right thing. I am so proud of you."

"Tracy, will you write to me?" he asked with a slight tremor in his voice.

I sniffled. "Of course I will, Pete. All the time. And I'll be praying for you, too."

"Thanks, Tracy. I'm going to need it. With this war ahead of us, we're all going to need it."

I buried my head into his broad shoulder and tried to burn the moment into my memory forever. More than anything, I didn't want time to march on, along with our soldiers who would be traveling to the ends of the earth, to fight in places they'd never even heard of before. Some of them would never come back. And while I knew it was terribly selfish of me, I silently prayed that Pete would be one who did come back. To me.

Later that night, after another few hours of dancing cheek-to-cheek, Pete drove me home and I invited him into our mansion for a nightcap. We strolled hand-in-hand to the parlor, only to find Nana talking to none other than Sammy himself. They were laughing and having quite the conversation. We joined them, and soon Hadley and my father came in, too. Benjamin even showed up and introduced us to Maureen, the dark-haired girl he'd been dating, who turned out to be a lovely person. And after Giles brought in drinks for everyone, Nana stood and tapped a spoon to her glass with a *ding, ding, ding*!

"If I might have your attention please," Nana said as she addressed us all. "I believe it is time to light the Christmas tree. My beautiful granddaughter and I worked on it all day, and now it's time to show it off."

With that, we all stood and gathered around the tree. Pete slipped his arm around my shoulders and I put my arm around his waist. Then Giles turned off the chandelier and Hadley plugged in the Christmas tree lights.

"*Oooooh . . .*" we all said at once as we stared at the tree full of sparkling lights and decorations.

"It's absolutely stunning," my father said. "Mother, you and Tracy did excellent work."

"Magnificent," was Hadley's only comment.

"Would you please sing us a song, Tracy?" Nana requested.

"Yeah, Tracy," Pete murmured to me. "Sing us a song. That would be swell."

So I did. I started out with "Hark the Herald Angels Sing," and soon everyone joined in.

It was so hard to believe it was almost Christmas. And it was hard to believe we were at war. This Christmas was going to be very different from any I'd ever known. But no matter what was going on in the world, it was still Christmas. And the shining star at the top of the tree said it all.

Once we'd finished singing, we stood silently for a moment, lost in our thoughts.

Until Sammy turned to me. "Excuse me, kid. I hate to break up the party, but could I speak to you for a moment in the hallway?"

I raised an eyebrow, nodded to Pete, and silently led Sammy out of the room.

Once we were just out of earshot, his tone became more serious. "Thought you might like to know, I made a decision about what to tell our clients, the mothers who hired me. The ones who lost their sons. The G-men don't want me to say anything about Betty being a spy, until they're sure they've caught all the Nazis nearby. So I thought I'd tell the moms that Betty was after money and jewelry, and that she fooled a lot of boys. I'll tell them she was killed, and just like the police said in the first place, by a jealous boyfriend. That should keep the moms happy, and we can keep Artie's good name out of it."

I nodded. "I think that's nice."

"He only did it in the service of his country. And, after all, there is a war going on."

I sighed. "There sure is."

"Tell me again how you knew Artie had killed Betty?"

I shook my head. "I put the pieces together after we talked to that FBI agent at the Polynesian Room. He mentioned something about my father having such an important role in the war effort. And suddenly I realized that's what Betty's murder was all about. Just like my father, Artie had wanted so badly to serve, and once he figured out that Betty was a spy, thanks to all her mail and more, I knew he would consider it his sworn duty to take out an enemy like her."

Sammy nodded. "So he killed her. And he even saved us at the end."

I took a deep breath. "He died a soldier, and he went out knowing he'd saved a lot of lives."

Sammy grinned at me. "You did a great job cracking this case, kid. Which brings me to the next thing I wanted to talk to you about. I'm going to need you in the office first thing Monday morning."

"Sure thing. What's up?"

"We've got a new case," he said. "And this one's got the Fifth Column written all over it."

"More Nazis? Didn't we just . . ."

"Get rid of them?" he finished for me. "Some of them, kid. Some of them. But we probably didn't get them all. And like Helmut said, even if we got rid of some, they'll just keep coming. And this time, it looks like they're after some kind of hidden artifact. But that's all I know."

Wasn't that just swell. More Nazis.

I gave my boss a little salute. "I'll be there," I told him. "First thing Monday morning. And we'll get to the bottom of this."

Somehow, I couldn't help but smile. Because, deep down I knew, from the pages of her books, Katie McClue would have been very, very proud of me.

About the Author

Cindy Vincent was born in Calgary, Alberta, Canada, and has lived all around the US and Canada. She is the creator of the Mysteries by Vincent murder mystery party games and the Daisy Diamond Detective Series games for girls. She is also the award-winning author of the Buckley and Bogey Cat Detective Caper books, and the Daisy Diamond Detective book series. Though she lives in Houston with her husband and an assortment of fantastic felines, people often tell her she acts like she's from another era, and that she *really* belongs back in the 1940s . . .

CPSIA information can be obtained at www.ICGtesting.com
Printed in the USA
LVOW11s2123161016

508873LV00003B/3/P